say

something

Also by N. Gemini Sasson:

Say No More (The Faderville Novels)
Say That Again (The Faderville Novels)

Memories and Matchsticks (#1, Sam McNamee Mysteries)
Lies and Letters (#2, Sam McNamee Mysteries)

The Crown in the Heather (The Bruce Trilogy: Book I)
Worth Dying For (The Bruce Trilogy: Book II)
The Honor Due a King (The Bruce Trilogy: Book III)

Isabeau: A Novel of Queen Isabella
and Sir Roger Mortimer

The King Must Die:
A Novel of Edward III

Uneasy Lies the Crown:
A Novel of Owain Glyndwr

In the Time of Kings

say something

A FADERVILLE NOVEL

N. GEMINI SASSON

SAY SOMETHING

ISBN 978-1-939344-13-7 (paperback)

Library of Congress Control No. 2016918475

For more details about N. Gemini Sasson and her books, go to:
www.ngeminisasson.com

Or become a 'fan' at:
www.facebook.com/NGeminiSasson

You can also sign up to learn about new releases via e-mail at:
http://eepurl.com/vSA6z

Editing by Lorelei Logsdon
Cover art by Ebook Launch

For all the dogs leading lives of service.

SAY SOMETHING

A runaway teen. A homeless drifter.
And how a stolen dog teaches them the meaning of family.

Not yet sixteen, Bellamy Larson — or Beam, as she'd rather be called — remembers *everything*. She has a condition called Highly Superior Autobiographical Memory. Truthfully, there's a lot she'd just rather forget. Beam never knew her father and doesn't ever want to. Her little brother died while saving her. And her mother self-medicates, leaving Beam to fend for herself.

Desperate for a normal life, Beam carjacks a rusty pickup and drives south to live with her grandparents in Faderville, Kentucky. Unfortunately, as Beam soon figures out, 'normal' doesn't exist. She could use a friend, but friends are hard to come by when you're an outsider.

Buzz Donovan knows what it's like to live on the outside. Luckily for him, he has a friend — a dog named Hush. It's because of Hush, though, that Buzz is homeless. But that's his choice, because if it weren't for Hush, he'd be dead.

When Beam runs into Buzz, her world is turned upside down. She doesn't trust dogs, and for good reason — she's been mauled by one.

chapter 1

Beam

They say pain fades with time. Not true. Not for me, at least.

Because I remember *everything*.

Every day. Every event. Every blessed moment.

Whether I want to or not.

Which was why I decided to leave. For good.

I breathed in, filling my lungs with wintry air, and looked down below.

It started in my palms. The slightest vibration. A faint buzz of molecules spinning, tumbling, colliding. The shiver crept up my arms. Settled in my spine until it built itself to a clattering roar, then burst through every bone in my body. It felt like my skeleton would shatter.

I gripped the edge of the platform, my fingers bloodless as I fought to hold on. Eyes clenched tight, I stiffened against the force of the wind as the semi blasted past, its horn a bellowing baritone. Diesel fumes flooded my nose and mouth, coating my tongue, spilling down my throat, gagging me. I retched, pulling my body back just before gravity tugged me downward.

1

They didn't build bridges like this anymore. Good thing, because they'd be scraping a lot more bodies like mine off the pavement below.

My name is Beam. That was what my little brother used to call me, because he couldn't say Bellamy. I hated the name Bellamy. Hated it with the power of ten thousand supernovas. It reminded me of something I never had: a father.

Sometimes people called me Bell. That was taking a lot of liberty. I hated it even more. It sounded like a Southern debutante who ought to be prancing around in a frilly ball gown. I'd sooner cover my body in tattoos and piercings, dress in black, and hang with the emos under the bleachers at the football games.

On occasion, I'd been called Bee, like 'a bee in your bonnet'. I wasn't always the friendliest person to be around, but I had my reasons. If they knew my full story, they would've understood why. But then, a lot of people *thought* they knew me. Which was why I'd ended up here: sitting on a steel beam (ironic, I know), somewhere in the Michigan countryside outside of Flint, staring at black asphalt in the dark from thirty feet up on the overpass while cars zipped obliviously by below.

Could've been they were just lazy and saying 'B', because, well, they didn't know how to say Bellamy, so they didn't even try.

If anybody actually knew I was here, they'd call the cops. Then the po-po would send a head-doctor to talk me down. I wouldn't have minded that, actually, because I could've used someone to talk to. But really, I didn't need a shrink. I wasn't here because I wanted to end my life. I just needed to think about it. Figure out why it was that I kept getting screwed.

Especially when I did everything right. At least I tried to.

Still, I couldn't catch a break. Everything, apparently, wasn't enough. I was starting to think it all boiled down to luck. And I hadn't had any of that. Not so far. Not even on the night I was conceived.

Twin rays of headlights torpedoed along the highway below, the broken yellow line in the middle of the road flashing as the car sped beneath me. As it disappeared in the opposite direction, it occurred to me that if I *had* jumped, I probably would've lived. It was only thirty feet down — and my aim was terrible, anyway. The car would've veered around me, blasted its horn, and I would've ended up with a few bruised ribs and a busted ankle.

Another rumble shook my bones, then another. Two cars, ten seconds apart. I wondered where they were going. Home to their families? Dinner waiting on the table? Hugs when they walked in the door? What would that feel like? Whenever anyone reached for me, I recoiled, sure I was about to get backhanded.

Pulling my feet in close, I wrapped my arms around my shins. I was cold but not shivering. I should've been. This wasn't right. And it wasn't right what happened to Oakley.

It shouldn't have been him. I was the one who ought to have died that night.

—o0Oo—

Now I was cold. So cold my bones could snap. I hated winter. Couldn't wait to be farther south.

I kicked my feet out, swung them from the beam of the bridge to get the blood flowing through my veins. Arching my back, I rolled my shoulders, reached out into the darkness, flexed my fingers around nothing but cold, cold February air.

Time to get going. I had a long road ahead.

I grabbed the truss overhead and pulled myself up and over. Clumps of ice fell to the concrete as I squeezed between the rusty beams and stepped out onto the road. No cars. Hadn't been any for more than an hour. I didn't even know what highway that was down below. I'd been on these roads before but barely knew their names.

Didn't matter. I'd never see them again. All I needed to know was how to get out onto the interstate. From there, it was a straight shot south for about eight hours, then a sharp right west and a handful of turns to Gram and Gramps' place. Flint, Michigan, to Faderville, Kentucky. I had it all memorized. Once I got to Faderville, I'd ask around. Should be easy.

Should be.

They weren't expecting me, but that didn't matter. I was family, right? I shuffled across the bridge toward my truck, parked off to the side of the road. Well, not *my* truck, exactly. I mean, I didn't even have a driver's license. For now, though, it was my ticket out of here. As long as it didn't drop the transmission in the next day or so.

A shiver traced its way down my spine. Bare hands tucked deep in my coat pockets, head down, I didn't even see the dog until it was almost too late.

If there was one thing I hated more than winter, it was dogs.

He stood in the middle of the road, planted squarely between me and the truck. Long black legs, lean like a racehorse's. Broad-chested. All muscle. A whip-like tail hung stiff and low behind his back legs. There were spots of brown on his toes, a patch of it on his chest and more on his cheeks. The muscles of his powerful jaws twitched. His tongue darted out between jagged teeth, flicked across his lips.

Even before the mongrel moved toward me or made a sound, I *knew* I was in trouble.

He tipped his nose up, sniffed the air. His lips quivered. A paw broke contact with the ground, inched forward. His head lowered. He took another step. And another. His black eyes fixed on mine.

I didn't look away. Couldn't. My feet were rooted deep into the concrete on which I stood.

I had no idea if this dog — this particular dog — was dangerous. But I'd been hurt before. And it wasn't the memory of teeth tearing into flesh that paralyzed me. It was the fear.

4

Yet if I stood here and did nothing, the fear would win. Again.

Somewhere in the distance, a coyote howled, long and mournful. It might have been miles away, but the dog, momentarily distracted, curved his neck to look off into a wooded ridgeline behind him.

Quickly, I looked around. A few feet in front of me was a fist-sized chunk of asphalt, a piece of what was now a pothole in the surface of the bridge.

Just as I lunged for it, the dog jerked his head back in my direction. I closed my hand around the chunk, rough edges pressing into my palm.

The dog crouched low, shoulders sinking, muscles coiled tight. He sprang at me.

I brought the chunk of road up to shoulder height, gauged its weight, calculated the distance, the trajectory — and lobbed it at him, hoping beyond hope that for once my aim would be good enough.

It wasn't.

The chunk hit the road five feet in front of him, exploding into a dozen smaller pieces that bounced and skidded.

But one tiny piece containing a sharp pebble nicked him in the toe.

He snatched both front feet off the ground in surprise, then landed with a shudder.

For a moment, I thought, just this once, I'd won.

That moment didn't last long.

chapter 2

Buzz

The old man, for a moment, couldn't see where he was going. Although it had been cloudy all day long, the storm had come up suddenly. In a matter of minutes it had gone from damp and dreary to ominous and blustery. Too quickly for Buzz Donovan to get out of the elements. He tried to keep his eyes on the white line, but his sight wasn't what it used to be. Sometimes, the edge of the road disappeared, lost in a jagged line of crumbling asphalt.

Buzz pulled his hood over his hat and tugged it forward. Icy rain slashed relentlessly at his whiskered cheeks. Yet even as the wind shoved him back, he trudged onward, one heavy step at a time. It was only a temporary inconvenience. A reminder that he was an insignificant creature adrift in a universe of untold powers.

Between broken hills, rutty fields of corn stumps spread out on either side of the road, broken intermittently by patches of woods, dense with old growth and tangled brush. These were the boondocks of Kentucky: sparsely populated, wild, unspoiled. Nature as it should be. The beauty of it all never ceased to astound him, when he remembered to look for it. Every mile he'd traversed offered a different view. The more he took it all in, the more he felt a part of it, less separate. That made him feel both big and small at the same time.

He'd started the trek from town back to this particular hiding place well before sundown — or so he thought. The problem was that there hadn't been a sundown. Not with those rain-choked clouds. Ironic that they hadn't spewed out the worst of their load until now, when he was halfway either way from decent shelter. For a while he'd tried to wait out the storm in an overhang behind some sort of union building in town, but there were too many cars coming and going down the alley, so he'd left, taking his chances that the rain would stop. It hadn't. In fact, it was raining twice as hard now as it had been an hour ago.

He wanted to stop, but that would've meant death for sure. Not the quick kind, either. No, someone would've discovered him the next day, lying in the ditch in a soggy heap, half-conscious. An ambulance would've shown up and hauled his old carcass to the hospital, where they'd keep him from dying. Then, they'd turn him back out on the streets, weaker and sicker than he was already.

No matter what, though, he couldn't go into the hospital. For a lot of reasons.

Nope, he wasn't having any of that. He'd just have to keep going. Get to the place where he'd hid his things. Dry off. Rest. Wait it out.

Besides, he couldn't die. At least not soon. No matter how much he'd like to, sometimes. He had something very important to do. Important to him, at least.

Anyway, his dog needed him. And that was enough to keep him going. Speaking of which —

Buzz planted his walking stick and stopped to look behind him. The dog slowed and then sat, his rump landing in a puddle. But Hush didn't seem to notice. He only had eyes for Buzz.

Buzz smiled, despite the conditions. He couldn't remember the last time he was this miserably cold and wet. No matter what his physical state was, though, as long as those eyes looked so adoringly at him, there was a reason to draw in his next breath, to look forward to tomorrow, to endure and forge on.

Squinting into the rain, Hush tipped his head so one ear was slightly higher than the other. Then he stuck his neck forward and nudged Buzz in the kneecap, as if to urge him onward. Hush was an Australian Shepherd, short on pedigree but long in loyalty. Had he been more regularly groomed, less road-worn, he might have been striking — stunning even, with his big black patches on his coat of silvery gray. The fur on his feet and face was smooth and short but on his britches and his ruff it was long and plush. His legs and chest were white, as was the blaze that ran between his eyes. Points of copper marked his cheeks and eyebrows, highlighting his every expression.

"Yeah, yeah. I know. You don't like being out here, either. You're free to go anytime, you know. There was a barn not half a mile back you could've run to. If you take off now, you could get back there and out of this mess in no time."

Hush sneezed, then gave a weak shake of his fur.

"I feel the same way," Buzz mumbled. "Guess we're stuck with each other."

Buzz turned back around and started forward. Instead of landing on solid road, though, his foot met a section of crumbled pavement and turned sideways. The right side of his body dipped. His knee buckled. His shoulder met gravel, the impact of his weight loosening it. His body, lean though it was, slid down the incline and into the ditch, where he slammed to an abrupt stop.

A jagged root scraped beside his eyelid before ramming into the skin of his cheekbone. The shock of the laceration was superseded only by the frigid water in which he lay.

Before Buzz could even attempt to push himself free, Hush was there, his cold nose rooting at Buzz's neck and armpit, soft little *woof-woofs* huffing in his throat.

"Get ... off!" Buzz smacked a wet-gloved palm against the dog's shoulder.

Indignant, Hush backed up. A tiny furrow of worry formed between his eyes of azure and golden brown. He woofed again.

"For crying out loud, I am *not* dying." Buzz finally freed the arm that had been pinned beneath him in the fall. "Not yet, anyway."

Actually, he'd died once before. A work accident. Live wires that he'd thought were disconnected. He'd been clinically dead for close to twenty minutes when they finally revived him in the emergency room. That was when they first discovered the tumor. At the time, he wished they'd let him die from that electrical shock. It's one thing to come back from the dead and have another chance at life; it's another thing altogether to learn your days are numbered.

He tried to push himself up, but he was lying at an odd angle, his feet up near the road and his head downhill. The more he tried to get out of his predicament, the more frustrated he became. He flopped his free arm behind him, but that only sent a jolt of pain into his lower back. He'd wrenched it again, damn it.

Worse than being stuck in a ditch, was being submersed in ice-cold ditch water. Carefully, he reached forward with his free arm, leveraging his other elbow beneath him. But he was neither as strong nor as agile as he used to be. Simple tasks like this were hard.

Somehow, he managed to sit up and pull his legs closer. Into the freezing water. The freezing, smelly water, rank with decaying organic matter trapped in layers of detritus. A series of grunts later and he was kneeling on the shoulder of the road again. Colder and more tired than he'd been a few minutes ago and caked in muck. But alive, which — at that moment — he wasn't so sure was all that wonderful of a thing to be celebrating.

He groped around for his walking stick. Where had it gone? Where was his backpack?

A faint silver glow lit up the road ahead. He'd hoped the overpass where he'd hidden his things earlier that morning was closer, but it was still nowhere in sight. The longer he sat there, the clearer that bleak fact became: he had a ways to go yet. He blinked at the sudden brightening, trying to make sense of it. It was still early night. And the clouds were still thick with rain. Where was the light coming from?

Suddenly, Hush crouched, his ears flattening as he twisted his head to look at the road before them.

Ah, a car. Maybe, just maybe …

Buzz braced both hands in the gravel, drawing one knee to his chest. Pain stabbed at his right hip. He ignored it and planted his foot on the ground, leaning his weight to that side. If only there were a tree or post close by that he could grab onto.

The car was bearing down on them. He looked at it as he pulled his other foot from beneath him. The headlights bored into his retinas: white, all-consuming light shining through the downpour. Rain slapping against the road. The aggressive roar of an engine. Louder and louder. Closer. Closer. Closer.

Its right tire hugged the white line at the road's edge. The same line where, less than a hundred feet away now, Buzz was crouched like a cement frog, unable to stand or move away.

A figure blocked the light. An iron fist clenched Buzz's heart.

"Hush, no!"

Buzz flailed a hand out, hoping to grab Hush's ratty old bandana, the stump of his tail, a lock of fur, anything. But Hush was too quick. The dog leaped into the road, planting himself in the path of the hurtling monster of steel, its radiant maw pouring light into the wintry deluge.

The car swerved, the arc of its headlights swinging abruptly to the other side of the road. Brakes slammed hard. The tires locked, rubber chattering over rain-slicked asphalt, squealing as the car careened toward the far side of the road. Its front end plunged into the ditch, then bounced over it. The car jerked back to the right as the driver regained control. But no sooner had it rejoined the road, than the rear end fishtailed. The car waggled from the far lane to the near and back again before slowing and finally stopping.

Like a shot of rocket fuel, adrenaline propelled Buzz to his feet. He nearly tripped over his walking stick, then picked it up.

His dog. Where was his dog now?

The glow of brake lights painted a watery swath of red over the wet road as the car began to back up.

Buzz's heartbeat pounded in his ears like storm-driven waves against a rocky shore. He scanned the road, left to right and from his feet to the approaching taillights. There was no sign of Hush, no flattened body ...

Then, on the near side of the road, half in the grassy ditch, Buzz saw it: a sodden lump of rain-darkened fur, inert, lifeless. His knees trembled, threatening to give out.

The car jerked to a halt next to Buzz. The near window powered down. A twisted, angry face glared at him.

"What the hell are you doing out here?" the man barked.

Waves of shame and guilt rolled off Buzz, crashing into his chest like a tidal wave so hard he stepped back.

The man pinched the steering wheel, then shifted the car into park, his expression softening. "Are you okay?"

"I'm fine, but —"

"Thank God, buster. 'Cause I could've killed you — walking down the middle of the road like that." Once again, his features transformed abruptly like a volcano erupting. "What were you thinking? Didn't you see me coming? And what the blazes are you doing out on a night like this?"

Anger surged within Buzz's chest, flooding him with energy. He stomped up to the car window and leaned in. Wetness streaked down his cheek. He touched a hand to it and realized it was blood. He was too furious to feel the pain. "You killed my dog."

The man drew his head back. "Your what? I did what?"

"Dog. My dog. You hit …" — the words lodged in his throat, but he forced them out between clenched teeth — "*my dog.*"

Buzz gripped his walking stick. He fought the urge to smash the man's front windshield with it. As soon as the thought entered his mind, he dampened it. He sensed the man's bluster was merely a mask to hide his humiliation. Still, the man ought to at least pretend to care about his dog.

"I didn't see any damn dog. I almost didn't see you." The stench of alcohol permeated the air. In the cup holders of the center console were two opened cans of beer. The man followed Buzz's gaze, then grappled at a newspaper in the passenger seat and covered the console with it. He yanked the stick shift back into drive. "And as far as anyone's concerned, you never saw me."

The man hit the power up button on the window. Buzz snatched his fingers away just in time to keep them from getting pinched. Through the rain-smeared window, Buzz saw him punch his foot at the gas pedal, but the wheels spun, flailing sprays of water behind them. Cursing, the man let up just enough so the tires made contact with the road again. The trunk of the car swung toward Buzz. He stumbled backward, falling on his hip as the car sped away. His stick clattered to the ground.

Buzz watched him go, the taillights fading to streaks of red through the sheets of black rain. A stone of heaviness sank his gut. It was dark. Pitch-black. Not even flashes of lightning to show him the way. He could only see the white line next to him, threading its way into the void beyond.

On hands and knees, Buzz followed the line, his stick clutched loosely. Rocks scraped at his palms. The water saturating his clothing weighed him down, chilled him. His teeth chattered. He shivered all the way down to his bones.

He didn't realize until several minutes passed that he had stopped. He couldn't go on. Could, maybe, but didn't want to. That bastard had run over his dog. Left him dead in a ditch and then just drove off without an apology. A decent human being would've offered help, a ride to the vet's, if there was even a chance …

Grief crashed through Buzz. Coiled itself around his organs, crushing him from the inside. He inhaled but couldn't get a lungful of air, so he captured it in little gulps before a sob ripped from his throat.

He folded to the pavement, pressed its roughness to his forehead. Rain pounded on his back, a relentless drumming, driving the misery deeper into his shriveled core. He'd come all this way, from California to Kentucky, with that dumb dog. *Because* of that dog. And now Hush was … Hush was …

Gone.

It seemed unfathomable. Like an ocean without water. A sky without sun or moon, stars or clouds. Life had been empty before Hush. After him it would be a black hole, devouring all joy, all life.

The breath leaked out of Buzz. Every last molecule. His mind was a vacuum. An empty space filling up with disbelief.

This couldn't be. It couldn't.

That car should have hit *him*, instead. If it had, what loss would the world have suffered? None. Buzz Donovan, a drifter, would have died on a country road somewhere in — Where was he again? — somewhere in the Kentucky foothills, and no one would have cared. Hush could've fended for himself. He might have wandered about for a few weeks, eating out of overturned trashcans or hunting small animals, but after a time he would have found himself a new human to tag along with. Dogs were resilient that way. He, Buzz, was not.

And now he had to go on alone.

The dog had gotten him this far. It was up to him to use that momentum and go the rest of the way by himself. Without his dog, maybe, but never really alone.

First things first. Retrieve Hush's body. Give him a proper burial. It was the respectful thing to do. The least he could do. He didn't have a shovel to dig with, but he could gather some rocks to build a mound.

The rain had let up a bit. It was now more of a gentle mist than a downpour. Buzz looked ahead into the darkness. The faintest silver outline of a dead body straddled the edge line ahead, not far across the road. He forced himself to his feet, trudged toward it. It wasn't moving or breathing.

But ... the color wasn't quite right. Hush was a deep, dark blue merle — a blend of black and shades of steely gray and silver — with copper on his legs and feet and a full white chest and collar. This animal's fur was dull, more tan than gray. Could be the darkness and wet fur, Buzz figured.

Twenty feet away, he stopped. That was no dog. It was ... a raccoon. Or was he just hoping it was?

He forced himself closer. Yes, a very bloated, very dead raccoon. Then where was —?

A sneeze sounded from somewhere to his right. Or was it behind him? And was he only imagining it? It was hard to tell with the steady patter of rain. He turned around, looked hard, but his eyes were playing tricks on him. At sixty-three, his vision wasn't good anyway, let alone trying to see anything at night.

"Hush," he said softly, "you there?" Then louder, more confident, hopeful, "Hush, come *here*."

Raindrops plopped in the ditchwater. Wind murmured in his ears. But in between, he heard the slightest exhalation. The crack of a twig. Then, feet wading through a puddle behind him.

Buzz wheeled around so fast he nearly fell over.

Head low, ears folded to the side, Hush limped forward. Licking his lips, he hobbled up to Buzz and leaned against him.

Laying down his walking stick, Buzz knelt at Hush's side and stroked his wet fur, his hand sliding down the dog's neck, past his shoulder, to his front leg. Between the dog's elbow and wrist, the bone made an abrupt angle. Broken, definitely broken. Unable to see well, Buzz gently probed it. Hush stiffened but didn't pull away. The bone wasn't protruding through. Still, this wasn't good.

"You lousy goat turd," Buzz muttered. "With you in this condition ... how're we gonna get to the ocean before I run out of time, huh?"

Hush flicked his tongue at Buzz's hand. The old man swatted at him, but his arm wouldn't do what he wanted it to. He lifted his head to look toward the overpass they'd been headed for. Wherever it was, it wasn't close enough. He didn't have time.

"No, no. Not now. Not here."

Hush licked Buzz's wrist obsessively. The harder and faster he licked, Buzz knew, the sooner it was going to happen.

"You should've warned me before now," he said, but the words came out all slurred.

No sense fighting it then.

Before he could lie down, a tingle of electricity speared through the right side of his head. A wall of cold walloped him. He shivered, his limbs trembling uncontrollably.

Then everything ... *everything* went black.

chapter 3

Beam

The dog was nearly all black, a silhouette of fury, scrabbling toward me across the pavement of the bridge like a hellhound unleashed.

My first instinct was to run. But to where? The truck? Unless I could levitate like an air-bender, that would've been a stupid move. The truck was *behind* the dog.

My second instinct was to crumple to the ground like a spineless jellyfish and protect my face. But that hadn't worked before. I had the scars to prove it.

There was no one around to save me this time. I was going to die.

Funny thing is, when death stares you down and charges at you on four paws, there's a certain clarity that descends. A calm detachment. Like floating above yourself, watching it all unfold.

A whoosh of cool air surrounded me. The lightest tickle brushed across the back of my neck, and then I heard a voice, a little kid's voice, soft in my right ear, as if someone were standing there beside me.

Be brave, Beam.

I ripped my jacket from my shoulders and wound it around my forearm like a bite sleeve.

"Hah!" I yelled from the bottom of my gut. I faked some Ninja moves. 'Fake' being the operative word. Really, I was scared to death. The chicken in me wanted to run, but to where? I shuttled back until my heels hit the framework of the bridge. I could smell the tang of rusty metal, feel the edge of the steel truss biting into my hamstring, see the strings of steamy saliva dripping from the dog's jagged yellow teeth.

Coal-black eyes glinted in the night. Nails scraped over the road in a drawn-out *click-click-click-click*.

I stuck my arm out, my feet braced wide for the impact — the impact that never came.

In an explosion of motion, the dog arced abruptly outward, its lanky form skirting the middle line as it dashed by. Swinging around, I saw it more clearly then. Saw its face as it skittered past. It looked more scared of me than I was of it.

Fifty feet farther on, the dog skidded to a halt. A discarded fast food paper bag lay on its side on the road. I could've sworn that hadn't been there when I'd driven over the bridge an hour ago, but maybe I just hadn't been paying attention. The dog crammed its nose inside and yanked out a half-eaten bag of fries, devouring them in three gulps before plunging its snout back in and rooting around in the bag again.

This was my chance to escape, before it decided I was prey after all.

I ran. Ran like my life depended on it. Because it did.

My heart burst against the inside of my ribs. Adrenaline zinged through every vein, flooded every cell of my body. Pure energy transforming me. Making me light and fast. A bullet fired from a gun. A hawk diving from up high. A high-speed train gliding along its rails as the world blurred by.

17

I'd parked the truck in a gulley just before the bridge so it was barely visible from the road. Half a dozen cars had gone by that evening, none of them stopping or even slowing to look as I'd perched on the side of the old bridge.

Too bad I hadn't thought to dig the key out of my coat pocket before I got to the truck. I grabbed the door handle. Panic squeezed my heart. I heard the click of nails again. Didn't dare look.

I looked. I really shouldn't have. Because the rabid beast had followed me.

Frantic, I unwrapped my jacket from my arm and groped for the pocket. I found it, but it was the wrong one. And, stupid me, I was holding the coat upside down.

The keys jangled as I turned the coat in my hands, feeling for the other pocket. But before I found it, I heard the clink of metal as they hit the pavement.

The dog's head snapped up. Tail tucked between its legs, it crept forward, curious. The nearer it got to me, the more it curled its body submissively. Like I was going to trust it. Fat chance. The thing had teeth. Sharp teeth. Lots of them. Jaws that could crush my facial bones.

Scooping the keys up, I flipped through them until I found the right one. Trembling, I punched the key at the keyhole. It wouldn't fit.

I turned it over, tried again. It slipped in; the lock clicked. I yanked the door open so hard I was afraid it would come off its hinges. Like an old arthritic man, it groaned in protest. This truck was older than I was and rust had taken its toll. Diving into the front seat, I slammed the door shut. Heart banging wildly, I pressed the back of my skull against the headrest as I put the key in the ignition and flicked on the headlights.

The dog, standing squarely in front of the grill, backed up and turned away. It went a good ways across the bridge before turning to look back. In its eyes, I recognized hunger and hard times and the toll they had taken, the fight for survival fading.

Bathed in the glare of the headlights, I could see it now in stark detail. Its fur was dull, patches missing. Its skin clung to a gaunt frame, every rib prominent. It stood as tall as a German Shepherd, yet was leaner than a Greyhound. It sniffed the air, then trotted away slowly, as if conserving energy.

A pang of sympathy plucked at my heart, but I shoved it down. I didn't like dogs. Hated them. Certainly didn't trust them. But, like me, this one had been down on its luck.

It wasn't a young dog. Somehow it had survived for years. What had happened to it that now it was a feral animal, wandering across the countryside, resorting to scavenging through trash and undoubtedly feasting on road-kill? Had it been dumped by the roadside recently? Had it been tied to a tree or doghouse and chewed through a rope to claim its freedom? Had it been a treasured pet that fled through a backyard gate when someone left the latch open, then explored until it was so far lost it couldn't find its way home? Had it lost its way by accident, or fled willingly like me?

If my crazy plan didn't work out, would I too end up a wanderer one day — no family, no home?

Then again, no loss. I didn't really have either of those anyway.

I started the truck and muscled the gearshift into drive and headed for the interstate. If I could manage to stay awake, I'd be in Faderville in time to have lunch with my grandparents. I hadn't seen them in over ten years, but that wasn't my fault. Not like I could drive down to see them anytime I wanted. Until now. I was still months away from being able to get my license, but that was a minor technicality, given the circumstances.

The shocks squeaked as I drove back over the potholed bridge. I had to be careful. One broken axle, one flat tire, one speeding ticket, and all my plans would go up in smoke. If anyone asked for ID or a credit card, well, I didn't have any. Even my library card was expired.

19

And I hadn't been able to find my Social Security card or birth certificate before I left. Heaven only knew where Lana had stuffed those.

Two stop signs and three turns later, the entrance ramp beckoned. I turned onto it, accelerating slowly. The highway stretched into the distance. Trucks and cars zoomed along. Palms slick with sweat as I gripped the steering wheel for dear life, I eased into the right-hand lane.

Only eight hours to go. More if I included bathroom breaks. I had a full tank of gas and by my calculations wouldn't need a refill until Cincinnati. As for food, I still had half a bag of hot dog buns, a mini bag of pretzels, an overripe banana, and two cans of Mountain Dew.

Enough carbs and caffeine to swim the English Channel.

—o00o—

I was drowning in pee. My blood had to be fifty percent sucrose by now. Before sun-up, I'd downed both cans of pop for the caffeine and sugar buzz. While adrenaline had fueled me for the first four hours, after that, keeping my eyes open had become a chore. I'd cranked the windows down, slapped myself in the face repeatedly, and started singing along to the radio — until it occurred to me that doing crazy stuff like that could draw attention and get me pulled over.

If I didn't relieve my bladder soon, I'd explode from the pressure. The only reason I'd kept going until now was that I had it in my head that Lana would call the authorities to claim I'd been kidnapped and there'd be a tri-state AMBER Alert out on me. Even though it was unlikely she'd care enough to bother, being seen in public was a risk I didn't want to take. I *could* take a leak into an empty can while driving, but that seemed dangerous. Not to mention messy. No, I couldn't take any stupid risks. That was the biggest reason I'd set out in the middle of the night. In the daytime, someone could've glanced my way from another car and seen me at the wheel. Sure, I could pass for eighteen with a little makeup and some grownup clothes, but what if Lana had woken up from her alcohol-dulled, medicated state and noticed I was gone — along with the truck? Count on her to have one lucid day out of a hundred just when I needed her to be a zombie.

And the truck, a Ford from the late eighties … obviously it wasn't mine. It wasn't exactly Lana's, either. One of Lana's many boyfriends — some loser named Drexel — had parked it in our back yard, saying he was going to fix it up and sell it. He'd never bothered. After half an hour of staring at the hood one day, he declared it dead and called the junkyard to come and get it. They wanted a hundred and fifty dollars to tow it, which he said he wasn't about to pay. He'd told Lana he and a friend would hook a chain to the front bumper and they'd haul it in themselves. At least he'd get money for the scrap metal then. But the next morning, after Drexel spent the night with Lana, they had a fight. He never came back. And so the truck sat there, weeds growing up around it, rust speckling the body, mice gnawing on the upholstery.

The neighbors probably saw it as an eyesore. I saw opportunity. You see, Drexel had left the key in the ignition. Since the engine wouldn't turn over, he figured it was as good as dead. Truth is he was just lazy. And broke. I didn't have the first clue about engines, but I knew someone who did. An eighteen-year-old kid known as Zapper lived a few doors down. Everyone knew he could hotwire a car, but as long as nobody squealed on him, he didn't bother anyone's car nearby. Most in our neighborhood weren't worth stealing anyway.

While Lana was at work one day, Zapper replaced a couple of spark plugs and the ignition switch. Problem solved. I told him it was a surprise for Lana's birthday, that she'd talked about fixing that truck up all of last year but just never had the money. I'm not sure he believed me, but he didn't pry, just like I didn't ask him how he got his spending money.

Twice, I took the truck, which I'd named Carlos because it was easier to cuss at something with a name, for a spin — once on a weekday evening after Lana left for work, and another time late at night when she was zoned-out on the couch. Lana never knew. And since the truck had been parked behind the detached garage, there was a good chance now she wouldn't figure out it was gone for quite some time.

It was Friday night, and I'd left a note taped to the fridge saying I'd be at my friend Morgan's for the weekend. Never mind that Morgan didn't even know we were friends. She'd stopped at our place once to pick up a shared homework assignment and Lana had answered the door. I figured that note would give me two days head start. Come Monday, Lana would be at work. That would probably buy me a couple more days. If she wasn't tending bar at the chain restaurant by the mall, she was out with a 'friend'. By the time she caught on, my grandparents would know the full story and would probably start custody proceedings by then.

In my head, it all made perfect sense. Completely logical and inarguable.

The problem was that I really didn't know my grandparents. I could only hope they were sensible people. They sort of had to be if they'd given up on Lana, the woman who gave birth to me and raised me for the first few years until I was old enough to figure things out on my own. Anymore, I pretty much took care of myself.

But the more I thought about my grandparents cutting Lana off, the more it bothered me. Because in giving up on her and shoving her out the door, they'd also given up on me.

If they'd thought Lana was such a lost cause, why had they allowed her to take me with her? They had to know about her issues. Why hadn't they insisted on providing me with a stable home? Plenty of grandparents did just that.

Maybe at the time they wouldn't have been able to prove she was an unfit parent. Maybe they'd tried to reach out to her and she was the one who had cut all ties. Maybe they didn't know how bad things had really become.

Yet I clung to the hope that a better life awaited me. It couldn't possibly be any worse.

An exit sign flashed by. Too late. I'd missed it. I went under an overpass and glanced in my rearview mirror. The brilliant gold and red of a McDonald's sign lit up the night sky. At 3 a.m., they probably weren't even open, anyway. A rest stop would've been perfect, but I'd just passed the last one fifteen minutes ago and there wouldn't be another until just outside of Cincinnati.

That was an hour-and-a-half away. There was no way I'd make it.

Funny, before tonight I'd never driven more than five miles at a time. Twice. I'd been so nervous then I'd almost come to a complete stop the first time another car approached in the opposite lane. I'd barely felt in control. The thought of operating several tons of steel, able to change speed with a tip of my foot or alter direction by turning the steering wheel just a few inches in one direction had damn near paralyzed me. But I'd taken this truck because I had to. It was my only way out. And here I was tonight, cruising down the interstate to some Podunk town two states away.

As long as traffic stayed light, I was going to manage just fine. But I still had to pee. Really bad. The last billboard promised an exit twenty miles away. At seventy miles an hour I could make that in less than twenty minutes. If I went eighty, I could cut it down to fifteen.

I sped up just a little. A minivan, with a pair of glassy-eyed parents at the helm and a trio of sleeping toddlers strapped in the back seats, passed me. It was followed closely by a box truck with giant sprinkle donuts and a cup of coffee plastered on the side. I pressed the accelerator down more. The speedometer climbed a couple of notches. I was now almost five miles an hour over the speed limit. And I kept getting passed like I was standing still.

23

Come to think of it, I hadn't seen a cop since I crossed the Michigan-Ohio border. Chances were there were very few of them out at this hour. The increasing discomfort was keeping me awake, but at some point I wasn't going to be able to hold it in any longer. I tucked behind a couple of cars going seventy-nine miles an hour. There *had* to be a gas station somewhere in this part of Ohio. You'd think.

The cars in front of me drifted into the left lane. Without changing speed, I quickly approached the bumper of an older sedan. I flipped on my turn signal to merge left, but a semi had already filled the gap. More vehicles came up from behind. I eased off the gas to give the car in front of me more distance, but after two miles of constantly checking my speed, I was getting impatient. Had to be an old lady driving, but why would *she* be out in the middle of the night?

I closed the space between my front bumper and her trunk. She puttered on, oblivious. The semi had passed, but in its place was a flatbed truck and behind that was a growing row of cars. I couldn't even slip back and join them, because another car had me trapped from behind.

A pothole swallowed one of my tires with a *thunk*. Carlos bounced hard, but amazingly held together. The impact, though, was not so kind to my bladder. I was one more pothole away from bursting in a spray of urine.

Finally, a space opened up to my left. A hasty glance in the mirror and I went for it. The truck's engine gurgled. At first, it didn't accelerate, so I let up on the gas, then pushed down slower. It responded with a weak surge, allowing me to slip in.

A horn blared at me.

Panic exploded inside my chest. I glanced in the mirror to see a pair of headlights bearing down on me. So I floored it some more. Eighty-four miles an hour. The truck's frame shuddered, threatening to break apart.

The moment I was ahead of the old lady — and it was indeed an

24

old lady — I switched back into the right lane, remembering a second too late that I'd forgotten to use my turn signal on both lane changes, which was probably why the last driver had expressed his road rage at me.

Anyway, I was still alive and that's what mattered.

Until I saw the spinning blue lights in my side mirror.

If I could've banged my head on the dashboard just then and still kept in control, I would have. I'd ruined my chances. Tossed them away just to get to a toilet five minutes sooner.

So much for well-laid plans.

The highway patrol car zoomed up behind me. The pounding of my heart in my ears warred with the wail of the siren. I let up on the gas as I began to rehearse my story.

"My grandma's dying and my mom was out stone cold. I couldn't wake her up. So I took the keys and went. I don't know if I'll make it in time."

Wait, no ... that story had more holes than a pair of acid-washed denims. And worse than being returned to Lana's care would be being handed over to foster care while they figured out what to do with me. I'd heard too many stories.

"I left my license at home —"

No, not good. That in itself would be an offense. If I had a license. Which I didn't.

"My wallet was stolen at the last rest stop. I'm on my way to see my dying mother ..."

Better. Except I was going south and the truck was registered in Michigan — and not in her name. At least I think the registration was in the glove compartment. I'd never actually looked for it. They were already probably running a check on the plates. Lana could have woken up, found my note, and in a rage reported the truck stolen.

I really should've made up a decent story before I started out, just for situations like this.

My nerves all knotted, I drifted onto the shoulder, double-checking to make sure my seatbelt was still on before coming to a full stop. My mouth went dry. My hands would've been shaking something terrible if I hadn't had a death grip on the steering wheel.

The twirling lights came closer, right up to me … and kept going. Right on past.

That was when I noticed the long line of cars ahead, the bright red glow of brake lights. Only four miles to the next exit.

I could hold it in that long. I had to. After all, I'd waited almost sixteen years for this day.

—o00o—

Four miles took thirty minutes. That was seven-and-a-half minutes per mile. I could run faster. No, really, I could. Thank goodness there was a twenty-four-hour truck stop at the next exit.

As I pulled into a far spot in the parking lot, I started to think this wasn't such a hot idea. The place looked pretty sketchy. If I hurried in, didn't make eye contact, and hurried back out, I could do this.

Maybe.

I hadn't even stepped foot out of the truck and two beer-bellied, tattooed truckers, leaning against the tire of an eighteen-wheeler, were ogling me. I tucked my ponytail into a Detroit Tigers ball cap and pulled my hood up. Wait, my sweatshirt was two sizes too big. I looked like I was planning to hold the place up. I tugged my hood back off. Before getting out, I reached under the front seat. There, amid fast food wrappers, loose change, and a few gel pens was the little plastic canister — my only weapon. I tucked it into the front pocket of my hoodie, got out, and locked the door.

I'd parked directly beneath a floodlight, but it made me feel more exposed than protected. Those two guys were the only people I could see and, even though I wasn't looking at them, I could tell they were

26

watching me. The lights were all on inside the truck stop and the neon sign in the front window said 'Open 24-7-365'.

Still, I couldn't see a single soul in there, not even someone behind the counter. It was one of those truck stops with a couple of fast food places in it, a mini-mart with cheap junk you didn't need until you discovered it there, mega-restrooms with about twenty stalls, and showers that were probably crawling with foot fungus. A dozen long-haul semis were lined up in a row in the gravel section of the lot to the rear of the building. Many of them had sleeping quarters behind the cab. Surely someone else was around.

Just before I reached the front door, I heard a catcall. If I'd been wearing hooker boots and a halter top, I might've understood, but a baseball hat, ratty old jeans, and an oversized sweatshirt? That was just creepy. I hurried inside.

A tall thin Indian man in a faded red uniform shirt and black pants turned away from the soft-drink machine long enough to say, "Welcome to Blue Dot." Then he went back to wiping down the counter with a rag that looked like it belonged in the bottom of an oil pan. Two middle-aged women stood in the snack aisle, tormenting themselves with artery-clogging choices. One of them glanced at me and smiled. Fear raced through me. What if they figured out I wasn't here with an adult? Then if they followed me into the parking lot and saw me get in the truck …

I ran to the restrooms and yanked open the first stall door.

"Agh!" A little old lady gawked at me in terror as she squatted on the toilet seat.

"Sorry, sorry," I offered, rife with embarrassment.

"The latch doesn't work." She slammed the door shut. "Knock next time, would you?"

I hurried to the last stall before she could get her pantyhose hitched up and come out and beat me with her overstuffed Vera Bradley purse. This time I peeked under the door before ducking

27

inside.

"Aunt Maude?" Another woman shuffled softly into the restrooms, pausing at the middle of the row of stalls. She waited before calling out again. "Aunt Maude, you in here still?"

My bashful bladder prevented me from getting any relief. I couldn't go when people were having a conversation practically next to me.

"Give me five minutes, will you, Bethany?" came the familiar irritated voice. "I'm eighty-six. These things happen in their own time."

"Sure, I'll be in the pain relievers aisle, waiting for you."

Aunt Maude took a lot longer than five minutes. Thankfully, once she left, no one else came in. Relief never felt so euphoric.

Several minutes and half a gallon later, I felt like a completely different person. I washed my hands and slapped cold water on my face. My stomach rumbled with a craving as I passed the donut display on the way out. I couldn't give in yet. I still had my pretzels and some hot dog buns to get me to my grandparents. They'd probably tell me I was too skinny and force food down my throat. Besides, I only had so much money. I had to save it for emergencies and put it toward my future — whatever that entailed.

I was fifty feet from my truck when one of the grease monkeys blocked my path.

"Hey, sweetheart." His lips drew up in a leering smile to reveal a gold tooth crowded by several discolored ones. "Traveling alone?"

"No," I lied. "My boyfriend's inside getting us some food."

He tipped his head back, glancing at the door. "Funny, I didn't see him go in with you."

"You must've missed him. He'll be out any second."

"That so? Sure is taking his time."

I was about to elaborate on my lie when it occurred to me I didn't owe this jerk an explanation. Unfortunately, he had me trapped between a semi and a row of cars.

"Excuse me." Feeling in my pocket for the pepper spray and my key, I dodged to the side.

He countered my move and stepped closer, kicking up handfuls of gravel.

I'd have to back up and go around the row of cars. I pivoted on my heel but pulled up. The second guy, who'd been behind me, was leaning against the trunk of a pimped-out Buick. He pushed away from it, looked me up and down.

"You figure she's lying about that boyfriend, Brandon?" the first one said.

"Probably," Brandon speculated. "But only 'cause she's, you know, not experienced. Just nervous, that's all." Then to me, "We don't mind, sugar. We'll take it easy on you."

Even from ten feet away — which was closer to the likes of him than I ever wanted to be — I could smell the alcohol on his breath. Brandon moved closer. "What d'you think, Luke? Pretty young to be wandering around here by herself at this hour, ain't she?"

"Way too young," Luke answered. "Then again, I like young."

"Yup, me too." Running a thumb under his belt, Brandon smiled knowingly at his friend. Then he tipped his head to the side to get a better view of my backside. "Fine-looking thing like you, hiding under those frumpy clothes. Keeps you warm, I s'pose. You got any girlfriends, sugar? Course, if'n you don't, Luke and I can always share."

Luke grunted. "Speak for yourself. I saw her first."

"Fine." Brandon sneered at him. "But you get her good and warmed up for me, hear?"

This encounter had gone from annoying to creepy to dangerous inside of a minute. For all the 'boyfriends' Lana had brought home over the years, some of them nothing but a quick wham-bam-thank-you-ma'am — none of them had ever come on to me. Sure, a few had flirted with me the past couple of years since I'd filled out, but none of them were lecherous enough to do something like this. For a few moments, it occurred to me that as much as I'd wanted to get away from home and all of Lana's problems, her choice in men was never as bad as this. I knew how to deal with her getting drunk or stoned or laid by some jerk. But this ... I was in way over my head.

Luke reached into his jacket pocket and brought out a clear glass bottle. "Want a taste? Loosens you up. You might like it. Jim Beam is a good friend of mine. He'll make things easier — if it *is* your first time."

"First time what?" Stupid question to ask, but I was stalling however I could.

They both laughed. Brandon doubled over and stumbled against a semi tire. Luke quickly dropped his smile, though, his eyes taking on a hard, intense look.

I felt like a mouse in the hawk's shadow. If I didn't get out of here, things were going to go south much too quickly. They were stronger than me, but drunk. I was faster and more nimble. I just needed an opportunity.

The front door of the building swung open. Aunt Maude walked out, leaning on Bethany's arm. Bethany had parked right in front of the truck stop, but getting Maude situated in the passenger's seat was taking her some time.

Luke sidled up to me until he was an arm's reach away. My heart was going ninety miles a minute. It took all my energy to keep my breathing under control. I backed up, but my butt hit the car. One more step and he had me pinned.

"Can I have that drink now?" I faked a seductive smile. I'd seen Lana flash it enough to know the look. "I could use a little courage."

Luke blinked at me, until it dawned on him that I just might give him what he wanted. He fumbled with the cap, unscrewed it, then lifted the bottle to my lips.

30

I shuddered to have him that close, inches from touching me. My skin crawled like it was coated with maggots.

When I hesitated, he shoved the bottle hard against my lips and tipped it just enough so some of the alcohol spilled into my mouth. In reflex, I turned my head away.

"Come on," Luke growled, his words sharp with angry impatience. "Just a little drink."

"A little?" I tried to laugh, but it came out sounding like a frog being strangled. "I think it's going to take more than a little."

He squinted at me, unsure if that was an insult or a challenge. This guy was as dense as he was smashed.

"Can I?" I reached for the bottle. He relinquished it willingly. The bottle was barely in my hands when I let it slip — on purpose. It hit the ground with a brittle crash. He looked down, mouth gaping in disbelief. Whiskey had splashed onto his work boots and darkened the bottom of his pants legs. He bent over to grab the pieces of the bottle, as if certain he could salvage some of it.

Luke took one of the shards in his hand. Unsure whether he was upset about losing his 'precious' or reaching for the sharp glass so he could cut me open, I pulled the canister of pepper spray from my pocket, aimed, and pushed the trigger. Right at his face.

"Holy shhhhhiiit!" he screamed.

One hand clutching his eyes, he fell to his knees. Right on top of the broken glass. He flopped over onto his side, finding more glass.

I scrambled over Luke's horizontal form as he cursed at me and flailed an arm my way. His hand grazed the back of my calf but I shook it free and was out beyond the Buick and headed back toward the building. I didn't care if someone else saw me. I didn't want to get pawed and poked by those bastards. And I didn't want to die. Not here. Not tonight.

I didn't get far before another pair of hands latched onto my shoulders. Brandon clamped down on me and dragged me back.

Before he could cover my mouth I shouted, "Bethany! Hey, Bethany!"

Brandon gave me a puzzled look, then glanced toward Bethany's car. She turned around, saw us.

"You there!" she shouted. "Stop!"

With a shove, Brandon released me. He hauled a bleeding, puling Luke up and toward their truck. They both climbed in. The engine started.

I stood trembling in the half-darkness. Bethany rushed over to me just as they were pulling out onto the road.

"Are you okay, honey? What happened? Did they hurt you?"

I shook my head. "No, I'm okay."

"Want me to call the cops? There was a highway patrol sitting in the median just before we got off at this exit. I'm sure he could be here in less than a minute."

"Don't bother. I'm fine. Really." Physically, I was fine. Emotionally, I was rattled to the core.

"You sure?"

"Yeah, I'm sure." As much as I'd needed her help, it was now making me uncomfortable. I couldn't let law enforcement get involved. "Anyway, thanks. I have to go now."

"Sure. Say ... how did you know my name, anyway?"

"I heard your aunt say it in the restroom."

"Oh." She glanced back at her car. "I suppose old Aunt Maude is having a conniption about now. That or she's asleep already. Or terribly confused. She forgets easily. Things like where we're going or what time it is. Sometimes she can't even remember my name. Anyway, you take care, okay? I don't know who those men were, but you look awful young to be mixing with their type. I mean, I know sometimes folks are hard up for money, that they have ... habits, but you look too nice for that sort of thing. Besides, you're not really dressed for the part, but you never know."

Had she just insinuated I was an underage hooker with a drug habit? I must've really looked like a wreck to be mistaken for a crack whore. Just like my mom.

"Thanks for your help." I turned away, got in my truck, and exited the parking lot just as a cruiser pulled in. Luckily for me the cops didn't get there five minutes sooner.

After that ordeal, I didn't need caffeine. In four hours' time, I'd almost been killed twice. That's what happens when delinquents like me run away from home, I suppose.

chapter 4

Buzz

It was always like waking up from a long, deep sleep. Sometimes Buzz lost hours when it happened. Like a videotape that had skipped ahead, from one frame to another.

The signals could be faint, almost imperceptible: a headache, a tingle throughout his body, a sense of being elsewhere. And then it was as if the stage curtain descended or someone had switched all the lights off. He'd learned to live with it, but it had meant giving up a lot of normal activities, like driving or regular work. Which pretty much meant he kept to himself. He was good at avoiding people. Until he needed them. Now was one of those times. Hush's broken leg was beyond Buzz's crude doctoring skills. The dog needed a veterinarian. First, though, Buzz had to get back to normal, however long that might take.

Before Hush came along, Buzz hadn't always had much warning about his episodes. With the passing of time they'd become more and more frequent — and more severe. At his last construction job, he'd hidden his condition from his boss and co-workers until the day he keeled over with a seizure while using a power saw. It had nearly cost him his left thumb. He didn't remember what happened exactly. Just that he felt … funny. Like his mind and his body were two separate entities. The next thing he knew, he was lying in a hospital bed, his thumb wrapped in gauze and medical tape, tubes snaking out of his arms, and some danged contraption beeping in his ears every time his heart pushed blood through his veins.

The nurse, who'd been changing out the IV bag hooked up beside him, called the doctor in. In the abruptness of her pained glance, Buzz sensed pity. *She knows*, he'd thought.

The doctor, a grim-faced young man too sober for his years, told Buzz, "We're going to run some tests —"

"No," Buzz interrupted, "you don't need to. I already know."

Buzz told him then. Not the technicalities of it, but the bare bones: he was going to die … eventually.

"We could refer you to another hospital," the doctor insisted. "There are some neurosurgeons at places like Mayo and Cleveland who specialize in this type of condition. They can run MRIs, pinpoint the location and tissue involved, prescribe drugs that …"

The doctor went on spewing his knowledge, making promises, tendering hope. It was all about cutting-edge experimental medicine, which meant volunteering to be a guinea pig. Buzz was no longer listening. He'd heard it all before and learned to live with what was. And he'd long since given up hope that things could be any different.

The first time he'd gotten the news, he was sure they were wrong — the whole medical team: three general practitioners, two neurologists, and an oncologist. Never one to accept bad news at face value, Buzz had done some research of his own. Turned out they were all right. Probably, anyways.

There was always room for doubt. Or hope, however you wanted to look at it. But Buzz was a practical man. 'Maybe', 'might', 'possibly' — he never risked living by those terms.

Faced with the inevitable, Buzz had succumbed to anger and depression, isolating himself. He stopped going out for beers with his work buddies. Not that any of them were real friends, the type you'd pour your heart out to, but they'd provided companionship, someone to kill the spare hours on weekends with. He stopped visiting the Descanso Gardens, the place that had provided him so much solace and peace with its sprawling live oaks and rose gardens. He stopped taking walks on the pier and going to the movies and rooting for the Lakers on TV. In short, he stopped living. He merely existed.

Soon after his accident, he quit his job. The bewilderment of his co-workers was too much to process. They didn't understand him distancing himself as he pondered his fate. Given both his current condition and that one damning mark in his criminal record, his options for a different career were few. Luckily, he could still get money. Disability, they called it. The point was that he wasn't working anymore. Not that he ever liked to, but it had provided a routine and given him a reason to get up every day. Not too long after that, he sold his neat little bungalow with its once lush green lawn and abundant rose beds, and moved into a basement apartment on the outskirts of the Green Meadows neighborhood.

Living in that place, it was easy to never raise your eyes and say 'hello', even to the people across the alley. Some of them you wouldn't want to know. You just hoped and prayed you never got on their bad side and every time you heard sirens, you wondered if it was the guy in the next unit, overdosed on heroin, or the old lady upstairs, sprawled in a pool of blood.

Eventually, going out got to be too dicey. Not because of the crime, because that was a given, but because of what might happen inside his head out of the blue. He avoided leaving his apartment unless absolutely necessary and tried to make his trips as short as possible. The episodes — or generalized convulsive seizures, as the last neurologist had called them — were becoming increasingly frequent. Twice he'd hit his head and suffered a concussion. Once he fell down a flight of stairs but didn't know it until he woke up in the hospital with his shoulder in a sling. They'd tried to convince him then to move into some kind of long-term-care facility, but Buzz knew that was just a fancy word for a nursing home. He was no spring chicken, but he wasn't *that* old. Besides, he'd had enough older acquaintances he knew go into nursing homes to know he couldn't afford the best ones — and the ones he could afford on his meager assistance weren't worth giving that money up for. Better to just go on like he was until he absolutely couldn't anymore.

In short, Buzz Donovan became a recluse in the middle of Los Angeles, a city of millions. Until the day he found Hush.

Buzz focused on the stars peeking from between the clouds as they raced across the night sky. It took him awhile to remember where he was and how he'd gotten there. Every time this happened, it was as though he had to gather his thoughts together again, like sheep that had scattered across the Scottish Highlands.

Highlands... Hills... Kentucky. Yes, that's where they were. He remembered now. But the name of the town they'd been in yesterday still escaped him.

Slowly, he sat up, his mind full of static. Rubbing at his head, his thoughts crackled and faded, then slowly returned. He hadn't been out long, but whether that meant fifteen minutes or three hours he had no idea. He pressed a palm to his coat and patted his breast pocket, then his hip pocket. Plastic crinkled beneath his touch.

It was still there, thankfully. The purpose for his journey. His greatest promise.

Ever diligent, Hush nosed his arm, then slipped his head beneath Buzz's hand to wait for a pet, the paw of his crooked leg held off the ground. Buzz was still too groggy and dazed to respond fully, but he let his hand rest on the dog a moment, if only because it reassured Hush that he was all right. They sat like that for several minutes on the roadside in the dark, just breathing, both of them hurting, yet grateful for more time together.

Although his limbs were stiff, Buzz forced himself to stretch. He'd learned it was best to get moving afterward and get on with whatever he'd been doing. But this time it was more difficult. His extremities were numb from the cold. He wondered if he'd hit his head again, but when he probed his skull, he didn't feel any lumps or tender spots.

His hands hurt. He peeled off his gloves to inspect for frostbite. A little blue, but no more so than normal for winter. Pressing his fingertips to his face he checked for sensation. Faint, but still there. His fingers actually stung a little now. That was good, he supposed. Hard though it was, he forced himself to stand. He needed to get back to the overpass and get his backpack. After that, they had to find a vet. He'd figure out how to pay for it later.

From a few feet away, Hush observed in quiet pensiveness, his feet — except for the injured one — tucked beneath him to ward off the cold. Anything Buzz did was a source of fascination for the dog. Whether Buzz was brushing his teeth or blowing his nose, hanging one of the three T-shirts he owned on a branch to dry, or re-packing his scant belongings to better fit them in his backpack, Hush was always watching, his quizzical copper eyebrows alternately lifting — unless he was asleep, which wasn't often, as far as Buzz could tell. Buzz couldn't so much as breathe without Hush studying the way his nostrils flared or take a piss without the dog sniffing the spot where his urine stream had hit.

It annoyed Buzz to no end. It also made him feel cherished in a way he'd never felt before. He'd never had anyone care about him as much as that dog did. As long as Hush was with him, he had a reason to get up every day, to go on living — no matter how much pain he was enduring, no matter how bleak the outlook, no matter how morose the purpose of their journey.

Buzz looked down at Hush. It was still hard to see how severe the damage was, but that leg was definitely broken. A shudder jarred Buzz's spine, knowing how much his friend must hurt. But aside from Hush squinting his eyes and leaning to one side so he wouldn't have to put weight on that leg, the dog didn't give much indication that he even was in pain. If Buzz had broken his leg, he'd be flopped over on the ground, helplessly sobbing until the next car came by — which in these parts might be hours yet.

Stooping down, Buzz gathered the dog and gently lifted him. Easier said than done. Twice, as he juggled the dog in his arms, he nearly dropped him. Hush was a calm dog, but obviously he had no idea what Buzz was doing and wasn't comfortable with it. So Buzz set Hush down on three legs, crouched beside him, and ducked his head under the dog's belly. Thighs straining, he stood. At fifty or so pounds, it was like carrying around a floppy sack of potatoes. Hush slid an inch to the right. Buzz instinctively grabbed a foreleg. The dog yelped in pain.

"Sorry, buddy, sorry." Buzz wound his fingers in Hush's mane. "I know this isn't comfortable for you, but we're gonna have to make do for now. Gotta get our things and then get you to the vet." Then like a parent reassuring his child, he lied, "We'll get you to the animal doctor soon. Real soon. He'll fix you up."

Soon, however, was a long ways off. Buzz figured his best chance was to go back to the small town they'd wandered into yesterday in search of food, even though he hadn't seen any sign of a vet's office. For all he knew, the nearest animal clinic might be fifty miles away. He'd walk five hundred miles to get help for Hush if he had to. Hell, they'd gone farther than that together already. So what if he had to carry the dog the rest of the way himself. Sure, it was still dark and colder than an outhouse in Siberia, but at least right now it wasn't raining any longer. Things could be worse.

They went slowly. Every time Hush shifted, Buzz struggled to keep his balance. He couldn't see more than ten feet in front of him at a time, but it was enough to avoid the potholes. His neck hurt, since he had to keep it bent forward. The blood was draining from his arms. His back had ached from the start. But he went on. Because you'd do anything for a friend and Hush was the only friend he had.

So on they went — an old man carrying a lame dog on his feeble shoulders.

The howl of a coyote sent a ripple of fear through Buzz's chest, but he told himself not to worry. Coyotes were after easy game and didn't bother humans. As far as he knew. Buzz couldn't help but notice how Hush was shivering, so he rubbed the dog's body as best he could while still holding on. And he sang to him, like he always did, because Hush never criticized the fact that he couldn't carry a tune. When he ran out of songs, he told him stories. Anything to keep his mind off their situation. Anything to pass the time. When you were on the road for months at a time, a dog your only companion, you got pretty good at talking to yourself, even if you had to make stuff up to keep it interesting.

Half a mile down the road, he had to rest before his knees gave out. He knelt and set Hush down. The dog immediately folded onto his side, which made it that much harder after a few minutes of rest to collect him again and put him back in position. They repeated this three more times before they rounded a curve beside a wood and the overpass finally came into view. By then the sky was lightening. Dawn would come soon and with it, hopefully, a car with a kindhearted soul who would give them a ride to town.

By the time they reached the overpass, the muscles in Buzz's legs and back were burning with fatigue. It was light out now. Small solace, but at least it meant someone would be by soon. Surely. As gently as he could, he settled Hush onto his side on the grass and patted him on the head.

"Stay there, buddy. I'll be right back." Then he pointed at him and repeated, "Stay." As if the dog was going to run anywhere. Hush would never leave Buzz's sight.

After a few more moments of rest, Buzz climbed up the short, rock-littered slope. By the time he reached his backpack, concealed by an old green blanket and wedged beneath the steel beams of the interstate, his palms were scraped up and there was a new hole in the knee of his jeans. He scrambled back down the hill, sending loose stones tumbling out onto the country road. By his estimate, he'd carried Hush at least two miles. So two back to where they'd come from and then probably four more back into town. Eight miles. At less than two miles an hour, it was going to take a *long* time.

Although the rain had stopped hours ago, it was now cold enough to snow. Judging by the gray clouds choking the sky, that was a distinct possibility.

Overhead, the highway was thick with traffic. He could've gotten a ride up there, but there was no way he'd get the dog up that steep slope on his shoulders. Besides, he preferred to keep a low profile.

Buzz rummaged through his backpack. "Let's see, old friend. What do we have? A fork with a bent tine, a knit cap with moth holes, a used hanky, some paperwork, a fraying wallet, a small skillet, a cup, an envelope of important papers, dirty socks, clean underwear ..." Buzz chuckled. "When I was a kid, my mom always told me to make sure I had on clean underwear, in case I was in an accident, but then I always thought, well, if I was in a wreck I'd probably pee my pants or ... well, didn't seem like it would make much difference."

After digging all the way to the bottom, he remembered why they'd gone into town yesterday and ended up staying after dark — to pick through dumpsters and trashcans, because Buzz was out of dog food and had to find something for Hush to eat. They'd scored a stale package of hamburger buns and cold French fries from some place called Harris's Outdoor Café. Luckily for them, it was midwinter and nobody was eating outdoors where they might have seen him lifting

41

the dumpster lid and fishing around inside. He'd found some breaded pork chops in their paper boats untouched, but left them. They could've been there all day, for all he knew. He'd learned his lesson weeks ago about eating cold meat out of dumpsters. Shame, because those chops had smelled really good.

He checked the inside pocket of his backpack. Crisp bills crinkled under his fingertips. Coins clinked as he dug deeper. All there.

Hush sniffed the air as Buzz took out a can of spray cheese and spread a large daub on a saltine cracker. Buzz had taken the cracker package from the restaurant when he walked in to ask directions. It wasn't stealing, really. Someone had left the package on a table after their meal. If he hadn't taken it, it would've been thrown out anyway.

Hush had been tied out back while he was inside. It was a routine the dog knew well: Buzz would disappear inside to use the facilities and hastily wash. Buzz preferred the single bathrooms, because then he could lock it and wash under his arms and brush his teeth. But he'd been run out of a few places. Some managers knew a vagrant when they saw one, so Buzz tried to stay presentable. As long as he kept himself neatly groomed, he got far fewer stares. Maintaining appearances wasn't always possible, however, when you slept outside in the elements. Still, Buzz had his dignity. He brushed his teeth at least once a day and never let more than two days go by without washing his face. Every few days, he washed his hair, sometimes with the soap in the dispenser, so he wouldn't have to use up his own shampoo. When he couldn't find a private bathroom to do his grooming in, he'd wash in a river.

He even made sure to keep Hush's coat brushed and free of burs. Couldn't let a dirty dog give him away.

"Here." He laid a cracker with cheese in his palm and held it out.

Without hesitation, Hush snapped it up. Buzz ate the second cracker, without cheese, because there wasn't much left. The third, and last one, he gave to Hush.

Still licking his lips, Hush twitched his eyebrows alternately. The blue marbling in his mostly brown eyes made him hard to read sometimes, so much so that strangers often kept their distance, even though he was an accepting, if not friendly, dog. Occasionally, people even asked if he was blind. His oddly colored eyes were a trademark of the Australian Shepherd breed, Buzz would explain. And like that, he found himself fielding questions about the breed in particular and talking about dogs in general to complete strangers. The conversation often drifted to other matters, and since Buzz was in no rush, several times it went on for hours. Twice, people told him their life stories. Buzz, the once soft-spoken recluse, began to look forward to these opportunities. For most of his life, he'd shut himself off from those around him. It was a means of protecting himself, as well as avoiding the awkwardness of not knowing what to say. What he learned was that people just wanted someone to listen, and that by asking questions of them, they often answered things themselves.

Even though it was just him and his dog traveling the breadth of America, he was discovering that people had more in common with each other than they were usually aware of. So instead of feeling more alone, he felt less so. Likely, he would never see any of those people again, but he'd touched their lives all the same. And sometimes been touched by theirs.

"That's all I got, buddy." Buzz stood and had one arm in the strap of his backpack when he realized he couldn't carry it and the dog. He sat back down, thought about it, but came up with nothing. The futility of their situation weighed down his chest. He pulled his knees up and bent his head forward to rest on them.

Sensing his friend's plight, Hush tried to scoot himself closer but let out a sharp whimper when his leg touched the ground. He stiffened and began to whine.

Buzz moved next to him to drape his blanket over the both of them and stroked his neck. "Shhh, shhh. It's all right. It's all right.

We'll just wait here until someone comes by."

But they waited. And waited. And no cars ever came.

Snow drifted down, dotting the road in clumps of frozen fluff. Exhaustion moored Buzz in place. He considered finding a path up to the interstate, but once he was up there, even if he got someone to stop and offer a ride, how would they get down here to get Hush? Still, how else was he going to get him help?

He took the leash from his back pocket and tied Hush to the guardrail. He couldn't take a chance on Hush following him, because that's just what that darn dog would do. Just as he reached for his backpack, Buzz thought about the long climb up the hill. He wasn't nimble anymore. His knees and back were bad. Sure, he could walk a long ways on a flat surface, but climbing? No, he hadn't done that in years. If there was any chance of him making it up there, he'd have to leave the backpack down here. Normally, he'd just let Hush guard it, but in Hush's current state, Buzz didn't think he'd be very effective at his regular duties.

After a few more moments of thought, Buzz left it where it was. And as hard as it was, he turned his back and left Hush, too.

Hush's whine, soft as a baby's sigh, tugged at his heart.

"I'll be back," he said, looking over his shoulder.

No sooner had Buzz started walking out from beneath the overpass than he saw a pickup headed toward them. Hope buoyed him. Waving his arms, Buzz moved out into the middle of the lane. He knew he could get hit, but he was desperate. That man last night had been a drunk, and it was dark. This was probably just some kind soul on their way to work.

The truck slowed and veered around him, then stopped about twenty yards away. The left rear taillight was missing a piece, so that while the brake was depressed a shark tooth-shaped patch of white glowed in a field of red. Then the truck turned around and came toward him. A younger man, in his twenties Buzz guessed, peered at him from behind the steering wheel, a cigarette dangling from the corner of his mouth. The man rolled down the window and flicked some ashes out as Buzz jogged up to him.

"Hey. Sorry to bother you, but I need some help." Buzz gestured toward Hush. "My dog got hit by a car. I need to get him to the vet."

The man took a drag of his cigarette, held it in his lungs for a few seconds before blowing out a puff of smoke. Menthol. Buzz remembered the taste of it. He'd smoked in his youth. Back when he was young and dumb.

When the man didn't answer, Buzz added, "Suppose you could give me a ride into town? I know you weren't going in that direction, but ... I don't know how else to get him there. Unless you know where there's a vet clinic closer by?"

The man shook his head, his lips pinched tight. He seemed nervous, like he was worried about something. "Ahhh, I don't know, man. It's kinda out of the way. I'd be late for work. "

Buzz's heart sank. He'd have to wait for another passerby. But this was a little traveled road. That could be another hour. "I can give you gas money."

"It's a long ways."

"Twenty bucks?" Not that he had much to spare, but he would've given his last penny to save Hush.

The man studied the dog and shrugged. Something in his demeanor shifted. "Okay, but the dog has to ride in back."

Buzz thanked him and rushed off to collect Hush. He grabbed his blanket as an extra measure. The man remained in the truck as Buzz labored to carry the dog. It was difficult, but he managed to flip the latch on the truck cap and pull down the tailgate without dropping Hush. Boxes and piles of tools and auto parts filled the bed. He placed Hush on the tailgate while he figured out where to put him. The ridges in the liner of the bed were full of dirt, so Buzz took his blanket and spread it out between two battered boxes smelling of auto fluids.

There was barely enough room for Hush to lie down, but it would have to do for now. The poor dog looked bewildered as Buzz closed the cap and latched it in place. He noticed the 'CHEVROLET' lettering on the back was a speckly faded white and the bumper dipped slightly to one side. The truck had probably done its fair share of work over the years. You didn't discard a good vehicle just because the shine had worn off.

Buzz opened the door to get in on the passenger side, but the seat was cluttered with work clothes.

"Forget something?" the man said, his voice a lazy drawl. He glanced back toward the backpack.

"Oh, yeah. Thanks." Buzz hurried as best he could to retrieve it. As he went back to the truck, he noticed the man bending down from his seat, then fiddling with something beside him, but figured he was probably just rearranging the mess in the cab so Buzz would have room.

When Buzz got in, there was a denim jacket wadded up on the bench seat beside the man. Buzz checked for a seatbelt but couldn't find one. The driver wasn't wearing one either. A bit disconcerting, but he'd only be riding along for a short time. He thought about introducing himself but decided not to. They'd never see each other again. What was the point? Anyway, this guy wasn't the friendliest of people. Best just to accept the favor without intruding, then go their separate ways.

No sooner had Buzz shut the door than the man pulled away, accelerating at a pace that made Buzz uncomfortable. He was glad there was no traffic on this road, but as they took the first curve, the tires on the right side clipped the gravel shoulder and Buzz's stomach catapulted into his throat. The moment the road straightened out, Buzz twisted around to look into the bed. He couldn't even see Hush but worried that too much jostling could hurt his leg more.

"Where is this vet clinic?" Buzz asked, now more concerned than curious.

"A ways."

"So it's not back in that town in the other direction?"

"All I know is where I'm taking you."

Buzz took that to mean the veterinarian was located someplace outside of town. Probably a farm vet.

For a minute, the man kept the truck in his lane, but he was speeding. Even without being able to see the speedometer, Buzz could tell. They topped a rise and for a split second the truck went airborne. It was like a ride on a rickety roller coaster, one that Buzz wanted to get off of but couldn't. His nerves were fraying bit by bit. Still, he was more concerned for Hush than for himself.

A front tire hit a pothole and the vehicle jounced to the left. Buzz gripped the armrest on the door. It was too much. Panic crept into Buzz's chest, tugging at him, sending a message he didn't quite understand.

"Can you slow down?" Buzz said, more command than question.

"What? Too fast for you?" The man had a distinct drawl. Buzz wasn't good at guessing accents, but he could tell his wasn't a Kentucky one. The man hit the gas a little harder, laughing as he took another curve at a dangerous pace. Too fast and too reckless.

"A little."

"You're the one who was begging for a ride. You want to criticize my driving?"

"No, but my dog has a broken leg. I don't want him to get hurt worse."

"Not very grateful, are you?" His words were bitterly sharp.

This was beyond uncomfortable now; it was dangerous. "No, I am. It's just —"

"Get out." He slammed on the brakes so hard that some of the tools in back slid in the bed and hit the front of it with a series of clunks.

All Buzz could think of was Hush. "What?"

The man glared at Buzz. "I want my gas money now."

"I'll get out if you want, but you haven't taken us to any vet clinic."

A snort ripped from the man's mouth. "And I'm not going to." His hand slid beneath the denim jacket. A second later, he was aiming a pistol at Buzz's head. "Give me the money *now*."

The barrel of the pistol gaped before Buzz. He wasn't afraid, though. He was mad. Mad that someone could pretend to be helpful, then pull a stunt like this. He didn't care what this guy's story was. What was *wrong* with people, anyway? Buzz reached for the zipper on his backpack.

"Get. Out." The man cocked the gun.

"Just getting the money!" Buzz barked.

"Leave the bag." He jammed the barrel against Buzz's forehead.

The cool imprint of metal pressed against bone. A very faint scent of sulfur curled inside Buzz's nostrils: a warning that this gun had been fired before, and not all that long ago. Buzz hesitated. Not only was his last hundred bucks in his pack, but his ID, some very important papers, and a few old photos that were all he had of his old life. Back before things went bad for him.

Yet none of that mattered as much as Hush. Not even his own life.

"Fine," Buzz growled between tight lips, "but give me thirty seconds to get the dog out of the back. He could die any minute in his condition. Then you'd have a dead body to dispose of. And if he doesn't die, he'll try to eat your face off."

A lie if he ever told one, but he had to give this derelict reason to let him have his dog back.

The man narrowed his eyes at Buzz, no remorse, no sympathy in his gaze. He grinned. "What makes you think I haven't gotten rid of a dead body before?"

Buzz had no doubt the man could, and would, kill him as well as the dog. But he owed that dog his life. It wasn't going to end like this at the hands of some heat-packing scumbag on some obscure road in the middle of nowhere.

Another pickup rounded the curve ahead, coming straight toward them. Buzz kicked the door open. This was his chance.

He stepped partway out but held on to the door. He'd let this psychopath drag him down the road if he had to. "Let me get the dog."

The man's eyes flicked to the approaching vehicle. He jerked his head toward the rear of the truck. "Hurry up."

Buzz left the door open, got out, and went to the back. The license plate was from Texas, but he didn't have time to memorize it. As fast as he could, Buzz opened the tailgate and slid Hush out, the green blanket gathered loosely around the dog's body. He barely had Hush free of the tailgate before the guy hit the gas. Tires bit into the pavement. Pebbles flew from beneath the truck and pelted Buzz's shins. The truck sped away, swerving over the center line to barely miss the oncoming vehicle.

The other truck veered away, then corrected. Too far. The grill was pointed directly at Buzz.

Buzz clutched Hush to his chest as it all played out before him: one truck zooming into hyperspace while another fought to maintain control on a collision course with him. The oncoming driver laid on the horn. There wasn't time to get out of the way. Not without diving to the pavement and hurting Hush. Buzz turned his body away, so the car would hit him first. Then he closed his eyes, held on tight, Hush's fur wound in his fingers.

With a drawn-out squeal, tires slid over the road. Rubber chattered over asphalt, trying hard to gain a grip.

Cold air rushed around Buzz. Hush shivered in his arms.

A bumper tapped against the back of Buzz's thigh.

Not until he heard a door slam and feet race toward him did he open his eyes.

"Sir, are you all right?"

Blinking, Buzz looked into eyes full of concern and kindness. This was a man of middle years, the slightest hint of silver tracing through the fair hair at his temples. He had on a pair of Carhartts, well-worn, but clean. He placed a hand on Buzz's shoulder.

"What just happened? Are you okay?"

The shock fading, Buzz nodded. He trusted him, although he didn't know why. He just did. "He ... he pointed a gun at me. I'm fine. But my dog ..."

The sandy-haired man looked at Hush, the realization sinking in. "His leg ..."

"He was hit by a car earlier. I was taking him to get help. The guy offered us a ride. And then ... he took my stuff. Almost drove off with my dog."

The man's eyebrows pinched together. "Get in my truck. We'll take him to my clinic."

Clinic? It was then Buzz noticed the embroidered patch on his coveralls: a staff with a snake coiled around it.

"It's okay," the man reassured him. "I'm Hunter McHugh, the vet here in Faderville. I was on a farm call, but it can wait. Nothing but routine hoof trimmings for a bunch of goats. Come on." He gestured toward the pickup: a long bed with a crew cab, the fanciest kind. "We're only five minutes from my clinic."

Buzz squeezed his eyes shut to dam back the tears. Up until now, it had been the worst day of his life. Worse than the day he got the news about his health. Worse than the day he was sentenced to jail. Worse, even, than the last day he saw his son. He swallowed back the lump in his throat, looked up at the sky where snowflakes were drifting down, and counted his blessings — the greatest of which was cradled in his aching arms.

Despite everything that had just happened, he considered himself lucky.

chapter 5

Beam

You know how they say some people are born under a lucky star? Yeah, well, mine was an unlucky star— and my bad luck started *before* I was even born.

Lana Adelaide Larson got stone drunk one night and got herself knocked up in the back seat of a Chevy Nova in a mall parking lot in Ann Arbor by some college boy. She didn't even know where he was from. I don't think she cared. Her parents had shipped her off to college two states away so she could 'learn some responsibility'. She got that in spades: me. Two months into her first semester, she dropped out of college. Severe morning sickness, she claimed. Whatever. On the same day her college classmates headed home for summer break, she had me in a hospital in Saginaw, where her boyfriend at the time — not my biological father — lived. He didn't stick around either. It became a routine: new boyfriend, new town, new crib, new job.

Apparently, I was the reason her life was so messed up — a fact that she never ceased to remind me of. Like I asked to be born. If I had, I would have chosen a better parent. Too bad there wasn't a way to track down my sperm donor. For all I knew he was a decent guy who'd just let his hormones lead the way and had a little fun. But I'm sure he never knew about me. Whoever 'he' was.

Bellamy was his last name, she once told me. Which was another reason I hated the name.

Lana seldom kept a job more than six months. There was always some reason: a co-worker she couldn't get along with, stocking shelves was boring, the customers were impossible to deal with, the boss came on to her ... I have no doubt that last one happened. She tended to flirt a lot. Flirting led to other things. Like me. And Oakley. It was what got her by in life. And what complicated her life, although she'd never admit to it.

When she didn't have a job, there was always a boyfriend to support her. Most of them were just as messed up as she was. They drank, they swore, they had bad hygiene ... One was even a hoarder who lived in a trailer park. She cleaned his place up when we moved in to make space for me and Oakley, but then when he wouldn't keep it tidy and griped at her for not picking up his stuff, she left him, too. Only one boyfriend was ever violent. The day he slapped me for not bringing him a beer when he woke up from his nap, she got us out of there. She had her standards. Too bad they were so low.

There were a couple, though, who did worse than drink. The first one just smoked a little pot now and then. Lana adopted the habit. 'Just to unwind', she'd claimed, because her job cleaning after hours at a doctor's office was so stressful. The smell made me sick to my stomach. So at ten years old, I would walk to the library ten blocks away, sometimes with Oakley in tow, and read all day. Just so I could get away from the stink. By twelve, I'd read all the classics and an entire set of encyclopedias. I hated holidays because the library was closed. The good thing about hanging out there was that I learned a lot. The librarians either knew I had it bad at home or they were thrilled to see a kid who spent more time with her nose in a book than texting. I wouldn't know about that. We were always too poor to even have cell phones. A lot of the time we didn't even have a landline. If you needed to get a hold of us, you had to show up at the door.

Another guy — Reggie was his name — got so high one night that he left a skillet with oil on the stove and fell asleep on the couch. The kitchen caught on fire. My little brother, Oakley, woke me up. Taking his hand, I went out into the hallway. It was thick with smoke. To our right was a wall of heat, flames cracking and hissing. To the left was a cloud of acrid smoke. Panicked, I started to cry.

Be brave, Beam, he said.

He twisted his hand in the tail of my shirt like a baby elephant trailing after its mother. I pulled him down, told him to crawl with me, to hang on. He answered me twice when I spoke to him. He said something about getting his kitten, but I told him not to worry about that right now, that she was probably outside already. I was sure he was there right behind me. Sure that he'd answered me.

When I finally made it outside, he wasn't behind me at all.

I tried to go back in, but a neighbor had a death-grip on me, wouldn't let me. I fought and clawed to free myself, but the smoke was making me cough so bad it weakened me. Later, when I got my breath back, I screamed Oakley's name so long and so loud that my vocal cords nearly burst from my throat. Meanwhile, Lana and Reggie stood in the background, both of them still foggy from the drugs.

They recovered Oakley's body the next morning from the smoldering structure.

After that, Lana started experimenting with drugs. If she couldn't invent some ache that would score her a script for painkillers, she'd find the local dealer and use whatever numbed her — although when I confronted her, she always claimed she never used the hard stuff. I didn't ask what that meant. It didn't matter. Drugs are drugs.

I understood grief. I felt it every day. Like someone had punched a hole in my gut and scooped out all the innards with a melon baller. I blamed myself for not holding Oak's hand and making sure he got out okay. But if he hadn't roused me, I probably would've succumbed to smoke inhalation before I ever woke up. Then I'd be the dead one, not him.

After that, it was like I didn't exist to my mother. Like I didn't matter. Not that she'd been all that great a mother before, but after that she might as well have not been around at all. She couldn't keep herself straight long enough to take care of me. When you're a kid, there's only so much you can do to try to make your parent get their act together. I brought home pamphlets from the library about drug abuse counseling and grief support groups for parents who've lost young children. I found out the name of the county agency that helped people get back on track after personal setbacks.

None of it mattered, though. *She* was always the victim. Not me. Not Oakley.

Because I witnessed her helplessness every day, I learned how to take care of myself. There was no way I'd ever let myself become like her. And I wasn't going to wait until I turned eighteen to get out of there. I couldn't let her ruin my life alongside hers. Not for another year. Not another month. Not another day.

Bad luck might follow me like a cloud, but I wasn't going to let it rain on me forever. As far as I was concerned, that black cloud was still sound asleep on a couch in Flint, Michigan.

Sometimes you just had to lose the dead weight.

Yeah, I'd learned a lot from my mother. I'd learned what *not* to be.

That was what I told myself as I drove down I-75 across the bridge spanning the Ohio River, and the rolling hills of Kentucky spread out before me. I was headed for a new life and a family that would support and accept me.

Just a few more hours to go and everything would be better. I'd leave my crappy childhood behind me and start fresh.

Pretty sober thing to say when you're not even sixteen yet.

—o00o—

Tracing a finger over the lines that were the roads, I estimated the distance remaining. Faderville was only a speck on the map on a wall of the rest station, but it was closer than I thought. Bladder again relieved and a fill-up from the drinking fountain and I was ready to go.

At the truck, as I took the key from my pocket, a young family straggled by. Judging by the pillow lines on the kids' faces and their bed-hair, they'd been on the road since before sunup. The dad carried a sleeping baby in his carrier and the mom balanced a toddler on her hip. Holding the mom's other hand was a little boy, same hair and eyes as my Oakley, and probably about the same age as when he died. A pang shot through my heart.

The little boy glanced at me and ducked behind his mother — probably because I was staring. I couldn't look away, the resemblance was so strong. Except his eyes weren't slanted and his head was normal sized.

They all traipsed up the sidewalk and to a concrete picnic bench. The mom spread out lunch items and got the two older kids started on their meal, while the dad helped the baby to a bottle. The parents chatted, the children laughed. I was transfixed. It was so … normal.

Even if I'd just had Oakley, I could've known some of that. He'd been a happy kid. Lana's shortcomings had never dragged him down.

"Beam, Beam. I can't wake Mommy up, Beam."

"I don't think she's going to wake up for a long time. We need food, Oak. I don't know what to do. I can't drive to the store myself."

"You brave, Beam. Brave and big. You walk there. I go, too."

And so I took ten bucks from her purse and we walked to the convenience store and back in falling darkness on the streets of

Kalamazoo, where we lived at the time. She never knew the money was missing. Never knew we'd been gone. I was twelve; Oak was four going on forty. Later, we did it again, going all the way to the big discount grocery. Eventually, I think she suspected it, but she never questioned me. In a way, by learning to get by, I took some of the responsibility from her.

When Oak first started to speak he called me Beam because he couldn't say Bellamy. I liked it so much I started introducing myself as Beam Larson and signed my name that way. Sometimes, when he was a little bigger, he would call me Sunbeam. A couple of times, when I got mad at Lana and argued with her, he called me Laser Beam, because I was like a light saber, he said. I sort of knew what he meant.

Oakley was … different. The wonderful thing is that he didn't know he was.

He didn't even know he had a father. Some guy Lana always called 'Wolf' who had taken one look at Oakley in his baby crib, asked what was wrong with him, and never saw him again. Guess he couldn't handle a kid with Down syndrome.

The little boy at the picnic bench looked at me and waved, smiling shyly. I waved back, returning the smile. Then I got in the truck and left, my heart a little heavier than it had been a few minutes before.

Sometimes you think you're running away from your past, but it just tags right along with you.

Oakley used to tag along everywhere. Like a lost puppy dog. I couldn't go to the bathroom without that kid standing outside the door, waiting to hear the toilet flush.

God, I missed him.

—o00o—

Evidently, I'd missed the sign that said: *Faderville, Kentucky. Population: Next to nothing.*

Seriously, you could walk from one end of town to the other in ten minutes. They didn't even have a General Dollar. Forget Wal-Mart. Where did the people in this town shop? Where did they go for fast food? Where were the doctors' offices and strip malls and movie theatres? What did they do if they needed to go to the hospital or had a dental emergency?

As far as I could tell when I pulled off the highway, this was nothing more than a crossroads. Sure, there were houses — small, well-kept, one-and-a-half-story homes hugging tree-lined streets — and cars occasionally driving up and down those streets, but I couldn't see where anyone around here worked. There weren't any shopping malls or chain restaurants, business parks or factories. Just the bare necessities: a place to gas up, a pizzeria, a couple of mom-and-pop restaurants, an elementary school, a post office, and a bank with a single car drive-thru. One old store front served as a senior center, and another, a used book store. I had a glimmer of hope with that last one, but the bookstore didn't appear to be open. Judging by the empty shelves, it wasn't even still in business.

After the last stop sign in town, I headed down a curvy stretch of state highway, then turned left onto another road. On the seat beside me was an envelope with a Christmas card in it from five years ago. The name and address scrawled in the upper left corner said: Roland and Noreen Larson, 1676 Victory Hill Farm Road, Faderville, KY.

The card had been buried in an old shoe box in the closet under a pair of Lana's black strappy heels. Those shoes got a lot of use. The card, however … it hadn't even been opened when I found it. I don't know why she would have hidden it in there, but maybe she hadn't hidden it at all. It had just ended up there, the same way Lana ended up in a different bed every few months and a different city every couple of years. I'd lived in six that I could remember. Flint had been the last stop — and the longest. You'd think I would be glad about that. I was anything but. Nobody wanted to stay in Flint. For certain, nobody moved there on purpose.

The Christmas card had been signed simply:

Love, Mom and Dad

P.S. How's the family doing? We'd love to see you all. Been a while.

Slowing, I pulled onto the shoulder. Before I even had the truck in park, my forehead was on the steering wheel, my breath coming in short pants. Tears stormed at my eyes.

Dang it. Dang it, dang it, *dang it!* I needed to get a grip. Be strong.

Leaning my head back, I dragged a sleeve across my eyes, then blew my nose on a used fast food napkin.

A truck appeared in my rearview mirror. I hunkered lower in my seat to hide as it swung out into the other lane to pass. It was a white truck, with the veterinary symbol painted in bright blue on the side. It went by so fast I couldn't see who or what was inside, but whoever it was sure was in a hurry.

I was so tired that all I wanted to do was keel over right then and take an eight-hour nap. But I was too close to do that now. Besides, parked on the side of the road wasn't a good place for that. After slapping myself a few times, I checked the directions I'd written down and went on. I almost didn't see the sign at the next turn, my mind was so foggy.

The only thing on Fox Hollow Road, besides a couple of farms, was a place called Fox Hollow Lifetime Care Center, where a sprawling, single-floor brick building was surrounded by short, leafless trees and winding paths through bare gardens. Must've been one of those retirement places. One path led to a gazebo and on it an older man pushed a woman in a wheelchair. What had caught my eye, though, was the dog trotting dutifully beside him, a nearly all black dog with white feet and chest and no tail. Amazing they even let dogs in there. I could imagine some sharp-clawed, rambunctious German Shepherd knocking an elderly person over and breaking their hip.

Four turns and twelve miles later, I came upon my grandparents' road. It was so far out of town, I couldn't figure out how this was even the same zip code. Marked by a weather-beaten hand-painted sign, Victory Hill Farm stood on the corner by the roadside, the house a good half mile back from the road. Two-story pillars supported a crumbling green shingle roof. A few of the shutters hung crookedly and overgrown bushes hugged the foundation. A rambling board fence was in sore need of repair and pastures were overgrown with thistle.

I slowed to read the numbers on the mailbox, squinting my tired eyes to focus. No, this wasn't their house. I kept going. Smaller pieces of property dotted with tiny houses followed. None of those addresses were even close. Fields and woods filled the gap that followed.

It took a long time until I came upon the mailbox that said '1676'. I pulled into the dirt driveway. My heart started to pound. Why was I so nervous? It was all going to be fine. They'd be happy to see me. Thrilled that I'd left my worthless mother behind.

I navigated around potholes, driving so slowly I could've pushed the darn thing faster. I pulled up to the house. It was an old farmhouse, a bit outdated, but well cared for. Off to the side was a barn almost as big as the house and a couple of sheds housing cattle. It was tidy and picturesque. Very Norman Rockwellian. The kind of place I'd dreamed of.

I pieced together the fragments of my childhood memories: the trumpet vine clambering up the trellis on one side of the house, the sprawling oak out front, the wraparound porch, the little creek ambling through a rolling pasture out back.

Yes, this was it. Just as I remembered it from that June morning, so long ago.

I turned the engine off and sat there, paralyzed, taking in the quiet, trying to think up what to say.

"Hi, I'm Beam ... I mean Bellamy — your granddaughter," I said quietly to myself, prying my cottony tongue off the roof of my mouth.

"I know I should've called, but ... I didn't ... didn't ..."

Didn't what? Why was my brain frozen?

I waited for thoughts to form, for my body to move. Butterflies flapped around in my stomach so furiously I felt like vomiting.

A little gray dog with a beard and cropped ears came bounding around from the back yard.

Yap, yap, yap, yap. Yap, yap, yap —

Holy crap. There was no way I was getting out of the truck now. He may have only been twelve inches tall, but those teeth were sharp. And the eyebrows, trimmed at an angle, made him look like some mad, little, dwarf version of the Grinch.

It had been over ten years since I'd seen my grandparents, but I didn't remember anything about a dog. If I'd known they had one now, I would've gone to more trouble to look them up, call them, and offer to meet on neutral territory. Dog-less. Or stay away altogether.

"Peppermint! Peppermint!" A woman wearing on oversized, paint-splattered flannel shirt came out the front door with a paintbrush dipped in mint green. She waved it at the dog. "Stop it this instant."

The dog glanced at her, paused for a breath, then went on yapping.

She peered at me. Stray black hairs surrounded a young pale face in vivid contrast. She couldn't have been more than in her late twenties.

"Can I help you?" she said from a distance. The dog raced in tightening loops between her feet and the door of my truck. "Are you looking for someone?"

I cracked the window, still too afraid to get out. "Roland and Noreen Larson. My grandparents."

"Sorry." She shook her head. "Doesn't ring a bell."

I glanced at the directions again. "Is this 1676 Victory Hill Farm Road?"

"It is." Holding the brush safely out from her body, she scooped the little dog up. He stopped barking but replaced it with distressed whining.

"But this is their address," I insisted.

She shushed the dog and shrugged. "We bought this place six months ago from Timothy Butler. Maybe they owned it before him? How long ago did they live here?"

My eyes sank to my lap. "A while."

This wasn't going well. Everything had hinged on them being here and now they weren't. I didn't know what to do or where to go. I'd rather live in my truck than go back to Flint. Just last week, someone on my block had been shot dead when they answered the front door. A month before, a five-year-old girl had been killed while sitting in her living room, watching cartoons, the victim of a drive-by shooting. That house was two streets over.

I startled when the woman tapped on my window. The little dog, shaking, whined louder.

"Peppermint gets excited when we have company. He just wants to say 'hi'. If you pet him, he'll calm down."

"I don't think so," I replied quickly, then added, "I'm allergic to dogs." I wasn't, but it always worked whenever someone tried to force a puppy on me.

"Ohhh, that's terrible. Anyway, I can put him away. Would you like to come in and we can make some calls? You look kind of upset."

Paranoia kicked in. I wasn't used to anyone being helpful. In Flint, you kept to yourself.

I pulled myself up tall and donned a strained smile. "No, I'm good. Just wanted to say 'hi'. Do you maybe have the address of the guy who lived here before you?"

"Do you want his phone number?"

"I, um, I don't have a cell phone."

Her eyes narrowed the tiniest bit. Like she couldn't believe a teenager in this day and age didn't have a smart phone. "I'll be right back."

I swear that on her way inside she looked at my license plate and memorized it. The plates had been expired for over a year. If she reported me to the cops, I was sunk. I slipped the key in the ignition and started the engine up.

Before I had a chance to put it in gear and back up, she hurried down the front steps with a phone book, her finger holding a place on the page. The dog was nowhere in sight, thank God.

She stood close to the window. "Says here he lives at 329 South Williams. That's on the south side of town, close to the interstate. Do you want directions?"

"I think I know where it is," I lied. I had learned a few things from my mom. She was good at calling in 'sick' when she'd had too much to drink or was still stoned. Anyway, I needed to get out of there before the cops showed up. "Thanks."

I put the truck in reverse as a signal for her to get out of the way.

She knocked on the window again. "His name is Timothy Butler. Don't know if I mentioned that."

She had, but it would have been rude to remind her. When I was about eight, I figured out that other people didn't remember things as well as I did. No wonder adults had called me a smart aleck and other kids snubbed me. I flashed a smile of thanks and hightailed it out of there. On my way out, I drove straight over the potholes.

I checked the fuel gauge. Just enough gas to get back into town. Hopefully.

—o0Oo—

Carlos was fading like an asthmatic in respiratory failure when I pulled into the gas station. After fueling up, I went inside to pay. The clerk looked like he didn't know what to do with real cash. He counted it again, his lips moving as he dropped the coins in the register.

"Can you tell me where South Williams is?"

He blinked at me. "Street or Drive?"

No way could there be both in this one-stoplight town. "Does it make a difference? I was just given an address on South Williams and was told it was on the south side."

His face brightened. "Oh, that makes sense now that you say it. Sorry, I'm not from around here. I don't know."

Wonderful. I'd have to go the three blocks to the pizza place and ask. I'd already spoken to way too many people for my comfort. Even in this backwoods I was afraid my picture had been splashed on the news.

"Hey, Brad," the clerk called out. He motioned to someone in the back of the store. "You know where South Williams is?"

Like I said, my luck was never good. Because a uniformed police officer strode from between the aisles and approached.

"Sure do." Styrofoam coffee cup in hand, he smiled at me. "In fact, I'm going that way on my way back to work. If you follow my car, miss, I'll lead the way."

A closer inspection at his uniform revealed he wasn't a cop at all, but some kind of campus security. A patch over his pocket read: Adair County Community College. He may not have been a real police officer, but the gun in his holster sure wasn't fake.

"Thanks, but, um ..." I pointed to the rear of the store. "I need to use the restroom. It might take a while."

Why had I said that? He didn't need to know I was constipated. Not that I was.

"Uh, how do you get there?" I prompted.

Hitching his thumb toward the rear of the store, Brad gave me a quizzical look. "The restroom's in the rear."

"I meant the address."

He winked. "Just joshin'. I knew what you meant. From the lot here, turn right onto Center Street, go two blocks, take a left on Harrison and it'll be on your left. Be careful out there by yourself, though. There was a robbery at the VFW hall outside of town early this morning. Old man Massey had just counted up all the money from their Monte Carlo event and had gone out the back door when some lunatic held him up at gunpoint. Got away with over three thousand dollars that was supposed to go to a disabled veterans' charity."

"Thanks, I will. Um …" I angled my body toward the back of the store.

He dipped his head in a nod. "You have a nice day, miss."

Without waiting to see if he was going outside to check my plates, I ran to the back of the store. Nothing but coolers full of energy drinks, sugary fruit juices, and processed meats and cheeses. Not even a door to a storage area. I went back up front.

"It's around the back." The clerk held out a key attached by a plastic cord to a hunk of wood. "Outside."

Did people in these parts regularly drive off with gas station restroom keys?

I grabbed it from him, ran outside, then locked myself in the bathroom for ten minutes. It reeked of toilet-bowl cleaner and engine oil. Used paper towels littered the floor around the trashcan. Right next to the tampon machine was a dispenser for … Really? So this is where the local guys came for birth control?

After a quick pee, I let myself out and ducked inside just long enough to return the key.

Dang. Sheriff Andy Taylor was still in the parking lot, standing next to his campus security car chatting it up with one of the locals. I waved at him. Either he was on to me or he wasn't. I might as well figure it out. He finally noticed me and waved back, then went on talking to his friend.

Dodged that bullet.

For now.

On to Timothy Butler's house, so I could find my grandparents.

—o0Oo—

Timothy Butler wasn't home. That or he wasn't going to open the door for some strange girl who looked like she'd just hiked the Appalachian Trail without a change of clothes. I needed a shower. And something to eat. And a bed.

I sank down on the top of the porch steps, so tired I could've just flopped over and gone comatose. I'd knocked on his door off and on for fifteen minutes, thinking maybe he was in the shower or hadn't heard me the first twenty times. There was a car in the driveway, a TV on in the living room visible through the picture window, and a half-eaten sandwich on the end table next to the recliner.

This was all supposed to be so simple: leave Flint for good, find my grandparents, and start over. Why did *everything* keep going wrong?

An icy wind scrubbed at my cheeks and stiffened my fingers as I traced the edge of the envelope in my pocket. I clamped my arms against my body to hold the heat in, but I was growing numb.

"Can I help you?" A well-padded middle-aged man in a plaid jacket stopped on the sidewalk in front of me.

"Probably not," I muttered, hoping this nosy passerby would just go on his merry way and leave me alone to wallow in my misery. The truth was I was ready to throw in the towel. Maybe even go back home. At the very least, I needed to drive somewhere out of the way and have a good long sleep. About sixteen hours' worth. After that, maybe I'd feel refreshed and ready to keep at this. Right now, I really didn't care. Everything had been going wrong since I left home. Everything always had. I should have taken it as a sign: nothing would ever change for me. Why even try?

The man shifted a grocery sack on his hip. "Well, you're going to have to move."

"I'm not sure I can." No joke. I'd burned up the last molecule of sugar in my bloodstream an hour ago. I was one blink away from a narcoleptic episode.

"You have to. You're in front of my door."

A tiny surge of hope lifted me up. "You're Timothy Butler?"

"No, I just buy his groceries." He waved me aside. "Yes, that's me. Now scoot out of the way."

Struggling to my feet, I moved aside. He fitted his key in its keyhole and jiggled it. I wasn't going to let him go inside without getting what I needed. "I was wondering if you could tell me something?"

"If it's the secret to the universe, no, I don't have a clue." He shoved the key in and turned it hard. The door popped open. "If it's my office hours, we open at nine on Monday. And no, I don't do emergency appointments unless you're a regular."

He wedged his hip into the space and had a foot inside when I tapped him on the back.

"I'm looking for my grandparents — Roland and Noreen Larson." At the mention of their names, there was a flicker of recognition in his eyes. He *had* to know. "You bought their farmhouse, then sold it to someone else. They used to live on Victory —"

"Yes, yes, I remember." He hugged the grocery bag to his body, then pushed the door open and stepped inside. "But there's something you should know."

He sounded very serious. Like when someone's about to give you bad news. Not that I expected anything else at this point.

"I bought the house in an estate auction. Your grandfather ..." Butler pressed his lips together. "He died. Stroke, I think. He'd had several. The medical bills and nursing care drained a lot of their savings, as I understand."

What little light I'd seen only moments before suddenly dimmed.

"I ... I didn't know."

I drew the envelope with their Christmas card from my coat pocket. My eyes felt watery again. Stupid tears. I'd only met my grandfather once. He'd been a quiet man, but kind. Between the two of my grandparents, it was him I'd taken to. He had smiled at me, ruffled my hair, pinched my cheek. My impression of my grandmother had been one of distance. Even then I'd sensed the friction between Lana and her. "My mom — she hadn't kept in touch with them. I'm not sure *she* knew."

He glanced at the envelope, then set the grocery bag just inside the front door. "I should have your grandmother's address in my paperwork somewhere. My wife is pretty good about filing things in labeled folders." He tilted his head to the side, drawing my gaze to a wide living room with a pair of tan couches flanking a glass-topped coffee table. At the end was a fireplace, logs and kindling already in place. I could fall asleep stretched out in front of it so easily.

He cleared his throat. "Would you like to come inside while I look for it?"

"That's okay. I'll wait out here," I answered, even though I really wanted to go inside just long enough to warm up. Caution held me back, though. In Flint, you didn't invite strangers into your house, and as a visitor, you didn't go into someone's house unless you knew them well. People here were so friendly that it was hard to accept.

With a nod, he left me shivering at the door. A few minutes later, he reappeared and handed me a piece of notepaper with an address and directions scribbled on it.

"Sorry about my handwriting. I wrote it all down quickly, figuring you needed to get on the road as soon as possible."

I took it from him. "Is this far?"

"Just a few miles outside of town. Are you sure you don't want to wait here until the weather clears up? My wife is at her sister's, two doors down, helping with the triplets. If you'd feel more comfortable with her here, I can call her. The news says there's a winter storm headed this way. Might be better to stay here. I could call information and get your grandmother's phone number to let her know."

I glanced at the darkening sky. It didn't look good, but he'd said it was only a few miles. That couldn't take long. "I think I'll be fine."

He gave me a dubious look. "All right. But if you need any more help, my phone number's on the back of that paper. I'm the chiropractor here in Faderville, by the way. Not that there's much business in a backwater town like this, but ... Oh, sorry, I didn't mean to say that. I'm from Dublin, Ohio, suburb of Columbus. Things are a little livelier up there."

"No problem, I get it. Thanks for the address." I didn't want to explain again that I had no cell phone.

Through daggers of freezing rain, I ran to the truck, the paper tucked into the pocket of my hoodie. I turned the key in the ignition. Carlos wheezed, then sputtered to life. The paper smoothed on the seat beside me, I headed to my grandparents' — grandmother's house.

In one day already, three people had come to my aid. Three people who didn't know me from Adam Lambert. There had to be a catch.

chapter 6

Buzz

The parking lot was empty when Buzz arrived at the clinic with Hunter. Together, they lifted Hush from the back seat and carried him inside on the green blanket.

On the way in, the veterinarian had called one of his techs and she arrived soon after they did. By that time, Hunter had Hush sedated.

"You can wait out front," he told Buzz. Clear fluid dripped from a bag on a pole and down a tube into Hush's vein through a needle. He checked the dog's heart and breathing rate again, laid out a pair of electric clippers, and then began to arrange his surgical instruments beside the operating table. When he noticed Buzz hadn't moved from his vigil, he tipped his head toward the doorway. "He'll be fine. I've fixed a lot of broken legs in my day. We'll let you know when it's over."

The tech, a petite young woman with a quiet, soothing nature, took Buzz by the elbow and led him to the door and down the hallway. She turned the overhead lights on and pointed to the waiting area. "I haven't had time to make the coffee yet, but everything's in the little cupboard below. Make yourself at home. There are some magazines on the shelf over there." She returned to the operating room and shut the door.

Buzz sat on the cold wooden bench directly across from the hallway, so he could see them the moment they came out. He tried reading a magazine but kept glancing down the hallway, sure that he heard something, that at any moment the technician or veterinarian would fling the door open and announce all was well. Or perhaps they would emerge grim-faced, telling him words he did not want to hear.

A knot of dread coiled itself inside his stomach. He knew there was nothing he could do as far as the operation, but he still wanted to be there to stroke Hush's fur and whisper in his ear that everything was going to be okay. Not that he knew it would be, but he was sure Hush would want to hear the reassuring tones of his voice.

At the back of Buzz's mind, another worry gnawed at him. The vet had never mentioned how much this might cost, although Buzz was sure it was more money than he had in the world. Throughout his life, Buzz had known of people who'd put animals down when the cost to fix them was too great. At the time, not being a dog owner, he'd understood. His priorities had been different then. But now, he'd pay a fortune to make sure Hush was healthy again.

Unfortunately, Buzz didn't have a fortune. In fact, he'd never had much money. Hadn't felt he needed it. Right now, he didn't have any at all. Not even a quarter in his pocket. His last hundred dollars, his extra clothes, the dog dish, his important papers ... they were all with that blasted thief, wherever he'd skedaddled to. The idiot had probably gone through his backpack, taken out the money, and tossed the rest on the side of the road somewhere. That could be anywhere.

Without ID, he couldn't get a job. Without a job, he couldn't make any money. Without money, he probably couldn't get his dog back. And without Hush ...

71

It was too much to reconcile.

Buzz probed inside the lining of his coat, felt the crinkle of the bag tucked away there. The only important thing was getting his dog back so they could finish their journey. He'd find a way. He had to.

For now, Hush was being taken care of. He'd figure out the details later.

Restless with worry, Buzz got up and made himself some coffee. As he cradled the warm cup in his hands, he looked down at his clothes, smudged with dirt and streaks of asphalt. He didn't have anything to change into or a comb to untangle his hair.

All he had was a blanket, the clothes he wore … and his dog.

—o0Oo—

Seconds grew into years as Buzz watched the door, but really only a little more than an hour and a half had elapsed. He'd downed two pots of coffee and eaten six donuts in that time. It wasn't the best of meals, but it was something. Nibbling and sipping had helped him pass the time. The caffeine had also made him jittery and he was afraid it might bring on another seizure, especially without Hush there to warn him. He remained seated as much as possible and stayed away from any sharp objects, just in case he did suddenly black out.

Since he'd been waiting, others had arrived, including a few more vet techs and some animal patients with their owners. A family with a black kitten in a carrier crowded the bench next to him, although the mother regarded him warily. The moment a row of seats on the other side of the room opened up, she ushered her three children to them.

When the mother got up to hand the kitten over to the vet tech, the youngest child came over to sit beside Buzz. She climbed up onto the bench, sat on her knees, and stared at him. He resisted for a minute, but finally glanced at her. They exchanged smiles.

"You hab a key-cat, too?" she asked, rocking side to side.

He shook his head. "Dog."

"Oh." She frowned sympathetically. "He sick, too?"

"No, hurt." Normally, Buzz would have been fine with the conversation, but today he was too riddled with concern. He just wanted time to hurry up, to have an answer, to know everything really was going to be all right.

Fidgeting, the little girl patted his shoulder. "Is otay. Dr. Magoo is good wif animaws."

Buzz smiled at the way she said Dr. McHugh's name. He realized, too, that even before she'd said so, Buzz had had the sense that he was a good vet, the kind who would go to great lengths to make them better, not just patch them up and hope for the best.

Still, he worried that might not be enough. That despite whatever Hunter McHugh might do that something could go wrong: an infection, a blood clot, hemorrhaging from unseen internal damage. He knew the risks. He'd seen all that could go wrong in situations like this. Even a simple bone break wasn't necessarily simple.

The little girl tapped him on the knee. "I hope your dog gits all bedder."

"Thank you. I do too."

"Ashley!" The mother stomped toward her daughter. "I told you to stay put. Now leave the man alone. You don't know him."

Inside, Buzz felt a little smaller and less worthy. He wondered if she would have told the girl the same thing had she spoken to one of the other, more presentable patrons.

After that, Buzz wasn't sure if anyone was giving him disgusted looks. He didn't want to know. Instead, he studied the veins and wrinkles in his hands and the dirt under his fingernails. When he grew bored with that, he counted the number of floor tiles in the waiting area. Once he figured that out, he began to observe the animals as they came in. Some of them were noticeably nervous in the same way he was. They were afraid of something bad happening. With its slick floors and antiseptic odors, the place didn't exactly promise fun and relaxation. One dog that pulled its owner in acted like it wanted to eat everyone around it, barking and growling, its hackles bristled. Buzz knew it was only a façade, that the dog was more scared than ferocious and was just trying to keep danger at bay.

The receptionist, who'd shown up thirty minutes after they had that morning, seemed to understand and left Buzz alone. He wanted very badly to lock himself in the bathroom and scrub every surface and crevice of his body, but he didn't want to abandon his post.

"Can I get you anything?"

Buzz looked up into the face of a woman wearing scrubs. Her nametag said 'Tracy'. She'd been the one escorting the patients and their families back to the exam rooms.

"I heard about your pup." Tracy gestured to the back room. "Poor guy."

What did that mean? Had something gone wrong? Was it worse than Hunter had first suggested?

"How is he?" Buzz asked.

"I don't know. Would you like me to find out?"

Hands gripping his knees, Buzz nodded. He was sick with worry.

She disappeared into the back and returned just a couple minutes later. "They're almost done. Dr. McHugh will be out soon."

As she turned to go, Buzz grabbed her arm. "Wait! Didn't he say anything?"

She glanced down at Buzz's hand but didn't pull away. Instead of stiffening, she melted into his touch, as if seeking comfort. She was worried, too, but not about Hush. "Just that he'd be out soon."

"Is my dog okay?" Buzz could barely control the tremor in his voice.

Tracy took his hand in both of hers and squeezed lightly. "He's still under sedation and will be for a while, but they're done with the surgery. Dr. McHugh will fill you in on the details."

All that told him was that Hush hadn't died on the operating table.

Small blessing. For now, it was hope.

Tracy started to go, but Buzz gripped her hands tighter. She needed ... something. If only a few words. He sensed it. "You don't need to worry. Everything's going to be all right."

Smiling faintly, she tilted her head at him. "Shouldn't I be telling that to you?"

With a shrug, he let go of her hands.

She walked away a few steps, then stopped and turned back to him. "Thanks, though. I needed to hear that. My little boy's been sick. I know it's nothing serious, but, well, I am a mother. I just don't like being away from him when he's not feeling well, you know?"

"Everything's going to be all right," Buzz repeated. Not because she didn't believe him. She did. But because he needed to believe it himself.

—o00o—

Hunter closed the door to the examining room behind Buzz and indicated a chair. Buzz sat, although he worried that the dirt on his clothes would rub off on the chair and leave a sign that he had been there. He didn't want to be noticed or remembered. He just wanted to take Hush and go on his way.

"Your dog — Hush, I think you said his name is, right? — he hasn't come out of anesthesia yet, but all his vitals are good. I had to put a pin in his leg. That will help the bone to heal straight. It will stay in there permanently, so don't expect to take him through airport security anytime soon and not have their alarms go off." Hunter smiled, trying to lighten the moment.

Buzz didn't find it funny. He didn't like being away from his dog. They'd been constant companions since they'd met. It was like having his heart removed. He rubbed the hem of his coat between his thumb and forefinger. "When will he be ready to go?"

Already, Buzz was trying to figure out how he was going to get Hush all the way to Virginia, where they'd been headed. Carrying him was out of the question. He couldn't have managed more than a few miles a day; besides, if he happened to stumble or have an episode and fall, he could hurt Hush even worse. He'd thought about making a stretcher out of tree limbs and a blanket. That would be slow-going, too, but at least it would be safer. Tree limbs would be easy to find, but the blanket would wear holes in it before he reached the state border. If he'd had a bicycle, one of those little carriages you tow behind and put small kids in, that would have been perfect, or even a little red wagon, but he didn't have the money to buy either of those. Besides, they had mountains to cross yet. How could they get over those if Hush couldn't walk on his own?

Hunter shifted on his feet. "I'm afraid I can't let him go for a few days. He needs to be monitored to make sure everything's healing properly and have his bandages changed regularly. Most of the time, I'd let them go home after a day or two, but … well, in your situation, I don't believe that's an option."

So, the vet was aware they weren't from around here and didn't have any place to go to. Even though Buzz knew it was obvious, it still made him feel ashamed whenever someone pointed it out.

"Also," Hunter went on, "there may have been a small amount of internal bleeding. Chances are good that he'll be all right, but he needs to be kept very, very still." He paused, as if sensing Buzz's dilemma. "Is that going to be a problem?"

He trusted this man completely, but it was sometimes hard to make others understand that Hush was as much a part of him as his right arm. The thought of even a few days without him … it was devastating.

"We were … walking across America. My dog and me. I don't

know …"

"Oh, I see. Quite an undertaking. Where did you start from?"

"Out west."

"You don't say? And you've come all this way?" Amazement brightened Hunter's face.

Buzz had run across many people in his adventures since leaving home. Hush had been the icebreaker for most of those conversations. The majority of people seemed to think he'd done this on some whim, like he was trying to 'find himself'. But it was so much more than that. Still, people's reactions surprised him every time. And he'd discovered more good people than bad, he had to remind himself. People like Hunter McHugh.

Hunter hopped up to sit casually on the counter. "I can't imagine how arduous that's been. Bet you've seen an array of wildlife, huh? All kinds of scenery. Endured all sorts of weather. Met a lot of folk." When Buzz didn't provide any details, the vet added, "Do you have a place to stay?"

"Not yet. I'll manage, but …"

"You're wondering how much it will cost?" Hunter finished for him.

Looking down at his hands again, Buzz nodded.

"Don't worry about that. I deal with a lot of clients in these parts who don't have much. They pay me when they can. *If* they can."

Buzz glanced at him. "Thank you." Tears filling his eyes, he looked down again and whispered, "Thank you."

"You're welcome, Mr. …?"

"Donovan. Buzz Donovan."

"We'll take good care of him, Mr. Donovan. Meanwhile, you're welcome to wait around until he wakes up. Should be another couple of hours. If you want, tomorrow is a Sunday, but you can stop by when Tracy comes in to take care of the animals in the morning. I'm sure Hush will want to see you."

"I'd like that." Although Buzz had no idea where he was going to go or what he was going to do in the meantime.

"By the way, is Buzz a nickname?"

Buzz nodded, but he didn't elaborate. He'd never liked his real name. He wasn't going to share it if he didn't have to. Besides, there were reasons he didn't want anyone to know it.

"Well" — Hunter hopped back down from the counter and stretched an arm toward the door — "make yourself as comfortable as possible in the lobby. It's a little early for lunch, but if you'd like, I can have Jeanette rustle up a sandwich or two from the fridge. Does that sound good?"

"Yes," he said softly, almost apologetically, "thank you."

It didn't seem like he could say thanks enough. He wasn't used to people being so kind. Civil, yes, but never so unbelievably accommodating. Buzz stood and angled for the door. He pulled it open, but again aware of his appearance, curled his fingers into loose fists so his dirty fingernails wouldn't show. Before he went out into the hall, he turned around. "May I use your restroom?"

"Of course. Let me show you where it is."

With relief, Buzz followed.

—o00o—

Hand towels, fancy soap, and scented moisturizer. It seemed a little extravagant, especially for a veterinary clinic, but Buzz stripped down to his drawers and used them all. He even found a container of floss and a small scrub brush in the cabinet next to the sink. The only things that would have made it a total spa experience for him would have been toothpaste, a toothbrush, and a stick of deodorant. Regardless, he felt better than he had in a long time.

Until he had to get back into his dirty clothes.

He put his socks and jeans on. Funny, he'd never felt self-conscious when it was just Hush and him. The dog didn't care if his hair wasn't brushed, the seams of his clothes were coming apart, or even if he hadn't bathed in the last month. Hush was content just being with him. As if life held no greater purpose than companionship.

Yet whenever Buzz had to step back into the world, as he had yesterday to go into town to forage through dumpsters for food, or today as he'd waited with the other clients, it made him feel not only terribly awkward and out of place, but reviled, like a leper — unwanted and feared. Although why anyone should be afraid of him was beyond his understanding. Had he really slipped so low? Or was it because people feared not him, but *becoming like* him?

The fall into disgrace was not as far as some might think. Sometimes, it only took a step.

He pulled the scrub brush through his beard, straightening the wiry whiskers as best he could. If he'd had scissors, he would have given himself a trim right there.

Buzz studied himself in the mirror. Bloodshot eyes stared back. His beard was so long and gray, his face so leathered from the constant assault of the sun's rays, and his cheeks so gaunt that he barely recognized himself as the man who'd left Los Angeles so many months ago. If he had to guess, he'd say he'd lost a good thirty pounds, if not forty — and he'd been of average size to begin with, not fat by any means. Now, he looked downright unhealthy. Almost skeletal.

He plucked a few bristles from the scrub brush and cleaned the food from his teeth. Damn thief had taken his toothbrush. He'd have a hard time finding another. He may have combed through dumpsters and trash bags frequently, but he seldom found what he really needed. Sometimes he found a treasure amid the refuse, but even most of that was stuff he had no need for: dated but functional dinnerware, boxes of never-worn women's shoes, an electric saw with just a little bit of rust on it, a package of brand new car seat-covers still in their Christmas wrapping paper. No, his chances of finding a toothbrush in the trash anytime soon were about as good as hitting the lottery millions with a single scratch-off ticket. If he wanted a toothbrush that wasn't splayed and stained, the store was about the only place to get one. And he didn't even have the two bucks to buy a cheap one.

One thing he wouldn't do was stoop to stealing. No matter how badly he needed something. If he landed in jail, he'd never make it to the coast. He'd lose his dog, too.

He wouldn't beg, either. He was too proud for that. He'd work for what he needed, he'd accept what was given to him. But ask? Never.

Leaning closer to the mirror, he noticed a mole on the top of his right ear. Had that been there before? Was it age or something more serious? Either way, it didn't matter much. He had one thing left to do in life and after that, well, who cared? He was just trying to fill the time in between now and the inevitable.

A knock startled him.

"Mr. Donovan?"

It was Tracy. He finished buttoning his shirt and tucked it in.

"Mr. Donovan, are you all right?"

"Yeah, fine. Just, uh, you know … age. It takes longer." He made sure his belt was cinched tight and pulled his sweater back on, one finger slipping through a hole in the elbow as he shoved a hand through the sleeve. "Be out in a minute."

"Oh, okay. Whenever you're ready, I can take you back to see Hush."

Excitement shivered through him. Everything was going to be all right. He sensed it. Hush was alive. In time, he'd be well.

Too bad Buzz couldn't say the same for himself.

—o00o—

The wire door swung open, but Hush didn't move. All Buzz could detect was the slow rise and fall of the dog's chest as he lay on his side in the bottom cage. Buzz crouched down, stooped forward to fit part of himself inside, and lay his head upon Hush's chest to listen to his heart beating. The dog exhaled and let out a low groan. Buzz pulled back to look at his best buddy's face.

Hush's whiskers twitched. His copper eyebrows lifted one at a time. An eyelid parted slowly, beginning at the inside corner until it opened fully. Hush lifted his head half an inch to gaze at Buzz for a few seconds; then, tiring, he laid it back down.

"Hey, pal." A tingly warmth flooded Buzz's chest.

The dog's cheeks bunched and his upper lip pulled back in a grin. That smile was a special talent of Hush's, although strangers often mistook it for a snarl, which always made Buzz laugh. Some people weren't good at reading dogs. It was easy for him, though. Always had been.

The longer he sat there with Hush, the better he felt. The fatigue and fog that had plagued him earlier that morning dissipated, replaced by relief and overwhelming love. So while Tracy flitted in and out of the room, Buzz spoke to Hush and stroked his fur, from his neck, across his ribs and back, and down to his hips. And the more he talked, the more awake Hush seemed. "The doc here fixed you up. But you can't go walking for a bit. First, you have to get better. You rest up, okay? Get well. I need you." He scratched behind the dog's ears — gently, though. Just enough to let him know he was there.

For close to half an hour, Buzz stayed with him, talking to and petting him. But after a while, Hush had a hard time keeping his eyes open. Finally, he drifted off to sleep, no longer aware of Buzz's presence.

Buzz sat back on his rump. The cold of the linoleum floor began to seep into his bones, reminding him how stiff his joints were these days. Although the tiredness had returned to his body, his spirit was lighter.

"Mr. Donovan?" Hunter came into the room. He'd replaced his Carhartts with a pair of clean jeans and a navy fleece. He held out the blanket Buzz had brought in with Hush. "We're all about to leave for the day, although someone will be by later this evening to check on Hush. Can I give you a ride somewhere? Into Faderville, maybe?"

His back and hips protesting, Buzz had to grasp the wires of the cages to help himself up. He took the blanket and clutched it to his chest. "No, I'm good." But as he said it, he regretted turning down the offer. Hunter and his staff had already done so much, though. It wasn't right to ask more. Besides, where would Hunter take him? It wasn't like there was a hotel in town, and even if there had been he couldn't have afforded it. He still had his blanket. He'd find a shed somewhere to stay warm in. There had been one less than a mile away, if he remembered correctly.

"You sure?"

Buzz nodded, not knowing what to say. He shuffled off but turned back at the door. "What time tomorrow?"

"Tomorrow?" The vet took a moment to grasp his meaning. "Oh, yes, you'd like to visit him tomorrow. Ah, between eight and nine, I suppose."

Right. He'd sold his watch three states ago to pay for a bag of dog kibble. He hadn't had much need of it, anyway. Even if he'd still had it, he'd be back here ahead of time. Just in case Tracy showed up early.

She caught up with him as he ambled down the hallway. "Hey, by the way, you were right. I talked to my mom a few minutes ago. She said my son's fever broke and he's been chattering up a storm."

He nodded. "That's good to hear. I'm glad."

Tracy looked like she wanted to say something more — or maybe hug him — but Buzz needed to go. Being around so many people when he wasn't used to it ... it was draining to him. He needed time to recharge.

The blanket rolled under his arm, Buzz showed himself out, giving a perfunctory nod and smile to the receptionist as he left. He was sure they'd be talking about him afterward — the condition he was in and where he might have gone — but Buzz was used to that. It still bothered him, though. Today, especially. Usually, he never had to see people again.

He didn't like to be pitied. If they knew him, if they'd understood his life, they might have regarded him a little differently. They would have known the courage it took him to face each day. They would have admired his dedication and resilience. And they would have realized that throughout his life, although he'd invited precious few people into his intimate circle, the depths of his love were boundless.

Pushing open the outer door, Buzz braved the cold. When he was beyond the shelter of the building, the frigid wind gripped him, slid its icy fingers beneath his coat, and filled his lungs. He walked across the parking lot and to the road. At its edge, he looked left, then right, and picked a direction. Not for any particular reason, other than the wind would be at his back.

He was just over the next hill when he realized he'd left his walking stick in Hunter's truck. He'd been so concerned about Hush that he'd forgotten all about it. Turning around, he could see the clinic was no longer in view. He'd get his stick back tomorrow. Right now, it was the least of his worries.

Buzz went on, one weary, unsteady step at a time. A few houses hugged the road ahead, but beyond that it was nothing but cattle pastures and hayfields. There had to be a barn somewhere ahead. He wouldn't go far. Thankfully, between the donuts, the coffee, and the sandwiches, he had enough food in his belly to get him through the day. Tomorrow was another matter entirely. If there was anything he'd learned in the past several months, it was not to think too far ahead when it was only going to get you down.

83

Less than a mile out from the veterinary clinic, the wind picked up some more. The barn he thought he'd seen on the way here never appeared. Buzz draped the blanket over his head and shoulders. His ears were freezing. He'd had a hat once, a sturdy canvas one with a brim. But one day a sixty-mile-an-hour wind in Oklahoma had snatched it from his head and whisked it across the open plains.

Soon, though, his coat and blanket were not enough. Knives of sleet drove down from the sky, stabbing the cold deeper and deeper, until it sliced into the marrow of his bones. Shivers gripped his body.

Then he saw it. Finally. Up ahead, a barn. Newer construction. A good roof. Walls without gaps. He could only hope there was one unlocked door on it somewhere.

Just a few minutes more and he'd be inside. Small consolation in wet clothes and cold temperatures, but at least it would be dry there.

Wobbling on his knees and pushed by the wind, he meandered away from the faded line at the side of the road and toward the road's center.

He didn't even hear the truck come up from behind him as it swung around the corner. But sensing something, he turned and saw it — a rusty streak of blue, barreling down on him.

chapter 7

Beam

I shouldn't have been driving so fast, but the weather had changed quicker than expected. Wind buffeted the truck, making it hard to stay in my lane. Thank goodness there wasn't much traffic. Actually, there wasn't any. Every car I'd seen in the last ten minutes had been parked. There wasn't anyone outside, either, which had me worried. Dr. Butler had said there was an ice storm on its way. Clearly, it was already here.

All I had to do was make it to my grandmother's house. Simple.

The address he'd written down was a few miles outside of town. Which shouldn't have been a problem, except that the spitting cold rain that had started five minutes ago had already turned to sleet. It pelted the windshield, piling up at the bottom and corners of it. The wipers had only two speeds: slow and slower. They couldn't keep up. Within a few minutes, the slush began to form a sheet of ice that gradually crept upward until it sat at the bottom of my line of vision. I contemplated stopping to scrape it off but wasn't even sure there was a scraper inside this tin can.

Twice, the wheels lost their grip on the road. Each time I felt them slip, I slowed a little bit more. I didn't have enough experience to handle conditions like this, but I didn't exactly have options at the moment. I sure couldn't go home. That was eight hours away in good weather. And it was just as far back into Faderville as it was to my grandmother's.

A mile or so outside of town, I made a turn onto what looked like a well-traveled road. It was wide and had recently had gravel scattered on it, which helped with traction and eased my nerves. I hadn't seen any salt trucks and doubted they had many this far south, unlike Michigan, where we expected winter storms on a regular basis. As the road straightened out, a veterinary clinic sat over to the right and a few houses lined either side of the road way up ahead. I sped up a little, impatient to reach my destination.

Moron that I was, I hadn't thought to check weather reports before I'd left home yesterday. I figured I was going south, so things had to be better down here. If anything, they were worse.

Sheets of ice now coated the road. I tried not to think about it, but it was practically *all* I could think about. I wanted to pull off to the side of the road, but sitting in the middle of nowhere while temperatures plummeted didn't seem too smart either. I *had* to get to my grandmother's.

If I'd had an ounce of sense, I would have called her. If not while I was on the road, at least before leaving Timothy Butler's. He would have let me use his phone. Then she would have been expecting me. And if I'd spent a few minutes on the internet back in Flint, I would have known my grandfather was dead. Nothing like having a stranger give you the news years after the fact. I probably could've figured out online where she lived, too. And then I'd already be there. Not wandering around some backcountry road to land on her doorstep during a winter storm, unannounced.

No sense in beating myself up. The fact was that I was on my way to her. Whether she was going to be happy to see me or not wasn't the point. The point was I had to get out from under Lana's roof or eventually something bad was —

I almost didn't see him. Just as I went around a corner where the road dipped ever so slightly, a man walked right out into the middle of it. The *middle*.

Instinctively, I yanked the steering wheel to the right. Too hard. So I hit the brake. Which was probably the worst thing I could have done.

The wheels lost their grip. The truck skated across the road. Launched itself from the shoulder. And went airborne across a broad ditch.

I had no control. None.

A helpless passenger, I watched as the truck sailed toward a fence post.

chapter 8

Buzz

His first thought, when the truck barely missed hitting him, was that this town was full of drunken, messed up people, and he couldn't wait to get away from the place. His second was that the driver was in trouble. Grave trouble.

The truck sped across the road, the vehicle unresponsive to the direction of the front wheels. It slid. And slid. And kept on sliding. Off the road. Over a ditch.

Then, with the gut-wrenching crunch of metal biting into wood, it slammed to a stop.

Before he could process it all, he found himself going toward it. The truck was now a full fifty yards away and slightly downhill. Caution told him not to run. Every footstep was a danger. His hands held out for balance — and to catch himself in case he fell, — he skated jerkily across the icy road.

Once on the shoulder, where the sleet had collected in tiny, frozen balls between dead blades of grass, the going was a little better. Ice crunched beneath his feet. He could see, now, the deep indent of the fence post in the front quarter panel. The truck had turned itself halfway around before sliding sideways off the road. Had it spun a couple feet more, the post would have impacted fully with the driver-side door.

Yet, why couldn't he see anyone moving inside? Why hadn't anyone gotten out to assess the damages? Maybe they were sitting safely inside, already on the phone to their insurance agent or the state patrol.

Or maybe they were hurt.

He reached the driver's side. With numb fingers, he pulled the door open.

Draped over the steering wheel was a girl, no more than sixteen, if that. Her brown hair was pulled back into a ponytail and covered by a baseball hat.

"Miss? Miss?" He touched her shoulder, her leg. "Are you all right, miss?"

She wasn't. But how badly was she hurt? It had been years since he'd had to remember what to do, but he reached into his memory and began to survey her for injuries.

He couldn't see any blood or broken bones. Her seatbelt was still on. There could be internal damage: head trauma, broken ribs, a spinal injury, a ruptured spleen, punctured lungs ...

It was important to keep her safe and get help. If another car came around that corner, it could slide right into them. He didn't want to move her ... but was it safe to leave her here? Hypothermia was a threat, so he had to get her warm. As for getting help, who knew when someone else might come by. No sense in going back to the clinic, either. Hunter had said they were all leaving for the day.

Carefully, he closed the door and went to the other side. He climbed in, checked her again. Pressing his fingertips to her neck, he felt a pulse — strong and certain. She was breathing normally. He looked around for a phone, in the glove compartment, on the floor.

Nothing.

"Miss, I need to call for help. You're hurt. Do you have a phone?" It seemed dumb to ask an unconscious girl questions, but he kept hoping she'd come to.

A backpack had slid to the floor in the wreck. He opened it and rummaged through it. Some clothes, a comb, a toothbrush ... He held the toothbrush for a moment, thinking of how much, not even an hour ago, he'd wanted one. Right now, though, it wasn't important. He stuffed it back inside and checked all the pockets, then went through it all one more time, just in case he'd missed a phone.

He looked under the seat. A wadded ski jacket lay under the passenger-seat. He pulled it out and felt a squarish lump inside one of the pockets. He slipped his fingers inside and pulled out a wallet. Maybe it would tell him who she was, so when help did arrive, they'd know how to contact her parents. Opening it, he found nothing but a library card and a couple of customer loyalty cards, none with her name on them.

Then he found something else: a stack of bills. Not a lot of money, but it would have been enough to get him and Hush to Virginia. He didn't count them — although he pinched a twenty between his fingers, thinking of how far that one bill would go for him. It would buy him a few days' worth of meals. And a toothbrush of his own.

For a few seconds, he understood why someone who was desperate for a basic need would steal. Only for a few seconds. He'd been hungry before. He'd sold his things and gone through trash for food, just to make what money he did have last a little longer. Sadly, he'd vastly underestimated how long their journey would take and how much it would cost.

Still, life was about choices. Stealing once, to survive, was understandable. Like Jean Valjean. Making a habit of it at the expense of others was not. He had no doubt the man who'd robbed him earlier that day had done it many times. He may have even harmed a few people along the way.

But that wasn't Buzz. Not even in the worst of times. Like now.

Closing the wallet, he put it back inside the pocket and draped the jacket over her shoulders, then continued searching for a phone, setting aside bits of trash and a piece of notebook paper. Occasionally he looked up and down the road, hoping a car would come by.

By now, ten minutes must have elapsed. It was getting colder inside the truck. The conditions outside were becoming increasingly hazardous.

Apparently, this teenager didn't have a phone. Unless …

She was wearing a hoodie. With a front pocket. And jeans. Also with pockets.

He didn't feel right fishing around in the clothes she was wearing. What if she woke up precisely when he had a hand inside one of those pockets? But if he didn't get help, they both stood to be in worse shape than they were now. He didn't really have a choice.

Buzz spoke to her again, shook her gently. When he got no response, he felt her front pockets. Empty, except for a well-used tissue.

That left the back pockets. But he was afraid to move her without help. What if she had a spinal injury?

A tiny, weak moan escaped her throat.

"Thank God," Buzz breathed. He touched her shoulder. "Miss, can you hear me?"

Her chest lifted with a deep breath. She shifted, rolled her head back. Her eyes were still closed, but she was waking up. Or trying to.

Relief washed through Buzz. He kept talking to her. "You were driving. I saw your truck go off the road. Do you remember it happening?"

Raising a hand slowly, she pushed herself off the steering wheel. Buzz helped her sit back. If her spine had been hurt, she would've cried out in pain, he told himself.

"I need to call for help," he said. "Do you have a phone?"

The back of her head against the headrest, she turned her face to him. Her eyelids fluttered, opened. Dark brown eyes gazed unfocused at him, confused but curious. She shook her head, then let her eyes drift shut again. "No ... phone."

"What's your name?"

"Beam."

"Beam? Like a sunbeam, then. Listen, the quicker we can get you help, the better. Where's your home? Is it around here?"

She moved her head as if to shake it again, but a grimace cut across her face. "Head ... hurts."

"You probably have a concussion." Or worse, but he wasn't about to list all the possibilities. He needed to keep her calm and comfortable. He took a sweatshirt from the floor and spread it across her lap to keep her warm, unlocking her seatbelt. "Do you live around here?"

Through barely parted lids, she looked at him. "No."

Then what was she doing out here on a stormy day in the middle of nowhere? "Do you live in ..." He searched his mind for the name of the town. What had the vet said? "... Faderville?"

"No, my ... grandma ..." Her fingers brushed over a piece of notebook paper, half-hidden beneath an empty pretzel bag.

He pulled it free. It had an address and directions on one side, and the name Noreen Larson. On the back was a phone number and, beside it, "Tim". "Your grandmother is Noreen?"

"Yes," she sighed.

"Don't worry, Sunbeam. We'll get a hold of her ... somehow."

He didn't know why he'd called her that, but it seemed to fit.

—o00o—

Another fifteen minutes went by. Or so he guessed. Buzz didn't really know. No watch, and the clock on the dashboard wasn't on. The truck had died when it hit the post and no amount of jiggling the key and pumping the gas had helped. Buzz didn't know the first thing about engines, or else he would have taken a look.

Even if the truck had started, chances were slim that he could have backed it out of the ditch. He'd gotten out to look once, just to make sure.

As much as he could, he talked to her, asked her questions to pass the time while they waited for help. Most of the time she didn't answer, just gazed at him groggily, mumbled something, and then drifted off again.

At some point, he couldn't wake her up at all. He contemplated carrying her to the barn in the distance, but he'd barely been able to carry Hush, and while this girl was pretty skinny, she was still a lot bigger than the dog. Plus, there was always the possibility he might drop her and do more harm than good. No, he'd wait. He had to.

Just as he was pulling clothes out of her backpack to pile around her and on top of her, he heard the faint hum of an engine above the steady *ping-ping-ping* of sleet on glass and metal. Looking out the back window, a familiar vehicle came into view: Hunter's truck.

Buzz closed his eyes and uttered a prayer of thanks. Not that he was religious, but he believed in a greater force in the universe. There were some things you couldn't explain otherwise.

The truck slowed, came abreast of them … and kept going.

Buzz's heart thudded as the rear bumper of Hunter's truck appeared ahead. A cloud of anger burst inside him. How could he —?

The brake lights lit up, then went off. Three more times they flashed. Hunter was tapping the brakes, Buzz thought, so he wouldn't go skidding across the road. Finally, the truck came to a halt, then began to back up.

When it was thirty feet away, it stopped, the exhaust still spewing out spires of diesel smoke. Hunter got out and jogged to them. Buzz reached across Beam's lap and rolled down the window. Even when the damp, freezing air rolled in, she didn't wake up.

"What happened?" Hunter said.

"I saw her go off the road. I didn't know what to do. There was no way to call anyone. So I've been waiting here for someone to come along and help."

"Help is here." Reaching in, Hunter checked her pulse and then asked Buzz a lot of questions about her. From his pocket, he took a penlight and shone it in one pupil, then the other. "Hmmm, yeah, concussion. You say she's been conscious?"

"Off and on."

"Did she seem lucid?"

"Didn't talk much, but yeah, I'd say so." Buzz handed him the piece of paper. "She said her name's Beam and this is her grandmother. Not sure who Tim is."

Hunter glanced at the paper. "The last name sounds familiar. I think … Yes, I remember a Larson — Ronald? No, that's not right. Roland, Roland Larson. But he died a while ago. Had a farm out on Victory Hill Farm Road. Raised feeder calves. But this isn't the place. Let me make a few calls." He excused himself.

Buzz rolled up the window. Still, the cold was pervasive, open window or not. Although Buzz was relieved the vet had found them, so far things were not progressing very quickly.

Hunter had pulled the hood of his coat up and was making a phone call. A couple minutes later, he returned.

Brow pinched, Hunter let out a big sigh as he looked up and down the road. "Tracy just told me it's a Level One state of emergency. I called nine-one-one. They said every vehicle they had was either already responding to an emergency or unavailable — two deputy cruisers and an ambulance were involved in crashes, that's how bad it is. I gave them this address and they confirmed it is Noreen

Larson's." He folded the paper up and put it in a front pocket. "They said they'd come as soon as they could, but it would likely be hours — if they could even make it today. Meanwhile, I tried calling the number on back. No one answered. But her grandmother's address is right up ahead. We'll go there and hope someone's at home. If not, we'll just invite ourselves in." He motioned to Buzz to get out of the truck. "Now, if you'll help me, I think we can manage to lay her down in my back seat."

Buzz hesitated. "Are you sure we should move her?"

"No, I'm not. Under normal circumstances, we wouldn't move her until the EMTs got here, but seeing as how they're not coming and we can't leave her here, then we sort of have to."

Getting her out of the truck was easier than Buzz expected. She couldn't have weighed a buck.

Hunter guided them to the other side of his truck. When the vet opened the door, Buzz saw an inert lump of speckled fur on the other side of the back seat. Hush's ribs rose and fell with each peaceful breath. They placed Beam inside, across from Hush on the same back seat, and then Hunter covered her with a spare coat that had been lying on the seat.

Buzz's heart twisted in concern. "You brought him with you?"

"I'd already sent Tracy home. She called me not five minutes later and told me how bad the roads were. So I decided to take him home with me and just hoped I'd find you along the way."

Gratitude overwhelmed Buzz. He turned his face to the freezing rain to blink away the prickle of tears. When the sting of the cold halted the surge of emotions, he went to the other side, one hand braced on the truck to keep himself upright. It was like being on an ice rink without the skates. Unfortunately, he'd never been good at skating, and so his muscles tensed with each step. Somehow, in the end, he made it.

Inside the truck, warmth poured from the heating vent. The slush

95

in Buzz's veins began to flow more readily, returning sensation to his extremities.

Carefully, Hunter pulled back onto the road. He went slowly, but the big tires and wide base of the truck made it steady, even on the sheets of ice now coating the surface.

Wet though he was, Buzz felt more human. His shivering lessened by the second. He glanced in the back seat to study his dog and Beam. Between the two of them, the girl concerned him most. "Will she be all right?"

"Honestly? I don't know. The next few hours will tell."

"Can't we just take her to the hospital?" The hills along the road were getting steeper. More than once the truck hit a slick patch and drifted to the side of the road a few feet before the vet corrected it.

"We could. But it's forty minutes away in good weather. In this? I reckon it'd take hours — and we'd run the risk of having another accident."

"What do we do, then?"

The vet shrugged. "We do what we can. Take her to her grandmother's, stay there a while, keep an eye on her ... and wait for an ambulance."

The truck crept along. Sleet pelted its exterior. Ice collected on fence wires and bent the winter dead blades of grass low to the ground.

Buzz wasn't even sure why he was so concerned about the girl. He didn't know her at all. Maybe it was the circumstances — that he had witnessed the accident.

More likely, deep down, it was the guilt. That he had caused her to go off the road. If he'd been off to the side, not stumbling about in the middle, she wouldn't have tried to avoid him and hit that patch of ice.

Somehow he felt he owed her. But what could he possibly give her? He had nothing and he couldn't do anything for her.

For a while, he stared out the window. Ice cloaked the tree limbs. If it hadn't been so dangerous, it might have been beautiful. "So were you going home this way?"

Hunter's jaw muscles twitched. "It's, uh, kind of the long way." He glanced in the back seat. "Tracy and I didn't leave the clinic for another half an hour after you did. We didn't know it was this bad or we wouldn't have let you go. Once we were aware of conditions, we became concerned about you. So she went one way, and five minutes later I went the other."

"You came looking for me?"

"I had to."

"Actually, you didn't."

"Buzz, the last thing I wanted was to wake up tomorrow and hear on the news how some guy froze to death in a barn."

"It wouldn't have been your fault if I had. I was the one dumb enough to walk out into the storm."

"Maybe so, but a lucky thing you did, huh? If you hadn't, you wouldn't have found the girl. Also, I wouldn't have come looking for you, and then this girl *and* you might have frozen out here."

Buzz didn't mention that he'd caused the wreck.

"It's only going to get worse, you know," Hunter went on. "They say once the freezing rain stops, the wind's supposed to pick up. And there's snow expected later tonight. This state's going to be crippled for days. I don't think there are even two snow plows in the whole county, let alone more than one salt truck." His face brightened as he bent his neck forward to peer out the ice-encrusted windshield. "There — is that it?"

A mailbox came into view. It sat at the end of a lane that led into the woods. That might have been encouraging except for a few things: the mailbox leaned to one side, the front of it was missing, and the lane looked to be in complete disrepair.

Squinting, Buzz tried to bring the numbers into focus. When he finally could, he read them out loud.

Hunter pulled into the drive. The lane was twisty, but thankfully flat. When they got to the house, it looked only slightly more promising. There was a light on inside, faintly visible through the side window closest to the driveway. To Buzz, that light was like the weak promise of sunlight through dreary clouds. A haven in the storm.

It struck Buzz that he didn't have a place to stay. He couldn't impose himself on this Mrs. Larson or Hunter, but what else was he going to do? And then there was Hush. Was Hunter going to take the dog home with him and leave Buzz without his best friend, his helper?

"Buzz?"

Buzz jumped at his name.

"I'm going to leave the engine running," Hunter said, "so it stays warm in here. Just in case no one's at home. Keep an eye on them, okay?"

Buzz nodded. It wasn't like either of them was suddenly going to jump up and run off.

The *ping-ping-ping* of sleet against the hood of the truck built to a quiet roar as Hunter trudged up the sidewalk, his hood pulled far over his face. He knocked on the front door and waited, then knocked again. After a couple of minutes, he glanced in the front window. Then he went back to the door and pounded harder.

When no one came, Hunter looked toward the truck and shrugged. Buzz lowered his gaze, relief and disappointment colliding inside him.

"Where ...?" The girl was awake. Sleepy-eyed, she blinked at him, as if trying to remember who he was.

"Hey there. We were getting a little worried about you." Buzz stuck his hand out.

Shaking her head, she scooted back, eyes fixed on his hand. "Who ...?"

His chest flooded with shame. He couldn't blame her. Even

freshly washed up, his clothes must've been a sore sight. And here she was trapped in a truck in an ice storm with a stranger she didn't know or trust. He pulled his hand back and turned around. "I'm Buzz. Dr. McHugh drove us to your —"

Hunter signaled to Buzz. Someone was there, after all.

"Grandmother's," he finished.

An older woman wearing a housecoat stood at the door, speaking to the vet as she held the storm door partway open. Then she went back inside and Hunter came down the front steps and along the sidewalk, careful of each footfall.

Had she turned them away? Buzz wondered.

Beam sat up, immediately clutching her head and making a face. "Dr. who? My what?"

Buzz wasn't sure if she hadn't heard him or didn't understand. Another glance told him she was confused.

Hunter opened the driver's door and smiled at Beam. "Good, you're awake. Your grandmother, Mrs. Larson, said to bring you on in." He looked at Buzz. "Can you help?"

As Hunter went around to open the back door, Beam sputtered and said, "My grandmother? I don't … What …?"

"It's all right," Buzz told her. But judging by the look on her face, she didn't believe him.

Beam glanced around the truck like she was trying to piece it all together. When her gaze fell on the sedated dog beside her, she threw herself against the door behind her, flailing for the handle to let herself out, as if she'd suddenly discovered herself in a den of lions.

"It's just my dog," Buzz reassured her. "He can't hurt you."

That was when Beam opened her mouth and let out a scream.

chapter 9

Beam

"Everything's going to be all right, Sunbeam," the homeless man repeated.

I wasn't so sure about that.

Dogs had teeth. They were descended from wolves. Hunters. Scavengers. Meat eaters. Pack animals. They even killed their own kind.

I clawed at the door handle, desperate for escape. But even as I pulled up on the latch, it wouldn't budge. It was frozen shut.

"He's right," the other man said, peering in from the now open door across from me. He was younger, maybe in his forties, and wearing a stiff pair of coveralls with a name stitched above his heart: 'Dr. Hunter Mc—' I couldn't read the rest of it because he had a winter coat on that was buttoned partway. "The dog's asleep. He just had surgery."

I dared a look. He was telling the truth. The fanged monster was totally out of it. I kept my eyes trained on him, just in case he sprang up from the shapeless heap he was and tried to take a chunk out of me.

"I'll go around to the other side and help you out in a second," the doctor said, after he lifted the dog's eyelids and looked in each one. The dog slept on. "I just didn't want to yank the door on your side open and have you fall out." He shut the door and tromped around the back.

Who were these people, anyway? The one guy, the doctor, looked all right, but the older one ... I'd seen a lot of junkies and homeless drunks wandering the streets in Flint, and while he didn't exactly look wasted, he didn't look huggable, either. My bet was the guy had slept on a few park benches in his day. Probably an alcoholic.

Still, something he'd said ...

The truck door on my side flew open and a blast of arctic wind raced in to snatch my breath away. I shivered. My head pulsed with a deep ache. The middle-aged guy stood outside, a reassuring smile on his face. "Hi. I'm Hunter McHugh, the veterinarian here in Fader-ville." He tipped his head at the hobo up front. "And this is Buzz Donovan, a new client of mine. We found you unconscious in your truck. Do you remember going off the road?"

"Yeah, sure." Really, I only had a vague recollection of it. This blasted headache made it hard to concentrate. The whole last day was kind of fuzzy too. I'd left Flint yesterday, driven all night, couldn't find my ... my what?

My grandmother. Right.

That's what this Buzz guy had tried to tell me. They'd brought me to her.

Crap. When she heard about the truck, she was going to kill me. Wrecked *and* stolen. Lovely.

Closing my eyes, I sank against the back of the seat and clutched the coat they'd tossed over me to my chest. The thing reeked of horses and hay. It was probably infused with manure, too.

I heard one of the front doors open, then ice crunching as Hobo

Buzz came around to stand next to Dr. Doolittle. I pried one eye open. "I think I'll just stay here. Thanks anyway."

They looked at each other, then at me.

"You really want to stay in here with the dog?" Hunter the Vet said.

I checked to make sure it hadn't started to rouse. Looked like it was still out for the count. I debated: an irate grandparent versus a disoriented, possibly starving canine. Seemed about even. Still, I wasn't ready to face her.

"I'll stay," I replied. I contemplated asking for a syringe filled with tranquilizers. For the dog, not me.

"Sorry to tell you," Hunter the Vet said, "but that's not an option. You have a head injury. We need to get you inside and keep an eye on you until we can get you to the hospital in Somerset."

"No," I said. "No hospital. I'm fine. Just got knocked out, that's all." I could see it now. They'd have me strapped to a hospital bed and the state police would show up. I'd be proclaimed a runaway and sent off to juvenile detention, where they'd probably make me see a shrink and put me on meds. No thanks. Just … no.

Ignoring me, Hunter reached forward, unbuckled my seatbelt, and pulled me to him. "Let me know if anything hurts."

If I'd been able to think a little faster, I would have screamed bloody murder again. That or clobbered him with my weak girl-fists. But before I knew it, he had me in his arms, lifting me as gently as a newborn lamb.

"Can you close the door, Buzz?" Hunter started up the sidewalk. The door boomed shut behind us.

Frozen rain pelted us. A stiff wind pried at the seams in my clothing. The cold assaulted every inch of my skin. If I hadn't been fully alert a few minutes ago, I sure was now. Hunter took small, cautious steps, making certain his forward foot was solid before he shifted forward each time. Before we made it to the porch steps, I heard the thud and crack of a body hitting ice.

Hunter turned carefully. "Buzz, are you okay? Buzz?"

I tried to look and for the first time noticed how stiff my neck was — as in I could barely move it to the right. On the ground lay Buzz, only he wasn't lying still like he'd gone out cold — his body was making little jerking movements. Before I could make sense of it, Hunter turned back around and hurried up the steps as quickly as he could. A woman in her sixties opened the door. As we moved past, she said, "Who's that and what the hell's wrong with him?"

Hunter set me down on the couch, grabbed a throw off the arm, and laid it over my legs. Then, without answering the woman, he rushed back outside.

The woman turned to stare at me, the space between her gray-laced eyebrows pinched tightly. In that one look, everything I'd dreamed and planned for the past few months disintegrated.

So this was my grandmother. I wilted inside.

The door burst open again and Hunter barreled in, Buzz tossed over his shoulder like a sack of cement. He made his way to the area rug in the middle of the cramped little living room and laid him there. He pushed a floor lamp away, and the old bag clucked at him in protest.

"Don't knock that over!"

Buzz's body twitched a few more times, then went still.

I sat up straighter, my neck and upper back immediately cramping. "Is he having a seizure?"

"Was." Hunter checked Buzz's pupils. Reflexively, Buzz turned his head away from the lamplight. "I think it's over now."

"Just make yourself at home," the old woman said snidely. She stood in the doorway between the living room and kitchen. The place wasn't so much overcrowded with things as it was just messy. Living alone all the way out here, I supposed she didn't see much of a need to straighten up, and seeing as how we'd shown up as a surprise, we could have just caught her at a bad time. Then again, she looked like she had a lot of those.

Now that I looked at her more closely, she wasn't actually all that old. Late fifties, maybe. Sixty, tops. Mostly it was her expression that aged her: her mouth turned down in a permanent scowl, her eyebrows crimped together, her eyes tight with mistrust. I'd seen that look often, back in Flint. There, surrounded by crime, unemployment, and poverty, it had been understandable. Here — what was there to be that way about here?

I contemplated going back to Flint. At least Lana had left me alone most of the time. Sure, she was a neglectful parent, but it had forced independence on me at an early age. She'd always been more concerned about herself than me. Apparently I'd traded apathy for outright disdain.

On cue, the old lady swiveled her head in my direction again. "And who did you say you were?"

Had Hunter not told her?

"Bellamy Larson," I mumbled, then added, "Lana's daughter. Everyone calls me Beam, though."

In my heart of hearts, I hoped her pruney old face would light up with a smile and she'd throw her arms around me in one of those squishy grandma hugs. Instead, she regarded me even more warily. I hadn't seen her since I was just shy of five. In between boyfriends and hard up for money, Lana had brought us south. For a 'visit', she'd said, although she'd probably been fishing for an invitation to move back in with them.

On our one and only visit to Kentucky, Grandpa had sat me on his knee and bounced me. He'd taken me on a walk through the woods and pastures. Beyond that, I couldn't remember what he said or what else we might have done, but he'd been nice to me. It wasn't until a couple years later that my ability to recall details and dates had sharpened. I did remember, though, that my grandmother — this stranger who now looked at me like I had just marched into her living room and demanded all her worldly possessions — had remained aloof back then. She hadn't done more than pat me on the head. In the end, she and Lana had an argument and we left after just two days at their farm. It was the only time I'd ever seen her before this.

"How do I know that's who you really are?" she asked.

What did she want — DNA proof? "If you want documentation, all I have with me is my library card."

"Forget your driver's license? That's convenient."

"I didn't forget." In a fit of bravery, I spat out the truth. "I don't have one."

She shot Hunter a look. "I thought you said you found her in a truck, wrecked in a ditch down the road."

"I did," he said.

"Was she alone?"

"She was until Buzz, here, found her."

"Then how was she driving if she doesn't have a license?"

Hunter held his hands wide. "Look, I don't know. It appears you two have some things to sort out. I was just trying to be the Good Samaritan. I went out looking for this man to give him a ride and happened upon your granddaughter, who needed help. Sorry to impose on you, but we didn't really have a choice."

She just stood there with her arms crossed, not even flinching. The woman had a heart of granite.

Hunter cleared the area around Buzz. Just as he stood up, Buzz stirred. Hunter knelt back down next to him and started asking questions, like Buzz had done to me in the truck: his name, what day it was, if he knew where he was. Buzz waved him off, kept telling him he was okay, that it was nothing.

"Hush," Buzz mumbled. "Where's Hush?"

"In the truck, still," Hunter answered calmly. "Don't worry, he's fine. You were only out for a few minutes."

105

Despite Hunter's soothing words, Buzz became agitated. He continued to ask about the dog and insisted on seeing him. Repeatedly, Hunter told him the dog was all right and that he'd check on him as soon as he had Buzz taken care of. Gradually, Buzz calmed, his clarity of mind and speech increasing. When Buzz tried to sit up, but failed, Hunter pulled a couple of throw pillows off the couch and piled them between him and the couch to prop him up, eliciting a scowl from the old lady.

"If you don't mind," Hunter said, sensing her disapproval, "I need to get these wet clothes off of him. Do you have a washer and dryer that I could use? Your electricity seems to be working just fine for now, so I'd like to get that done before the lines go down."

I had to admire the guy for taking charge.

"I do mind," the old lady huffed, like she didn't like being told what to do. "But I don't suppose I have much of a choice, do I?" She tipped her head toward a short hallway. "Spare bedroom's back there. There are some extra men's clothes in the closet that should fit him — they were my husband's. You make sure he doesn't come out here in his birthday suit, got it?"

Hunter nodded, but before he helped Buzz up, we glanced at each other. Funny how you can make allies just like that.

The door to the spare bedroom clicked shut. The old lady went into the kitchen and turned on a TV on the counter. Reports of the storm rolled in: semis jackknifed on the interstate, a thirty-car pileup, downed power lines, and farther west roofs blown off by gale-force winds.

While the old lady was in the kitchen, I could hear Hunter's and Buzz's muffled voices through the closed door. A few minutes later, Hunter appeared with an armload of clothes. The old lady directed him to the basement. His feet pounded on the wooden steps as he went down. Dials clicked, water gushed, pipes groaned, the lid banged shut. The whole time, the old woman never came out and asked if I needed anything or how I was feeling. It was like she wanted us all to go away and leave her alone.

If I could have, I would.

Hunter came back upstairs. Scampering after him was an older black and white kitten. It batted at his heels as he paused to open the door to the spare bedroom. He nudged it away with his toe. "You stay out here for now."

The door shut behind him, leaving the gangly kitten to stare at the knob, its striped tail swishing back and forth. A few seconds later, the kitten lost interest and began zooming around the house. The old lady got up to see what all the commotion was about and sighed as the little imp skidded to a halt in front of her, then leaped up in the air, claws outstretched. It hit the hardwood floor, pivoted, and darted behind the curtains.

I started to laugh, but it made my head hurt.

"It's not mine." The old lady walked across the room to peer out the front door.

"Are you watching it for someone?" I asked politely, wondering what it would take to fracture her protective shell.

"It showed up on my porch this morning. I couldn't leave it out in this weather, now could I?"

So she was slightly human, after all? There was hope for me yet.

Just to break the ice, I asked, "You *are* Noreen Larson, right?"

She plopped down in the recliner. "Of course I am."

"Humph, got any ID?" I mumbled.

"Smart aleck." She picked up the remote control to flip through the channels, even though she hadn't turned the other TV off.

Hunter returned. I swung my feet to the floor to give him space at the end of the couch. He sat on the edge of the cushion, as if unwilling to let himself get comfortable. His fingers laced together, elbows resting on his knees, he gazed absently at the TV screen as Noreen flicked from one station to another to another. After a dreadfully

107

awkward minute, he broached the silence. "I'm sorry about your husband, Mrs. Larson."

"That was five years ago," she said sharply, not even looking at him. She stopped on a PBS show about the Great Wall of China. "But thank you, anyway. We sort of kept to ourselves. Not a lot of folks turned up at the funeral. It's been hard, living by myself." In her sigh, I heard the ache of loneliness and empty days. I'd often felt that way myself since Oakley died. He'd been both my little brother and my best friend. The only one I could rely on to always be there. Moving in the middle of a school year, every year, sometimes more than once per year, didn't give you many chances to form lasting friendships. Out here, I could see how easy it was to isolate yourself without even trying.

In the corner of the room was a fireplace, still filled with ashes from the last fire. I wondered if she used it often. This place was freezing and I hadn't heard the furnace kick on yet. Noreen's gaze drifted to the window next to her. Outside, a gutter hung loose to angle across the window.

"A lot of things need fixed around here," she said softly, a trace of longing in her voice. "Roland used to do all that at our farm. I just don't have the know-how to do any of it myself."

"I can understand," Hunter said "I hire out work myself as much as possible. More of a time factor for me, but I find it's worth it to pay for help when you need it. If you ever need any names …"

He left it unfinished, like he didn't want to force anything on her or suggest that, yes, the place was a crumbling eyesore. I wondered why she'd moved here in the first place. Unless money was an issue, which would explain a lot. Dr. Butler had said medical bills had forced her to auction off the farm. Maybe this was my chance to win her over.

"I could help," I offered.

Noreen looked at me sideways. "What could *you* do? You can't even drive."

Actually, I *could*, although I wasn't supposed to. Still, I wasn't about to let her dismiss me so easily. "Paint, clean up, tear things down ... I mean, if you needed some demolition, I could do that. And I'd do it for free ..." — my words grew quieter — "if I stay, that is."

Her eyebrow arched. "Stay?"

I wiggled back against the cushions, hoping to find a crack I could slip into. The truth was, I needed somewhere to stay until I was old enough to be legally independent. I'd rather deal with Granny Grumpy-Pants than go back to Flint.

As if he sensed the mounting tension, Hunter excused himself and went outside.

Floorboards creaked. A shadow appeared at the opening to the hallway and soon Buzz shuffled out. He wore a pair of green slacks rolled up at the ankles and a striped shirt straight out of *The Brady Bunch* era.

He shrugged at me. Then he turned and continued on, wobbling each time he stepped forward. He stopped in front of Noreen and waited for her to look his way. When, after half a minute, she said nothing, he broke the silence.

"Thank you ... for the clothes."

Her eyes flicked over him. "Roland was taller than you."

Buzz nodded slowly. "I suppose he was taller than most people." He held his arms out. The sides of the shirt fanned out like a loose tent. "And maybe a little wider."

She blew out a *humph* and returned her gaze to the outside.

The only empty seat was the end of the couch where I was — between me and Noreen. Instead of joining me, Buzz settled on the floor and slouched against the pillows Hunter had left there, his hair matted to his head on one side and sticking out in fifty directions on the other.

The doorknob jangled. Noreen stayed put. Buzz tried to push

himself up, but he just as quickly sank back down, one hand covering his forehead. Since I was closest to the door, I got up.

Big mistake. Everything around me flipped upside down. I staggered backward, bumping into the couch, and put a hand out just in time to keep from collapsing into a puddle of Jell-O. My vision narrowed to a small circle of light. My knees threatened to give out.

Hands took hold of my arms, guided me gently back onto the couch.

"Stay right there," Noreen said. As I felt around for the blanket, she stormed off and flung open the front door. "You could've —"

The dog lying limply in his arms, Hunter brushed past her without a word. He went to Buzz and laid the dog down beside him.

Noreen marched after him. "You can't bring that creature in here. I don't allow dogs in my home."

So, she didn't like dogs? She may have been auditioning for the Wicked Witch of Faderville, but at least we had something in common.

She jabbed a finger at the door. "You take him right back out there. He's not staying in here."

Standing, Hunter looked down at her. "Buzz's dog alerts him to seizures before they happen so he can lie down in a safe place. That way Buzz doesn't get hurt. Now if you want a lawsuit on your hands ..." He left the threat hanging.

Seizure-alert dog? That explained a lot. Still, it didn't change the fact that any dog can bite.

"Are you threatening me, Dr. McHugh? Why don't I just call Sheriff Bowden and have the lot of you removed?"

I was torn. While I didn't want the dog in here, I didn't want Hunter to leave, either.

"You go right ahead," Hunter said. "I'll even speak to Nate myself. He and my stepdad, Brad, go way back. I'm sure he'd be happy to come right over, say, oh ... tomorrow or the day after. Right now, I don't think this is reason enough for him to come all the way out here when he has accidents to attend to."

"This is my house. I won't have animals —"

"You have a cat!" he shouted.

"It's not my cat!" she shouted back. "It's a stray. Besides, it's a kitten."

"I don't see the difference."

"How can you not?"

"Stop," Buzz said in a quavering voice. "She's right. It's her house. We'll stay in the garage. Do you have a space heater, ma'am?"

"Buzz, no," Hunter told him. "It's freezing out there. You both need to stay warm." Then to Noreen, he said, "Hush is a service dog, Mrs. Larson. By law, he's allowed anywhere."

"Service dog? I don't see any vest or tags on him. No, sir, take that fleabag right back outside."

Whispering words of comfort, Buzz ran his hands over the dog's ribs and back, careful to avoid the bandage covering the shaved area that went from the foot of the dog's front left leg all the way up to its shoulder. With a soft whimper, Hush lifted his head, but only an inch and only for a moment.

Defiant, Noreen planted her hands on her hips. For the longest time, no one spoke. The only sounds were the chatter of the TVs and Hush's drawn-out sighs as Buzz stroked his fur.

And then … the kitten raced through the living room, circled Noreen, and, from four feet away, vaulted into my lap. Motor purring, he butted his head against my chest. Unable to resist, I scratched along his spine. After a few circles to find the proper spot, he curled up on my lap and closed his eyes, content.

Noreen let out a long exhalation. Then, muttering, she stalked off into the kitchen.

And just like that, the tension dissipated.

Except there was a dog not ten feet from me. So much for a good night's sleep.

Within minutes, Buzz drifted off to la-la land, one arm slung over his dog. Hunter phoned home. After a short conversation during which his wife apparently assured him all was well at the little house on the prairie, he announced he was staying put until the roads were declared safe for travel once again.

The furnace kicked on with a clang and a rumble. Noreen slipped away to her bedroom and locked the door. The rest of us huddled down in our spots in the living room, listening to the rhythmic *swish-swish* of the washing machine and the endless reports on the local news station about the cataclysmic ice storm as the wind roared outside, branches clattered, and sleet hissed against the windows.

chapter 10

Buzz

"He can stay in the garage," Noreen Larson grumbled from her recliner.

Buzz sat at the kitchen table, nibbling on toast with peanut butter and trying to act like they weren't talking about him. He'd kept his chair where he could see Hush sprawled in the middle of the living room floor, mere feet from Noreen. Every time she so much as glanced at the dog, she emitted a huff of indignation.

"I'm sorry ... what?" Hunter turned away from the window to pin Noreen with a challenging glare. "I thought we already discussed this."

It was nearly dark out now. After another call home to his wife, Hunter had been commanded to stay put. He seemed eager to escape this place, but he wasn't senseless enough to risk driving.

"I said he" — Noreen hitched a thumb toward the kitchen — "can stay in the garage with the dog. This is my home. I'll say who goes where. You're free to have the spare bedroom, Dr. McHugh. The girl here, she can sleep on the couch."

"Buzz said he'd be fine on the floor, that he'd prefer it, actually. I'll take the couch and Beam can have the bedroom. All we need are a few spare blankets and —"

"I don't know him." Noreen's gaze flicked to Buzz.

Embarrassment filled him. Granted, he was wearing clean clothes and looked slightly less scruffy now, but he still had a long way to go. Noreen's late husband's clothes hung off him like adult clothing on a small child. Roland Larson had obviously been a big man, more tall than wide, but not svelte by any definition. Buzz was lanky, most would say underweight, and of average height. Rather than look more presentable because the clothes he now wore were clean, Buzz viewed himself as a caricature, not unlike the Scarecrow from *The Wizard of Oz*.

Bundled up on the couch, Beam seemed more intent on making sure Hush didn't come a foot closer to her. The girl was petrified of the dog. A dog who, in the past two hours, hadn't moved from his blanket on the floor other than to lift his head from his paws. Still groggy from the anesthesia, Hush returned an innocent gaze, as if trying to tell her he meant no harm.

Noreen aimed the remote at the TV. "I barely know the two of you, as it is. This might be hard to hear, but I'm more than a little uncomfortable opening my home to strangers. He can stay in the garage — *with* his mutt. There's a space heater out there. All he has to do is plug it in. Place heats up like a furnace."

Hush wasn't a mutt. He was a purebred Australian Shepherd, even though he didn't have papers. Buzz wasn't about to correct her on the matter, though. It was irrelevant to her. The dog and Buzz were unwelcome intruders. They all were. But it was easier to draw the line with a vagrant and his four-footed mongrel than a long-lost relative and a respected citizen of the community.

"Excuse me, but that's ridiculous," Hunter protested. "It's supposed to get down to single digits tonight."

Buzz had to admire the guy for sticking up for him, even though he knew it was a lost cause. He'd suffered a lot of rejection and disdain in the past year — and in a way understood it — but any decent human being would have made an exception on a night like this.

Downstairs, the dryer buzzed weakly. No one moved or spoke for a good minute. Finally, Noreen said, "I'm *not* changing my mind."

Although there were three others in the house, Buzz had never felt so alone, or so low. Unable to bear being the topic of conversation any longer, Buzz got up from the table and went into the living room. "It's all right, Doc. I understand. I'm a stranger around here and" — he stole a shy glance at Beam — "not a relative or anything. The garage is better than out of doors."

"Hold on, Buzz. I'm not giving up so easily." Hunter stepped in front of the TV, blocking its light. "Mrs. Larson, reconsider, please. We'll be out of here as soon as possible. These are hardly normal circumstances. My wife, Jenn, says it's not safe out there. Half the state is under warning to stay put. We're lucky that the electricity has —"

The TV emitted a breathy *pop* as the screen went blank. The room darkened.

"Never mind," Hunter said disgustedly. He moved away from the TV and went to lean against the window.

Floorboards creaked as Noreen made her way to the kitchen. Buzz scooted out of her way and into the living room, careful to move toward the faint light of the window. A few moments later, Noreen was rummaging through a drawer. A match hissed in the darkness, unseen. From the kitchen, a single candle glowed. She returned with an armload of candles and, one by one, lit them and set them at intervals on the mantel, the tops of bookshelves, and atop the very old boxy TV set.

It might have been quaint had the place not been such a fire hazard.

"Power goes out at least a couple of times a year in these parts."

115

She lit one last candle and set it on the end table next to Beam. Selecting a book from the nearest shelf, she placed it on the couch arm next to Beam in offer. Then to Hunter and Buzz, she said, "There's a wood pile on the back porch."

It wasn't a fact relayed; it was a command.

Without a word, the two men filed through the kitchen. The wind slammed the storm door shut before Hunter could close it. Buzz clung to the deck railing, still unsteady on his feet. The back porch was roofed, but the wind had blown the sleet a few feet underneath so that every step was treacherous. Thick ice coated every surface, including the end of the tarp over the wood pile. Hunter picked up a thick stick from the floor and cracked the ice with it until he could pull the tarp back.

"I'm sorry, Buzz." He handed him a small armload of logs. "Who knew she'd be so ... so ..."

"Difficult?"

"That's putting it kindly." Hunter grabbed some kindling from another pile and placed them on top of the logs Buzz was holding. "Mostly, I feel sorry for the girl. I don't know what her story is, but for the time being, she seems stuck here. At least you and I will be gone tomorrow."

Buzz lowered his head. Sure, Hunter had a home to go to. Him? Where was he supposed to go?

"Are you taking Hush with you?" Buzz asked.

"Of course. I certainly can't leave him here. And I can't take him back to the clinic, since we don't know how soon we'll open up again." Hunter took a bigger load of logs and kindling in his own arms before pulling the tarp back over the pile. "So, yes, I'm taking him to my home — and you're welcome to come along, since you need to be with him anyway."

Buzz had hoped he would offer, but now that he had he wasn't so sure. There was something about the girl, though. He felt a curiosity about her, a connection to her.

"I'll ... I'll think about it."

Nodding, Hunter shifted the bundle of wood in his arms. "Don't be shy, Buzz. It's the least I can do. I already talked to my wife about it. She's in total agreement. Maura, my oldest daughter, would love to hear about all the things you've seen. She's been bugging us to take a vacation out west. The younger one, Hannah, might be a little unsettled with a stranger in the house, so don't be surprised if you don't see much of her. She has Asperger's and has trouble with her social skills, but she's getting better. You should see her paintings, though. She has a rare gift, if I do say." He grabbed the door handle but paused before opening it. "You know, we have one of those carriages you attach to a bicycle — the kind you put little kids in when you go cycling. We haven't used it for years. I bet Hush would fit inside nicely, once he's healthy enough to go."

"Nah, I can't ride a bike with my condition." Buzz normally didn't like to talk about it, but they all knew, so there was no sense pretending it never happened.

"I'm sure we could rig it up so you could pull it. Until he's strong enough to walk all day. It'll take him some time to build up to that, though."

"How long?" Buzz asked tentatively.

Hunter's face fell. "A couple of months, probably."

And was Buzz supposed to pull the dog along all that time? He wasn't sure it was possible. Besides, he might not have a couple of months. He might not ever get to Virginia to —

Buzz's hand went to his pocket. No, not *his* pocket — Roland's pocket.

Just as Hunter opened the door, Buzz clamped a hand on his shoulder. "My clothes! You washed my —"

Sticks tumbled from his grasp to clatter upon the porch flooring. He looked down, and just as he did so, the shift in his stance caused one of the top logs still in his arms to slide off his precarious pile. It fell on his foot, causing him to jerk his leg back, and the rest of his armload toppled to the floor. His back thudded against the outside wall of the house.

The door flew open. Her housecoat pulled tight across her chest, Noreen stepped outside. "What's going on out here?"

Buzz bent to pick up the wood. "Just dropped it, that's all."

Disbelief and anger boiled inside him. He'd been too muddled after the seizure to think of removing the plastic bag from his coat pocket before Hunter took it away to wash it. How could he have been so stupid? He didn't have a reason to continue his journey now. This whole trip had been an absolute waste of time.

"I'm afraid I gave him too much," Hunter explained to Noreen.

"Huh. You two were taking long enough. Throwing a party?"

"We're both fine," Buzz said, straightening so he could look her in the eye, "in case you were wondering."

She pulled her chin back and nodded. "Good. I was afraid someone had fallen." Stooping over, she picked up a handful of sticks, then stood. "Remember, we can't get an ambulance out here anytime soon."

Hunter rolled his eyes so only Buzz could see as the door shut behind Noreen. He shifted the wood to one arm and placed a hand on Buzz's shoulder. "I checked your pockets before I put your clothes in the wash, Buzz. What ... what's in the bag, anyway?"

Looking away, Buzz drew in several breaths, until the panic in his chest eased. He didn't want to say. It was too ... personal. Still, he owed him an explanation.

"Ashes," Buzz whispered.

With a nod, Hunter removed his hand. "I thought so. They're in the top drawer of the dresser. I forgot to tell you." He nodded toward the door. "Come on. It's blasted cold out here. You any good at starting a fire?"

A smile crept over Buzz's mouth. "I wouldn't have made it this far if I wasn't."

chapter 11

Beam

Dry warmth and the musky scent of wood smoke curled around me as I pushed my blankets away and crept past sleeping bodies. The kitten had disappeared from my lap and was nowhere in sight. One hand on the wall, I went down the hallway in search of the bathroom. In this small of a house, it wasn't hard to find. I opened the door wide, let the glow of the fire spill in while I memorized the layout. Then, I shut the door and felt my way to the toilet in total darkness.

The power was still out. Probably would be for a while. Days, maybe, Hunter had said.

I eased down onto the toilet seat until my barely warm skin made contact with cold, cold porcelain. My relief was immediate. I hadn't gone to the bathroom in, oh, ten hours, maybe. I'd either been sleeping off my Texas-sized headache or hiding beneath my blankets, pretending to sleep so I didn't have to talk to anyone, mostly Noreen.

In the living room, it was toasty warm. Verging on desert-like. Here, it was an arctic outpost.

Cold air leaked around the ancient window next to the toilet. I shivered as I sat there, eager to get back to my little cocoon on the sofa.

Hours ago, Buzz and Hunter had hauled in load after load of wood from out back. After a hasty inspection of the flue and sweeping aside of old ashes, Hunter had declared the fireplace safe. Steepling the lightest of logs, Buzz placed wads of newspaper underneath and added kindling. Then he lit the newspaper with a box of matches that Noreen brought from the kitchen. She'd piled on more layers of clothing, but even from across the room I could see she was shivering as she stood in the doorway to the kitchen, keeping her distance.

Noreen had tried to go to sleep in her own bedroom with the door left ajar, but the cold must've gotten to her eventually, because when I woke up a few minutes ago, she was asleep on a pile of blankets on the floor at the other end of the couch.

When I finished my business, I decided not to flush. The last thing I wanted was to wake someone up. This brief snatch of peace, tentative as it was, was the calmest I had felt in years. For once, I didn't have to worry about Lana's condition, or if one of her boyfriends was going to come staggering in drunk and punch a hole in the wall. For once, I could just *be*.

I stood and groped my way back to the door, all of six feet. Floorboards creaked beneath my slight weight. The metal of the knob was cool to the touch. I turned it, pulled, stepped beyond the threshold ... The hinges let out a ghostly moan.

Devil eyes stared me down. Glowing discs of translucent blue, marbled with bands of gold. Looking into those eyes was like gazing directly into a savage soul. The dog was possessed. I was sure of it.

Panic squeezed my chest like a vise, crushing the breath from me. Flashes from my childhood pulled me under: me bending over to pet a dog, his muscles stiffening under my touch, his tight gaze sliding to me, the almost imperceptible twitch of his lip as my hand ran farther down his back, and then ... teeth piercing my arm, tearing at flesh, my own screams a distant realization.

My heart banged in my eardrums, so loud I thought it might burst my ribs wide open. I fought to breathe.

Hush lifted his muzzle, sniffed the air, and whimpered lowly.

I backed up, flailed a hand behind me. Then, my fingers found the doorknob.

The dog took two steps toward me, his head lowering.

"Stay ... the hell ... away," I warned.

Sitting, the dog cocked his head.

"I mean it. You stay."

His lip lifted. Rows of jagged teeth gleamed in the wavering light of the fire.

Screaming, I jumped backward, into the bathroom, and slammed the door so hard the walls shook like the first tremble of an earthquake.

I was inside. A door between me and Cujo. Why didn't I feel safe, then? Why couldn't I calm down? Why hadn't Buzz put that monster outside?

Out in the living room, human feet hit the floor, then pounded down the hallway. A voice murmured softly. And then, "Beam, are you okay?"

It was Hunter.

My headache stabbed behind my eyeballs. I tingled all over as I tried not to hyperventilate. I couldn't see anything but the barest outline of the sink, tub, and toilet. When I tried to reach out to find the toilet to sit on, my balance tipped. Everything around me spun wildly.

I wanted out, wanted to run away. Somewhere, anywhere.

"Beam?" Hunter knocked softly on the door. "Can I come in?"

Somehow I found the toilet. I sat, put my head between my knees. Told myself to *breathe*. In, out, in, out, in ... out.

Finally, when I found my voice again, I answered, my words

muffled in the cloth of my jeans. "Come in, but ... make sure the dog's not with you."

A pause, then, "Oookay."

The door latch snicked. A vertical sliver of light appeared, widening slowly to a band, then a rectangle. Hunter wedged himself through the beam of light. "Is something wrong?"

Lifting my head, I peered past his knees and saw the light waver as a shadow moved across it.

"He's behind you," I warned.

Hunter looked back into the hallway. "Who?"

"The dog!" I squeaked.

"Oh. He just stood up. He's still where he was."

"Come in. Shut the door."

"All right." He did. There was barely enough room for the two of us. He could've reached out and touched me, it was that small. "You're afraid of the dog?"

"He snarled at me."

"Snarled?"

"I saw his teeth! He pulled his lips back and snarled at me."

"Did he ... growl?"

"Doc?" Buzz said from behind the door.

"Yeah, I'm in here ... We're in here, I mean. Beam and I."

"Uh, why?"

Hunter cracked the door open. Light poured in.

"No!" I jumped into the tub and pulled the shower curtain closed. Like it was some magical force field that could repel evil beasts.

"Apparently," he said to Buzz, "she's afraid of the dog. Said he snarled at her." Then to me, "Beam, come out of the shower. You're fine."

"No way."

"Hush snarled?" Buzz asked, squeezing into the tiny cube. Now there were three of us in a space meant for one. I could tell by the glow that he held a candle. "Did he growl? Did his hackles go up?"

"I ... I couldn't tell," I said. "It was too dark."

He shuffled closer and tapped on the curtain.

I peeled it back just far enough to see his face.

"Like this?" He lifted his upper lip, showing teeth that were yellow with age and one that was chipped.

"Yes, like that. Exactly like that."

Buzz snorted, then chuckled. He set the candle on the counter. Soon, he was clutching his stomach with laughter.

"What?!" I shouted. "It's not funny. What are you laughing at?"

Swiping a hand across his eyes, he shook his head. "Sorry, Sunbeam. I can't help it. Hush was grinning at you. It's what he does when he likes someone."

"Likes someone? Well, I don't like him. I don't like dogs at all. Hate them. All of them. So keep him away from me."

"That's going to be kinda hard to do, seeing as how we're all cooped up in this shoebox —" He lowered his voice. "Sorry, you didn't hear that from me. Anyway, we all have to stay near the fire tonight, so you're just going to have to get used to him being there, 'cause he sure as heck ain't leaving."

With that, he turned around, collected his candle, and shuffled back down the hall. The dog took one look at me, then gimped after him. It took Hush a long time to make it just partway down that short hall. The paw on his bad leg held off the ground, he hopped on three feet. Each movement was an awkward ballet.

Seeing the dog in distress, Hunter grabbed a towel off the shower curtain rod and abandoned me. When he caught up with the dog, he looped the towel under Hush's belly to hold him up. At first, Hush blinked in confusion, but when Hunter urged him on, the dog hobbled forward a step, and then another, and another.

After shutting the door and locking it, I stood in that tub for a good ten minutes before sinking down to its bottom. I pulled two more towels off the towel rack behind the toilet and laid them over me. Then, my head resting against the faucet, I curled up tight, waiting for my own body heat to warm me. But the towels were thin and scratchy, and the porcelain of the tub was cool, and a winter draft hissed incessantly through the window.

No one came to ask if the dog had hurt me, or to guard me on my way back. Noreen didn't even come to usher me out. They didn't understand how real my fear was.

—o0Oo—

I woke up, shivering. The murmur of voices drifted from beneath the bottom of the door. It was hard to make out all the words, but I could hear some of them, mostly Noreen's.

"What about the Faderville Motor Hotel? They could stay …"

Then Hunter's muffled reply. "… first place I …"

"Surely, they could make an exception for —"

"… not the dog … stairs are the …"

"Oh, I didn't think of the veranda. That place is a national landmark, did you know? Maybe someone could …"

Another low, barely controlled reply from Hunter.

"Full? How could they be full?"

Hunter's voice came a little more forcefully this time, revealing his frustration. "…worst ice storm in fifty … people sleeping in the …"

She spoke hurriedly, like she had to get the words out fast or not at all. "What about you, then? Why can't you …?"

"I didn't know until just this morning. I was planning on taking them with me, but Jenn says the girls —"

The back door thudded shut and I heard Hunter say, "Morning, Buzz! How's Hush doing today?" A polite reply ensued, followed by the gentle reassurances of Buzz's voice along with the tap and scrape of claws on the kitchen floor. They must've been outside while Hunter

125

and Noreen were sorting out what to do with them.

As much as I wanted to stay in that tub and hide, my stomach clock was telling me it was long past time for a meal. I started to sit up, but I suddenly felt lightheaded. My neck was so stiff I couldn't turn it to the right at all. My headache seemed to have relocated from the front of my head to the base of my skull. I forced myself upright but immediately regretted it. A cramp tightened the muscles between my shoulder blades. I bit my teeth together hard, trying to keep them from clattering.

The palest of dawn light filtered in through the window above me. The splat of freezing rain was gone, but in its place a fierce wind howled.

In the kitchen, bowls plinked on the countertop. Glass containers rattled. A cupboard door banged shut. Voices mingled in forced congeniality.

Still, no one came for me. Sooner or later, though, someone would have to pee. I sure did. But I didn't want to shed this paltry little cocoon I'd built.

I wanted so badly to sit close to the fire, to let its heat thaw the ice in my veins. I tried to bend my fingers, but they were painfully stiff from the cold.

Noreen's voice pitched in a question. Hunter laughed in reply.

I wanted to be warm, like them. I wanted food.

But … the dog. The dog was out there.

My breathing quickened. My stomach flipped. Tears trailed their way down my cheeks, leaving rivulets of ice. Damn it. I'd planned this for months. Made it all this way. By myself. And now I was going to freeze to death in a bathtub or possibly starve because of some stupid dog.

I never for a moment thought this would be easy. I just had no idea how hard it would turn out to be. My stomach contracted in hunger. More tears welled. I was tired and my head hurt and my back ached and I was so stinking, unbelievably cold that I —

Knuckles rapped sharply on the bathroom door. "Bellamy?"

It was Noreen. I sucked down a glob of tear snot. "Yes?"

"There's a bowl of cereal and milk out here for you." The mention of food sent my appetite into overdrive. I was feeling weak from the lack of calories. At this point, I didn't care if she offered me stale rice cakes. And then — "If you come out soon, you can say goodbye."

A hodgepodge of feelings bubbled up in me. If Hunter left, he'd also be taking that hobo and his mutt. Surely. Then, I wouldn't have to worry about getting mauled. But that would also leave me alone with Noreen the Ice Queen. No matter how I looked at it, there was no way to win in this scenario. Everything had been going downhill since I left Michigan. Here I thought I was saving myself, forging a better future. I blew my nose quietly on my sleeve. "Dr. McHugh's leaving? Now?"

"Yes, now. Hurry up." Without another word, Noreen plodded down the hallway.

He couldn't go. He just couldn't. How could he abandon me like this? He was the only normal person here. Not counting myself. Now he was going home to his wife and kids. Two kids who had two normal parents. Those kids had probably lived in the same house all their lives, too. Bet the older one had never had to pry a joint out of her baby brother's mouth or go around the house and dispose of all the half empty beer bottles. Bet Jenn and Hunter hugged their kids and told them they loved them, every day. The more I thought about it, the sadder I got.

Like it or not, I had to say goodbye. If Hunter hadn't come down that road when he did, I might've frozen to death in that storm.

Gathering my courage, I climbed out of the tub. Before I opened the door, I stretched, took a dozen deep breaths, and told myself over and over that the dog would be gone soon and then, *then* I could relax.

127

Carefully, I opened the door and made my way to the living room. Morning light spilled through the big window by the front door. There, Hunter stood with his coat on.

He smiled shyly. "Hey, Beam. I'm heading out in a minute. Jasper Buxton's prize mare decided to birth her colt on the worst day of the year and it's not going smoothly. He's only a few miles down the road, so —"

"Sure. Bye. And, uh … thanks for … you know." Shrugging, I turned away and made for the kitchen. I wasn't interested in any long, drawn-out explan—

I stopped dead in my tracks. That blasted dog was sprawled out on a blanket on the kitchen floor, right next to the table. Why wasn't Buzz getting ready to go too?

Noreen was washing dishes in the sink, oblivious. She turned around long enough to wave toward the chair opposite Buzz. "Sit there, Bellamy. I only have Frosted Flakes. The milk's still cold, so it shouldn't have spoiled yet."

When I didn't move after several seconds, she set a pan down on the counter hard enough to get my attention. "Sit, I said. The dog won't bite. He can barely move."

Says you, I thought. Last night he'd made it to the end of the hallway on three legs to hunt me down.

My back to the wall, I made a wide arc around the dog. Without lifting his chin from his paws, his ghost eyes tracked me like laser beams trained to a target. I pulled the chair out from behind, then scooted around it and sat. Noreen slid a bowl of corn flakes in front of me. Hardly appetizing. There were days in my life I'd had nothing but cereal — breakfast, lunch, and dinner. Still, I needed to eat. I picked up a spoon and stirred, hoping a few raisins would float to the top. Hush stretched his neck to watch, and I flinched, my heart ramping up its cadence for several seconds until the dog closed his eyes again. I kept a close eye on him anyway.

Never trust a dog, I reminded myself. Never. No matter how calm they look. It's all a ploy, like the mountain lion stalking a chipmunk. Lay low, still, and quiet. Yawn, feign boredom. Until your prey lets its guard down. Then —

Hunter stepped into the kitchen, the brim of his ball cap bent in his hands. "I just wanted to tell you, Beam, how glad I am to have met you. Maybe we'll see each other again soon? Maura's about your age. I'm sure she'd be glad to show you around the high school if you need a tour."

"Yeah, sure," I said, less snidely this time. "That would be nice."

Although who knew if I'd be here a month or even a day from now? Anyway, he was assuming I still went to school, which I didn't. Interesting story to that. I never bothered explaining it to people anymore because I could tell by the way they squinted at me that they didn't believe it.

Any moment now Buzz was going to stand up and head on out that door with him. Any moment.

Buzz scooped a spoonful of cereal and munched it slowly. He needed to hurry up. Hunter was being way too patient with him.

"And soon as the ice thaws," Hunter added, "I'll be back to help you get the truck out of the ditch."

Right. Forgot about that.

I couldn't help but notice the disapproval in Noreen's glance. Sooner or later, the manure was going to hit the fan about the truck. I wondered if she already knew.

"Bye, Mrs. Larson." Hunter lifted a hand in farewell. "Buzz. Maybe once the girls get over their strep throat, you could come and stay with us for a while."

Wait. What? I plunked my spoon down on the table. "You mean Buzz isn't going home with you?"

"No, he can't right now. Jenn said both the girls had sore throats last night. This morning they came down with fevers. Strep is going

129

around. I don't want to expose anyone else to it."

My heart sank as the two men clasped hands. Buzz started to get up, but Hunter waved him back down, pointing at him. "Take care of yourself, sir."

"I will, Doc. I will. Thanks ... for everything. I mean it."

As he put his hand on the knob of the front door, Noreen called out. "Wait ... What about the girl? Shouldn't she go to the hospital? You said she had a concussion."

"I'm not seeing any signs of one. I think she's fine, but keep an eye on her, okay?"

Hunter left then, the front door clunking shut like a bank's vault door. Resounding. Final. Impenetrable. As Hunter's truck rumbled off into the distance, I regretted not having thrown myself at his feet. I would've happily suffered strep throat to escape this crew.

Instead, I was stuck here with a crotchety old grandmother who was about to throw the book at me at any minute, and a homeless man and his spooky-eyed dog. Just wonderful. My nightmare. I pulled my feet up and tucked them underneath me. If the dog lunged, I could more quickly jump up on the table this way.

In the poor, cramped neighborhoods where I'd grown up, people kept dogs for two reasons. The more law-abiding citizens kept them to protect themselves from thieves who needed drug money. The thieving druggies kept dogs to warn them if the cops came by.

Maybe there were some dogs in this world that had no intention of doing harm. Possibly. As I saw it, though, better safe than sorry. I didn't want to be around any of them, plain and simple.

I ignored my bowl so long the cereal flakes became milk-logged and started to sink. Every so often, Buzz would rub at his forehead, as if to erase the furrows there. By the time I dipped my spoon in to eat, I got a mouthful of mush. I forced it down. Except for some junk food and a couple of sodas, I'd barely eaten yesterday or the day before.

Spoons pinged, dishes clattered in the sink, and a dog snored softly. For ten minutes, no one spoke. I emptied my bowl and refilled it. The dog, eyes still closed, stretched his legs, and Buzz bent down to rub his spotted ears. Noreen dried the dishes and began to put them away. As much as I'd hated the constant clamor of the city, right now I desperately wanted to hear the wail of sirens or confusion of traffic noise. Even the senseless chatter of a talk show or soap opera. Anything to distract from the tension.

Finally, I couldn't stand it anymore. "Well, *I'm* not sleeping in the tub tomorrow night again."

"Nobody asked you to last night," Noreen snapped. She closed a cupboard door and grabbed her winter coat from a peg by the back door. "I'm going outside."

"What for?"

"What do you mean 'what for'?" she shot back with a hostile glare.

I put my feet down carefully and slid my chair back. The dog went on snoring. My eyes never left the monster as I tiptoed across the floor and set my bowl in the sink. "I mean, it's nothing but ice out there. You aren't leaving, too, are you?"

"No, I'm not leaving. Work's canceled again today. Ever heard of cabin fever?" She crammed her arms through too-tight sleeves and began to button up. Evidently she'd bought this winter coat thirty pounds ago. She wasn't obese by any means, but she'd acquired the comfortable padding of late middle age. If she hadn't been so cranky, she might've been huggable. "I'm going out to salt the sidewalk. Once it melts a bit, it'll be easier to shovel the ice off."

I raced into the living room to find a pile of my belongings beside the couch. Apparently Hunter had taken the liberty of grabbing some of my things from Carlos before bringing me here. I dug my coat out. Noreen was still struggling to pull on her boots when I came back into the kitchen. By then, Buzz was on the floor with the dog, inspecting

131

its bandages.

"What are you doing?" Noreen asked me. "Shouldn't you be lying down, recovering from your accident?"

My neck still felt screwed on wrong and my shoulders were bunched up tighter than banjo strings, but the bump on my head had shrunk to marble-size. "My headache's gone." Not true, but I was going to have one no matter what. Better to be outside, freezing my buns off, than inside being constantly watched by that wolf. "Can I help?"

In answer, she grabbed a pair of mittens and a knitted cap from a basket beside the door and handed them to me. A moment later she was out the door.

As soon as I had my winter gear on, I scurried after her.

The screen door slapped shut behind me. The shock of the cold hitting me was like diving into an icy river. Snot froze in my nostrils. Breath shattered inside my lungs. My face hurt. I wanted to run back inside and spare myself from the polar winds slicing over the hills and rattling through the trees. Thank God I had my puffy ski coat on, fit for a Michigan winter, or else I would have frozen to death where I stood. But I wasn't about to go back in, for two reasons ... No, make that three. One — the *dog* was in there. Two — if I didn't start sucking up to the old hag, she was going to ship me straight back to Lana. And three —

It was beautiful out here.

Overnight, a light snow had fallen. For a moment I forgot to breathe. Every surface sparkled with a pale blue iridescence. Prisms of sunlight bounced off icy branches. Every tree as far as the eye could see was a living ice sculpture. Snow glinted on the garage roof and in the crooks of trees and across the lawn.

It was a world made of crystal. Fragile and wicked and terrifying. And captivating.

Before Noreen got too far, I asked, "How long are they staying?"

Halfway to the garage, she stopped and regarded me carefully. "I could ask the same of you."

Suddenly I felt very … guilty? Like I'd imposed on her, like I wasn't welcome here. Where else was I supposed to go, Child Protective Services? No, I knew how that would go. It wasn't an option. Instead, I'd held the hope that Noreen's signature at the bottom of that Christmas card along with the word 'Love' had meant something. When I'd left Flint, I hadn't allowed myself to consider that she might reject me and now that the possibility was real, it sucked a hole in my soul as big as Lake Superior. I'd accepted long ago that it wasn't in Lana's capacity to truly love another human being, but for a while I'd had Oakley's love to offset that. Until he died. I'd been bitter ever since, knowing that I'd survived and he hadn't. If I had perished and Oakley had been left in Lana's care, he never would have known she wasn't a normal mother. If she'd just fed and clothed him, which somehow she'd always managed to do, that would have been enough. But that was just another what-if among a thousand. And, why had Lana and her bum boyfriend been spared in that fire? That was one more injustice in a string of many. If karma truly existed, they would have been the ones not to make it out alive. So since the universe wasn't going to set things straight all by itself, I had taken it upon myself to do it. When I got in that truck and drove south two days ago, I figured things here would *have* to be better. She couldn't turn away her own flesh and blood.

Maybe all Noreen needed was time to accept that I wasn't going anywhere. After all, I had no place else to go.

"I'm sorry," I muttered. A lump clogged my throat.

"For what?"

I sniffed. Was it the wind stinging my eyes, or more tears? "For coming here. For not calling first."

She scoffed. "Well, you're here now. I suppose we'll just deal with it one day at a time until it all gets sorted out."

133

Sorted out? By who — and how? Her words hung, fragile, in the brittle air. Were they a threat or a challenge? I wasn't sure what she meant, but I didn't want to ask. All I knew was it wasn't what I'd needed to hear.

I needed someone to care for me. To tell me everything would be fine and that I was welcome here. I needed a champion. A protector. A parent.

Noreen's boots crunched across the snow. I stepped from the porch to follow her and immediately regretted that I only had a pair of old running shoes with worn soles on. Every step was treacherous. The layer of snow was deceptive. I was used to snow being something you could just kick out of the way, or at most would sink into. But this was a sprinkling of glitter atop a thick sheet of glass. With every step, I had to punch through it or else my foot would slide over the surface. Snow got into my shoes and melted from the heat of my body, making my socks wet by the time I reached the garage.

"Here." Noreen handed me a large tool with a long handle and a thick straight blade at the end, speckled with rust.

"What's this?"

"An ice breaker. Haven't used it for ages. Almost threw it out when I moved. Good thing I didn't." She hefted a bag of salt onto her hip and hobbled over the sidewalk, casting handfuls of salt pellets to either side as she went, like an ancient farmer sowing seed.

She was halfway back to the house before she turned around and glared at me. "Are you going to stand there all day, or help like you said you would?"

"Like this?" I lifted the tool a few inches, aimed it down, and ... *thwack*! It impacted with a dull thud. Stooping to get a closer view, I couldn't see that it had done anything.

"Isn't much art to it," Noreen said. "But you'd better work a little faster than that if you expect to get done before suppertime."

She whipped around and flung salt in swooping arcs before her.

Ice popped and crackled wherever the pellets landed, then hissed as it melted.

In front of me, little ice-free pockets were forming. I lifted the ice-breaker and dropped it in one of the more melted areas. A tiny crack spread outward. I chipped at the edge of one of the pockets. A chunk about four inches square broke loose.

"Faster!" Noreen barked, not even looking.

I pounded harder, slamming the edge down with newfound resentment. It was very cathartic. I lifted the tool and banged it on the edge of my slowly widening patch. A tiny flake of ice chipped off. No, shoot, that was a piece of concrete.

"I said faster, not harder. Don't ruin my sidewalk."

I tapped at the ice. Left, right, left. After a while, my right arm and shoulder got exhausted, so I switched to my left.

Chip, chip, chip. Chip, chip. Chip... Chip.

Pretty soon my hands got so tired I could barely grip the handle. A trickle of sweat worked its way down my breastbone. My muscles were knotting up so tight they burned. I stopped to rest.

Noreen surveyed my progress from the top porch step, the empty salt bag wadded in her hand. "What are you quitting for?"

"I'm not quitting," I grumbled. "Just resting."

Her chin dipped in the smallest nod. "Well, as soon as you feel like it, get back to work. You're doing fine." She started for the door, then turned back around. "Oh, and we'll come back out later with the snow shovel and clear the rest off."

Was this how it was going to be — her ordering me about like a drill sergeant? What a complete one-eighty from Lana's absolute apathy. I wasn't used to this. Might as well join the army and go to boot camp. At least I could make a career out of that.

Must be one of those cases of 'be careful what you wish for'. I'd wanted someone's attention. Now I had it. I only wished I could've happened upon something in between. I wanted concern and unconditional love, not micromanagement and child slavery.

Before I went back to chipping ice, I took another minute to look around me and admire this new land I'd stumbled into. The hills, rugged and wildly beautiful, rose up around Noreen's homestead. Ice glittered on naked tree branches. Snow sparkled beneath an amber sun. This was nothing like Flint. Not even on its best day. Hard to believe it was even on the same planet.

Yesterday, when I'd first arrived in Faderville, I'd missed the conveniences of city life: fast food, mega stores, the businesses and industry. Evidence of humankind's productivity and consumerism. Now ... I wasn't so sure those things were even worth missing. Because without them, it was easier to notice that beauty could be something as simple as an icicle capturing and bending the color and light around it.

The wind carried my sigh away. Up hills. Over mountains. Through steep-sided valleys. Past rivers winding lazily through deep woods. All the way out to an ocean I'd never seen.

When I thought of things that way, my troubles seemed pretty small.

It didn't make them go away, though. One look toward the house — at the kitchen window where my grandmother, Noreen Larson, stood sipping from a mug as she glared judgmentally at me — and I was reminded that my day of reckoning might very well be today.

There was something about that woman's gaze that could flay flesh from bones.

chapter 12

Buzz

Buzz set the drawer into its guides and slid it back and forth several times. It glided smoothly on the tracks and closed without gaps. A simple home repair, but it made a big difference. So far today he'd fixed three drawers, replaced the handles on the lower kitchen cabinets, greased all the door hinges, and hung a new coat rack in the mudroom. He had never loved home remodeling or construction work, but he'd been proficient at it and it was the type of work that kept him busy from start to finish with a different task every day. There were always problems to be solved and useful things to be created. It hadn't been his first choice as a career, but at the time, it was the only job he could get. He'd started off almost thirty years ago as a laborer for a homebuilder when he'd gotten out of jail —

The doorknob rattled and Noreen stomped in, snow falling from her boots in fluffy clumps that instantly began to melt into puddles. She shrugged her coat off, although it took some effort to free her arms of the too-tight sleeves. One glance from her in Buzz's direction and he instantly felt exposed.

Did she know? How could she? If she had, she never would have agreed to let him stay.

Still, he didn't have anything to feel guilty about. The charges, the conviction — they'd all been a setup. Everyone who'd known him back then knew it was true. Yet it was there on his record. He'd admitted to it. He'd had to. Or so he'd been led to believe.

As Noreen crossed the kitchen floor, Hush lifted his head and struggled to stand. Buzz went to the dog and pushed his shoulders down. "Stay," he commanded lowly. Hush complied, although he followed Noreen's movements with interest. She pulled open a narrow drawer and the contents rattled as she fished through them.

Buzz took a seat beside where Hush lay and waited for Noreen to remark on how easily the drawer opened, to ask him what he'd done to fix it, but she seemed not to notice that it didn't stick anymore.

"When would you like to go over the other work that needs done?" Buzz prompted.

Closing the drawer with more force than she needed to, she turned around. "There are a lot of things that need fixing around here, Mr. Donovan. It's not like I don't have the money. But you know what? I don't trust contractors any further than I can throw them, which means not at all. I learned long ago not to advance them any money. In the past two years alone, I've had four who either did shoddy work or stopped showing up. Several others who never returned calls or even came out at all. Do you know how many days of work I've missed just waiting for some electrician, plumber, or carpenter to show up? I can't convey the level of frustration I've experienced. This place was supposed to be an investment. A nice piece of property in the country, halfway between Faderville and Somerset, where I could live out my final working years in peace before I retired to Florida or Arizona or maybe even some Central American country where houses are a fraction of the price they are here. If I sell now, it would be at a loss. Instead, I'm stuck here waiting on some self-employed worker who obviously doesn't want or need the money I'm offering. Mr. Yoder was the only one I trusted, but he — God rest his soul — got killed when a speeding car rear-ended his buggy. One decent carpenter in all of Adair County and he had to die on me like that. Haven't had a good worker since."

It was the most he'd heard her speak since he got there. Too bad it was full of vitriol. No wonder she couldn't get anyone to show up. The amazing thing was she'd managed the whole speech on two breaths. He understood her frustration, in a way, but if she kept looking for the negative, then that was what she was bound to find. "I don't think he died to spite you."

"Who?"

"Mr. Yoder."

She waved a spatula at him like a swordsman squaring up for a duel. "Don't mock me, Mr. Donovan. Your kind is not reliable. You overcharge, show up late, skip out early, and —"

"You said you had a long list that needed done. Can you show me?" The only way to change this woman's mind about him was to prove himself. She wasn't going to make that easy. If she wasn't convinced by the time he got done, then she didn't want to be convinced.

"It's up here, Mr. Donovan." She tapped at her temple. "I don't have it written down anywhere … yet. Forget the home improvements for the time being. Right now, I'm just trying to take care of the basics, like how we're supposed to keep warm or eat or have light to see by if this lasts another night. I only have one flashlight and no extra batteries. Once, back in the seventies, Roland and I went a week without power after a winter storm. We melted ice over an outdoor fire for water and bundled up in layers to keep from freezing to death. We were survivors, not complainers. Practical people, not baseless dreamers. Maybe when the roads get cleared I can drive into town, but I'll wager there's not a single battery, loaf of bread, or jug of milk available, unless you drive all the way to Lexington. So your list" — she waved her hands in the air like she was conjuring up a magic spell — "will just have to wait until I do what needs to be done to keep us alive."

Hanging on to the table edge, Buzz rose slowly from his seat. His vision blackened momentarily and he felt the familiar muffling of sounds that went along with it. At his feet, Hush stirred, rolling over onto his belly. When shapes began to sharpen, Buzz drew a long breath, trying to remember what it was he was about to say. Through the kitchen window, he could see Beam driving a heavy metal tool into the sheets of ice to clear a path with all the enthusiasm of a convict on a chain gang. From what he could gather in bits yesterday, she had driven overnight all the way from Flint, Michigan, to southern Kentucky, on her own and without a license, just to get to her grandmother's house. A grandmother she hadn't seen in ten years. The girl was either an enormous fool or a courageous young lady.

Then, he remembered. "I've kept myself and my dog alive for over two thousand miles, Mrs. Larson. There's a lot I could do to help."

"In your condition?"

"I've lived with it a while. Unless the dog says otherwise, I'm fine. And you did agree to let me work for room and board until Hush was well enough to leave with me."

"Only because Dr. McHugh couldn't take you in for now, on account of his kids being sick. It's a big risk I'm taking, Mr. Donovan, letting a stranger like you into my home. Just so you know, I don't leave valuables or paperwork with personal information lying about. It's all locked up and secure. So don't bother looking for any of it, 'cause you won't find it."

The woman didn't mince words, yet he didn't hold it against her. She had a lot of old thorns still embedded in her. Mistrust was about fear. Chances were she'd been hurt or betrayed before. When the time was right, when she'd softened to him a little, he'd get her to talk. Right now, though, the walls around her heart were too high. She'd only take questions as an intrusion. "We'll be out of here as soon as we're able to leave. Until then and until the power comes back … what can I do to help around here?"

She pretended to rummage around in yet more drawers. "I … I don't know. I spend most of my time at work, so I don't have to come back to this empty house and be faced with all the projects that never get done. Lately, I've just given up on them. So I just make do with things as they are. Today, I can't go to work because of the roads and I have all the time in the world on my hands and I wouldn't know where to start. I can't start, because there's no electricity and I'm stranded here with … with 'guests' I wasn't expecting and no way to feed them or keep them warm."

"I'm sorry, Mrs. Larson. I didn't plan to end up here. It just —"

"I know, I know you didn't," she interrupted, clearly exasperated. "I was about ready to boot you out the door with Doc McHugh but then it came up that you knew all about houses and fixing them and I thought … I thought, well, maybe this was — what do they call it? — oh, yes, serendipity. What a strange word that is. Ser-en-dip-ity." She bobbed her head with each syllable. "Sounds like some kind of medical condition."

She said it like it was the plague.

While she blathered on, Buzz could see her façade crumbling, like the exterior of an old industrial building falling away one brick at a time. Maybe she didn't hate company as much as she appeared to. Maybe she *wanted* someone around but just couldn't let herself admit it.

Loneliness, that's what he sensed. She clung to it like a familiar pain.

Noreen turned in a circle, as if studying in turn the bits of unfinished drywall, exposed wiring, and loose tiles. "I thought living

141

alone would be easier here than on the farm with all the animals, but if anything it's been harder. There's something about having to get out and take care of someone other than yourself. Even if the animals never said so, you knew you were needed. But now, no one relies on me. I just rely on myself. And apparently I can't rely on anyone else."

He didn't say anything back. This woman harbored more self-pity than anyone he'd ever met. Being in the same room with her was like having your spirit siphoned away.

If there was one thing he'd learned since he started his journey with Hush, it was that you did what you had to do, and if every time something bad happened you asked 'Why me?', then you were just setting yourself up for a lifetime of suffering. Better to just deal with it, look for the lesson, and go on. And whenever possible, focus on the good. In this case, he had a roof over his head. He should be grateful for that. She was making it hard, though.

"If you'll allow me" — he inspected an outlet where a tangle of wires twisted around itself — "maybe I can figure out what needs fixed most, other than the odds and ends I've already attended to. Sometimes it's just better to start somewhere than never start at all. See, dangerous bits like this ..." He carefully tugged at the wires to pull them farther out so she could have a good look. "Now this should be a priority."

"Why that?"

"Could be dangerous. Wouldn't want your house to burn down. Or for you to get electrocuted. Things like a crooked drawer are in inconvenience, yes. But they're not a safety concern."

"Do you even know electricity, Mr. Donovan?"

"Please, call me Buzz. And yes, I do. Carpentry was my specialty, but I've helped wire enough houses to light a town the size of Faderville twice over. On a construction site, you were expected to be able to do more than one thing because sometimes you had to cover for your co-workers when they were out sick."

Or hungover. Or in jail. But Buzz didn't mention those things because they would only confirm her opinion of contractors. Most of them were generally good guys fighting daily with their demons. They worked hard, but sometimes they just made stupid choices. He'd been that way once, too. Little did he know the impact those choices would have on the rest of his life.

Arms crossed, she pinched her lips together in thought. "Fine. Have a look around. You let me know what you think is a priority — as long as it's within your knowledge base. But run it by me first." She pulled open the last drawer and retrieved the flashlight. One flick of the switch and its light beamed up at the ceiling. "But whatever you do, don't presume to call me by my first name. We don't know each other that well and I don't imagine we ever will."

With that, she marched from the room and down into the basement.

"Come on, buddy." After putting on his borrowed coat, Buzz roused Hush with a good hard scratch on the neck. "You and I have work to do. Let's go outside for now, so you can do your business."

Upon hearing the word 'outside', Hush's ears lifted. The dog tried to push himself up, but with one leg being bandaged straight and his pain meds still making him woozy, he couldn't quite manage without his feet sliding out from under him. So Buzz took the towel that had been lying beneath him and slung it under the dog's belly. Once Hush was standing, Buzz helped him out the back door and down the steps. It was an awkward dance — Hush gimping along, Buzz trying to keep step — but somehow they managed, adjusting to each other like a pianist's two hands coordinate to play a song, harmony complementing melody.

Pausing in her chores, Beam regarded them warily. Mostly it was Hush she kept an eye on.

She could stare all she wanted. Hush wasn't going to do anything. The sooner she figured that out, the easier her life was going to be.

143

For now, though, she interpreted every move as a potential offense, Buzz could tell. Maybe she'd just never grown up with a dog.

"He won't hurt you." Buzz helped his dog to where the grass was so he could pee. Hush squatted like a girl dog, his cheeks bunched in a smile of relief as his steaming urine hit the pristine white snow. "Even if he wanted to — which he doesn't — I'm pretty sure you could outmaneuver him at the moment."

"Sure," she muttered, both hands on the tool like she was ready to wield it as a weapon.

A couple minutes later, Hush finished his business and Buzz helped him back inside. After settling the dog down under the kitchen table on the blanket, he went back outside and claimed the snow shovel that was leaning against the wall of the back porch. He scooped a load of ice chips and snow and tossed it into the yard. Soon, he and Beam had cleared the back sidewalk all the way to the garage and had gotten a good start on the driveway.

Sweat trickled warmly down Buzz's chest, dampening his borrowed shirt. He unzipped his coat to cool off. A wave of lightheadedness swept over him and he leaned against a fence post for security. His vision grayed. Still clutching the shovel in one hand, he held on to the post for dear life with the other.

His world narrowed to a tunnel, through which he drifted, half-conscious. He was barely aware of his own thoughts, heard only a muted buzz in his ears.

"Hey …? Hey, are you okay?"

The voice was soft, distant. A girl's.

Buzz forced himself to focus, to swim toward the sound. Soon, the familiar knife of pain in the back of his head slammed him back to reality. He blinked repeatedly. When he felt for the shovel handle, it wasn't there.

"Are you having another one? Should we go back inside?"

Light hands braced his shoulders. He saw her through a fog, like a fairy floating in the mist. Beam stood before him, looking up at him. Somehow he'd remained standing. The wind had picked up. It was a wonder it hadn't knocked him over.

"No, no, I'm fine."

Her fingertips pressed against his cheek. He sensed their pressure but not whether they were warm or cold. Beam frowned at him. "You don't look fine."

"Relatively speaking, I mean. I'm still standing, aren't I?" he joked. Judging by Beam's reaction, she didn't take the incident lightly. Funny how perspectives can differ, depending on your circumstances. She was youth and new beginnings. He was merely clinging to whatever small graces he was granted, day by day. His episodes were new and frightening to her. To him, they had become a part of who he was. He'd long since stopped lamenting the way things were or dreading what was to come.

Nearby, a crack sounded. A branch, high in a tree, splintered and plunged earthward. When it hit the ground, not fifty feet from them, the casing of ice shattered, chiming as it plinked in crystalline shards upon the crust of packed snow.

Beam flinched, but Buzz was still too numb to react. The wind gusted, causing more branches, heavy with their frozen burden, to clatter and moan. He observed it all with an innocent wonderment, as he often did nowadays, like he was seeing it all for the first time.

Or the last.

Beam's head swiveled to take it all in, her eyes widening in wonder. Above the hills, through the tangled stands of trees, and over rough pastures, the wind raced, a hushed roar, mighty yet understated. A power often present but seldom noted.

"I've never really heard the wind," she said quietly.

"Never?" He eased his grip on the post, the earth now firm beneath him. "How can you not have heard the wind?"

She cocked her head indignantly, as if perturbed he didn't

understand her meaning. "I *know* it's there. It's just ... I've never heard nothing *but* the wind, you know? Where I come from, it's never quiet like this. There's always traffic and people shouting and music playing and ..." — she looked down, staring at nothing — "sometimes gunshots."

Shrugging the thought off, Beam picked up the shovel and handed it to him.

"Is that why you left Michigan?" Buzz asked. "To get away from the violence?"

"Yeah ... no. I mean, partly." She was older than her years. A worn soul in a vibrant young body. Yet she was the opposite, too: spring's first tentative bloom after winter's long assault. Buzz had no doubt she'd seen things no child should ever witness. But somehow, she'd endured. She looked at him boldly, unafraid. "Mostly I left because my mother was going to kill herself. Somehow, someday. Not on purpose, you know. But eventually. And I didn't want to see it happen. Or become collateral damage."

Frozen balloons of breath billowed from her lips as she gazed at the distant hills. Her eyes were an earthy, golden brown, like a doe's.

Buzz thought she was going to go on, but when she didn't, he said, "I'd say you were smart to leave."

A sheen of tears glistened in Beam's eyes, but she sniffed them away. "Yeah, well, she wasn't interested in changing."

Buzz wanted to reassure her that all was not lost, but he knew differently. If someone didn't want to change, well, there was no way you could make them. It wasn't worth spending your time hoping they would become what you wanted them to be. He'd learned that with his former wife at an early age.

From a side window, Noreen gazed out at them momentarily, then moved into the shadows indoors. Beam must have glimpsed her, too, and when she did her shoulders rolled forward.

"Your grandmother ..." he began, unsure how to say what he

meant, "she's a bit crusty around the edges, but I have the feeling she's not all that bad."

Scoffing, Beam rammed the icebreaker downward. "Yeah, well, she doesn't seem too happy about me being here, now does she? How'd you swing board here, anyway? Yesterday she didn't want you or your dog to step foot inside."

"To tell the truth, it was Hunter who facilitated the arrangement. Mrs. Larson kept complaining about all that needed done. I offered some suggestions and it came out that I have a background in construction work. I can do a little bit of everything. So, she needed work done. I needed a place to stay. Somehow she agreed to let me sleep in the mudroom on a cot. Sounds humble, but it's far better than sleeping on a piece of cardboard under an overpass. Between you and me, I'm surprised she agreed, too, given that she doesn't know me from Adam. My guess is she's feeling a little ambiguous about having company."

"Ambiguous?"

"It means —"

"Spare me the definition, Webster. I know what it means. Ambiguous about what?"

"Even people who like to be alone get lonely. I have a notion she'll come around about you, given time."

She arched an eyebrow at him, mulling it over. "I'll believe that when I see it."

For another hour, they worked on, clearing the snow and ice. Without Hush around, Beam was less guarded. More amicable. Even though they'd known each other less than a day, there was an easiness between them, like old friends who didn't have to worry about what they said — or if they said anything at all.

At first Buzz had found being outside invigorating, but now the cold and all-too-familiar fatigue were dragging him down. He was pressing his luck staying so far from Hush, never knowing when a

147

spell might hit. He shivered inside his borrowed clothes, which today included a heavily insulated coat that had belonged to Roland Larson. He could've fit two of himself inside that coat.

Something made him look toward the house. Noreen was there again, her face tight with expectation. She glanced behind her, toward the kitchen.

"I, uh, need to go inside and see to the dog." Using the shovel as a cane to steady himself over the icy ground, Buzz headed toward the back door. Light, quick feet followed him.

"How'd he get hurt, anyway?" Beam asked, close on his heels.

"A car was about to hit me." They climbed the back steps and stomped the snow from their shoes. Buzz rested the shovel against the wall. Beam propped her tool beside it. "He put himself in the way. Saved me."

A sideways smile tilted Beam's mouth. More of a smirk, really. "You sure? Dogs get hit by cars all the time."

"I'm sure." Through the frost on the window, he could see Hush raise his head from the floor to gaze at him. Warmth filled his chest. "I know my dog."

Sometimes he didn't feel worthy of that dog's love, but he accepted it all the same.

They went inside, but Noreen wasn't in view. Except for the gentle drip of ice melting from the eaves outside and the howl of the wind, the house was quiet.

Beam stepped out of her shoes, curled her toes under to hide the holes in her socks. She glanced warily at Hush. "Seems like he's going to be laid up for a while. Why not just leave him behind and go on by yourself? You could always come back for him later."

"Leave him? Why would I do that?" Buzz hung his oversized coat on the new coat rack inside the door. "Besides, who would take a lame dog in and care for him? You?"

"Noooo way. Not me. But maybe someone else would, like Dr.

McHugh." With a twist of her shoulders, Beam removed her coat and hung it beside his. "Anyway, wouldn't it be easier to travel without him?"

Buzz snorted without meaning to. He was pretty sure Hunter had plenty of animals of his own to take care of, as well as a family, and Buzz wasn't about to hoist a charity case on him. If only this poor girl understood the loyalty and friendship of a dog. He faced her. "A lot of things would be easier without a dog. But life wouldn't be the same, now would it?"

"I don't get it."

"No, I don't imagine you do." He almost added that she didn't know what she was missing, but something told him not to. People were most believing of things when they figured them out on their own. Bellamy Larson was a smart kid. She'd figure it out. Eventually.

chapter 13

Beam

The way Buzz talked about that dog, you'd think it was his best friend. Maybe it was. For the life of me, though, I couldn't get the connection. A dog was just a dog. It wasn't like you could have a deeply meaningful conversation with it.

While we had been out clearing the driveway, Noreen had set out a lunch for us: two slices of bread each on a couple of saucers and a jar of peanut butter. Which would have been just fine, except there was a conspiracy underway.

With one swipe of his paw, the kitten knocked two slices to the floor. They landed, conveniently, between Hush's front paws. Before either of us could say a word, the dog gulped down both slices like he hadn't eaten in days.

Instead of reacting in anger, Buzz merely waved a hand at the kitten. "Scat."

The kitten hopped onto the floor, then scampered off into a corner, his black tail flicking playfully. He crouched into pounce mode, peeking around the edge of a cabinet like a stealthy black leopard hiding in the jungle, waiting to ambush his prey.

Shaking his head, Buzz tilted the jar toward me. There was clear evidence of a small tongue having lapped up a good chunk of that peanut butter.

If I'd worked up an appetite that morning, I didn't have one anymore.

Hugging the perimeter of the room, I kept an eye on the dog and peered into the living room. Noreen wasn't there. The bedroom door was closed. Without electricity and a TV to watch, she must've decided to take a nap. Cupboard doors closed softly one after another as Buzz searched through them.

"What're you looking for?" I asked.

The kitten was at his feet now, twisting between his legs as it looked up at him. He shut the last top cabinet and started on the bottom ones. "Bread, but I'm getting the sense Hush ate the last of it. Not much here that you can eat without a stove or microwave. Unless you want cold soup." He turned a can in his hand, then tossed it in the trashcan. "Never mind. It expired last June. Hmmm, I think I can rustle up some spoons, if you want to share what's left in the peanut butter jar."

My stomach convulsed. The cat had just licked inside that jar. Who knew where his tongue had been lately?

"But ..." I gestured at the kitten, which was now busily washing the evidence from his face, not appearing the slightest bit guilty. Seconds later, he was rolling on his back, white-mittened paws stuck in the air, eyeing us innocently. Meanwhile, Hush gazed expectantly at Buzz, as if waiting for him to lob a few more slices his way.

"Aha!" Buzz pulled a box of saltines from the corner cupboard.

I hadn't looked through the cupboards myself, but from what I'd seen, there was no rhyme or reason as to where things were. Whenever Lana and I had moved into a new place, it had been my job to put things away, so I always grouped like things together. Usually

151

that wasn't much more than you could fit into the trunk of a gas-guzzling sedan. Actually, our food supply never amounted to more than you could fit in a laundry basket. The rest of the trunk was always full of Lana's low-cut tops, tight skirts, and fancy shoes. Lana also liked her cars big and flashy, which meant she bought cast-off luxury cars that were on their last leg. One even had heated leather seats. Except the heat didn't work and the leather was ripped in multiple places. That car didn't work half the time, either. We lived in that car for two weeks once, until Lana found herself a new boyfriend. At least she was good at something. Oakley thought we were on vacation, driving around central and western Michigan in that big boat of a car. When we got to Lake Michigan, Lana told him it was the ocean and that the whitecaps were shark fins. He believed her; he was that gullible. Oakley believed everything anyone ever told him. It was what made him so … pure. So perfect. And yet, so vulnerable. He didn't understand that people lied. He couldn't fathom why they would.

Buzz set the cracker box on the table, right next to the peanut butter jar. My stomach gurgled. Okay, so maybe I was hungry enough to pretend the cat hadn't drooled in that container. I could only hope he wasn't carrying bubonic plague.

The kitten jumped up in my chair, but Buzz snapped his fingers near the kitten's head and he darted away, hind legs churning as he wheeled around the corner and down the hallway in search of more mischief.

Easing down in a chair, Buzz pushed the last two pieces of bread across the table. "Go ahead. Hush and I will make do with the crackers."

"What about the cat? What are we going to feed him? Pretty sure there's no cat food around here, either."

"Second cabinet from the right." Buzz pointed. "Couple cans of tuna on the bottom shelf."

I retrieved one. "Can opener?"

He indicated a drawer that didn't quite close all the way because it was stuffed with kitchen gadgets. I dug the can opener out, tried to close the door, and gave up. I hadn't even half opened the can when the kitten was at my feet again, pawing softly at my kneecaps in a begging gesture. I spooned a little bit into a bowl and set it down before him.

"You like fish, little man?" I scratched him between the ears and his motor revved. How he could purr and eat at the same time I don't know. "Fisher — that's what we'll call you."

The kitten meowed softly in agreement.

Unimpressed with the cat, Hush whimpered as he struggled to lie down on his blanket behind Buzz. Once he was settled, I returned to my usual chair. The one wedged in the corner, where I could see everything in the room and a wide span of the living room, including the door to Noreen's room. Of course, if the dog suddenly bolted upright and came at me, I was trapped, no route for escape. But at least I'd see my end coming.

"Is there any jam?" The thought of eating a dry peanut butter sandwich didn't appeal to me.

"Pretty sure not. But there is butter."

"That'll work."

"Over there." Smiling, he pointed to the counter behind him, where a stick of butter sat on an old china saucer.

I hesitated. I'd have to pass close to the dog to get it.

Buzz scooped spoonfuls of peanut butter onto several crackers, hiding a pill in one of the globs of peanut butter. Then he set one right between Hush's front paws and told him to 'Wait'. "Did you want me to fetch it for you?"

It took me a moment to realize he was talking to me and not the dog. Hush stared cross-eyed at the cracker. A thin string of drool dripped from his lips and he licked it away, his teeth clicking softly as he did so.

"Um, sure, that'd be nice."

"Can't," he said. "Can't get up and down too often. Makes me lightheaded." He told the dog 'Okay' and Hush snarfed the cracker down in two bites. "So go ahead. Help yourself."

My mouth watered. I looked at the butter, a softened brick of creamy yellow. Then I looked at the dog, his long tongue flicking over speckled lips. Buzz tossed a cracker in the air and Hush snapped it up with perfect precision.

"That's okay," I said. "I don't really need it."

He went on eating three crackers to Hush's one, while I forced down a dry sandwich. Bread stuck in my throat like clumps of cotton balls. I reached for the cup sitting by my plate, but when I lifted it, it was empty.

A tiny smirk tilted Buzz's mouth. "There's a little milk left in the fridge if you want it. And water from the tap. Probably enough pressure left in the pump for you to get a glass of it."

Considering the fridge was next to where the butter was sitting — in a direct line with the dog — I decided on water. Somehow I managed to make my way to the sink without turning my back on the canine predator in the room. I flipped the lever up on the faucet and let my cup fill. My heart rate had doubled since entering the room minutes ago. My nerves were on edge, every sense razor sharp. Water splashed over my hand and I jerked it toward me so hard the cup smacked against the side of the sink. The cup crashed from my hold and landed in a bowl filled with dirty dishwater, splashing wet gunk halfway up my hooded sweatshirt. I grabbed a dishtowel and mopped it dry, one eye on the dog as I did so. Buzz didn't look up, didn't say a word. The dog barely glanced my way, then trained his sights again on the cracker Buzz was slathering. As quickly as I could, I refilled another cup, my hands shaking the whole time.

I'd barely sat down again when Buzz said, "Does your mom know you're here?"

"I left her a note."

His shaggy gray eyebrows made the slightest twitch. "Oh?"

I didn't have a chance to even think of an answer, because just then Noreen came into the kitchen. I must've been so fixated on the mess I was making at the sink and the dog that I hadn't heard her come out of her room.

She fixed me with a stare. The kind you couldn't look away from.

"I need your mom's phone number," she said.

"I can give it to you, but last I knew, it wasn't working." Which was the truth.

Noreen huffed. "Give it to me anyway." She took a pen and piece of note paper from a drawer and handed them to me.

I scribbled Lana's number down. She drew a cell phone from her pocket, dialed, waited. Her eyebrows pinched together in concentration. I could barely make out a recording on the other end.

"No longer in service, it says." She pushed a button and dropped the phone back into her pocket. "How do I know that's her number?"

"You don't. But it is."

She sniffed, walked around to the other side of the table, her eyes never leaving me. "Right."

"It *is*." I stifled the urge to slug her. If I was disappointed at first that she hadn't greeted me more warmly, now I was getting mad at her for insinuating I was a liar. "Guess you'll just have to trust me, huh?"

Buzz cleared his throat. Or I thought he did. He was trying to act like he wasn't a part of this, which he wasn't, but it was clearly making him uneasy.

"How do I know you are who you say you are?" Noreen began. "After all, you show up unannounced on my doorstep, in the middle of a storm, no less, and you figure I'll just roll out the red carpet? Wouldn't you be a little suspicious, if you were me?"

I let several breaths lapse before I replied. "No, I wouldn't."

"Well, I am. And if you are who you say you are, it shouldn't be

155

that hard for you to give me some proof. What's your mother's full name, anyway? Tell me something about her. When was she born? Where does she live?" She slapped the flats of her palms on the table. "What's she been doing all this time?"

Heat fanned through me. Rage, almost. I clung to it, weird as that may seem. Because it was better than breaking down in tears. Because it gave me courage. I clenched my teeth together, let my breath out slowly through my nostrils like I was opening a vent to let off the steam before my head exploded.

"Whatever happened between you two," I said lowly, "is not my fault."

Buzz coughed, and Noreen glanced his way. But he wasn't looking at her. He was patting his dog on the head.

It was enough to yank Noreen off whatever track she'd been on. She drew back, looked out the window. "How am I supposed to get in touch with her to let her know you're here?"

"I can tell you where she works: Harrigan's Brewhouse. In Flint. I don't know the phone number, though. You'll have to look it up."

"I can't do that until the power comes back on." She said it like it was my fault or something. "The only computer I have is an old desktop in my bedroom. My phone isn't fancy enough to get on the internet."

"Sorry. That's the best I can do."

One shoulder lifted in a half-shrug. She laid the pen and paper in front of me again. "Write it down. I'm no good at remembering."

I did as she asked, then got up from the table and started out of the room.

"Where are you going?" she called.

"To get your proof," I said over my shoulder. A minute later I returned and placed the old Christmas card in front of her. "There."

She read it twice, stuffed it back in the envelope, nodded slowly. Then she took a long look at me, trying hard not to let on that she'd been wrong to doubt me. "All right. But I *am* calling your mother. You can stay until we get this straightened out."

Gee, thanks. She acted like that card hadn't changed a thing.

As she turned to leave the room, I said, "Aren't you going to ask why I left?"

She stopped but didn't turn around. Just kept her back to me, frozen in place. "If I did, I'm sure I'd get your version of the situation. If there's one thing I've learned in this life" — she turned her head just enough to look over her shoulder at me — "it's that there are always two sides to a story."

With that, she returned to her room, closing the door firmly behind her.

"Well, that's a start," Buzz said.

"Hardly." I took a few swallows of water, wishing I could turn the TV on and disappear into some other world. The shelves of books in the living room called out to me. There had to be something there I could get interested in. What else was I going to do until this all got 'sorted out'?

Buzz waved a butter knife in the air. "Ah, but you see, that was probably huge for her. High walls are hard to overcome. If there's no gate through, you have to breach them one stone at a time."

I herded the bread crumbs on the table into a small pile with a paper towel. I wasn't about to leave a mess, however small, and give Noreen one more reason to hate me. "I have no idea what you're talking about."

"Just a hunch, but maybe her ... reluctance or disapproval or whatever you want to call it —"

"That's putting it mildly."

"I know, I know. But maybe it isn't about you. Maybe it's about something between her and your mother."

I shrugged. "Maybe." After sweeping the crumbs into my palm and dumping them in the trashcan, I carried my cup over to the sink.

157

"But why make me pay for it, whatever 'it' was?"

I wasn't about to say it, but I had a suspicion that 'it' had a lot to do with me being the result of my mother's irresponsible behavior.

"Because sometimes," Buzz said, "clinging to pain keeps us safe from further hurt. At least, that's what we tell ourselves."

What was that supposed to mean? My brain hurt just trying to figure this guy out. Obviously there was a lot more to Buzz Donovan than you could tell at first glance. Made me wonder what *his* story was.

Yet the more I thought about what he'd just said, the more I wondered if he was talking about me.

Deep in thought, I almost tripped over the dog. He was sound asleep. Or thoroughly drugged up. The whole time he'd been awake, he'd been more interested in Buzz's crackers than me, but I wasn't about to let my guard down. Maybe Hunter's kids would get better soon, so he could take Buzz and his dog in. Then, at least I'd be free of them part of the time.

Time was something I had a lot of now. Not much I could do around here. Except read.

From a shelf in the living room, I pulled out a few books, then snuggled up on the couch. In the kitchen, I could hear Buzz unscrewing switch plates and tugging at wires. The dog snoozed peacefully in a drug-induced slumber, his upper lip folded in one spot, exposing a shiny fang. For several minutes, I watched him, his furry chest rising and falling with each sluggish breath. Like the slumbering tiger, there could be beauty in a beast capable of terror. At the moment, the dog seemed as incapable of springing up and attacking as I was of running away. My head ached. My neck was wrenched. And I felt like I'd just swum the entire length of the Mississippi.

Opening the book, I fingered pages yellow with the years. I wasn't four pages in to *Les Misérables* when sleep swept away my fears.

—o00o—

A murmur tickled inside my ears, tugging at my consciousness. A voice — low, furtive, insistent — buzzed at the perimeter of my awareness. I waded above the fog of sleep, opened my eyes, shivered at the cold. The flames in the hearth had dwindled to a faint glow, the log now little more than a charred chunk with one end glowing.

The voice came again and I looked toward Noreen's door. Peeling chips in the lower corners of the door revealed layers of paint. For the first time I looked around the house. Really looked. It wasn't filthy, by any means. Lana and I had lived in far worse places, riddled with cockroaches and rodents so bad that I remember waking at the age of four to find my legs covered in bug bites. This place wasn't that bad. But it was old. Very old. And unloved, if a house could be that.

It couldn't have been later than midafternoon, but as I unbent my neck from the odd position I'd fallen asleep in, a cramp flared between my neck and right shoulder. Ever since the accident, I'd felt twisted out of shape, like a wrung-out washcloth. The headache was still there, too. And no matter how much I slept, I still awoke tired. I wondered if I'd suffered whiplash or a mild concussion, but I didn't want to say anything for fear that Noreen would drag me off to a hospital after all and then Lana would have to get involved. I'd bounced back so quickly that everyone had apparently forgotten how the accident might have affected me.

"I called Information and talked to her at work. She's mad as hell at you, do you know that?"

I looked up to see Noreen standing across the room, phone in hand.

"Really? I thought she'd be happy to be rid of me."

In the moments that she studied me, I thought I saw the faintest smirk flit across her wrinkled lips. It was hard to tell though, because she had this permanent scowl on her face that made her look mad even when she was relaxed. That is, if she ever was.

159

She moved stiffly across the room to sit in her tatty recliner. Really, she was more worn than old. Beaten down, kind of. Like life had been difficult.

Her exhalation whistled through pinched nostrils. She drummed her fingers slowly on the armrests, like she was thinking hard about something, trying to piece words together.

"Don't know about that," she said, "but you stole that truck."

"Not like she was using it."

"She threatened to press charges."

I didn't say anything. Just stared into the wavering fire, suddenly aware of the chill in the room. It didn't surprise me, but I was pretty sure she wouldn't follow through on it. Lana was all drama. She'd string it out as long as she could, use it to make me feel about two inches tall, until something else stole her attention. If I was lucky, she had her sights on a new boyfriend.

Still, if she was mad enough, I realized I could get in really big trouble. As in grand theft auto. Wouldn't look too good on my college applications.

"I told her the truck was totaled."

I kept my gaze on the dying fire. Things had gone from bad to abysmal inside of a minute. "Is it?"

"Not quite. I gave Dr. McHugh the keys before he left and he swung by it on his way home. Still wouldn't start, but he said there's a cracked hose and a few other things that might be the problem. He's picking Mr. Donovan up tomorrow to help him tow it to the mechanic's. The body damage is pretty significant, though."

There was more she hadn't said yet, but I knew what was coming. She'd shame me, try to make me feel bad. She could guilt me all she wanted for taking the truck. It was true. I had. But the wreck was an accident. It could've happened to anyone.

"It was the ice," I mumbled. Before I knew it, it all spilled out. All the urgency and anger and indignation and resentment. "I just wanted

160

to get here. Somewhere safe. So I could be away from *her*. Before something really bad happened. I almost made it. Almost. I drove for over eight hours. Eight hours. Farther than I've ever gone. It scared the hell out of me. Aside from taking the truck — a truck nobody was using, that didn't even work until my friend fixed it — I didn't break any laws. I had to ask around to find you, because I was too dumb to look you up before I came, thinking you'd be living in the same place you did before, when I was little. I didn't know you'd moved, but people I don't even know were nice enough to help me, for no reason at all. But I came all that way and did all that myself, because there was no one I could rely on, so I had to rely on me. Sure, I could've called first, but I figured if I just showed up, you'd have to take me in and we'd work it out, because I'm your granddaughter and you would believe me, knowing my mom. So I took a chance and I came. All this way." By now I was shaking, I was so worked up. I needed to be heard. I needed to matter. Being fifteen shouldn't make you invisible. "I thought I'd made it. I knew I was close. Then, I went over a small hill and there was Buzz, out in the middle of the road. Probably didn't hear me coming. There wasn't time to honk at him. I barely had time to react. I swerved, but —"

"I believe you."

My mouth hung open. She was dead serious. But I had to ask, just to see what else she'd say. "You do?"

Her left eye twitched as she lifted her chin. "Doesn't mean I'm letting you off the hook. You were driving without a license." She pointed a finger at me, but her tone was more matter-of-fact, less patronizing. "You took a vehicle that didn't belong to you — without asking. That truck may have gotten you here, but how did you figure you were going to get it back to its rightful owner? Or did you even think that far? And, you're a runaway. Offenses like that can land you in juvenile detention until your eighteenth birthday. If you're lucky enough not to be tried as an adult."

161

She picked up the remote, aimed it at the TV, and clicked. Nothing happened. "Damn power's still off. Anyway" — she set it back down and pinned me with a victorious gaze, like she had me trapped and knew it — "I offered her a thousand dollars for the truck. She couldn't say 'yes' fast enough. Except that it's not hers to give away. She claims the guy who owns it never knew it was gone, so she was going to tell him that she'd have it towed away if he'll sign it over to her. She's supposed to call back later, but I suspect she'll be able to swing it. Lying seems to come easy enough to her."

She didn't say it, but I sensed the implication that the fruit didn't fall far from the tree and she wasn't about to take everything I said as truth. I resented that, yet she'd covered for me — and for that I was grateful. This change in her had me perplexed, though. I got why she would start to understand who Lana really was and that my reasons for leaving might be legit, but the real mystery was why she would offer to buy the truck.

"Why would you want that truck? It's a rust bucket, barely starts, *and* I just wrecked it."

"I figure it'll come in handy around here. If it can be repaired, that is."

I scoffed. I hadn't meant to. It just came out. I might've been more mature than most people my age, but teenage sarcasm just leaked out of me.

She gave me one of those looks that demanded I explain myself.

"I just don't see you driving a truck around, that's all."

"It's not for me."

I still didn't understand what she was getting at.

"Wait … Not for you? You're going to sell it?"

Crossing her arms, she let out a sigh of exasperation. "No, I'm not selling it. It wouldn't be worth what I'd have to put into it. The house needs repairs. We still have to come up with a list and work out the details, but Mr. Donovan will be doing all that. The truck is good enough for hauling supplies from town to here, at least for as long as it works."

"But Buzz can't drive. I mean, I don't know, but my guess is he can't with his —"

Buzz cleared his throat. My heart jolted. He was standing in the doorway between the living room and kitchen, a plastic box of sorts in his hand. He'd been so quiet I hadn't even thought of him listening in. Anyway, it wasn't like I'd said anything bad. The guy had seizures. That was a fact.

"Excuse me, Mrs. Larson." He held the box out so Noreen could see, showing a place where it had partly melted. "You'll have to take my word for this, but you've got some faulty electrical outlets in this house. At least in the kitchen there. I'll check the other rooms later, but I wouldn't be surprised if there were more like this."

Unimpressed, she sniffed. "So what does that mean? Do I need to hire a professional electrician and have him pull permits? Suppose that'll cost a lot of money."

"No, don't think so. They're old as dirt, is all. I just need to replace them. It'll take me a couple days, at most. But I do need to get to a hardware store. Might take a few trips as I figure out exactly what I need and how much."

"Klinger's Hardware is on this side of town, just over ten minutes away. You get whatever you need. If I call Johnny, he'll run me a tab and I can settle up later."

Settle up later? Sounded like an episode from *Little House on the Prairie*. In Flint, you didn't 'run a tab'. You paid up when you bought something. Cash or credit card. A lot of places didn't even take checks anymore, they'd had so many bad ones.

Buzz nodded, but didn't move away. He waited a few seconds before asking, "So will you be able to take me there? If not, I suppose I could ask Hunter for a ride, but I'm not sure when he'd be available."

"Today I can. After that, I'm not sure. I'm the loan manager at Hilldale Savings and Loan in Somerset and as soon as the power's back up, I'm going back to work. Place grinds to a halt without me."

"And after that? Doc Hunter has to go to work too. I don't want to impose on his free time, since he has a family and all."

"If you tell me what you need, I can pick it up on the way home. Or" — she glanced at me — "maybe you can supervise a certain young driver with a learner's permit."

Permit? I tried to digest this. The Bizarro-factor had just ramped up to interplanetary levels. If Buzz helped me get my driver's license that meant his dog would have to ride along. I weighed whether getting a license was worth putting my life at risk.

"It's been a while since I've driven myself, but the laws haven't changed much, if any. I suppose I could."

"Good, then. It's settled. I'll call the body shop about having that piece of lead towed in for work. If it's not astronomical, we'll get it fixed up. Then Bellamy here can take you into town whenever you need something. That is, until you finish the work around here and move on. Meanwhile, Bellamy can assist you with the odds and ends." She redirected her glare at me. "I have some painting that needs done, but you're to help Mr. Donovan whenever he needs it, understand?"

I was still trying to decode this all in my head when she spoke to Buzz again. "I'll have that to-do list for you by this evening. I suppose I need to think about it, prioritize things. Then you can give me some idea of how much it'll cost. Did Dr. McHugh tell you how long it would be before your dog's able to walk on his own again?"

"He couldn't say exactly, but anywhere between six to ten weeks. Just depends on how fast he heals and if there are any complications."

"You could get a lot done in six weeks. You need food for him?"

"Yes."

"I'll pick some up on the way home from work tomorrow. That is, if the ice melts enough to clear the roads and the power's back on at work."

"Thank you, ma'am. But just one request."

"What? You aren't going to ask for fresh cooked meat and raw vegetables for him, are you, because I'm not cooking for a dog. I barely cook for myself. And don't expect any of that gourmet dog food. He'll get what they have at the local grocery."

"No, nothing like that. Just, no corn. He doesn't digest it well. Runs right through him. So you have to check the label, make sure there's no corn."

"All right," she said, her lids fluttering as she rolled her eyes. "No corn. Got it. That it?"

"That's it. Thank you. You can deduct it from my pay."

"Forget about it. Consider it a perk."

He blinked at her several times, just as shocked as I was, then thanked her again before shuffling off to poke around at some more wires in another room.

"What?" she snapped.

I jumped at the sound of her voice. I'd been staring. With my mouth open. "Nothing."

She placed her hands on her hips. "Look, you may think I'm a little testy, but I'm not as mean as you make me out to be. I'm just used to telling people what to do. And to having the house to myself."

In other words, I'd imposed. And I was judgmental. Both true. But she was cranky. Not to mention anti-social. In a contest of undesirable social traits, we were at a draw.

"One more thing. In my little conversation with your mother, she told me a thing or two about you. That you got expelled in fifth grade."

I didn't flinch, didn't shrink from her, or hide my eyes. "They thought I was cheating. That I'd stolen the teacher's grading sheet for a test."

"Did you?"

I scoffed. "No."

"Then why did they kick you out?"

"Because I got all the answers right. All the time." Fifth grade had been a yawn-fest. Most kids as bored as me would have acted out. Yet in my naiveté, I kept trying to prove how smart I was. That might go over well in an upper-class suburban educational setting, but try that in an inner-city school where half the class is reading three grades below level — if they can read at all.

Noreen leaned closer, her voice lowering. "That's not all she told me."

Whatever Lana had to say about me, I was ready to defend myself. Bring it on, Granny.

"She also said you're some kind of genius. That you were so far ahead of your classmates, they didn't know what to do with you in school, so they let you take online classes and you graduated early and started college courses." Crossing her arms, she straightened. "As soon as the power's back on, you can use my computer for your classes."

"Won't matter."

"Why?"

"Because Lana won't pay for any more." I didn't go into all the details about how she'd told me college was a waste of time and I needed to go out and get a job. Never mind the fact that I wasn't old enough to do anything but babysit.

"Then I'll help you out."

Help *me?* There had to be a catch. "Why?"

"If you have to ask that, maybe you're not as smart as you think you are."

With a shake of her head, she began to stalk off, but she paused at the threshold to the living room. "I suppose I ought to make sure you have a phone. It won't be one of those fancy ones. Just one for making calls and sending texts. In case you ever need help or anything.

I'll pick one up in Somerset this week."

I was too stunned to thank her before she turned back around and left.

The air in the room lightened, but I was still dizzy with confusion. Sucking in a breath, I pressed my fingertips to my forehead.

It didn't sound like Noreen was going to send me back. At least not right away. Problem was, I wasn't sure how I felt about that.

For a while, I closed my eyes and listened to the sound of my own breathing. I heard a faint whimper and looked to see Hush in his usual place in the kitchen, ears perked, head tilting side to side like one of those bobblehead dolls. Buzz wasn't in the kitchen with him. What if he was about to have an episode?

I swung my feet down from the couch and padded to the doorway between the living room and kitchen. Just as I touched the wall between the rooms, a weak click sounded, followed by the hum of the refrigerator. Then the TV on the counter made a breathy buzz. The screen lightened. An image appeared: a college basketball game.

The electricity was back on.

Good. Tomorrow, Noreen would go to work and when she came home she could turn the TV on and ignore me again. I inched toward the cupboards, suddenly craving mac and cheese and wondering if there was any in there.

Toenails clicked unevenly over the linoleum. I flattened myself against the wall. My head bumped a corkboard, knocking loose a push pin. Several raggedly clipped coupons drifted to the floor. I let them fall. Because the dog was closing in on me.

Hush hobbled across the yellowing flecked linoleum, setting his bad leg down gingerly before lurching forward every other step. The whole time he was coming at me, his back end was wiggling like a hula dancer. Three feet away, he stopped, sat, and looked up at me, swirly blue-and-brown eyes studying me with curiosity. His cheeks bunched into a deceptive smile. His upper lip twitched. He flashed his

167

teeth at me.

I pointed at him and, in my most threatening voice, commanded, "Stay!"

He replied with a sneeze.

Hugging the wall, I crept around him until I was almost back at the entryway to the living room. Feet stomped up the basement steps. The door swung open.

Buzz looked from me to the dog and back again. Shaking his head, he placed a pair of pliers on the counter, then opened a drawer and took out a screwdriver. "Don't you think if he'd wanted to bite you, he'd have done it by now? Face it, he's had plenty of opportunity."

I gave him my best squinty-eyed glare. That comment was so dumb it didn't deserve a reply. If all dogs charged at and bit the first person they saw, they'd all be dead. Or wild. No one would have ever domesticated them. What they did was lie low, watch you with those wolfish eyes, and wait. They couldn't be trusted. Ever.

"He's trying real hard, you know." Buzz picked through an assortment of screws from the junk drawer and carefully selected a handful.

"What?"

"The dog." He dropped the screws in his pocket. "He wants to be friends with you. Heaven knows why. But he has a sense about people. Knows the good from the bad."

"So, what? You're saying he thinks I'm a good person?"

"Not at all. He knows you are." He took a screwdriver and twirled it between his fingers. "And I've never known him to be wrong."

chapter 14

Buzz

Buzz gave the screw one final twist and tapped at the outlet plate around the edges to make sure it was secure. He'd had all the outlets in the kitchen pulled out and two in the guest bedroom when the power came back on. Back on the job — when he had a job — his co-workers would have ribbed him for being too productive. There was an unwritten code that you only worked as fast as it took to make it look like there was some kind of progress each day. Too slow and customers would complain. Too fast and they'd come to expect that sort of output every time. Buzz hated it. He liked to stay busy and it made him feel lazy. To fill the idle time, he did the work of others. They'd claim a problem, feign ignorance, and call on Buzz to fix it for them. He knew what they were doing, but he never let on about it. As long as he stayed busy — and stayed employed — he didn't mind. He'd known too many men who got let go because they tripped up on the job and made a mistake. Sometimes it was just because a customer wasn't happy with the work and so the boss had to blame someone. It wasn't easy to get another job once you'd been fired. Working home construction may not have been the career of his dreams, but it had kept a roof over his head and money in the bank. For a while, anyway.

Funny how one event can change your life so drastically.

As he leaned over the counter beside the sink to affix the last outlet, the glare coming in from outside made it hard to see. He stole a look out the window. Wispy clouds laced the sky. Yesterday's frigid danger had passed, leaving in its wake a world both sunlit and soggy.

By late afternoon the wind had lessened and the sun was shining. It was still cold and ice still clung to every surface, but the earth was just warm enough to turn the slick roads into ribbons of slush. Noreen's driveway was marked by twin rivers of ice water where Hunter's truck had driven the day before.

Hunter was set to come by after work. Until then, Buzz kept himself busy. Time passed more quickly that way. And the more hours and days he could fill up, the sooner he and Hush could be back out on the road.

It was nearly 5 p.m. when Hunter returned, his big white truck bumping and splashing up the driveway. He'd brought supplies from town for Buzz. Just like Noreen had said, the hardware store owner just added the total of the receipt to a tab. Then, Hunter and Buzz set off to retrieve Beam's truck from the ditch.

The drive was less treacherous than the day before, but it was still slow going. When they got there, Hunter hooked a chain to the back bumper of Beam's truck and fixed the other end to the trailer hitch of his. Buzz stood across the road and gave the signal.

Hunter hit the gas. The dually wheels of his truck spun over wet pavement, and Buzz shook his head. Hunter turned the wheel a few degrees, backed up six inches, and then shifted into drive again. This time the wheels spun so fast that steam billowed off the treads. After setting the parking brake, Hunter retrieved a large sack from the bed, ripped the corner off, and flung a few handfuls of gritty matter near the wheel tracks.

"What's that?" Buzz asked.

"Kitty litter. Comes in handy in these situations. You can also soak up spilled oil with it. But you have to use the old-fashioned clay litter. None of that new-fangled stuff with absorbent gel or the eco-friendly kind made out of corn husks."

He climbed back in the truck. This time the wheels hit the granules of litter and bit down. The truck lurched forward. The chain tightened. Beam's truck heaved from the ditch like a sunken boat being raised from the depths. Buzz pointed his thumb up.

"Just a couple more feet and you're clear," he called.

Hunter kept his foot steady on the gas until Beam's truck was fully on the road. After making sure the chain was secure and her truck in the right gear, he and Buzz both returned to his truck. Hush stretched his neck to nuzzle Buzz, but couldn't quite reach him from the back seat. Buzz gave him a pat on the head. They started toward town with Beam's truck in tow.

"So how's it going over there?" Hunter kept his eyes on the road.

"Honestly? It's like watching a dynamite fuse burn. Just waiting for the big explosion." Buzz looked out the window at a world of gray. The ice had melted quickly that day, leaving behind a watery mess. "It's like they're both mad at each other, but they don't know what for. If they'd just get it out in the open ... Well, it occurred to me if they'd just say why, they'd stand a chance of getting past it all and moving on. Life's too damn short for that nonsense."

"Hmm, living in a house full of women, I can tell you that sometimes I'm not even sure *they* know what it is they're mad about. Heck, half the time it's about nothing. Just last week, Jenn got herself all in knots because I said I'd clean out the garage. She thought I meant I was going to do it right then. I didn't say 'now'. I meant when I had time. You know, eventually. She stomped around half the day before she finally blew a gasket. Here's the kicker — I must've asked her four times before then what was wrong. You know what she kept

171

saying? 'Nothing.' Guess I was supposed to read her mind."

They both went silent. They'd said the basics. No need to overanalyze the situation. Besides, Buzz wasn't comfortable delving into people's lives.

Hunter punched the volume down on the radio. "Buzz, I've been meaning to ask you..."

Buzz steeled himself.

"Those ashes..." Hunter glanced at him as he pulled up to the stop sign before the state highway that led to Faderville. "Whose were they?"

"Someone close to me."

"Didn't reckon they belonged to a stranger."

"Very funny."

"So why are you carrying them around? Does it have anything to do with you walking across the United States?"

"It might."

"A war buddy?"

Buzz smiled at him. "Nice try, but I'd rather not talk about it."

A box truck drove by and Hunter pulled out after it, headed south. "And yet you think Noreen and Beam ought to open up? Ironic."

Another minute crawled by, Buzz with his face turned to the window as he watched the hills slide slowly by in the distance, Hunter intent on the road before him.

"So where did you say you were from?" Hunter said finally.

"Don't believe I did."

"Alaska? Oregon?"

"California."

"California, huh? That's a big state."

"It is."

More silence. More hills. A four-way stop. Hunter looked at Buzz.

"They're my son's," Buzz said, figuring if he gave him that much, he might let it go.

Hunter looked both ways before crossing the intersection. "Your son's?"

"Ashes."

"I'm sorry. Was this recently?"

"No. Years ago." He hadn't meant to give out so much information, but Hunter was easy to talk to. Like Beam. Noreen, not so much. But even sharing that little bit seemed to expose a raw place in him, like a scab that had been pulled loose.

"How… how did he …?"

"Die?"

"Yeah."

"War."

And that was all they said until Hunter pulled into the auto body shop. Hunter deposited the keys in a slot in the front door, since it was after hours. On the way back, they stopped at Harris's Outdoor Café to get meals for Noreen, Beam, and Buzz — because Noreen hadn't yet been to the grocery store — and shakes for Hunter's daughters, Maura and Hannah.

As they left the drive-thru, Hunter handed Buzz his fountain Coke and set the food bag on the console between them. "There shouldn't be any wars."

"Got that right." Buzz opened the bag and inhaled the cooking oils and saltiness. He helped himself to a few fries. It had been weeks since he'd had any fresh ones. "You ever lost anyone close to you?"

"Besides my childhood dog?"

"Yeah, a person." Although losing your dog was sometimes harder than losing a human family member. It was a shame that dogs never lived as long as people. Cruel, in a way.

"My dad and grandpa. I was only five when it happened."

"Both in the same year?"

"At the same time, actually."

Buzz could barely fathom it. "What happened?"

"They were moving a manure pile around. Tractor overturned. Killed them both." He took a long drink, then glanced at Buzz. "I saw it happen."

Not knowing what to say, Buzz said nothing. Hunter had just confided his deepest hurt, even though they'd hardly known each other a day. To Buzz, it seemed far too personal a thing to share so soon. He had secrets of his own, but he wasn't ready to reveal them right now. Perhaps ever.

Yet wherever he went, people had a habit of telling their stories to Buzz. Probably because he was a better listener than a talker.

Hunter's jaw worked as if he had more to say. He fidgeted in his seat. Finally, the words tumbled out. "I didn't speak for years, except to my mom. Looking back now, I realize I was mad at the world. Can't figure out how that was supposed to solve anything. Guess maybe I blamed myself, thought I could've stopped it from happening because I'd been watching them, thinking it looked dangerous, that at any moment that big heap could collapse ... and then it did." He waited a few breaths before continuing, his eyes on the road but his mind very obviously churning through his past. "Goes to show you that when people are mad, that sometimes what they're mad at has nothing to do with who they're with at the time or what's going on right then ... If that makes sense."

"Yep. Perfect sense."

They passed the local feed store, a tractor sales lot, and a horse farm that had seen better days. Homes ran the gamut, from trailers from the 1950s sitting in weedy lots to grand colonials with pillared two-story porches and pastures outlined with white or occasionally black board fences. Buzz was taking it all in when Hunter cleared his throat, the signal that he was about to start a conversation again.

"So yesterday, that guy robbed you, and it occurred to me that we never called the sheriff to report it. Why don't I pick you up tomorrow morning and drop you off at the station while I go on a farm call? After that I can take you back to —"

"Don't bother. Not worth it."

"What do you mean?" Hunter looked at him so long that Buzz was afraid he'd go off the road. Before that could happen, Hunter looked back, but his face was twisted in vexation. "He took your wallet and all your stuff, didn't he?"

"I didn't have much. Sure he's figured that out by now. Besides, he's probably long gone."

"Even if he is in another state already, the sheriff can relay it to the highway patrol."

When Buzz hesitated, Hunter continued, more insistent. "Buzz, he held you up at gunpoint! He needs to be apprehended before he does it again. Before he kills someone."

Buzz couldn't think of an argument against that one, even though the idea of walking into a police station and giving them personal information didn't sit well with him. There was too much at stake. But if he said no again, Hunter might become suspicious and start asking more questions. For now, he had to go along with it.

"All right, then. What time?"

"Seven a.m.? I have to tag some of Kip Shipley's new calves, but that won't take long. I'd be back in an hour."

Buzz nodded. Between now and then, he had to figure something out. He couldn't tell the sheriff his real name.

Before they knew it, they were on the road that Noreen's house was on. In the back seat, Hush raised his head, his breath coming in soft little huffs. Struggling upright, he somehow sat to look out the window.

A light rain had begun to fall, but this time it was warmer. Droplets plopped in scattered puddles to ripple outward. All traces of ice and snow from the storm were now gone, leaving behind muddy earth and naked tree limbs. But in the ditches and on the ground far below the lacework of bare branches, here and there a pale green bud pushed through soft earth.

Even in the ugly aftermath of a late winter storm, there were new beginnings.

Buzz hadn't planned on being waylaid like this: his dog hit by a car, his last few personal items stolen, his only means of shelter to be housed with a troubled teen and her bitter grandmother. But then, there wasn't much he could do about it. He couldn't just pick up and leave. Not without Hush.

They reached Noreen's house just as the sun was setting. Hunter helped him unload Hush and then escorted them just inside the front door. He told Buzz to call him on his cell if he needed anything and then excused himself, saying how he'd be late for dinner once again.

Buzz found Beam in the kitchen, wiping out cupboards, which seemed to Buzz like an odd thing for a fifteen-year-old to do with her time, but maybe Noreen had given her a list of chores for the day. Even odder was the intensity with which she attacked her duty. All the canned goods had been herded onto the counter and organized by food type: vegetables, fruits, soups, and some sort of miscellaneous category that included pickles, sauerkraut, and evaporated milk. Cleaning supplies had been piled into an empty laundry basket and, by the looks of it, she'd already rearranged all the dishes and cookware.

On her hands and knees by the corner cabinet, Beam finally looked over her shoulder. Her face brightened momentarily when she met Buzz's eyes, but just as quickly it clouded over as her sight fell on Hush. She spun around, crouching on the balls of her feet, a bottle of spray cleaner gripped in her left hand.

Instead of guiding Hush to his blanket, Buzz crossed the room with his dog at his side, one stilted step at a time.

"What are you doing?" Beam said, her voice rising in pitch.

Hush halted, cocked his head at her.

Buzz coaxed him forward. "Pardon?"

"I mean it." She clutched the trigger in both hands. "Stop!"

"Stop what?"

What was the matter with her? She should know by now that Hush was no threat.

The dog seemed more concerned than alarmed. Hush kept his head low, a submissive gesture, but to someone who couldn't read dogs it might appear like he was sizing her up, ready to pounce. Buzz didn't care. He wasn't going to live in this house with a girl who was frightened to death of his dog. A dog who'd never laid teeth on anyone — although heaven knew he'd had cause to a few times during their travels.

Beam scampered backward until she was pressed tightly into the corner, a small stack of plastic mixing bowls toppling behind her in the commotion.

Three feet away now.

She dropped the spray bottle. It hit on its bottom and fell sideways, knocking the trigger assembly askew. Blue liquid poured out. Beam wrapped her hands around her head, elbows over her face protectively, feet tucked up under her rump.

"Stoooopppppp!" she screeched. Then a shaky, indrawn breath. She held it an impossibly long time.

Hush crept forward silently, pressed the leather of his nose to the crown of her head, and snuffled.

The words poured out of her rapidly, like one long multi-syllabic utterance. "Stop-it-stop-it-stop-it-stop-it—"

He licked her. First on top of her head, then her arms and hands. He whimpered softly. The kind of whimper a mother dog makes when her newborn pups wander out of reach.

"Stop ... it." A tiny wail leaked from behind her arms, like air escaping from a flattening tire. "Stop. It."

Hush lay down. Which wasn't an easy thing to do, given that he couldn't bend the one leg, so he more or less had to flop sideways at a certain point. A small groan of distress escaped him as he gazed forlornly at the bandages covering his leg. He tried to reach his head forward to lick at the wrapping, but his position didn't allow it and readjusting himself was clearly too much trouble. So he groaned again. Longer, a little sadder.

Beam's elbows parted ever so slightly. Buzz couldn't tell for sure, but she was probably peeking at the dog. Hush let out an exasperated sigh. It was the first time since the accident that Buzz had seen him give any indication that the broken leg was causing him any trouble. Any human being would've bellyached a ton by this point.

"Does he need a pill?" Beam whispered. Like she was afraid of startling him.

"Soon." Buzz approached them. He knelt down, the stiffness in his knees slowing him. Getting up would be difficult, but he felt the need to be close and speak softly to her. "Has a dog ever bitten you?"

She gave a small nod. Buzz wasn't sure how he knew. He just did. It was the only way to explain her reaction.

"How old were you?"

Shrugging, she sucked back tears, swiped a hand over her eyes. "Five, I think." Her eyes stayed on Hush, but for the first time, they weren't wide with fear. "No, I must've been six. It was a month past my birthday. Early May. A Saturday. I know, because I'd just learned to ride a bike that week. Not mine, though. I never owned one. It belonged to some kid who lived on our block. He was a couple years older, so the bike was a little big, but he let me borrow it and helped me learn."

"Was that the day it happened?" He kept the questions simple. People usually talked as much or as little as they were inclined to. He never forced it. Trust came gradually to some. For others, it poured out like a broken dam. Like now.

Again, Beam nodded. "Not right then. Later. After the kid had left. His name was Joshua. Not Josh. Joshua. I think he was Jewish.

178

He was wearing a white button-up shirt, jacket, and long shorts, and I thought that was really odd, but then again I had on jeans with holes in them and ... Sorry, the details get stuck in my head sometimes and I get sidetracked. Anyway, his mother saw us and made him leave. As they were walking away she told him never to play with me again, because she knew my mom. At the time, I wasn't sure why that was such a bad thing, but I was starting to figure it out. After they left, I was by myself. There were other kids there, but I didn't know them and they were older, so I just sat on the swing. Not lonely, really, but kind of happy not to be at home. Mom ... Lana was expecting a baby soon. I was excited about that and kind of mad. She barely paid any attention to me. What was going to happen with a new baby around?" Beam gathered a strand from her ponytail and twisted it around her index finger. "Anyway, I was just sitting there on the park bench next to the basketball court where I'd been riding the bike, when this dog trots up. I thought, 'Oh, cool. Maybe he's a stray and if I feed him, he'll follow me around and be my buddy.' He looked friendly enough, and kind of hungry. So I took a fruit roll-up out of my jacket pocket — that was Lana's idea of a packed lunch, by the way — and I held it out to him."

Slowly, she extended her hand, her fingers pinched together as if she were holding it that very moment. Hush's eyes shifted, but he didn't raise his head to sniff, just watched her, as if each word held a key, any of which might unlock some magical secret.

A crease formed between Beam's eyebrows as she tilted her head. And then, suddenly, her breath caught and every muscle in her body jerked. Her face contorted into a grimace of pain. Raising her left hand, she fisted it. The sleeve on that side fell away from her arm, revealing a long, crescent-shaped white scar. Her mouth opened, as if to scream, but nothing came out.

Buzz reached toward her shoulder to comfort her, to tell her everything was okay. But the moment his fingers grazed her upper

179

arm, she recoiled, collapsing into a wad of helpless horror, her eyes screwed tightly shut as the memory of it played out inside her head.

Hush raised his head, ears cocked forward, his eyebrows twitching in concern.

"Beam, Beam, it's okay." Tentatively, Buzz tapped her arm once. But when she pulled tighter into herself, he took her firmly by the arms. "It's okay. You're here now, not there. That was a long time ago. Almost ten years ago. Sunbeam?"

He gripped her harder, wanted to shake her out of her nightmare, but something in her finally yielded to his touch. A shiver rippled through her and then, with an exhaled breath, the terror of it left her.

Shaken but not broken, Beam pried her eyes open. She didn't look at Buzz, though. She met Hush's gaze squarely and it was as if something passed between them.

"You don't have to be afraid anymore, Sunbeam," Buzz told her. "Hush would never, ever hurt you. He's the kindest, gentlest soul you will ever in this life meet."

For a while, Beam didn't respond. She merely blinked at the dog, studying him quietly. Then she shook her head and said to Buzz, "She left me there."

"Who?"

"Lana."

"But the dog ... Were you hurt badly?"

"Yeah. Some older kid beat the dog off with a baseball bat. They called an ambulance. Took me to the hospital. It took forty-eight stitches to patch me up and later two plastic surgeries."

"Where was your mom?"

"They couldn't find her at first. Finally, some neighbor clued them in that she'd gone to the hospital to have her baby. That was Oakley. But she'd shooed me off to the playground that morning because she wasn't feeling well and then she forgot about me. Never sent anyone to get me when her labor started or once she got to the hospital. I suppose she just figured I'd wander on home eventually and let myself in. Not that she'd given me a key or anything." Scoffing, she rolled her eyes. "I was six. *Six* for God's sake. Who does that kind of thing?"

Keys jangled behind Buzz. He twisted around to see Noreen in the entryway to the kitchen, two plastic grocery sacks dangling from one hand, a beaten-up old briefcase in the other.

"There are more groceries in my car, if you want to fetch them, Bellamy." It was more command than request. "It's in the garage, but the side door's open."

"Yeah, sure," Beam said softly. She straightened an arm, her hand dangling curiously close to Hush. For a moment, it looked like she was going to pat the dog on the head. But then she hauled herself to her feet and out the door.

As difficult as it was, Buzz stood, using the counter to steady himself. He sensed the blood draining from his veins, pooling in his legs. For a few seconds he didn't move at all. Even looking up or turning his head would be enough to send him crashing to the floor. A waspish buzz rose to a murmur. Noreen was talking.

"— she been doing around here? Good Lord, that's not where I put the canned tomatoes. And the dishes … How am I supposed to find anything now?"

Before her words could drift away, he lassoed them and formed a response. "Looks like she's doing a fine job to me."

Lifting her chin, Noreen settled her hands on her broad hips. The bags, heavy with their contents, crinkled against her thighs. "Hah, well, I don't know about that."

Buzz pointed to the grocery sacks. "You need help putting stuff away?"

"We'll let the girl do it, since she's the only one who knows where things go now."

"My guess is she just wants to be useful. Which I suspect we all do. Doesn't sound like her childhood was all that easy."

"Not everybody's is, Mr. Donovan. Her mother had her share of problems. We did our best. In the end, she thumbed her nose at us. Never once said thanks for all we did for her."

"Pardon me, but what does that have to do with Beam? She's just a kid."

"There's a lot you don't know, Mr. Donovan —"

"Please, it's Buzz."

Her lip twitched. She set the bags on the counter, the cans in one thunking metallically. "Like I said, there's a lot you don't know. Having Bellamy here just invites Lana to waltz back into my life and I don't need that kind of trouble. I've long since given up on my daughter."

He took a soup can from the bag, found where it belonged. "So you're giving up on Beam too?"

"I'll do what I feel is right, thank you. And spare me your high and mighty lectures. I didn't ask for a charity case. She was supposed to be her mother's responsibility, not mine. I don't know where you think I owe that girl —"

The back kitchen door swung open. Beam stared at Noreen, neither willing to look away.

"Put things where you want," Noreen told her granddaughter, setting her briefcase at the end of the counter. Then, as she stalked across the living room, she said, "And if you want to be even more helpful, make some burgers for us for dinner. I've had a long day. I need to unwind for a bit."

Lumbering into her bedroom as if she bore the burdens of the world, Noreen shut the door and cranked the volume on her TV.

For some reason, Buzz knew it was loud, and yet it sounded like it was a million miles away and he couldn't quite make out the words.

"Buzz? Buzz?"

Beam grabbed his arm and started tugging him downward. He

looked at her hands, confused. He tried to resist but couldn't. His limbs were growing light, weak.

"Huh ... what?" He was on his knees now. But how did he get there?

Hush had scooted over to him and was licking his legs, then his arms.

"It's happening again. You're about to have another one."

"Another?"

"Seizure."

"I ... am?" He wasn't even sure he'd said the second word. His tongue felt thick and clumsy, like someone had stuffed a towel in his mouth.

"Yeah, but don't worry. You're okay. Just lie down, all right?"

Seconds later, a seat cushion slid under his head. Everything was sideways. He was lying down. A paw, gentle at first, then more insistent, nudged him onto his back. Above him, kaleidoscope eyes of golden brown and glacial blue peered down into his. Hush had flattened himself across his chest so he couldn't flail around too much and was licking at his face. Sparks flew through Buzz's brain and extinguished, quenched by a darkness that seeped from within. His vision went grainy, colorless holes widening until all was night. Through it all, Beam spoke to him, her words a soothing melody. Then, her voice dimmed.

And the persistent *flick-flick-flick* of Hush's wet tongue faded — but the loyalty of the dog remained.

—o0o—

A feeble sun had barely pushed through broken clouds above the Kentucky hills when Hunter picked Buzz up the following morning. Buzz was greatly relieved to find the radio playing and Hunter busily sipping from a tall coffee mug.

"Morning, Buzz," Hunter mumbled in between slurps.

"Morning, Doc."

"Where's Hush?"

"Asleep."

"Good, he needs the rest."

And that was all either said until Hunter pulled into the Adair County sheriff's station fifteen minutes later. It was right next to a little mom-and-pop grocery that, amazingly, was already open.

Buzz was halfway out the door when Hunter spoke. "Want me to come in with you? I know I only saw it from a distance, but I figure if they need another statement, well, I'd be happy to give it."

"I'll, uh, I'll ask them if they need anything from you." Then before Hunter could insist, Buzz added, "How long did you say you'll be?"

"An hour, at most. Kip's place is just a couple miles down the road."

"See you then." He shut the truck door and started for the station, waiting to hear Hunter's truck pull away. But it didn't. He turned to look.

Hunter powered down the window. "Just wanted to make sure you made it in okay, because ... you know."

"I'm fine. Really." He waved toward the road. "Go."

With a goodbye, Hunter put the window up and pulled away slowly, looking in his rearview mirror until Buzz, reluctantly, went inside the building. It seemed like the only way to get rid of Hunter for the time being.

A friendly voice chimed, "Can I help you, sir?"

Behind an oversized old desk sat a perky twenty-something gal who looked fresh from a beauty pageant. Her honey-colored hair was piled on top of her head in a loose bun and she wore eye-shadow in a brilliant shade of blue that even Buzz realized had gone out of fashion thirty years ago.

Standing, she started toward him, eager for a task to keep her occupied in what seemed like an otherwise idle workplace.

"Uh, next door ..." He hitched a thumb in the direction of the grocery. "You know when they open? I didn't see any cars in the parking lot."

"Haskell's?" Perplexed, she veered from him to peer out the glass of the front door. "That's funny. They should be." A moment later her face lit up. "Oh, yeah! Lights are on. They're just not busy yet."

He thanked her and ducked out before she could ask anything else. To make a show of it, he went into the grocery and ambled up and down the aisles for ten minutes or so — he wasn't sure of the length of time because he'd long ago sold his watch to buy dog food — before nodding to a sleepy-eyed cashier and walking back out. A chilly rain pelted his face. He drew Roland's coat tight against his chest, wishing he'd asked Noreen for a hat. He used to have one of those, too.

He wanted badly to stay out of the rain but certainly wasn't going back into the sheriff's station. If he stayed in the grocery too long, they'd have him arrested for loitering. A few other buildings sat along the road near the station, including an insurance agency and a dentist's office. None were places Buzz could walk into without raising a few eyebrows.

Pulling the collar of his coat up as high as it would go, he walked down the road as far as the insurance agency. Rain slashed at his face, beating hard and cold against his skin. He turned around, back the way he had come. By the time he was halfway to the station, his hair was matted to his head and his coat was nearly soaked through. With each waterlogged step, his shoes made a giant squishing noise. He wanted to keep walking, he was used to it, found it invigorating, but he had no idea where he'd go. Like always, he'd only be running away from what he'd left behind. He certainly couldn't leave Faderville without Hush. Besides, if Hunter came back early, he wasn't sure how he'd explain

185

being out in the rain, so he went back to the grocery store.

Inside, he stood dripping by the front door, more aware than ever of how oversized his clothes were. He looked around and saw only a distracted cashier, her thumbs tapping away at her phone. A clock hung from the wall above the deli case. By Buzz's estimation, it would be half an hour yet until Hunter came back. He glanced out the front door. Yes, even through a steady rain, from here he had a good view of the station parking lot.

The cashier stopped playing with her phone long enough to utter a greeting at him.

"I'm expecting a ride, but I got here early," Buzz explained. She wasn't looking at him anymore, but he wanted to make sure she didn't think he was a vagrant who was bent on robbing the store. Because he was sure that's what he looked like. He figured the more polite he was, the more at ease she'd feel. "Mind if I wait inside until they come? It's raining out and kinda cold."

"Oh, sure. No problem." She tucked a lock of overgrown bangs behind an ear and went back to tapping at her phone, her face scrunched in concentration. "Dang. Stuck on level twenty. You know how to get past the exploding grapefruit stand in the orchard?"

She held her phone out toward him, showing what Buzz could only assume was a game of some sort. As if he could see the tiny screen from twenty feet away.

"Sorry, no."

Mumbling a curse, she punched the screen a few more times, then stowed the phone in her pocket. "Who did you say was picking you up?" she asked.

Buzz pushed on the door handle. "I think that's him. Thanks."

He went outside and tucked himself against the corner of the building, sheltered from the worst of the rain by a narrow overhang. But every time the wind gusted, the rain splashed over his pants legs. Shivering, he bounced on the balls of his feet, but after a while it exhausted him. So he crouched down and huddled against the ice machine, his arms wrapped around his knees, waiting for what seemed like forever for Hunter to come back for him.

He waited so long he was sure Hunter had forgotten him. Finally, he went back inside to check the clock. An hour and fifteen minutes had passed.

"Still waiting?" The cashier walked briskly toward him. "You need to borrow my phone to call them?"

Buzz looked outside, desperation building in his chest. A pair of deputies exited the station and walked to a cruiser, got in. Where was Hunter? He tried to remember — had Hunter given him a card with his phone number on it? No. No, he hadn't.

"Hey."

Buzz jumped.

The cashier was standing at his shoulder, a meek but sympathetic smile on her kind face. "It's okay. You can use my phone. I'm not a germophobe or anything."

"I ... I don't know his number. I didn't think I'd need it."

"Anyone who lives around here? I think there's a phone book in the back office."

"Yes. Could you ...?"

"Be right back. Wait here. Inside, that is."

As she scurried off to the back, Buzz looked out the rain-smeared plate glass of the front door. Far down the road, a white truck crested a small rise. From this distance yet, he couldn't tell if it was Hunter or not. He was vaguely aware of sounds coming from the back of the store.

"Hang on," the woman called from a doorway in the back. "I know it's here somewhere. I'm sure I saw it not too long ago."

The truck came closer, dually wheels in the rear sending up sprays of rain, Buzz thought he saw the faint red pulse of a turn signal from one of the front lights.

187

"Don't bother. I think he's here," Buzz said, not even sure if she could hear him.

He pushed the door open and darted for the adjacent parking lot. If he angled his approach, it might look like he was coming out of the station.

The truck slowed, turned in.

By the time Hunter pulled up, Buzz was standing on the corner of the station's sidewalk, as if he'd been waiting there all along.

He climbed into the truck, shutting the door as fast as he could. Water poured off him, soaking the seat, pooling at his feet.

"Really coming down now, isn't it?" Hunter asked with an amused smile.

"Yeah." Buzz wiped the rain from his face.

"How'd it go?"

"Oh, fine, fine. Didn't take long, really. Just a short interview. They wrote everything down. Said they'd get back to me if they needed anything else."

"Huh, okay." Hunter finally started driving. But before he pulled onto the road, he sat there a moment, drumming a finger on the steering wheel. He shot Buzz a look. "So that's all, really? Did they have you look at mug shots or anything?"

"Not today, no."

"Who'd you talk to? Was it Deputy Martinson?"

"Sorry, doesn't ring a bell."

Hunter eased out onto the road, his speed slower than normal, like he was about to turn back and go into the station himself.

An uneasiness built inside Buzz, like acid eating at his stomach. It left him with a sour feeling. He didn't like deceiving Hunter, but he had his reasons.

Before Hunter could ask about his supposed police statement again, Buzz said, "Suppose you can take a quick look at Hush again today? He seemed a bit warm to me. Just want to make sure he's okay."

"Of course, Buzz. I'd be happy to."

And then Buzz asked him about Hush's injury again and what his prognosis was. It was enough to keep Hunter talking all the way back to Noreen's.

When Hush greeted Buzz with wags and happy little monkey sounds, Buzz knew he'd done the right thing that morning, even as deceitful as he felt about it. He couldn't imagine ever lying to Hunter for any other reason. That dog meant everything to him.

When you loved someone, you protected them at all costs. No matter what.

chapter 15

Beam

If I could forget half of what happened in my life, I'd consider it a gift. A good memory is an asset for playing trivia games; it's a curse if your childhood has been a social worker's nightmare.

It's not the details of my life that trip me up, even though I recall more of those than I'd like to. It's reliving the experiences, the good and the bad. The way they made me feel inside: the disgust of finding another man I'd never seen before in Lana's bed, the maddening despair that filled me when baby Oakley cried to be fed and Lana was out stone cold, and the loneliness that swallowed me the morning after he died and I realized it was just me and my mother ... Okay, there was way more bad than good. That's what I hate about the way I am. It's like being stuck on a repeating loop.

But what started to happen with Buzz's episodes was that I learned I could handle his medical emergencies with calmness and clarity. Buzz needed my help — and that alone made my life less futile.

More than two weeks had gone by since his last incident. He'd put on weight, shaved, and I'd even trimmed his hair for him. I was starting to believe he might get better. But in my heart, I knew it was only a short reprieve. That normal meant nothing was a given. That anything could happen at any time.

Even when things were 'normal', they weren't necessarily ideal. I'd woken up that morning to Buzz hammering and sawing. At half past nine. Much too early, in my book.

Noreen's computer, an obvious relic from the Univac days, clicked and whirred as it went into its fifth minute of booting up. I resisted the urge to kick it. While I waited for its life force to be resurrected, I fetched a cup of mint green tea, a bruised apple, and a granola bar from the kitchen. When I returned, the screen was starting to blink to life. The next gauntlet was connecting to the satellite internet, which I'd quickly learned failed whenever it rained. By the time that was done, I'd finished my breakfast, which by most people's standards was lunch, given the hour. Mornings weren't my thing. I wondered what kind of job I could get that didn't start before noon: third shift at the coroner's office as a forensic scientist, maybe?

Distracted by the small furry creature rubbing his head against my shins, I ran my nails over Fisher's spine. He arched against my touch, then spat something small and wet at my feet: his favorite paper wad. Plucking it up, I tossed it out into the hallway. He brought it back, looking up at me expectantly. An offering, I guess. I threw it again. And again. Each time, he raced to it, picked it up in his mouth, and pranced back to drop it at my feet.

"Are you a dog or a cat?" I asked him.

He bounded into my lap and curled into a ball, purring in answer.

Unable to leave my seat, I logged onto my assignment page for calculus and took the last few sips of a second cup of now lukewarm tea. Differentials and integrals, sequences and series, derivatives and infinitesimals. Great stuff if you wanted to go into Quantum Physics and ponder the invisible forces of the universe. I still hadn't showered yet that day, but there wasn't much incentive when you never left the house. Noreen was always up before dawn and off to work, seldom home before sundown.

An odd silence tugged me from my mathematics trance, but only for a few seconds. With forced focus, I finished the last three problems, scanned my work for errors, and hit send, then clicked on my next class. In the kitchen, Hush knocked against a chair leg as he struggled to upright himself. Probably just needed a drink and had to make his way to the other side of the room. His bandages had been off for a couple weeks now, but he was still learning to use all his muscles again and was pretty clumsy.

With a blink and a rattling buzz, the page popped up before me. I perused the homework list and test schedule for World Literature 115. Crap, another reading assignment. If I hadn't yet felt inclined to a nap, I soon would. I wrote the pages down and, setting the kitten gingerly on the ground, got up to retrieve the textbook from the living room where I'd last been reading it.

Hush met me in the doorway. Stopped me dead.

His jowls puffed out with two breathy barks. *Woof, woof.*

Now this was unusual. Did he want to play? Have to pee?

I waved a hand at him, trying to shoo him away. He leaned away from his bad leg but didn't move. The walk from the kitchen appeared to have exhausted him, because his tongue was hanging out and he was panting rapidly. He whined softly. Must have to pee, I concluded. Buzz was just going to have to take him out, because there was no way I was jumping into the role of dog-sitter. Not my responsibility.

I took a step to my right. "Excuse me, buddy." I pointed past him to where my textbooks were stacked in a tottering pile on an end table. "I just need to get something. So, if you would … go back into the kitchen, okay?"

Woof!

"Please?"

More slowly this time, I took another half a step. Hush took three. Straight at me. I scooted backward.

"Buzz? Can you come and get your dog? I think he has to go out." I knew the dog wasn't going to do anything to me. Or at least he hadn't tried to. Yet. But he had this wild, anxious look and there was saliva dripping from his fangs onto the floor. It had me kind of worried.

A lot worried, actually.

The first thing I was going to do after this was Google 'rabies'. Because that dog sure looked like he had it.

"Uh, Buzz?" My voice climbed higher. "Your dog?"

The kitchen clock replied with a sluggish *tick … tick … tick*. From the attic overhead came the tiny *scritch-scritch* of a rodent's teeth sawing at a cardboard box. Birdsong permeated the thin windowpanes of the house as a pair of quarrelsome sparrows alighted on a pine tree right outside the bedroom window.

"Buuuuzz!"

The birds flew away. The mice stopped gnawing.

Except for the clock, everything was quiet. A strange, worrisome kind of quiet.

He wasn't in the kitchen or the living room. The bathroom door was wide open. Maybe he was outside. Usually, he didn't go anywhere without the dog, not even to the bathroom. Except —

The moment I thought it, Hush had spun around and was ahead of me. He limped toward the basement steps, his whines pitching to a frenzied alert. The basement door was wide open. Hustling there, my fear of the dog forgotten, I gazed down into the dank cavern that was Noreen's basement. The light from down below shone dimly.

"Buzz?! You down there?"

Hush moved his splinted leg forward onto the first step, shifted his weight. With a sharp whimper, he pulled his leg back.

"Stay there," I told him. "I got this."

I bounded down three at a time, my heart five steps ahead of me.

Hush howled with concern. At the bottom, I saw nothing, which at first seemed good. Buzz hadn't fallen down the stairs at least. It took my eyes a few moments to adjust to the half-darkness. There were two light bulbs in the cramped basement and only one of those, the one nearest the stairs, was on. The support beams were low — just over seven feet — but ductwork, plumbing, and a snake's nest of wiring hung down. I tried not to think of how many spiders were lurking in the dark crevices all around me.

To the right of the stairs was a row of shelving crammed with boxes that hadn't been opened in years. Some were labeled, some not. A few had mildew creeping up from the bottom where dampness had invaded. Ahead of me were the washer and dryer, circa 1960, topped by two old plastic baskets filled with a pile of haphazardly folded laundry.

Left of the stairs, the basement took a ninety-degree right turn. While my eyes adjusted, I shuffled in that direction like a mummy, waving my hands back and forth at the ends of stiff arms, searching for the string on the light bulb there. It had to be close —

My toe struck *something*. I looked down, focused. Before me stretched a dark lump. It twitched. I stepped to the right, flung my hand out to grab the string, and gave it a sharp tug. A cone of light illuminated the area.

Buzz lay on the floor. A thin slash of blood ran from his temple to his cheekbone. Not a deep cut, but a long one. Close by sat a dusty old bench littered with tools and jars of screws, bolts, and nuts. Atop it was also a drill press and next to it a bench saw. He could've cut his head on any of those things. Each day, when my schoolwork was done, I'd go find Buzz. He was easy to locate. All I had to do was listen for the bang of a hammer or the buzz of a saw. Buzz had taught me the names of all the tools and explained the steps to rewiring a room, repairing a leaky J-trap, and how to replace a doorknob. Really, I didn't care about any of those things. It was just that when I wanted to talk to someone, he always listened. At the end of my confessional, he'd ponder it all and ask questions like "What did you learn from it?", or even "Why do you suppose she said that?" Instead of playing a loop over and over in my head with the same outcome, Buzz's questions made me look at things from a different angle.

I crouched before him, looking closer at the gash. He must've nicked the vein there, because it was pulsing scarlet onto the grungy basement floor to congeal in a dark red puddle beneath his head.

If not for the fading tremors in his limbs, I might have thought him dead. A knot in my stomach that I hadn't known was there drew tighter on itself.

He was still in that dazed stage, past the worst of it but not yet fully out. Laying a hand on his shoulder, I spoke to him. Even if he didn't understand my words at first, he'd want to know someone was with him.

In the two months since I'd been at Noreen's, I'd sifted through as many medical articles as I could find about seizures, reading the ones that sounded most like his. The best thing was to keep him as still as possible in a clear area and wait for it to pass.

He twitched a few more times and slowly the rigidity melted from his body. When his breathing finally evened out and his eyes focused fully on me, I smiled at him.

"I'm going to call Hunter to come and check on you, okay?"

"What? No, no … don't. I'm fine. I am."

"You're bleeding."

He blinked at me. He was slow to process things afterward sometimes. "Where?"

I touched below the cut, showed him the red on my fingertips. "Here, see?"

With a shaky hand he probed the area, then dabbed it with his sleeve. "Nothing a cold washcloth won't fix. Bring me one?"

"Sure." I ran upstairs, past Hush who was crouched like a sphinx at the top of the stairs, and retrieved one from the bathroom. When I returned, I wiped the blood from Buzz's cheek.

He flailed a hand weakly at me. "I can do that. Just give —"

"No. You can't even sit up yet. Besides, I need to see how bad it is. You might need stitches."

"For Pete's sake, Sunbeam, I don't need surgery. You're making too much out of this."

I ignored him and kept sopping at the blood. It almost seemed like the more I dabbed, the more it gushed. I'd read up on first aid recently too, and it finally occurred to me that I needed to stop the bleeding. So I went to the dryer and grabbed one of the washcloths buried in the laundry basket there. God only knew how long it had been there or whether it was even remotely clean, but if he bled to death I supposed none of that mattered.

Pressing the cloth to his head, I told him to be still. He complied with a grunt.

"So have you always been this way?" I asked.

"Cantankerous, you mean?"

"You're hardly that. Epileptic. I mean, I know some people are born with the condition, some acquire it as a result of trauma or illness or tumors —"

A grimace flashed across his face. "You studying to be a doctor? Or do you just Google a lot? Sure do spend a lot of time at the computer."

"I haven't decided what I want to be yet. Mostly I just study whatever sounds interesting."

"I hear engineering is a good field to get into."

"If you like math and machines." He had a habit of changing topics whenever the conversation drifted his way. I wasn't about to let him avoid answering me. "Tell me. Have you always had these?"

He hesitated. If he could've walked out of the room just then, I'm sure he would have. "No, not always."

I thought he was going to say more, but he pressed his lips together, like nothing was going to get out. I dabbed some more. The bleeding was slowing. It didn't look so bad now. Maybe a Band-Aid would do the trick.

Dang it, for once in my life I just wanted to be the kid, not the adult taking care of everyone else. But at times like this, you just did what you had to. Anyway, I was never one to walk away from responsibility, whether I'd chosen it or not.

"Tell you what …" Gently, I peeled the washcloth away to peek at the gash one more time. Still bleeding, although barely. He'd have a nice scar, stitches or no stitches, but it didn't look like he was going to bleed to death after all. The next step was to get it cleaned up so a staph infection didn't set in. "If you tell me how you got this way — and I do mean every little detail — I won't call Hunter, all right?"

He blew out a puff of air. "It's not that interesting," he said with a lopsided smile, "but all right."

—o00o—

A hot May sun blazed down on us as we sat on the back porch steps. Noreen's property abutted a cow field edged by a falling down fence. The neighbor's Angus cattle hadn't yet been moved to the adjacent pasture and the weeds were already bursting in abundance. In the woods that fringed the fields, the last of the redbud blossoms were fading and the phlox had made its debut. Virginia creeper intertwined with the sagging woven wire fence and atop a fence post sat a rusty blackbird, cocking his head side to side as Hush hobbled about the open grassy area beside the garage out back.

"When they first told me, I was sure they were wrong." Buzz took a chug of Noreen's sweet tea, so saturated with sugar that it was more of a slurry than a beverage. Might as well just hook an IV up to a bottle of corn syrup. Setting his glass on the step beside him, he rested

197

his elbows on his knees.

"But they were, right?" I said.

"An oligo-dendro-glioma." He pronounced it slowly but precisely, each syllable a stone too heavy to hold on to. "Inoperable. Not cancerous, but ..."

But. Funny how that one word can erase all the ones before it. "And there's no treatment for that? Nothing they can do?"

He laced his fingers together, studied them. "There is. But it wasn't promising."

"Why didn't you do it?"

His gaze fell upon Hush briefly. "And what was I supposed to do with my dog? Even if the VA had paid for the treatment, they weren't going to spring for dog boarding."

"Back up a second — VA? Veteran's Administration? You were in the military?"

"At one point."

"You left?"

"Not exactly."

"What does that mean?"

"It means, as your generation so often says, it's complicated." The ice in his glass clinked as he brought it to his lips. Half a glass later, he went on. "Besides, you wanted to know about my seizures. Last I knew, I wasn't dictating my autobiography to you."

"You know, the more you play 'mystery man' and refuse to talk about your past, the worse I imagine. Did you kill a man? Embezzle millions? Employ refugees in a child-labor sweat shop?"

"You do have quite the imagination, don't you?"

"I've read a lot of books. But I also read the news. Regular-looking people like you do crazy stuff every day."

He fidgeted, took another drink. "Nothing crazy, I assure you."

"Then spill. After all, you know way more about me than I know about you."

"I didn't force it out of you. You chose to tell me."

"Buzz," I growled. By now I was getting irritated. I couldn't begin to guess what he might have done to get kicked out of the military, but sooner or later he'd have to tell me. Maybe not today, but I'd milk it out of him eventually.

He nodded at Hush. "That dog has saved my life more times than I can count. I knew if I went into the hospital, there was a very good chance he'd end up in a shelter and then —" The softest of sighs emptied his lungs. "I couldn't let that happen. Not after all he's done for me."

"You've had him a long time?"

"Not really. Less than two years, I suppose. I'm not even sure how old he is. Before Hush came into my life, I'd almost stopped living. Out of a job and collecting welfare. Sold my house and moved into public housing. Hellhole of a place. Living there, you understand why people get messed up. They're just angry because they've run out of hope." When he looked at me then, it was the first time I'd ever felt that someone understood. *Really* understood. "From what you've said about your mother, I get why you wanted to leave."

"Thanks. I appreciate that. I just thought that when I came here ..." I didn't know how to finish that. Or if I even needed to.

"Noreen will come around. Just give her time. She's already done better by you than your own mother, hasn't she?"

I hated that he was right. But still ... "She could be a little less, I don't know, cold, unfriendly, terse, grumpy —"

"She could be a lot worse."

We'd been down this road a dozen times. Nothing had changed much since the beginning. Noreen hadn't kicked me out. She'd paid for my classes. I'd thanked her, only to have her reply with a grunt and a shrug. At least my life was no longer in danger every day. Yes, I was safer. But beyond that —

At any rate, I was tired of talking about it. Tired of hoping

Noreen would change. In a small way, I was beginning to understand why Lana herself may have left home, and in that, I blamed her a tiny bit less. But I'd far from forgiven her.

Out in the yard, Hush snapped at a dandelion. The seeds exploded in a puff and drifted along the ground. Something in the grass drew his attention and he lay down, his nose pressed between his paws as he sniffed in breaths, drinking in the smell of the lawn.

"You didn't have anyone," I asked, "who would've taken care of Hush until you got out? Family? Friends?"

"Not really. My parents both died before I was twenty. I had no siblings. Any cousins I may have had I never met. As for friends, no one that could have kept him for weeks. Besides, I was living on the street by then."

"What? Why?"

"Wasn't supposed to have a pet where I lived. One day a neighbor ratted on us, so we had to go. Any place I could afford wouldn't allow a dog his size — like being under fifty pounds makes a dog less of a problem somehow. I decided I'd rather do without a home than give up my dog. Because without him, I would've been dead more than just the once."

"You mean you almost died once?"

"Not almost. Did."

I squinted at him. "Explain."

"Electrical shock. Died. Dead. As in not breathing. No heartbeat. No blips on the little machine. Clinically dead. Clinically." He drew his chin back. "What? You don't believe me?"

"You *are* sitting here talking to me right now. If you did 'die', how did they bring you back? What'd they do to, you know, 'resurrect' you?"

His hand on the pillar, he stood. Slowly. Whenever he got up, he always looked woozy, like you could've pushed him over with a fingertip. "They didn't do anything."

Hush trotted over to us, but stopped at the bottom steps. With his stiff bandages now off, he could walk better lately. Just not up steps. Or down.

"Right," I muttered. "So you just spontaneously came back to life? All on your own?"

"Something like that. They later told me I flat-lined. They weren't even sure why. But apparently it wasn't my time." He eased his stiff body down one step at a time and onto the sidewalk. Lifting Hush, he grunted with the effort. At the top of the steps, he set the dog down and straightened, then kneaded at his lower back. "I figured I was sent back for a purpose. That I had work left to do in this world."

"Like rescuing a dog?" I followed them into the kitchen and started rummaging around for something to prepare for dinner.

"Maybe the dog was meant to rescue me?" He tilted his head, pondering. "Lately, though, I've started wondering. That maybe the reason Hush saved me ... was so *I* could save *you*."

"Me?" I pointed at my chest. "In case you forgot, you're the reason I went off the road and crashed into that fence post."

His left eyebrow lifted ever so slightly, crinkling the bandage at his temple. "I suppose if you look at it that way, I almost killed you."

"That's not what I meant." I took a bag of potatoes from a bottom cupboard.

"Let me be clearer, then." Buzz set a colander in the sink and went to work washing the potatoes. "If I hadn't been walking down the middle of the road, you would have just kept on going. Let's say you ended up here at Noreen's by yourself. Would you have stayed, given how she is?"

"I ... I don't know. I guess I would have had to, considering I don't exactly have any options, short of living on the streets." Which is exactly what Buzz had been doing, until Noreen took him in. "Okay, I see what you're doing. You're trying to make me feel grateful toward Noreen, is that it?"

201

"I'm not trying to make you do anything, Sunbeam. You're pretty smart all on your own." He let that sink in. Buzz was never one to tell you what to think. He just asked questions and let you figure stuff out yourself. "There's something more, though. Something that maybe hasn't come together just yet. I believe everything happens for a reason. Sometimes it just takes a while to figure out what that reason is."

"You're full of it, Buzz."

"Am I?"

"Yeah, loaded. Crap's practically oozing out of your pores."

He chuckled. "I do like your sense of humor, crude as it is."

"Thanks. I think."

I started paring the spuds at the counter while Buzz filled a pot with water.

"Sunbeam?"

I dug the knife into the potato and pushed hard. Too hard. The blade skipped over the peel and nicked the pad of my thumb. Dropping the knife, I sucked in a breath. The cut was shallow, but long. I rushed to the faucet, flipped the spigot to the side so I wouldn't contaminate Buzz's pot of water, and stuck my thumb under the cool stream.

"You okay, Sunbeam?"

"*Why* do you keep calling me 'Sunbeam'?" I snapped.

He blinked innocently at me. "Want me to stop?"

"No ... I just ... I just want to know why."

"I don't know why. It just came to me when you first told me your name. Why do you ask?"

I shrugged. Memories pushed up from deep inside. Lined themselves up like a row of dominoes, waiting to be knocked over. "Oakley's the only one who ever called me that, that's all. Every time you say it ..."

"You don't like me calling you that, is that it?"

"No, that's not it." I didn't know how to say what I meant without getting all mushy, so I just said it. "Oak and I had this ... connection. And when you call me that ... This almost sounds creepy, so don't take it wrong, but when you call me that, I feel that with you, too. Like if I'd ever had a dad — the real kind, not just some sperm donor — that's what he would have called me."

There. It was out. I hadn't even realized I'd felt that way until that very moment. And who'd have ever thought I'd identify with a homeless man as a sort of adoptive father? I suppose that just goes to show you that jobs and titles and possessions don't define any of us. What matters is how we treat people, and with Buzz I felt accepted. Cherished, even.

"And if I'd ever had a daughter," he said, touching me briefly on the shoulder, "I would have wanted her to be just like you."

I looked down, avoiding his eyes. I'd never heard words like that. Never had anyone but Oakley treat me like anything special. I'd thought no one ever would again.

A moment stretched into a minute. The floor squeaked as Buzz inched closer. Part of me wanted to run, like I didn't deserve his love. Another part of me —

His arms, light and comforting, went around me. But only for a few seconds. Long enough that I'd know he meant what he'd said.

A nose wedged between us, forcing us apart. Hush stared up at us, his bobtailed hind end wiggling playfully. He picked up a stick that he'd stolen from the wood pile before coming in and darted a few feet away, inviting us to play.

"Not inside, buddy." Buzz took it from him and placed it on the counter next to the back door.

"Buzz, you were going to say something."

"I was?" He filled Hush's water dish to the brim and set it down before him. Hush lapped sloppily.

"Before I interrupted you about my name."

203

He thought a moment. "Oh, that's right. I remember now." Sitting down at the table, he stretched his thin legs out and rubbed the sides of his knees. "What do *you* think happens when we die, when our bodies shut down?"

"What do you mean 'what happens'? Nothing happens after that. You're dead."

A grimace flashed across his face. I wasn't sure if it was because of my reply, or that some part of his body was hurting. Until he spoke. "Ahhh, I sure hope you're wrong, Sunbeam. Because if you aren't, well, I, for one, don't have much to look forward to."

Now that was a morbid way to wrap up a conversation. Yet it was exactly like Buzz to plant the seed of a thought, to make you think just hard enough to maybe change your mind. Not that I was ever going to.

Dead was dead: no heartbeat, no breath, no neurological impulses.

A thing either was or wasn't. There was no in between.

chapter 16

Buzz

"I'm not sure that's such a good idea." Buzz slid a grilled ham-and-cheese onto Noreen's plate. "After all, I haven't driven in … well, three years. And, well, you know …"

It was a Sunday. The most awkward day of the week. Because it was Noreen's day off. Not much about either Buzz's or Beam's routines changed on Sundays, but Noreen never knew quite what to do with herself. As far as Buzz was concerned, the only thing she was good for was getting in the way of everybody else's business.

"You seem to be managing your condition well enough. If it happens, she can just pull over and attend to it. Not like you'll be driving the truck. Besides, it's not like it happens every day."

Buzz decided not to point out that since she wasn't home all that much, there was a lot she missed, like his episodes. She never asked about his day — or Beam's — when she came home. The only time the topic ever came up was if Beam mentioned it.

Pressing the sandwich between her knife and fork, Noreen flipped it over, inspected it thoroughly, and deemed it edible. She cut it precisely in half. "But you remember how to drive, correct?"

"Sure, I do. It's like writing in cursive. Most of it's muscle memory."

"I trust your license is current." Next to her plate sat a small box. Inside was a new phone for Beam. Not a simple flip phone. A smart phone. She took a bite of the sandwich, chewed slowly. When Buzz didn't answer, she repeated, "I said is it current?"

"Sorry, I didn't realize that was a question at first." Actually, the phone had stolen his attention. He'd looked at phones like those in a store out in Arkansas one day on his journey when he'd needed a place to get out of a torrential rain. They were expensive. And complicated. He hadn't the slightest idea how to use one. "It was."

"What do you mean *was*? I'm talking right now. This year. Is it?"

"Technically, yes."

She put the sandwich down. "Was it revoked?"

"No, it was stolen, remember?"

"Humph." Her eyebrows jumped, like she didn't really believe him. She pushed her glasses higher up on her nose, studied what was left of the sandwich, turning it on her plate with her fork like there was an ideal angle from which to attack it. Buzz had bent over backward to carry his weight around the house — washing his own laundry, fixing things he hadn't even been asked to fix, cooking full meals with whatever happened to be in the cupboards — yet he was never confident that his efforts were ever appreciated, or even noticed. By Noreen, that is. He never doubted that Beam was aware of how much he did, even though she didn't say much. It was just that with Noreen, he always felt judged. And not in a good way.

"That's right — stolen," she added cynically. "Must have been harrowing. All your possessions, gone just like that. No trace of them. Pity."

Buzz ignored her jab. He understood it was meant to get under his skin, to incite him to defend himself. Yet he felt no need to. He'd been robbed at gunpoint, his life threatened. His dog had nearly been stolen after almost dying earlier that same day. His backpack and belongings had mattered little in light of all that.

A few long minutes later, Beam joined them in the kitchen. She shared a glance with Buzz and he detected the slightest of eye rolls from her. Sitting down at her usual place, she took one look at the phone sitting on the table and asked, "Did you get yourself a new phone?"

Noreen nudged it at her with a fingertip. "It's yours."

Beam's mouth flopped open. "Mine?"

"Yes, yours."

"But" — she opened the box, powered it on — "I thought I was getting a phone just for calls and texting?" It chirped to life, and she immediately began swiping and tapping, working her way through all the tiny icons that to Buzz looked like a bunch of cartoon pictures.

"It's the plan that costs, not the phone, really. They practically give those away. I figured since you're not from around here, you need maps and access to information. Anyway, don't go crazy with it, playing games and all that. I'll know when you're over your limit." She leaned in Beam's direction to peer at the screen. "I've put all my numbers in there already: home, cell, work. But don't call me at work unless it's necessary. I have a lot of client appointments throughout the day and interruptions will put me behind."

Squinting at the contacts list, Beam made a face. "Dr. McHugh? Why would I call Dr. McHugh?"

"Who else do you know around here? Anyway, in case you ever need to call him about the cat or the dog."

Just then, Fisher skidded around the doorway, bounded across the floor, then did a one-eighty and rocketed in the other direction, his tail pointed straight in the air like the tailfin on a jet plane.

Beam nodded absently, her fingers dancing across the screen. Moments later, concentration turned to fascination. She held the phone up, pointed it directly at Buzz. "Look, it has a camera!"

Just as her thumb pressed to take a picture, Buzz blocked her with his palm.

The last thing he needed was his picture floating around the internet.

She lowered it, scowling. "Why'd you do that?"

"Put that thing away," Buzz said gruffly.

"Just wanted to see how it works." She aimed the camera eye at him again. "Anyway, it's not like anyone's going to see it. Who would I share it with? I promise I'll delete —"

This time Buzz batted it away. "I said no pictures!"

"What the —?"

"Put the phone away, Bellamy," Noreen warned. "It's rude to play with those during mealtime."

"Play?" Beam drew herself up tall. "I wasn't 'playing'. I was just —"

"It's also rude to take photos without asking."

"And it's rude to interrupt, too."

They stared at each other for a good fifteen seconds, Beam gripping the phone possessively, Noreen with her hands flat on the table. Defiant, stubborn. Very much alike.

It was like watching two lionesses square up for dominance. After taking a quick swallow of water, Buzz set the glass down firmly, so it clunked on the table. Noreen's eyes snapped to him, but Beam's were still locked on her grandmother. He cleared his throat, loud and long, until Beam, too, turned her face to him. "Sorry, Sunbeam. I didn't mean to cause a ruckus. I just don't like having my picture taken, that's all. Never did. Even more as I get older."

When her eyes narrowed at him, he added an apologetic smile.

Finally, Beam looked down at her plate. "You're vain, Buzz."

"S'pose so."

"No one cares if you have wrinkles." She speared a broccoli

fleurette and devoured it in two bites. Then, her mouth twitching in a grin, she winked at him. "They're marks of experience."

He laughed softly. "If you say so."

Like a misty rain that fades, the tension dissipated, and Buzz focused on finishing his meal so he could get back to clearing the leaves out of the gutters and securing the downspouts.

"Why do you want to know if Buzz has his driver's license?" Beam asked her grandmother.

Noreen peered at her over the rims of her glasses. "Because someone needs to supervise while you get in your hours for your learner's permit and I don't have the time. Since you and Buzz —"

Buzz almost jumped in and said something about her calling him something other than 'Mr. Donovan', but he let it go. Probably just a slip, but if she made a habit of it, he'd be sure to return the favor.

"— seemed to be joined at the hip, I thought he could fulfill that role. Might as well do something useful around here until he can move on."

Again, Beam and Buzz shared another glance. Buzz rolled his eyes. There was no pleasing the woman. In many ways, he'd be happy to leave and put Noreen's bad moods behind him. But in other ways, he wasn't ready to go. Didn't want to. Maybe ever. Beam was here. He'd taken to the girl. Saw a lot of promise in her. And for some inexplicable reason, he felt the need to make Noreen see what he saw in Beam. She just made it so damn hard. Yet given the time he had left — which wasn't much — it was a worthwhile project.

At any rate, as much as he detested confrontation, he also wasn't about to let this woman bully them around with her snide comments.

"Useful, huh?" He sat across from Noreen and looked directly at her. "Have I not been useful so far?"

He realized he sounded like a chided husband of fifty years, but it had to be said.

"You have." She held his gaze with all the authority of a Fortune

500 CEO. "And you've certainly made a difference around here, Buzz Donovan. Don't think I haven't noticed. But soon that dog of yours will be mended and you'll be off to far horizons, back to being the drifter that you were. Thanks to you, this house will hold together long enough for me to retire somewhere warmer. In the meanwhile" — she took the last nibble of her sandwich, then dabbed at her mouth with a paper towel before continuing — "I need someone to help my granddaughter gain her independence. She may want to go to graduate school one day or find herself a job. I don't think she'll want to stay here forever. I know putting up with me is no party. But if you can't, she'll just have to wait for Sundays, and I'll —"

"Buzz," Beam pleaded, "say you will. Please. Hush would like the car rides, don't you think?"

Folding his arms over his chest, he sat back. "Let me get this straight — you want the dog to ride along?"

"He'd have to. If you came, I mean."

"You *want* him to?"

She looked toward where the dog lay on his back, legs spread wide, his lips fluttering with dreamy snores. Then, as if suddenly aware of her, his eyes snapped open. He wiggled, groaning as he rubbed his spine over the floor, and stretched long. Still upside down, he curled his head around to get a better view of her. His cheeks bunched into something resembling a smile.

"Yeah," she said softly, "I want him to."

"I thought you were a cat person."

"Oh, I am, I am. But you need the dog to stay with you, so ..." She shrugged, like that should be enough of an explanation, never mind the truth. She'd taken to Hush, although she wasn't going to admit to it just yet.

As Beam turned her face away from the dog and gobbled down her grilled ham and Swiss cheese, Buzz saw the scars along her jawline, faint but clear.

Love, especially a dog's love, can change a person.

—oOOo—

With a jarring clunk, Beam shifted the truck down into second. The gears ground in a nerve-shredding rasp. Carlos lurched, then chugged up the steep, bumpy hill with intrepid determination.

"You left from where?" Beam asked. As they topped the hill, the crowd of trees embracing the road parted and a green valley opened up before them. She shifted up, the truck now coasting happily downhill.

"Los Angeles." She'd done it again, gotten him to talk about himself. Wore down his resolve is how she did it. A man can only sidestep so many questions before the truth inevitably slips out.

"When?"

They'd begun these drives almost a month ago. Sometimes they were in the car for as much as three hours a day. Beam was determined to complete them as quickly as possible, and since she already knew how to drive, even a stick shift, and knew all the laws by heart, there wasn't anything Buzz could tell her that she didn't already know. The truth of it was that she knew more than him by a long shot. Not that he'd ever admit it.

"Four-way stop coming up," he reminded her, if only because he felt otherwise useless.

"I know, Buzz. We came this way yesterday, remember? And three times last week. Monday the twelfth, three p.m. You'd just finished securing the downspout by the bathroom window and didn't want to start another project." They cruised toward the intersection a bit too fast for Buzz's comfort, while Beam chattered on. "Then Thursday the fifteenth after Hush dropped that termite-infested stick in my lap. And Saturday —"

"Just don't want you to go into autopilot, that's all." Instinctively,

211

he gripped the inside door handle. "Pay attention."

Twenty feet away, she punched the brakes, grinning. "I am."

Whimpering, Hush braced his front feet on the seat. His bandages were long gone, and while he could walk on his own now, he had a distinct limp and it was still hard going for him.

Buzz grabbed his seatbelt. "Sooner next time."

She snorted. "Wasn't anyone coming."

"Lucky for us."

Swiveling her head left, then right, then left again, she crept out into the intersection. They continued north. "You didn't answer me — when?"

"When what?" In truth, he'd forgotten the question. She was like a butterfly in search of nectar, easily distracted, yet determined. At first he'd sidestepped the barrage of questions. Bit by bit, though, he'd caved. It was as if she were conducting an investigation, filing away bits of knowledge for later use.

"When did you leave L.A.?"

He hadn't meant to ever name where he was actually from. It had just slipped out one day. "Nine months ago, give or take a couple of weeks. Slower than it should've taken, but we made progress almost every day."

"And you *walked* all this way? You never hitched a ride or took a bus?"

"Didn't have the money for a bus. Besides, they wouldn't have let Hush on. Unless I got him one of those fake Service Dog vests. Which also cost money. Anyway, I can't stand the smell of diesel. Makes me sick. As far as hitchhiking ... only twice. The first time in a terrible thunderstorm out in Oklahoma. The sky had that look like a tornado might drop out of the clouds at any moment. A trucker gave us a ride, but it was only about fifty miles before he needed to take an exit heading a different direction from the way we were going. We hung out at a gas station until the threat was over. The second time ...

that was the day you and I met, earlier that morning. Hush had been hit by that car. I had to get him to a vet and didn't know where one was. The man offered me a ride, but then he robbed me, took all my clothes except what I had on, my money, my wallet ... every last thing I owned. He would've driven off with Hush, too, if I hadn't begged him not to."

"That's terrible. I hope they catch the guy." She allowed a brief pause, but Buzz knew it was only because she intended to take the conversation in yet another direction. "So you never said — where is it that you're headed, anyway?"

So that was the point of her line of questioning. Buzz knew the tactic well. She'd learned it from him. Start at the beginning. Let them open up gradually. "Chincoteague Island. Ever heard of it?"

"I think ... Yeah, I have. In Virginia, isn't it? Isn't that where the wild horses are?"

"Ponies, technically. Descendants of escapees from a wrecked Spanish galleon, over two hundred and fifty years ago."

"Neat. But why go there? Why not, say, Florida or New York City or the farthest point in Maine? I hear Acadia National Park is stunning."

Buzz shrugged. He didn't want to say. Some things you just kept to yourself. "No reason, really. Just something from a book I read once. It was on the bucket list." Before she could ask him anything else, he aimed a question at her. "Aren't there things you want to do someday?"

"'Someday' as in before I die, you mean?"

Her words dug deep. Practically shot a hole through his gut.

Until now, he'd accepted his fate. Not willingly, certainly not eagerly, but with a sense of profound knowledge that his existence consisted of more than just the bodily shell he inhabited. His only regret had been that he'd have to leave Hush behind one day.

He turned to Beam. Looked at her so hard and so long that she jerked her face in his direction. The truck whipped to the right. The front wheel dipped off the shoulder. A rusty red gate, pillared by two splintered posts, loomed ahead.

Buzz slapped both hands on the dashboard. "Whoa!"

A second later, Beam righted the truck. It bounced back onto the pavement and sped on down the road like nothing had happened.

"Are you *trying* to kill me?" he accused.

"No!" she bit back. "It's just that ... you had that look, like you were losing focus, about to go out. Only Hush wasn't doing anything."

"I'm fine, Sunbeam. Just fine."

"Then why were you staring at me? You're creeping me out, Buzz."

"I wasn't staring."

"Oh yeah? Then what do you call looking at someone and not averting your eyes?"

"I was ... thinking."

"Thinking, huh? About what?"

He couldn't ask. Shouldn't. Not right now. It was too soon.

But if not now, when?

"Sunbeam ... if anything, you know, happens to me, will you take care of Hush?"

For several moments, she had no reaction, gave no reply. Then, soft as the trickle of water from a drippy faucet, she laughed. It welled up from her throat, bubbled out. Louder, she laughed, clutching her stomach. "Oh, God. Sorry. I should pull over. I had no idea. Am I that bad a driver? I thought I was doing okay, but sometimes my mind just wanders, you know." With a shake of her head, she sobered. Both hands clenched the steering wheel. She stared straight ahead, worry carving deep furrows in her forehead. "Man, I'm in trouble, aren't I? You aren't going to tell Noreen I went off the road, are you? I can do better. I can. Really, I can."

"Beam, will you take care of him?" He rubbed his thumb over the well-worn surface of his walking stick, resting between his knees. These days, he needed it more and more.

Snorting, she rolled her eyes. "You're *not* going to die, Buzz. That's all there is to it. No sense in me answering a question like that." They neared a gas station at an intersection and Beam slowly decelerated before pulling in and up to a pump. Inside, the female clerk glanced at them through dirty plate glass as another customer ambled up to the counter. Beam pulled the key out, the hot engine making little pinging noises. She pulled her wallet from beneath the seat and counted out bills. Noreen had given her fifty bucks for gas — enough to fill up the tank and afford a couple of fountain drinks — although she'd also given Buzz fifty a week ago, in case of emergency. Beam tucked the bills in her pocket and glanced at Buzz. "But if you want to know if I'll take care of him if you're ever in the hospital, then sure, I'll do it. For you. When you get back out, though, he's all yours. I'm not a dog person. If anything, I'm a cat person. In case you forgot."

Not the enthusiastic response he'd been hoping for, but at least he could have some peace of mind now. Beam cared for that dog more than she'd ever let on.

"If you say so." Buzz held on to Hush's collar while Beam kicked her door open. The rusty hinges made a sound that was half squeal, half groan. "Want me to pump the gas?"

"No, I got this." Then the door boomed shut as Beam hopped out. She spoke through the open window. "Besides, just easier if I do it. I don't have to keep a dog glued to my leg."

Hush scooted over to Beam's seat to watch her, his head cocking as the keypad of the pump beeped its messages at her. He studied her with childlike curiosity. Finally, the nozzle clicked off and Beam hung it up. As she walked toward the store to pay, Hush rested his good paw in the frame of the open window, watching intently. Beam put her hand on the door handle to open it, paused as she looked back, then quickly pulled her phone out to snap a picture.

Buzz pressed the back of his head against the headrest. He was pretty sure he hadn't been in the picture, but just in case, he'd ask about it when she came back out.

Even though the windows were down, heat was building inside the truck like a blast furnace. Buzz dragged the back of his hand across his forehead to keep the sweat from running into his eyes and stinging. He was thirsting for a tall, cool drink.

Scratching Hush behind the ears, Buzz flipped the key on and fiddled with the radio knobs. Only a few country stations would come in, on account of all the hills. Buzz settled on an old-time country station playing Roger Miller's 'King of the Road'. A welcome calm flowed through him. A knowledge that all was as it should be — and would be. He might never complete the journey he and Hush had set out for all those months ago, but maybe his real purpose had just been accomplished.

Cold pain stabbed through Buzz's skull. Not again. He rubbed at his forehead, but all that did was intensify the searing pain behind his eyes. He wanted to lie down, to retreat into darkness, even though he knew that doing so had never helped him feel better any sooner. Most of the time, he just went on doing whatever it was he had been doing, not letting on about his headache if anyone was around. But they were getting more frequent — and sometimes more severe. Like now.

Whimpering, Hush shifted on his front feet. Buzz wondered why it was taking Beam so long to pay. Maybe she was picking out some cold drinks for them? But the snack aisle was right in the front of the store and she wasn't there. Maybe she'd gone to the bathroom? He looked to the right of the building on the outside where the restrooms were. No, she definitely hadn't come out of the store. He'd have seen her.

Another truck, the cab partially hidden from view, sat at an angle just outside the restrooms, the engine still idling. What idiot leaves his car running? That was just asking for it to get stolen. Good thing there wasn't anyone else around to do just that.

Impatient, Buzz looked toward the checkout counter but couldn't see the clerk anymore. Or Beam. Just the other customer with his back to the storefront. It looked like he was leaning over the counter, dragging a couple of cigarette cartons into his arms —

Something tugged at Buzz's gut, light, but sharp as a fish hook. Buzz jerked his head back toward the other truck parked next to the building. Then it smacked him with the force of a steel door slamming.

The other truck. Buzz recognized the back end of it: the faded lettering on the tailgate, the cracked taillight, the way the bumper dipped to the right —

That was the truck of the man who'd robbed him.

chapter 17

Beam

Buzz was probably wondering what was taking me so long.

"Not those," the man in front of me growled. He'd been staring at those cigarettes since I came in. "Gimme your best."

The clerk, a grandmotherly old woman with a slight overbite and a bad dye job of pinkish strawberry blond, put her elbows on the counter. "Best, huh? What brand do you like?"

Why did people smoke? Might as well stick your head in a chimney flue or roll around in campfire ashes if you wanted that tough-guy smoky odor. It would be a lot cheaper.

The man plunged his hands deep into his jacket pockets like he was digging for change. By the looks of him, he couldn't afford a pack, let alone a carton. "What's your most expensive?"

She drew a pair of leopard-print reading glasses from her smock pouch and turned to squint at a board behind her, listing them all. Fifteen or so seconds passed before she figured she needed a closer look. Stepping closer, she ran a fingertip down the list, then back up. The woman must've been legally blind — I could see it from where I stood, a good ten feet away.

When she started saying them all out loud, I had to refrain from leaping over the counter and pulling off a carton to hand to the guy. At some point she lost her place, started over, and then lost her place again. The guy cursed under his breath and she turned around. "What was that?"

"The blue-and-gold carton. That's the one."

"My late husband, Newton, used to like that blue-and-gold kind. Swore by it. Asked for it for his birthday every year until —"

"Just give 'em to me, damn it!"

"Which one?"

"I don't care!"

Talk about nicotine withdrawal. This guy needed a patch *and* an intervention. He was starting to scare me.

"Suit yourself." The clerk pulled the closest carton off the shelf and set it next to the register, between a spare penny tray and a sign that said 'No personal checks accepted'. She peered at him peevishly over the rim of her glasses. "Just one?"

"Yes, just one. Now how much?"

"You need anything else, honey? A soda? Snacks? Fuel —"

He slapped his palms on the counter. Tiny beads of perspiration sparkled against his beet-red face. A vein in his neck throbbed so big, I was afraid it was going to burst open and start spraying blood like a loose hose. He grabbed the far edge of the counter, but the lady didn't flinch. "Just the cigarettes, okay? Now hurry up, would you?"

She shrugged. "Suit yourself." Then she turned around to look at the price list. Again.

"They're twenty-eight ninety-nine," I piped.

A thin-lipped smile split her old face. "Thank you, honey. Nice to know some young'uns still have manners."

There are some things you don't say around people with a short fuse. That was apparently one of them.

The next thing I knew, the guy was waving a pistol barrel in her face. "Open the fucking cash register, you old witch, before I blow your goddamn head off!!!"

And he probably would have. Except I was standing right behind him. And I might have groaned.

"What are you staring at?!" He flipped the gun in my direction, his finger twitching on the trigger. "Lie down," he growled.

Did I look like a dog? I wasn't about to —

He shoved the barrel at my nose. So close I could smell that it had been recently fired. "Lie down!"

I did.

Dropped was more like it. Face down. He hadn't specified that, but I'd already gotten a good look at him. Besides, if he was going to kill me anyway, I didn't want to see it coming.

"You, too, bitch!" he yelled at the clerk.

She'd started to cry. Big blubbery sobs. "Oh, my heavens. Oh my, ohhh … ohhh …" A strangling sound, half wail, half whimper, leaked out of her.

"Now!"

"I'm trying, I'm trying." She sobbed again, this time more like she was in pain. "My knees, they just don't —"

"Open the register first!" He fired a shot into the stacks of cigarettes.

I couldn't *not* look any longer. The guy had the shakes, like he needed a hit or a stiff drink. Sometimes it was hard to tell the difference between an alcoholic and a druggie. At least Lana had never sunk this low. Amazingly, she'd managed to stay out of jail and keep us fed and housed, even if it meant swapping out boyfriends every few months.

Trembling, the old lady hurriedly punched a few keys like she was making a transaction. The register beeped and kicked the drawer out — right into the flabby paunch of her belly, knocking the air out of her. In a terrified daze, she gulped in two short breaths. The color drained from her face. Her eyes fluttered upward, her head rolled back, and she plummeted to the floor with a colossal *wooompf!*

The guy hurled himself across the counter like a kid on a water slide. Stuff went flying off: chip bags, packs of gum, a stack of real estate flyers, and a handful of pennies. Something flew at me and I instinctively pinched my eyes shut. The corner of the cigarette carton jabbed me in the back of the skull, but I stayed put.

Changed rattled and clunked as the robber scooped coins into a plastic bag. Bills crinkled as he crammed those, too, inside.

At that point I was sure he'd hightail it out of there. A quick glance around revealed there weren't any security cameras. This county probably hadn't ever seen an armed robbery. Break-ins and graffiti, sure. But nothing like this.

He was stuffing cartons of cigarettes into another bag when he caught me looking at him again. A sneer tugged at his upper lip. He raised his gun at me.

Cold fear trickled through me.

This is how I'm going to die, I thought. *This is it. Right here. Right now.*

What really struck me wasn't that my time was up. It was that I hadn't done a darn thing to make a difference in this life. I hadn't cured any diseases, built any bridges or dams, saved any dolphins … I hadn't even taught a kindergartner their ABCs. I hadn't kissed a boy, or stayed up all night gabbing with a friend, or gone off to college and soaked in all the knowledge I could. I'd just been stomping around like I was mad at the world while I stewed over my sorry excuse for a mother, meanwhile kicking myself for letting my little brother die.

In that moment, I felt very, very small. Insignificant. Pathetic. Unworthy.

And very determined to be something nobler — if, by some miracle, I made it out of this alive.

On the other side of the counter, the clerk whimpered. "Don't

221

shoot me," she pled. "I got eight grandbabies who need their mammaw. I love my babies. Ever' one of 'em."

For a few seconds, he managed to ignore the woman, his arm extended, one eye narrowed as he stared down the barrel at me.

Then, she added, "You got a mammaw, don't you, son?"

He laughed dryly. "Yeah, I got me one. Had. She was a drunken whore. Used to beat me. Till I shut her up." Unblinking, he turned his head to glower at her, the gun still pointed at me. "For good."

His arm swung sideways and down. A gunshot cracked. The woman's scream sliced the air, vibrated the floor beneath my body, rattled the glass refrigerated cases in the back of the store. Packs of cigarettes tumbled from the lowest shelf.

"Sweet Savior," she blubbered, answering whether she was dead or alive, "please, nooooo. Don't hurt me. Please don't hurt me."

"One more frickin' word, grandma, and I'm gonna blow your stupid brains out. Got it?"

Long ragged snuffles. A drawn-out moan rising in pitch. Then a squeaky, "Uh-huh."

His arm stiffened. I tensed for the fatal shot. Waited for him to snap, to make good on his threat. But instead of the explosive signal of gunfire, I heard a tinkle, soft and clear and distinctively out of place.

The front door eased open. But there was no one there. Summer heat rolled in in oppressive waves. Birds chattered in the nearby branches of a juniper, oblivious to the scene unfolding inside.

The robber flapped his eyelids in confusion. "What the —?"

I'd barely noticed the walking stick wedged at the bottom corner of the door, nudging it open, when a streak of spotted gray blazed through the gap and down the aisle. A shot cracked. The bullet whizzed past. The glass of the entry door shattered into a million tiny bits.

Undeterred, Hush barely made eye contact with me as he bounded over my head and around the counter. His gait was jerky but unbelievably fast for a dog that still couldn't flex one front leg.

The robber didn't have time to take aim again or defend himself. He spun around, fired blindly, and brought down a cardboard candy-bar display. Wrapped bars rained over the floor, a landmine of chocolate, caramel, and cookie centers scattered in bits and chunks across the checkered tiles.

Above the chaos, a throaty growl rumbled. The plastic bags filled with money flew from the robber's hold, coins plinking everywhere. He spewed curses. Fired again. The growls escalated in ferocity. Teeth sank viciously into flesh. Tore sinew and pulled limbs.

This time, the man screamed.

And Hush — the gentle soul turned raging beast — leaped up, caught the man's exposed wrist in his jaws, and clamped down. The gun clattered to the floor.

Until then, I'd been too stunned to react. My brain wasn't wired to function at lightning speed.

I should do something. Help Hush somehow.

Work boots stomped past my head as I lay there, still thinking about what to do.

Before I could process it in full, Buzz stormed behind the counter, bent over, and then stood, the gun in his hand. By the way he gripped it, I knew he'd held one before and knew how to use it.

"Ma'am," Buzz told the clerk, his aim on the robber now squirming on the floor in Hush's fanged grip, "you might want to scoot out of the way, case I have to fire. My eyesight's not what it used to be."

I couldn't see her from where I was, but I heard cigarette packs sliding across the floor as she crawled around the corner into a recess.

"You got a phone in here?" Buzz asked.

"Cell's in my pocket," the lady answered in a quaking voice.

"Call the sheriff, will you? Tell them to send an ambulance too."

She tapped at her phone. A few moments later, she started to give the dispatcher the information.

"Call your goddamned dog off!" the would-be robber shouted. "Before he kills me!"

"Hah," Buzz said with a chuckle. "Here you were shooting a gun at innocent people, and now you're saying *you* don't want to die? Pretty ironic. What've you got to live for, anyway?"

"Just get him off, okay?" His screams broke into wails of desperation. "I wasn't gonna kill nobody, man. I just needed the money. And the cigarettes."

"Oh, all right, then. You seem like a nice enough fellow. Leave it, Hush," Buzz ordered firmly but calmly.

Hush chomped down. Denim ripped.

Buzz let the dog go on for a half minute more while the man puled hysterically.

"I said leave it!"

Hush's whine was muffled by the cloth of the robber's pants leg.

"He won't hurt us, buddy," Buzz reassured. "He can't now." Then, more calmly, quieter, "Let go."

On hands and knees, I crawled around the checkout desk. The robber's face was long with terror. I remembered that feeling from the dog attack when I was young. But this time, instead of spiraling back into that vortex of paralyzing fear, I felt flushed with triumph. Not only had I survived this ordeal, I had learned the power of a dog to protect. Hush knew the difference between an innocent child and a violent stranger. He was gifted with the ability to judge a threat quickly, loyalty to those he loved, and the courage to defend them.

Even at the risk to his own life.

Hush huffed a few more breaths before loosening his hold on the man's pants. The moment he let go, the robber yanked his leg back, yelling in pain as he did so. Dark blotches seeped through the material. Just below the man's right knee, a wide hole in the jeans revealed a deep set of teeth marks, ringed in blood. At his wrist, skin flapped loose, exposing sinew. Not a large wound, but a deep one.

The man wailed again and Hush coiled tight, as if ready to spring. I touched him on the rump, his fur deceivingly soft. As he snapped his head toward me to look, I instinctively pulled my hand back, that old familiar fear flickering through me.

He took me in, his face softening. His whole body quivered and his tongue hung long, saliva mixed with blood dripping onto the floor. His head sank beneath the level of his withers.

"It's okay, Hush," I said, my voice trembling. "It's okay. Come here."

Folding to the floor, he crawled to me. He looked spent, confused, and overwhelmed — not like some rabid canine gone berserk. He'd launched himself into the gaping maw of danger to spare the lives of me, Buzz, and a woman he'd never before met.

I wrapped my arms around him, wept into the soft fur of his collar. Tears of relief and gratitude.

Buzz nudged the robber's good leg with the toe of his boot.

The man's eyes, red-rimmed and bleary, shot up. "Damn vicious dog. Soon as they see what he did to me, they're gonna —"

"Don't you remember us?"

"Never seen you before."

"Close to three months ago, I think it was. Day of that big ice storm. My dog and I were on a country road, not far from the Cumberland Parkway. Needed a ride. You picked us up."

His eyes widened with the tug of a memory, but he shook his head in denial.

"You put a gun in my face," Buzz went on. "Stole my things. Took off."

The man shook his head again, more emphatically. "You're lying. I got no idea what you're talking about. No frickin' idea."

From behind him, "They're on their way." The clerk's bosom heaved as she stepped tentatively forward. Perspiration ran down her face and neck. She laid a hand on her chest, pulling in deep, calming breaths. "I told them how you and that dog there saved us. Thank the Lord you showed up when you did."

Buzz gave the faintest of nods. He motioned her over. She stepped around the robber to stand beside him.

"Hold this." Buzz handed her the gun. "Keep it on him."

The clerk held it loosely, like it was coated with a poison that could be absorbed through the skin. But she did as Buzz asked and pointed the barrel in the general direction of the robber. "What am I supposed to do with it?"

"If he moves ... shoot him."

Closing his eyes, Buzz brought a hand to his left shoulder and pressed it. It wasn't until he drew his hand away to look that I noticed the blood on his fingertips.

"Look at that," he muttered. "Bastard got me."

With that, he crumpled to the floor, unconscious.

—o00o—

One glance in the rearview mirror and Noreen grimaced. "Can you make him sit still?"

Whining, Hush hopped back and forth on the rear seat of her car to look from one window to another as we sped along the state highway. She'd laid out a raincoat and an old fleece on the seat, but Hush had already kicked them off in his franticness to find Buzz.

I lowered my window part way, so Hush could get a breeze. The air conditioning was on, but it didn't seem to be reaching in back. "Don't think so," I said.

"Well, he's slobbering on the windows."

"I'll clean them later."

"And shedding."

"I'll vacuum."

When the ambulance had arrived at the filling station fifteen minutes after the county sheriff showed up, they'd taken Buzz first. The second deputy on the scene loaded the robber into his patrol car to transport him to the hospital. As wicked as the guy's wounds looked, they'd deemed them not life-threatening, despite his protests that he was dying, even as Buzz lay on the ground unresponsive.

Thankfully, Buzz's heartbeat had been strong and the bleeding not profuse. Still, I worried about him. Obviously Hush did too. I even think Noreen — her knuckles white as she gripped the steering wheel — was concerned. Or maybe she was ticked off that we'd somehow landed ourselves in that situation. It was hard to tell with her.

"Sorry you got called out of work," I said. The cops had released me to her after a cursory interrogation, with the promise that they'd follow up at the hospital once we got there.

She flipped on her turn signal at a stoplight in the middle of nowhere. A sign pointed left: Somerset 2.0 miles. "Don't be."

"Well, I am. I know you don't like to miss work —"

"The place would fall apart without me, that's all. If they'd hire more competent people, maybe I wouldn't have to manage every little mundane detail, but it's not exactly a place with jobs that require a lot of skills, so we get whoever will take the work. Then I get stuck …" The light changed to green. She waited for another car to pass, then turned. "I suppose I shouldn't be complaining at a time like this."

That seemed so out of character for her that I couldn't help but stare at the side of her head to see if she was suddenly going to shapeshift from a troll into a unicorn.

"Look, I know I'm not always easy to live with —"

I let that one go. I was sure it hadn't been easy for her to say, but I wasn't really interested in her side of things right now.

"But I've gotten used to living by myself, and —"

Here we go with the excuses. I turned my attention to the smattering of wildflowers on the roadside and halfway tuned her out.

227

Buzz was lying in a hospital emergency room, the life leaking out of him, and she was trying to make herself feel better about being such a witch by rationalizing her behavior. Whatever.

Untended land gave way to neighborhoods as we entered the outskirts of Somerset. Modest brick homes with tidy yards crowded together. Every now and then a strip mall or convenience store or used car lot broke up the monotony. There was more going on here than in Faderville, but that wasn't saying much. As backward as this area was, though, I was getting used to it. Heck, I could stay around here a while. Maybe forever. As long as Buzz was here.

A wet nose bumped my ear. Hush snorted. I pressed my fingertips to his soft muzzle and gazed into those wild eyes, half-blue, half-brown. Eyes that, not so long ago, had terrified me.

" — Lana wasn't ..."

I snapped to attention. "Wasn't what?"

Noreen glanced at me. "Haven't you been listening?"

"No," I confessed. "Sorry, I was thinking about Buzz."

We turned into the hospital parking lot and Noreen found an empty space in the first row by the Emergency entrance. She turned the ignition off and stared out the window, looking like she'd just lost her last best friend.

"Lana wasn't ours by birth. She was adopted."

"Oh." For a minute, that was the only word I could manage. I'd never questioned the fact that Lana looked nothing like Noreen, figuring maybe she'd favored Roland or some other ancestor.

Then it dawned on me. I wasn't Noreen's granddaughter. Legally I suppose I was, but still, that little bit of news was just too big to get my head around.

"Bellamy?"

Instead of answering, I fumbled around for Hush's leash. It took me a few moments to realize I'd left it in the truck back at the gas station.

"Bellamy ..."

My hand went to my waist. I hadn't worn a belt. If I'd had a belt on, I could've used that as a leash. How was I supposed to keep Hush from wandering off in search of Buzz? Maybe Noreen had a bungee cord or some rope in the trunk.

"Beam ..." She placed a hand on my shoulder, light and surprisingly gentle. Her thumb rubbed at my sleeve. "There's more I need to tell you."

I popped open the console between the seats. An auxiliary cable. Perfect. I looped it through the leash ring of Hush's collar, got out of the car, and then let him out, stooping by the open window just long enough to say, "I'm going to check on Buzz."

"Bellamy, you can't take that dog —"

I sprinted across the lane, hopped over the sidewalk, and barreled up to the revolving door. My left arm jerked backward as Hush put the brakes on. How was I supposed to get Hush through that?

"Bellamy, wait!"

How many times was that woman going to screech my name?

Over to the side, an automatic door whooshed open. A young mother dragging a bleary-eyed toddler stepped through.

"When we get home, I'm giving you a piece of my mind, young man." She half-swung him around to face her and crouched down, taking him firmly by the shoulders. "You do not ever, ever, EVER stick peas up your nose, do you understand me?"

Fingers in his mouth, he nodded dully, but wouldn't look at her. His eyes were all red and puffy and his cheeks drenched.

"Do you understand why I'm telling you this?"

His gaze wandered to Hush, whose ears were flattened to his skull. Hush's tongue hung down, strings of saliva dripping onto the pale concrete to form a dark pool. That was when I noticed the blood stains on Hush's front legs and neck.

"Tobias Bartholomew Norton." The mother shook him once

lightly, her voice stern. "Do you?"

He shrugged.

Behind me, Noreen huffed her way across the parking lot.

"Because" — the mother swept the hair from her son's forehead — "it could go down the wrong pipe and you could choke. You'd stop breathing, then, and when you stop breathing, you die." Her arms enclosed him, his small head buried in the lengths of her dark brown hair. "I don't want to lose you, Toby." More softly, "I don't know what I'd do without you."

Toby turned his head to peek at Hush, but Hush's sights were fixed on the now closed door. The dog barked once, then lurched toward it. I let him pull me. He came to a stop in front of the door and tapped at it with his paw, whining.

A sticker in the middle of the door said: Service Dogs Permitted.

"Bellamy," Noreen barked, "you can't take the dog —"

I hit the big button on the brick wall and the doors slid open. Cold air wafted out. Hush took one look at me, as if to make sure I'd follow, then darted in, head low, his nails scrabbling at the slick floor.

We went up to the receptionist's desk, Noreen trailing behind, grumbling about how we were going to get kicked out.

"We're here to see Buzz Donovan," I announced.

The lady behind the counter looked up at me. Where she was sitting, she couldn't see Hush and apparently she'd been too busy reading her paperback romance novel to notice him walking in. There were only two other people sitting in the waiting area and they didn't seem to be too stressed out, so I figured there wasn't much else going on at the moment.

She laid down her book and clicked the mouse to wake her computer up. "Bubba Donaldson, did you say?"

"Donovan. Buzz Donovan," Noreen said. "Just came in with a gunshot."

"Ohhh, him." The woman sat back, the chair creaking under her weight. "Yeah, he's back there. Don't get many gunshots here. Hunting accident?"

"Robbery." Noreen glanced down at the dog, her lip twitching as she took in the blood on his fur.

"Robbery — really now?" Her head swinging side to side, the receptionist clucked her tongue. "He the victim or the perpetrator?"

"Hero," I said. Hush was, too, for that matter, but if she wasn't observant enough to see the dog, I wasn't going to bring him to her attention. "Can we see him now?"

"Are you kinfolk?"

Kinfolk? Who used that word in this century? I spoke up before Noreen could ruin our chances. "Yeah, we are."

The woman leaned closer to her computer screen, tapped at a few more keys. "Immediate family?"

"He doesn't have any immediate family," I told her, pretty sure it was true. "We're it. I'm his niece. This is my grandmother."

"Funny, you two don't look anything alike."

"I take after my father."

Noreen coughed. Or gagged, I wasn't sure.

"I'll have to check if you're allowed to see him. He's still under emergency care." She picked up the phone and dialed. When a voice came on the other end, she made a quick explanation, giving us both the squinty-eyed, sideways look of suspicion.

The two older ladies camped out by the TV had begun whispering and pointing at Hush, whose butt was pressed against my leg. He was watching a door to a hallway, his nose twitching as he sniffed at the air and his back legs trembling anxiously. I had my makeshift leash wound so tight around my fingers they were losing circulation.

"Uh-huh, yes, send Porter. In the meanwhile ... All right, I'll tell them." The receptionist hung up and pointed to the waiting area. "Have a seat. Someone will be out to talk to you."

231

"Soon?" I asked.

"Eventually."

"Is he okay?"

"He's being treated."

That still didn't answer my question. He could be hooked up on life support, for all I knew. I shoved myself against the counter ledge, my agitation climbing. "Look, lady, I was in a gas station waiting to pay when a man held the cashier up at gunpoint. Buzz saved us. I have to see him."

"You will. For now, you need to have a seat. Now please don't make me call security on you, because I will."

Noreen marched off without further warning, but I stayed glued where I was. Hush was pulling so tight on the leash that I knew if I headed anywhere in the direction of that door he was staring down that he'd drag me across the floor like a sled dog on the Iditarod trail. And yet, I couldn't stand at the desk all day. Maybe I'd wait until the lady disappeared into her book again.

That was when she got up and peered over the counter edge. And a security guard sauntered through those swinging doors to the back hallway, his badge flashing and his gun hanging menacingly at his belt.

"Thank goodness you're here, Porter," the receptionist said, her gaze finally sliding to Hush.

"There a problem, Maxine?" He hooked both thumbs in his belt to rearrange it on his narrow hips. Milk-faced and scrawny, the guy could've passed for a high schooler. He came toward us, his head tilting as he took Hush in. I felt Hush's chest vibrate with the barest of growls. Apparently the guard didn't hear it, because three feet away, he knelt down and held out a hand, palm down, for Hush to sniff.

Hush wasn't the least bit interested, though. His eyes were still glued to that back door. He tugged toward it again, but I held firm.

"Hey there, buddy," the guard cooed. "Aren't you a beaut?" He looked down at Hush's blood-stained legs. "What'd ya get into, anyway? Lost a fight with a coon, did ya?"

"Porter, that's a dog," Maxine said. "It doesn't belong in an emergency room."

Reluctantly, he drew his hand back. "Oh, right." Standing, he hitched a thumb at the outer doors. "You'll have to take him outside."

"It's a hundred degrees out there," I protested.

He scratched at his neck before saying to Maxine, "She's got a point."

"So fetch him a cup of water," she said, "and show them to the maples on the other side of the parking lot. Plenty of shade there."

This wasn't going well. I hadn't thought it through. Maybe if I created a diversion … No, I should just ask nicely. Tell them how Buzz and Hush had saved us. They couldn't possibly turn us away then.

The guard motioned toward the exit. "I'll show you a nice spot. I can probably even rustle up a bologna sandwich from the cafeteria for the little fella." He started walking away, like he was sure I was going to follow.

Hush yanked my arm so hard he about pulled it out of the socket. I tried to pull back, to dig in my heels, but the cord whipped through my fingers and out of my hold. Hush flew across the waiting room, his nails barely clicking on the hard surface before he hit the space between the two doors full force. They swung open so hard they hit the stoppers on the inside of the hallway wall with a bone-jarring *bang!*

Before I could call out his name, another voice sounded.

"Beam?"

Hunter McHugh emerged through the revolving door, his wavy hair all puffed up from the humidity.

The guard had already taken off after Hush. The receptionist was on the phone, undoubtedly calling in reinforcements. Noreen looked from the door to me, and back again. And the two old ladies sat there taking it all in as if it were a circus act.

"I came as soon as I heard." Hunter dragged an arm across his sweat-drenched forehead. When he got to me, he surveyed the room, nodding to Noreen. "What's going on? Is Buzz okay?"

I stared at the doors to the back hallway, dread sucking at my insides. The guard had a gun. What if he used it on Hush?

"Hey, Beam." Hunter waved a hand in front of my face, but I leaned to the side to look past him. "My stepdad, Brad Dunphy, said he got word that Buzz had been shot, but it didn't appear to be life-threatening. If he's in the back, then where's —"

From somewhere down the hallway, a crash sounded: metal clattering and skidding across the hard floor. Shouts followed. Glass shattered.

My heart clogging my throat, I ran for those doors, willing to take a bullet for the dog who had saved me.

chapter 18

Buzz

"Don't leave, Buzz. Don't leave, okay?"

"He's unresponsive. Pulse rate?"

"I need you ... Hush needs you."

"No excessive blood loss. Bullet doesn't appear to be lodged in his arm."

"And this hooligan pulls a gun and starts shooting at anything and everything."

"Hang in there, Buzz. Everything's going to be all right, yeah? Just like you always say."

"That old man sicced his dog on him and snatched that pistol right out of his hand."

"Blood pressure ninety over sixty — and dropping."

"But the bullet only grazed him ..."

"Oh, my Lord, is he ... dying? Please, not on my shift. I'm probably going to lose my job as is. I don't need that on my conscience, too."

"He has a brain tumor. He has seizures, sometimes."

"Thanks, that helps to know."

"Are you a relative?"

"No, just a friend."

"I'm sorry, you can't come with us, then. We're taking him to Somerset Community Hospital."

"Is he going to be okay?"

There was a pause, a short one, but an ominous one.

"I don't really know. We're doing everything we can."

"Heart rate falling rapidly. Fifty beats per minute ... Forty-two ..."

"Buzz?"

"Thirty-six ... Thirty ..."

"We have respiratory failure."

"Get the defib ready."

"Stand back."

"Buzz! Buuuzzz!!!"

—o00o—

Buzz not only heard every word, he understood them all. And yet, strangely, he had no reaction. No worry, no fear, no roiling rage or murky fog of grief. He merely processed it all like an unconcerned observer.

What he wasn't quite sure of was whether or not he could actually *see* those around him. He certainly didn't *feel* anything, not in the physical sense. Fuzzy shapes floated before him — or sometimes beneath. He seemed to be hovering. Two images were vaguely recognizable: one human, one dog. He was drawn to them. Not attracted so much, as connected.

The girl, full of promise, was mired by her past. She desperately wanted to accept the goodness offered her, but questioned its permanence in her life.

The dog had tried relentlessly to show her that nothing mattered more than the moment in which they lived, aware and alive. And it *had* made a difference. Buzz sensed her fondness for the dog and for him, flowing forth like a newly sprung spring. Yet the love had always been there within her.

Who was she? Who —?

Ah, yes, Bellamy … Beam. That was her name. And the dog — he was Hush.

He observed them, poised at the hospital doors, one straining to enter to find him, one hesitant of what she might discover. Loyalty and loss. Hope and apprehension.

After them straggled an older woman. Noreen. She'd suffered disappointment too. Learned to guard herself against love in order to protect her heart. There was more control that way. But with it also came loneliness, and she had tired of the solitude, although she had not known that until recently.

Below him, a team of unfamiliar faces busied themselves with dire purpose. Their work was selfless, comprised of a series of rapid decisions, followed by tedious stretches of waiting and observation. Their eyes wearied, their motions were often automatic. Still, they persisted — cleaning the blood from his wound, stitching the laceration in his flesh, monitoring every bodily function they could. He was a stranger to them, and they to him. Yet they would not relent. They were intent on rejoining his consciousness to his body. The soul to the corporeal.

Despite the fact that he could take all this in, there was an uncertainty. Like a question was being asked of him that he didn't fully understand. A choice to be made.

He resisted looking above him. He knew the view was clearer there. That there was light and color dazzling to the eye. That taste and sound and sight all blended together in a glittering nebula of musical notes and a bouquet of aromas, a symphony to the senses. A place where pain and fear, hate and envy, greed and despondency failed to exist. Where joy, peace, and love were ever present, and time was entirely absent. Where yesterday and today and tomorrow were all one and the same. Where here and there merged, each molecule and parcel of energy the element of an entirety, inseparable.

And yet, there was uniqueness in the moment, the single, the solitary. Wonder in the workings of the parts of the universe. The past gave meaning to the present — and direction for the future. Here and now could not exist without there and then.

Buzz was not ready to depart from all that.

So, he decided to return. To stay as long as he could. Long enough to matter.

—o00o—

A nose — cool and damp — jabbed at the tender hollow of his armpit. Buzz pulled in oxygen, his ribs aching as they expanded. A muzzle, as soft as it was insistent, burrowed between his neck and shoulder, emitting a loud snort. A body nudged his arm aside, formed itself to his. Buzz drifted along, letting his senses awaken slowly, savoring each breath, his heartbeat synchronizing with another. He stretched his hand, pulled it closer to the warmth beside him. Fur tickled at his fingers.

"He's waking up," a voice murmured. Then, as if in surprise, "He's waking up!"

Another voice from farther away, a woman's: "What are you ...?" Footsteps. A pause. "Where'd that dog come from? Who let it in here?"

"I don't know. I just left for a minute and on my way back I heard something. I got here to find them like this. Wasn't he in a coma?"

"Unresponsive — and slipping rapidly. His organs were on the verge of shutting down."

"Then how —?"

"Don't matter, does it?" the woman said, her voice thick with the syrupy twang of the South. "Some things you just don't question."

"If that don't beat all. Never seen anything like it. I thought he was a goner for sure."

"You and me both."

"Should we get the dog out of here?"

"No, not yet. He's not hurting anything. Besides, what would we do with him? It's like he came out of nowhere."

"I'll call Dr. Anderson. Let him know the patient's awake."

"Hey, do you think ...?"

"Think what?"

"The dog. Do you think the dog had something to do with him waking up?"

"Like some sort of guardian angel? Maybe. Like I said, some things you just don't question."

—o0Oo—

"Say something, Buzz," Beam pleaded. Then, in a tearful whisper, "Say ... *anything*."

Until then, he'd only wanted to sleep, but the suggestion nudged him upward. Buzz pried his eyelids open, yearning toward the sound of the familiar voice. Every muscle in his body screamed with fatigue. If he didn't know better, he'd have thought he'd just raced an ultramarathon, climbed Mt. Everest, and been run over by a fleet of semis all at once. It took all his energy just to will the blood through his veins.

But that voice ... That voice buoyed him. Toward a light more radiant than any he'd ever seen.

"Sunbeam?" The word barely registered in his own ears, but he'd

239

felt it rustle in his throat and flutter across his tongue, as light and airy as a dragonfly's wings.

She must have heard him. Because she smiled. And his heart beat stronger.

"I'm here. I've been here for hours." Beam sat on the edge of his bed, a droopy but relieved half smile on her face. "I told them I was your niece, but I don't think they believed me, because they weren't going to let me in here until Hunter came along." She tilted her head to the right.

On the other side of the bed stood Hunter, fresher-looking and more alert than Beam. "Quite the day you've had." He came closer. "One of the deputies on the scene showed up at the hospital not long ago. He said one of the Lexington TV stations is sending a crew to interview you."

It took a few moments of hauling it up from the depths of his chest, but Buzz finally found his voice, as rough and heavy as an unhewn timber. "They'd best speak to Beam. Not fit for much talkin' myself, just yet."

Hunter nodded. "I suppose they'll want the dog in the segment." He ruffled Hush's coat, then raked the hairs back into place with his fingers, as if anyone cared.

"Keep Hush out of it too," Buzz uttered hoarsely. "All those damn cameras ... He doesn't want the attention either."

In today's world, news spread all too quickly. One picture, one video on the internet could reach millions in a matter of hours. Then, days, months, or even years later, it could still be dredged up. If anyone in their old L.A. neighborhood saw Buzz or Hush, recognized them from before —

"Maybe later, then," Hunter said. "When things have settled down and after you're back on your feet."

"Probably not."

"If you say so. You two just take time to rest up. Someday I'll tell you the story of how our Aussie, Echo, saved my daughter Hannah. When you're up to it."

Buzz smiled his consent. Words were too much of an effort. He'd known since the day he met Hush how special his kind was. Hush had already saved his life countless times. Still, he didn't feel the need to crow about it. It was just the way things were. How it was supposed to be.

"Take as much time as you need, Buzz." A hand patted him tentatively on the shoulder. It was Noreen. He'd sensed her, but her presence hadn't registered with him until then.

"Don't plan on staying here any longer than I have to," he grumbled.

"Well, you aren't leaving today, I can tell you that. Bellamy and I are fixing up the mudroom tonight, more permanent like, so you'll have a place of your own when they say you're free to go. Dr. McHugh is going to pick up a twin bed from the secondhand store in Faderville tomorrow. There's just enough space for it over to the side, and we can squeeze a dresser in there and put a TV on it for you. And you don't have to worry about traffic coming through. We can use the front door just as well. You stay as long as you want. I don't care what anyone says. They can flap their jaws all they want. You're welcome in my house."

Even though he still felt like he'd be imposing on Noreen, it was much more appealing than being here. He didn't like hospitals. It wasn't the anti-septic smell of them, or all the needles and tests and pills. He didn't like being fussed over and feeling helpless. He'd much rather keel over dead in the middle of doing something meaningful than fade away hooked up to machines that breathed for him.

Either way, at least he didn't have to worry about who would take care of Hush anymore. That was settled.

The nurse who'd been there when he first regained consciousness came into the room and said something to Hunter. He motioned to

Noreen and they left together. But Beam stayed.

She reached across him to lay her hand on top of Hush's paw, pressed atop his chest.

"Promise me you won't do that again," she said.

"Save your skinny rear end?" He tried to laugh, but it came out a raspy cough instead.

She waited until he had his breath back. "You almost died on me, Buzz. You can't leave us."

Technically, he *had* died. Again. Yet he kept getting sent back. Maybe 'sent back' wasn't the right term. Turned away? No, that implied a gatekeeper and he hadn't seen hide nor hair of any such thing. Called back? That was more like it. But for what reason? Or was it just chance?

Whatever it was, eventually it would happen again and he wouldn't return.

He lifted his hand to brush her cheek with his thumb. "In case you haven't noticed, I'm not the healthiest of individuals. I'm not going to live forever, you know. No one does."

"Buzz ... don't say things like that."

But he'd had to say it. Truth didn't disappear just because you refused to look at it. Better to confront it, acknowledge its presence. Otherwise it was like a bogeyman riding on your back, breathing fear down your neck.

A long silence stretched between them, the words unsaid more profound than anything they could have spoken.

Down the hall, the nurse introduced a doctor to Hunter and Noreen, who directed them through a set of doors. A few moments later, their voices were gone, but Buzz knew the conversation was about him and that the news was grave.

A sheriff's deputy passed by in the hallway, pausing just long enough to read the room number on the plaque by the door. He glanced toward the hospital bed, took one look at Hush, and backed around the corner.

Buzz tucked his fingers beneath Hush's collar, not ready to let him go.

They knew now. They had to.

Beam's dark hair was gathered low on her neck in a disheveled ponytail. Her jaw quivered with the tremble of an indrawn breath.

Somehow he had to make it easier for her. Yet not right now. She'd been through enough already. For that matter, so had he.

He didn't want to have to choose between Beam and Hush. Shouldn't have to.

But the dog had been with him first. The dog had saved his life more times than he could remember. The dog had slept beside him on cold, dark nights when all his possessions fit in one ragged backpack and he'd had to leave his own past behind.

Besides, Beam's life wasn't in jeopardy anymore.

The dog, though ... the dog deserved to live.

chapter 19

Beam

Noreen sat across from me in the hospital cafeteria, stirring a cup of steaming black coffee with a spoon, her face pinched in a look of perpetual irritation.

"Bellamy ..." Her spoon rattled against the bottom of the porcelain mug. *Ting, ting, ting.* "I spoke to the surgeon after the shooting" — her gaze flicked from her coffee to me, then back again as she went on stirring it — "about Buzz."

She'd left work at midmorning to bring me to the hospital to visit Buzz, but upon hearing I hadn't eaten yet today, she'd insisted on feeding me. Not that I had any appetite to speak of. Last night I'd been unable to fall asleep until halfway through the night, my concern about Buzz too great to push aside. At least they'd allowed Hush to stay with him.

Picking up my fork, I pushed the fruit cocktail around on my tray, dividing the grapes from the cherries, the pears from the oranges, then piling them back together again. In a separate compartment, the mashed potatoes sat untouched in a lopsided lump, congealed gravy oozing down the side. Finally, I gathered a few crumbles of meatloaf onto my fork to shove into my mouth. I forced two forkfuls down before I realized I wasn't even remotely hungry. But if I kept eating, I wouldn't have to talk. And so I ate, oblivious to what any of the food tasted like.

Noreen was halfway through carving up her open-faced turkey sandwich before she spoke again. "He has a tumor ... in his brain." She didn't look up from her plate, but she was cutting slowly now, like she could hardly saw with the knife and arrange the words at the same time.

"I know."

Laying down her knife, she wiped at the corner of her mouth with a paper napkin. "You do?"

"Sure. It's what causes his seizures."

Relief softened the harshness of her features. "Oh, all right. I didn't know if you knew." She speared another forkful of her sandwich, popped it in her mouth, and swallowed. "It isn't cancerous."

"I know."

She folded her napkin neatly and placed her fork beside it, right between her knife and her spoon, so it looked like an unused place setting. "It *is* growing, though."

Did she not know the definition of a tumor? It was tissue growing out of control. Replicating cells that didn't have an off switch. The question was: how fast and how out of control? But the way she said it ... I wasn't sure I wanted to know more. Still, I had to know there was hope. "There's a treatment for it, right?"

"There is, but ..." Folding her hands in her lap, she looked up. The same look you gave a little kid when their hamster was dying and there was no way to save it. "If he had sought treatment sooner, there might have been more hope. But now ... it's hard to say. They could try, Dr. Anderson said. It would involve experimental drugs ... Some kind of cyberknife, too; although some healthy cells could be damaged by the radiation. It would mean months in and out of the hospital. Unfortunately, the place for the treatment is nowhere close to here. He'd have to go far away. And he'd likely get sicker before he got better" — her voice faded almost to a whisper — "if ... if he did at all."

If ...

I hated that word. Especially when you said it all by itself. Such a short word. So much it could mean.

Through the second-story window, I watched people in the parking lot down below come and go, wondering if they were here to visit a newborn baby, a friend who'd just had knee surgery, or an elderly relative who was dying.

I had no idea what Oakley would think in a situation like this. He probably thought people lived forever. As long as someone remembered them, I suppose in a way they did.

Panic hit me like a bullet to the chest. Unexpectedly. Out of nowhere.

I couldn't stay here. I had to see Buzz and Hush.

Picking up my tray, I stood to look for the trash receptacle so abruptly I bumped the table and sent a glass filled with ice toppling on its side. I swept the cubes onto my tray and blotted at the puddle left behind.

"Sit down and eat, Bellamy."

"I'm not hungry."

I started toward the tray return counter, an inexplicable urgency bubbling up inside me.

"Where are you going?" she called after me.

I didn't have time to explain. Couldn't, even if I'd tried.

I just *had* to get out of there. Had to find them.

A trio of nurses turned around in their chairs to watch as Noreen got up to follow me. I weaved through a scattering of round tables and plastic chairs, as people pulled their feet out of my way and scooted their chairs in. I slid the tray onto the metal shelves without bothering to empty my food into the trash.

With a shove, I pushed the release bar on the door. Long banks of fluorescent lights flooded the corridor in either direction. To the left against the wall, a gurney sat empty.

I started that way, uncertain whether it was the shortest way to Buzz's room. Or even the right way at all.

An elderly volunteer stepped out of the way just in time before I plowed him over.

"Sorry," I mumbled, trying to regain my bearings. The place was a maze of hallways and bends and doors that all looked alike.

He waved his hands at me. "You're all right. I wasn't looking where I was going."

With a nod, he continued on, a clipboard tucked beneath his arm.

Then I heard footsteps — quick and heavy — behind me. The other way down the corridor, a deputy appeared through an opening beside a sign with an arrow pointing in the direction he'd just come from. Beneath the arrow, it said 'Elevator to Emergency'.

He pressed a button on his shoulder mic. "Got it. Headed that way."

Then he took off in the other direction. I followed him, not even sure where he was headed, but certain it had something to do with Buzz. Sometimes your gut just knew things.

—o00o—

Buzz's bed lay empty. The only sign he'd been there was a crumpled set of sheets and an indented pillow.

A small huddle of hospital staff and Porter, the security guard, blocked the doorway to Buzz's hospital room. Stepping to the left, I stood on tiptoe to get a clear view into the bathroom, but it, too, was vacant.

No Buzz. No Hush.

The deputy was in the room, pulling out drawers and checking items on the portable tray table. Not that there was anything to find, but it was almost like he was searching for clues.

"Bellamy."

I spun around to see Noreen hurrying toward me. The closer she came, the more worried I got. Halfway down the hall, she grabbed a passing nurse and spoke lowly to her. The nurse shook her head several times, shrugged, and went on.

My first thought in not seeing Buzz in his room had been that something had happened to him. But if he'd died, they wouldn't have taken him from the room so soon. And if he'd suffered a medical emergency, there wouldn't be a security guard and a deputy there.

Porter joined the deputy in his search of the room. I tapped on the shoulder of the male nurse in front of me. Intent on the conversation between the other nurses, he ignored me. I tapped harder. Nothing. I tugged on his sleeve. "What happened? Where is he?"

Without looking at me, he held up a hand.

"Where's my friend Buzz?"

Finally he turned around. "Who?"

"Buzz. Buzz Donovan. I was just here with him, less than an hour ago."

He shook his head. "There's no Donovan on this floor. You must have the wrong room."

"But I was just here with him!"

"Porter," he called, curling a finger in the air, "come here for a second."

Bewildered, I searched Porter's face for some sign that there was a simple answer to this. That they'd merely moved him to a different room, taken him for an X-ray, anything that would make sudden sense out of this. But Porter merely took me by the arm and led me down the hallway. Away from the whispering nurses and nosy deputy. Toward Noreen.

She spoke before he could say anything. "I heard the gist of it. How on earth does something like this happen?"

"*What* happened?" I said, that jittery sense of panic mushrooming to atomic proportions.

Wearing an expression that was half sympathy, half concern, Noreen tilted her head. "It appears Buzz slipped out of the hospital this morning."

"In broad daylight?" But the place was filled with people. There were doors to get through, hallways to navigate. He hadn't even been on the ground floor.

"Don't worry, miss," Porter said. "He can't get far in his condition. And with a dog, someone's sure to spot him."

chapter 20

Buzz

Coming up with a plan had been easy enough. It was the execution of it that was proving difficult.

Earlier, an orderly had wheeled Buzz two floors down for an MRI — as if the X-ray and CAT scan hadn't shown enough of his insides to map all his internal organs down to their mitochondrial DNA. On the way, just around the corner from his room, they'd passed a door marked 'Laundry'.

The convenience of it hadn't dawned on him until the paranoia began to settle in. He had to get out of here. They would figure him out. Or already had and were just putting everything in order. Soon, they'd haul him off to jail again. But that wasn't the worst part. If they took Hush, if they knew the dog's record, he'd be a goner. Dogs were never 'innocent until proven guilty'. If someone said a dog bit a person, the dog was put to sleep. No trial. No due process. Just a death sentence. All because some neighbor had a bone to pick.

When the same orderly later parked an empty gurney across the hall from Buzz, opportunity had arrived. So Buzz forced himself out of bed, battled dizziness, and crept to the door while listening for footsteps. The morning shift change had already occurred. Many patients were still asleep. The nurse at the central desk was busily typing away. The dog at his knee, he tiptoed down the hallway and into the laundry room.

Buzz pulled the green surgical cap lower to cover his bushy eyebrows. He put a pair of scrubs over the T-shirt and jeans Noreen had brought him from home. For extra measure, he borrowed a pair of eyeglasses from the patient next door, who'd been snoring away. Anything to disguise his identity. Then he coaxed Hush onto the gurney, covered him with a sheet, and told him to stay.

That proved to be the tricky part.

Hush was a dog, after all. He liked going on rides. Any kind of ride. He got excited about them. A hospital bed on wheels was no exception. The long lump posing as a corpse sat up, tenting the sheet.

"Lie down," Buzz mumbled.

Reluctantly, Hush collapsed onto his side. A few seconds later, the leather of his black nose poked between the sheet and pillow.

"Be *still*," Buzz growled, tugging the corner of the sheet up as far as he could.

The nurse at the station desk glanced up. Smiling, Buzz nodded at her. She grunted a greeting, then went back to work shuffling paperwork and stacking clipboards. Buzz passed four more doorways, but only one patient was awake and looked his way. An older woman, probably in her nineties. He was pretty sure she couldn't see that far. He hurried past to the elevator. There, he punched the ground floor button and waited. And waited. And waited.

Still weak from his ordeal, he leaned heavily on the gurney. It would get him out of this place, but he'd have to find a new walking stick somewhere, since no one had bothered to return the one that had taken him three-fourths the way across the continent.

The numbered lights beside the elevator blipped agonizingly

slowly. *Ding!* The doors burped open to reveal an empty elevator. Good. Moving past a distracted nurse was one thing, but standing for a minute in close quarters with someone else was too risky. Buzz pushed the gurney in, mumbling another 'stay' command. Just as he moved around to the other side, a doctor dressed in full surgical gear sprinted toward him.

"Hold the doors!"

Buzz panicked, searching for the button that closed the doors. Just as he reached toward the panel, one of Hush's back feet kicked outward to peek beneath the edge of the sheet nearest the open door. Quickly, Buzz grabbed the corner to rearrange it. The doors began to close. Relief washed over Buzz.

Until a hand wedged between the rubberized edges of the elevator door. Four inches from freedom.

The door whooshed open. A short, young, female doctor hopped in.

"Whew!" She swept the cap from her head. Dark curls tumbled out. "That was close. Thanks for holding it."

He hadn't, but he wasn't about to argue with her.

A few seconds of silence. And then, "You must be the new guy. Rick, is it?"

"Yeah." If she wanted to call him Rick for now, so be it. He'd never see her again. Or Beam.

A little pang shot through his heart.

No, he couldn't think about her. She'd be mad as hell at him, but he'd send her a letter later, explaining everything. She'd forgive him. He hoped.

"Nice to meet you, Rick," the doctor said. She had the weary look of a resident on her fourth straight twelve-hour shift in four days. Still, she was bubbly. Like if she let herself slow down, she'd keel over from exhaustion.

The door finally closed and there was the gentle shift of gravity beneath them as the car started downward. Buzz stared at the numbered buttons, as if he could will this ride over with quicker. Hush's breaths puffed softly beneath the sheet.

"I'm Nikki — Nikki Hildreth. You can skip the 'Dr.' part. I'm still not used to it myself. Always surprises me when people say it: *Dr. Hildreth, Dr. Hildreth*. It's like they're talking to someone else. Takes a moment to register. But anyway —"

There was an awkward pause. Buzz's gaze drifted to her. She'd stuck her hand out to shake his. A headache pulsed behind his eyeballs. His vision blurred until he saw two of her.

"Oh, sorry." She pulled her hand back, looked down at the lump beneath the gurney. Then in a more subdued voice, "I should be more respectful. On your way to the morgue, huh?"

He nodded. The glasses slid down his nose. His heart was racing. Cold sweat trickled over his temples. If he hadn't been leaning on the gurney, he might have fallen over. He blinked hard and his vision sharpened.

"Are you okay?" she asked.

A bell dinged and the doors parted.

He forced the words out. "Fine, fine. Just ..." — he looked down at the lump, aware of Hush stretching a leg, and placed a hand on it to still it — "these things stay with you." He stressed the word 'stay', hoping she wouldn't think his behavior strange and alert anyone.

"Gotcha," she said.

Buzz's heart skipped a beat.

"I feel the same way. You'd think after all those cadavers I'd get used to it, but not really. Especially not when it's a kid."

She stepped off before him. Just as he was about to push the gurney through the doors, she turned around.

"The morgue is downstairs," she said.

"Sorry, I wasn't paying attention. Thanks."

He let the doors go shut, rode down the extra floor, then came

253

back up. It seemed to Buzz like it took half an hour, even though it was probably only an extra couple of minutes. When he finally got out at the ground floor, an emergency exit plan map was taped to the wall opposite.

One turn and a short hallway later, they arrived at a rear exit. He held his breath, looked up and down the hallway, then parked the gurney in an alcove near some vending machines. A supply closet door stood on one wall. He released Hush from his hiding place and ducked inside the closet, where he shed his borrowed hospital attire and glasses.

As he tucked in his shirt, the stitches in his arm pulled tight. His muscles there were sore. So sore he couldn't raise his arm above waist level. Small inconvenience. He'd survive. For a while, at least. Hopefully long enough to get where he was going.

Which was pretty far away yet, once he thought about it.

Tentatively, he exited the closet. Voices echoed down the hallway. Buzz leaned against the wall, his energy level already sinking. The excitement of yesterday's robbery, the stress of being held captive in a hospital, the threat of having his best friend taken from him — it had all been too much. He needed to get out of here. Go far away. Be alone. Just him and his dog.

When the voices were gone, he ventured forth again, toward the outside exit. There were no alarm warnings posted by the door. No security guard. Just a camera with a blinking red light that would undoubtedly record his escape.

"Let's go," he said to Hush. Keeping his head down, he went out the door.

Out into broad daylight. Into the suffocating heat. Onto a sidewalk that wound around an endless parking lot. Across from which stretched a road heavy with traffic. In sight of hundreds of eyes.

—o0Oo—

No one stopped them. No one — not that he noticed, at least — even stared. He and Hush simply walked down the sidewalk along the main road until they came to a cross street that led through a sleepy neighborhood.

The shade there was dense. Hush's tongue hung down. His panting was heavy. So heavy that Buzz regretted taking him out in this. They'd go a ways, get farther from the hospital, then find a shady spot out of the way to hide until nightfall. And food. They'd need to find food. Problem was, he had no idea where to find any around here. Nothing but houses around here and he couldn't raid trashcans in the daytime. Maybe he should've waited to leave the hospital until after they'd brought him breakfast. But the place would have been busier then. No, it was better they left when they did.

In contrast to the main road, the side street was relatively empty. Apparently, everyone was either at work or hiding in air-conditioned comfort. Buzz and Hush headed that way. They passed a pair of young mothers pushing jogging strollers, but the women were too absorbed in their own conversations to even look his way.

Two blocks later, Buzz and Hush walked by an older man washing his car in his driveway. Where the stream of soapy water ran from the driveway to spill over the sidewalk, Hush stopped abruptly. He sniffed the water and whined.

"Your dog thirsty?" The man approached, dragging the hose beside him.

Buzz didn't want to stop long enough to let the man get a better look at them, yet Hush was thirsty. For that matter, so was he, but asking the man for a drink from the hose for himself would call too much attention to them.

"They say it's supposed to get up near ninety-five today." The man adjusted the nozzle so the water came out in a gentle spray. Hush bit at the water, gulping it down between slurps. The man let him drink until Hush was obviously done. "Gonna be a hundred out in Missouri."

"That so?"

The man turned the hose back on his car, rinsing the remaining suds onto the ground. "Yup. Humid, too."

"It is." Buzz's tongue stuck to the roof of his mouth. The thirst made his insides feel heavy. He wanted a drink. Needed one. But couldn't ask. Would have liked to stick his head under that cool running water. Bathe in it. Instead, he patted his leg for Hush to follow him and started down the street. "Thanks."

The man touched flattened fingers to his forehead in something like a salute. "Anytime."

A car turned down the street behind them, its engine humming. Buzz glanced over his shoulder. It was a police car. Buzz didn't speed up. Didn't look again. Didn't stop. Just kept going.

Until Hush hiked his leg on a bush. Just as the police car came up behind them.

The car slowed. Buzz looked down at the sidewalk. Waited for the car to go by. And for Hush to finish peeing. Which was a lot. A river, practically.

The car passed them, then stopped about ten feet ahead. The window powered down.

A satisfied look on his face, Hush trotted back to Buzz. He couldn't turn around. Not without being obvious. So they continued on the way they'd been going.

"Hi there," the officer called, leaning across the seats to peer through the open window.

"Hey," Buzz returned. He was sure the police officer would ask where he was going, if he'd heard about the man who escaped the hospital, if it was him.

Instead, the officer simply said, "Might want to head on back home. The sidewalks and roads really heat up on a day like this. It can burn a dog's pads."

"Thanks, I will." Buzz canted his head toward the bush that Hush had peed on. "I think he's done, anyway."

"I'll say. Dog must've drunk a gallon not long ago." He studied Buzz a bit longer, as if he were trying to memorize his face, before adding, "You have a nice day."

With a nod, he pulled away. Relief cascaded through Buzz. Two blocks later, he still couldn't shake the feeling that the police officer had been watching him. He had to get out of this town somehow. And the sooner the better.

—o00o—

Buzz didn't get far before Hush began nosing the back of his kneecaps. He almost stumbled twice as Hush circled around him, whining in agitation. The signs were unmistakable: the crackling of electricity throughout his body, the feeling of disconnecting, the cleaving pain in his head. He departed from the shoulder of the country road he'd been walking along, slid down a grassy embankment, and waded through knee-deep ditchwater. The drainage swale passed beneath the road, where a rock-filled culvert cut through.

It was cool in the culvert, invitingly cool. But right now that was not his main concern. The rocks were too dangerous. He needed safety.

So he lay down on the grass, where the hill met the ditch, his feet in the stagnant muck — and hoped that he wouldn't roll into the water and drown in six inches of it.

—o00o—

Points of light pulsed against a black screen. Buzz was both fascinated and perplexed by the sight. It took him a long time to realize where he

257

was and that it was now night.

His legs were wet halfway up his shins. Pulling his feet beneath him, he tried to get up, but his knees wobbled like an infant who hadn't yet learned to walk. So he just sat up, waiting for the world to stop spinning and for the day's memories to resurface.

A lazy yawn reached his ears. Buzz saw only an unrecognizable shape creeping through the tall grass nearby. He couldn't have run if he'd tried.

Then Hush sneezed his greeting and bounded the last few feet to Buzz, his hind end waggling like Buzz had gone someplace far, far away and just returned. In a sense, he had. But he was back. For now.

It must've taken hours for him to climb that hill. Hush's patience humbled him. Several times he had to sit down and rest. Getting back up was hard, but he forced himself to go on. As tired as he was, he was also starving — and growing weaker.

Hush was dragging tail, too. Even Buzz could tell.

But he went on because the dog did. And the dog forged onward because he did. Neither would have quit because neither would have let the other down.

As he'd done so many days and months before, Buzz followed the white line at road's edge. Circumstances had forced his stay in Faderville and it wasn't until now that he realized he liked the place. Still, he didn't know the area well, wasn't sure which way was east, which was west, whether he was going to or away from Somerset. But his objective had changed since that morning.

First, he needed food. Where there were people, there was food. If the two of them didn't eat something soon, one or both of them were going to end up dead. And he hadn't come all this way just to die, lost, out in the middle of nowhere. For no reason.

Which is when it struck him — he didn't have the ashes with him. He'd left them in the plastic bag in a drawer at Noreen's. Right where they always were.

He sank to his knees. Realized the hopelessness of his situation.

He couldn't go back to Noreen's, though. He had to keep Hush safe. Reaching out, he stroked the dog's head. Hush looked at him; he looked at Hush. The loyalty went both ways.

And the love ... the love was infinite.

Several vehicles passed them before one slowed down, eventually coming to a stop about fifty feet ahead of them. Buzz was not at all relieved to see the car had no blue lights or police markings. Not that he wanted to get picked up by the state police or a sheriff. It was that his last two experiences with passing motorists hadn't gone well.

A burly black man in a sleeveless white T-shirt got out of his big silver sedan and tromped over the gravel toward them. The dog huffed softly, his shoulder pressed against Buzz's side.

If the man had stopped to rob him, Buzz thought, he was going to be sorely disappointed. At any rate, Hush wasn't going to let that happen. He knew that now.

"Car trouble?" The man stopped about ten feet away, as if he were as uncertain about a bedraggled old man and his dog as they were about him.

But the more Buzz looked at him, the less afraid he became. The man had a fringe of white around his head and walked partially stooped over. He was older than Buzz. Concern gleamed in his dark eyes.

The man pointed into the darkness, back the way Buzz had come from. "That car back there yours?"

"Uh ... yeah." Buzz had no idea what car he was talking about. He didn't remember passing one, but maybe someone had abandoned one in the time he was out cold.

"Man, that's a looong way to hike in the middle of the night. You must be dead tired."

Buzz didn't answer. He figured his condition spoke for itself.

"I take it you don't have a cell phone." An observation, not a question. The man motioned toward his car. "Come on, then. There's an all-night truck stop by the highway. I'll drop you off there. You got someone you can call?"

"Sure." Although he wasn't going to call anyone. Not yet. But this guy didn't need to know that.

When Buzz didn't get up, the man put his hand out. Buzz took it, stood. Gathered himself to make the arduous trek to the car, even though it really wasn't all that far. When they got there, Buzz started to open the back door.

"Ah, no, no. You both sit up front," the man said. "It ain't but a few miles from here. Little dog hair don't bother me none."

When they were all situated in the front seat, the man said, "Name's Gander, by the way. Not my real name, but everybody from here to Paducah knows me by that."

Buzz wasn't about to tell his real name, either. He tried to think of something ordinary. "I'm Ed."

"And the dog?"

"Buddy." It was all he could come up with on the spot.

"I had a dog named Buddy once!"

All the way to the truck stop, then, the man yakked about his dog, Buddy. Some kind of poodle mix that lived to be twenty-one. Buzz didn't absorb any of the details beyond that and didn't share any of his own. He was just thankful for the ride, and that today luck seemed to be in his favor.

—o00o—

The lights from Tipper's Truck Stop blazed like a beacon from two miles away. Sixty feet tall, a scrolling sign flashed prices for diesel fuel, coffee, and bags of ice. Gander parked at the side of the store, even though there were no cars in front. To the rear, a fleet of semis lined the gravel lot. Most of Tipper's patrons must have been asleep in their cabs, because there were only a few people inside that Buzz could see. He wasn't even sure what time it was, except that it had to be the middle of the night. Which made him wonder what Gander was doing out at that hour. He decided not to ask.

They all got out of the car.

"You take that dog everywhere without a leash?" Gander asked, pocketing a heavy ring of keys.

Buzz tried to remember the last time he'd actually had Hush on a leash. He was sure he'd had one in his backpack, before that thug stole it. "Just sometimes," he lied. It was getting easier. "Left it in the car. Wasn't thinking."

"I know how that is. Crap happens and you get all discombobulated. Anyway, looks like he don't need one."

Gander pulled the entry door open, but Buzz stopped short.

"Problem?" Gander said.

Buzz tapped at a sticker in the window that clearly said: *No pets allowed.*

"Maybe if we told 'em you broke down?"

Buzz shook his head. "That's all right. I'll just find him a spot and tell him to stay. He won't go anywhere without me."

There'd been lots of times that Buzz had needed to go inside a building — a restroom so he could wash up, a fast food joint for a hot cup of coffee, a highway welcome center where he could look at the map and see how far they had yet to go — and Hush had never once not been where he'd left him when he came out.

"Man, that is some dog you got there. My ol' Buddy acted like he didn't even know his own name. If you opened the front door, he was outta there."

While Buzz situated Hush near a fence surrounding a dumpster, Gander waited by the building entrance. When Buzz returned, Gander just shook his head. "Yeah, some dog. Some dog. Well ..."

A pause, and Buzz could tell this was the moment they were

about to part ways and one more person was soon to come and go in his life, never to be seen again. Funny how someone could be in your life for less than an hour, yet have more of an impact than someone you'd known for years.

They stepped inside. Gander dug his hands in his pockets, nodded like he needed to shake the words loose from inside his head. "Gotta get home to my wife. Just gonna use the little boy's room and head on out. You need anything else?"

"No, no, I'm good." Tipping his head back toward the dumpster, he added, "We're good."

Gander offered his hand. "Nice meeting you, Ed. Good luck with the car."

"Thanks." Buzz took his hand, shook it light and quick. He cleared his throat to dislodge the bad taste of the lies, and added, "For everything."

For saving his life. But he wasn't going to say it. That would only invite more questions — and Buzz had never been comfortable with questions about himself. He'd rather ask them of other people. He didn't want anyone to know his full story.

—o00o—

"Where ya headed to?"

Startled, Buzz looked up from his coffee to find the waitress hovering on the other side of the diner counter with a carafe of black coffee in one hand and a saucer with a slice of pie in the other. He wanted that pie. In the worst way. But he only had the fifty bucks on him that he'd left the house with the day of the convenience store robbery. That was supposed to have been extra gas money for Beam and had been given to him by Noreen. He felt bad taking off with it yesterday, but it was all the money he had access to.

"Sorry, was that too nosy?" The waitress topped off his cup.

Her nametag said Miranda. Buzz wondered if she was wearing someone else's nametag, because she didn't look like a 'Miranda'. She didn't act like one, either. 'Miranda' was far too serious. This woman had an uplifting warmness to her. A way of making you feel like you weren't bothering her if you asked for a refill, like she was happy to do it. The biggest reason Buzz hadn't left already was that he'd been sitting there wondering how his life might have been different if he'd met her a year or two ago and gone out of his way to talk to her.

She tilted her head at him. Smiled. Set the carafe down and leaned her elbows on the counter, like she had all day. Not in a lazy way. Like she was interested in him. "I'd ask if you live around here, but you have that look like you've been on the road a while, so I assumed you're from out of town. Always interesting to hear where folks are headed to and why. Just last week there was an elderly couple in here on their way to a cat show in Baltimore. Said they'd been together for fifty-eight years. I've barely been alive that long. Same day there was a neurosurgeon headed to the Appalachian Trail. Wanted to spend some time alone after his divorce. Looked like he could use it. Couple weeks ago, I had a woman in here fresh out of prison. Tattoos everywhere — at least everywhere I could see. Claimed she was framed for drug possession, but whatever. Not the sort you'd want to tangle with, but I'm sure she's had an interesting life so far. Believe me, sometimes I hear more than I want to."

"I can imagine."

"Anyway, just asking. Kills the time. 'Specially when you work the night shift. But if you'd rather not say, I can respect that. Although some days I think I could write a book based on the stories I hear."

"No story here," he said. "Honest."

Two days ago, he might have told her. Not everything, but some of it. But now ... he couldn't afford to.

"I hear ya, sugar." She picked up the carafe, swirled its contents around. "Moving on."

263

Buzz gazed out the window to see Hush lying next to the board fence, his chin resting on his paws. Every once in a while the dog would cock an ear, open an eye, stretch a leg. But he hadn't moved from that spot in the hour Buzz had been sitting there, nursing a bottomless cup of coffee as he recovered from the day's events.

The coffee was bitter and tasted slightly burned, like the pot had been brewing for hours. Still, Buzz drank it, adding spoonfuls of sugar to chase away the bitterness. He knew he really ought to pay up and go, but the caffeine was a lifeline. The longer he sat there, the more normal he felt. Relatively speaking, that is. He hadn't felt truly normal, health-wise, in a couple of years. But he did remember what it was like to have a spring in his step and to not feel like he was drowning in fatigue. It was like he'd aged thirty years in the last three.

The waitress returned the coffee pot to its warming plate and went to work wiping down the counters. Two other men sat chatting in a booth. The cook prepared meals, then disappeared for minutes at a time into the storage room. Every now and then, a customer came into the store section, grabbed a few items, and paid up.

Mindful of being discovered, Buzz kept his face turned toward the TV fixed to the wall. The sound had become white noise. A late, late-night talk show with a couple of quasi-celebrities Buzz didn't recognize. Eventually, a rerun of the local news came on. After a brief preview of the weather and sports, the anchor started talking about a murder in Lexington, then an overturned semi that spilled tons of corn onto an interstate cloverleaf ramp.

Buzz tuned it all out, trying to convince himself it was time to leave, but inertia kept him there.

And then ... he heard Beam's voice.

"That's right. Buzz has a medical condition. His dog helps alert him to oncoming seizures."

Beam was standing outside, Somerset Community Hospital in the background. Just behind her was Noreen, a reassuring hand on her shoulder. They both looked weary. And worried.

Then the camera panned wider to bring a reporter into the picture — a young woman with kinky blond curls who looked fresh out of broadcasting school. "And do they know for certain if the dog is with him right now?"

"Has to be. The security cameras showed them leaving together."

The screen switched to a short loop of him standing by the back door to the hospital and glancing up at the camera. Hush was waiting obediently at his knee. But like all security camera videos, the picture was grainy.

The two men who'd been eating at a nearby booth now stood at the cash register, both of them watching the TV.

"Is there anything you'd like to say to your friend?" the reporter said.

Beam's face appeared in a close-up. "Yeah," she said softly, banishing a tear from the corner of her eye. She turned her gaze from the reporter to the camera, as if speaking directly to him. "Buzz, wherever you are, come back. Please. We know Buzz Donovan isn't your real name. We know why you ran. Hush isn't in any danger. You have to trust me. You're safe — both of you. So please, *please* ..." — her voice faded to a tearful whisper — "come home."

Just like that, everything was out in the open. The real reason he'd left L.A. The reason he'd been living on the streets. The reason he'd chosen a different name. The reason he didn't like to talk about himself.

He felt exposed. And ashamed.

He'd been lying to Beam all this time. Surely she'd be angry with him. And Noreen would have even less reason to trust him now.

But ... he found it hard to believe Hush was exonerated. He'd spent almost the whole last year running, trying to keep him free. It couldn't all be erased that simply — could it? How?

Just as he was about to leave, a picture of Hush flashed up on the screen — and behind him, Buzz. Beam had snapped a photo with her phone right before going into the convenience store. Hush was hanging out the truck window, his head tilted to one side, and right behind him was Buzz in profile. Both were clearly revealed in the picture, their identities unmistakable. Hush's spots. His copper eyebrows. The dark patch around one eye. The deep lines in Buzz's face, each fold and wrinkle like the rings on a tree, evidence of years gone by. His beard and hair a peppery gray. The slight hook in his nose, the result of having broken it playing baseball when he was younger.

The camera was on the reporter again. "Again, yesterday this man known as Buzz Donovan" — his picture flashed across the screen again, this time a close-up of just his face, which on the large screen TV set made his head look four times as big as it was — "and his dog, a blue merle Australian Shepherd called Hush, stopped an armed robber at the Pump-N-Go gas station nine miles northeast of Faderville. The robber is in custody at the Adair County Regional Jail, but Donovan, which again we understand is not his real name, slipped away from Somerset Community Hospital yesterday early morning. While his actions are being heralded as nothing short of heroic, authorities are actively searching for the man and his dog. Donovan was shot during the holdup and although his injury is not life-threatening, he did have a pre-existing medical condition which needs monitored. So if you see him, please call the —"

Buzz's chest tightened. He spun around on his stool, took one step away, and nearly stumbled into the broad chest of one of the truckers.

"Going somewhere?"

Buzz stared up at the man, a good six inches taller than him and half again as wide.

"You know, you look a lot like that guy they just showed on TV." The trucker leaned to his side and said to his friend then, "Don't you think so, Jimmy?"

"Yup, sure does." The man behind him plunked a handful of change on the counter. He winked at the waitress. "Keep the change, sugar-pie."

But the waitress wasn't paying any attention to Jimmy or the money lying on the counter. Instead, she was staring at Buzz's arm. She walked from behind the counter and up to Buzz. "Ohhh, honey . . . looks like you're bleeding there." Her fingers grazed the sleeve over his bicep. "What'd you do to yourself?"

"Do to himself?" the big trucker said. "Didn't do nothing to himself, Mandy. He's the one who got shot." He studied Buzz intently. "Yeah, that was him all right."

Hemmed in by the counter, the waitress, and two truckers, there was no escape route. Yet instead of feeling trapped, something in Buzz's resolve shifted. Like the last wave of a storm rolling back into the sea. Relief, almost. For over a year now, he'd been running. Well, not running, exactly. But constantly on the move, denying his identity so he could get to the Atlantic, pay homage to his son, and keep his dog with him.

But if what Beam said was true, there was no reason to keep running.

All this time he'd been preaching at her to let go of her past. Now she knew — he'd been a hypocrite all along.

He glanced down at his arm. A spot of fresh blood was staining his sleeve. He could feel its faint trickle tracing a path down his arm. The bandage was soaked. He must've pulled the stitches loose somehow.

He sat back down and said to Mandy, "I need to use the phone."

chapter 21

Beam

The buttery yellow light of morning spilled into the living room, stirring up dust motes as Fisher raced along the back of the couch and vaulted onto a lower bookshelf. A moment later, he landed on the floor, eyes of emerald sparking with wonder and curiosity.

A new dawn. A new day. Yet I'd never felt more tired or more ready to crawl back into bed and sleep the day away. But I couldn't. Not yet. I had so much to say. So many emotions logjammed inside of me, trying to get out.

I planted my rump on the coffee table and pushed the newspaper aside. Buzz's picture was plastered on the front page, complete with the story of how he'd had a neighbor in L.A. who'd complained that Hush had bitten him and threatened a lawsuit. When authorities showed up at Buzz's place to investigate, he and the dog were gone — along with the remaining funds in his bank account. After a few more attempts to reach him and no close relatives to call on, they eventually abandoned the case. The accuser, it was soon discovered, had a history of betting on dog fights. He'd suffered a nasty bite the night before at one of his events, wound up in the emergency room, and in order to deflect suspicion had pinned his injury on Hush, the harmless dog next door.

"Why didn't you tell us, Buzz?"

Hands clasped loosely together as he sat on the couch, Buzz blinked at me. His gaze drifted to the floor. His lips parted, then closed.

"Did you think we would dump you back out on the street? Or call the cops on you?"

More silence.

The phone rang. Again. Noreen walked into the kitchen and pulled the plug. The reporters had been relentless. Going public right now was the last thing any of us wanted to do. Least of all Buzz, evidently.

"I guess you don't know us all that well, then. Because we wouldn't have done either of those things."

I felt like a parent lecturing a child. Nothing new. I'd been Oakley's parent, since Lana hadn't been interested in the job. Thinking back, I couldn't remember once when she'd ever sat me down and given me a good talking to. She'd been too wrapped up in her own life. Too busy assembling sexy outfits, hunting down her next date, recovering from her last hangover, lining up her next boyfriend, then scrambling for a new place to live whenever the latest man-of-the-day didn't work out. You'd think she would have noticed a cycle.

Two months ago just thinking about her would've launched me into a loop of righteous anger and self-pity. Now … now I had a whole new outlook.

It wasn't worth caring about people who didn't care about you. If you were important to a person, they made time for you. They went out of their way to do things for you. They made sacrifices for you.

Had that been what Buzz was trying to do when he left the hospital? Did he think he was going to spare us the pain of eventually

269

losing him? Or was there something more to it? Something he was hiding? Or had it all been about saving Hush, since he thought the dog was still in trouble?

I wanted to know and I didn't.

Then again, not knowing the truth sometimes was worse than the truth itself. There wasn't much more he could say after the last couple of days to surprise me.

"Tell me one thing, Buzz. Just one for now — and I'll leave you alone until you're ready to tell me more. Or you don't have to tell me anything else. Ever. I won't force it. But you've saved my life twice now, damn it. So we have this thing ... this connection. And you owe it to me."

Two words, finally. "What's that?"

Just then, Noreen's cell phone rang. Her sigh carried all the way from the kitchen. She looked at the display, groaned, and put the phone to her ear. "Hello?"

A long pause as she listened. Then, she cupped her free hand to the speaker and spun away, like she was afraid of us overhearing something. "Hold on." Grabbing her coffee cup from the counter, she went out the back door.

Probably some reporter who'd gotten her number from a co-worker. Or the state police ... again.

I turned my attention back to Buzz and spit it out. "What were you *afraid* of?"

He met my eyes but only for a moment. "Afraid of?"

"Why else would you try to run away?" As soon as I said that, the irony of it hit me: I'd run away not so long ago, too. But my reasons had been understandable.

He took a few breaths. "You know ... I never intended to stay here so long."

"But Hush was hurt. You had to. And I'm glad it worked out that way. Even Noreen is — although I'm sure she's never told you that.

But when she got the call about you being shot … She cares, Buzz. She does. We both do."

He pointed a finger at me. "That's the problem, you see. Right there. You care. And I …" He wiped at his eyes before the tears could escape. "I care about you, too."

And like that, all my anger diffused. It didn't matter that he'd left, or that he'd even lied in the first place about his name or why he'd fled L.A.. He'd been found. That was all that mattered.

The truth can hurt. It can also heal.

Because what he meant … what we both meant — was that we all *loved* each other. But it felt strange to say the word when you weren't used to it. Some people used it all the time. To the point where it didn't mean anything. But in this case, it meant something huge. Something bigger than I could comprehend. Something so strong and binding that its power was almost frightening.

I stood. Didn't move for a few heartbeats.

Finally, I started toward the kitchen where Hush lay sleeping, a bone beside his paws.

"Sunbeam?"

I stopped but didn't turn around.

"I didn't find him on the streets."

I waited for him to go on. When he didn't, I said, "Where did you find him, then?"

"Tied to a dog house. Sitting in a patch of dirt. Yard filled with junk. No shade, no water … I walked down to the corner store, bought a bottle of water and asked for a cup, then took it back to him. For two more days, I took him water and fed him. You've never seen an animal more grateful for a slice of bread and a hunk of cheese. On the third day, just as I was about to go through the gate into the yard of that house, a man came out. I asked if he needed a home for the dog, because I was looking for one."

"So he gave him to you?"

271

"Not exactly."

"You bought him?"

"I tried to, but he wasn't budging. Claimed he'd paid five hundred dollars for him as a pup. By then he was getting pretty riled up. Told me to get the hell off his property."

"I see. You stole Hush."

And that was the tiny kernel of truth on which all Buzz's actions had hinged.

He nodded. "You could say that. I prefer to think of it as I rescued the dog, but call it what you like. Do you know why I named him 'Hush'?"

It hadn't occurred to me until just then that the dog might have had some other name before. "I have no idea."

"Because when I went back to get him, the guy was on the back porch. For hours. Drinking by himself. Every once in a while he'd lob a bottle at the dog. Call him curse words. Yell at his wife inside. She'd come out and they'd argue some, then she'd go back inside. But he stayed. And drank. And cursed some more. After things got quiet for a bit, I finally got up the courage to open the gate and have a look. He was passed out in a lawn chair not thirty feet away. The dog heard the hinges creak and woofed at me. Not in a watchdog sort of way. More like he was happy to see me. The guy stirred, flopped over the other way. I told the dog to 'hush' and he did.

"I wasn't going to call the dog warden only to have them throw Hush in a shelter — or worse, leave the dog with that no-good loser and have him take his anger out on Hush somehow. Just made more sense to get Hush out of the situation. He deserved better. I was going to find him a home, but then ... well, he proved we were supposed to be together, I guess. The next day was when I had my first seizure alone. He was trying to alert me ahead of time, but I was too dumb to know he was being anything other than obnoxious. Took a few more times of it happening for me to catch on. Amazing what animals can do that people can't, isn't it? Like they have these special abilities."

Superpowers, if you ask me.

My fingertips wandered to the faintest ridge of a scar along my jawline, then to another above my wrist: reminders of a horrible event and how I'd survived it. For years, I'd generalized, thinking I was keeping myself safe without realizing what I might have been missing. Not all dogs, I'd since come to realize, were bad. Some were good. A few were exceptional. Hush was one of the rare ones, with a heart as big as any mountain. Yet before Buzz rescued him, he'd been relegated to being chained in a back yard, neglected, unappreciated. He could've turned out mean or scared. But he hadn't. He'd chosen love over hate, courage over fear, loyalty over mistrust. Made you wonder how many dogs there were just like him, all that love and maybe even some instinct going to waste because the humans were either too stupid, busy, or selfish to notice.

I sat back down in front of Buzz. "I don't think anyone's going to take Hush away from you now. You're a hero in these parts. He's a legend. Everyone knows you belong together. And you both belong here."

"Maybe. But then there's the reason we were headed east." He took a plastic bag from his back pocket, held it up for me to see.

"Are those ... ashes?"

"They are." Before I could ask whose, he told me. "My son's."

Noreen pushed open the back door so hard it hit the wall with a bang. Both Buzz and I jumped where we sat. Buzz slid the bag back in his pocket.

She marched directly to me, held the phone out. I took it, expecting another reporter, which I honestly didn't have the energy to deal with right now, but maybe if I gave them a few pat answers they'd leave us alone for a while.

I put my hand over the receiver end. "Who is it?"

Noreen's face twisted with a mixture of emotions. "Your mother.

She saw you on the news. All the way up in Michigan."

Shaking my head, I tried to give the phone back, mouthing the word 'no'.

Noreen kept her hands at her sides. "Talk to her, Bellamy. She sounds worried. Almost frantic. Just for a minute, that's all. If you don't, she'll keep calling."

Talking to Lana was the last thing I wanted to do right now. I was about to hand the phone back, when Buzz nodded at it.

"Talk to her, Sunbeam. Let her know you're okay."

Outnumbered, I put the phone to my ear, dreading the sound of her voice and the memories it would dredge up. I walked to the window, fixed my gaze on the distant hills, reminded myself I was hundreds of miles away from her.

Half a minute must have passed before I managed one word. "Yeah?"

"Beam? Beam? Is that you? Are you okay?" She didn't sound so much concerned as she did irritated at me. "Oh, my God. I can't believe what I heard. You could've been killed!"

In some situations, that might have come across as concern. But she said it like I was a little kid who'd just put my hand on a hot stove after being told not to and she was about to whoop my ass for it.

"Uh … I'm fine, thanks for asking."

"I was going to ask, damn it. It's just that I'm still in shock. Not every day you see your little girl on the network news. I mean, you run away without a word, then don't talk to me for weeks and the first I hear about you is on TV, traveling around with some old pervert and his rabid dog."

Where did she get these ideas?

Before I could compose a sensible reply, she really lit into me. "And that robber … Didn't you learn anything living in the city? You don't trust strangers. Ever. For God's sake, the guy had a gun, Beam. A gun! He could've blown your head off."

Did she think I didn't know that?

Instead of snarking back, though, I let it slide. Because strangely, the fact that she actually called to lecture me was something I couldn't recall her ever doing before. I wasn't sure what to make of it. So I just let her go on, waiting for her to finish. Which took quite a long time. She had a lot to say. Something about what it was like to be alone, to not know what I was doing or if I was ever coming back.

"My life has been crazy since you left. I almost called the cops to go find you. But to be honest, I didn't even know you'd been gone until two days later because your note had fallen off the fridge and onto the floor. I thought it was a piece of junk mail. Meanwhile, I figured you were at the library or out on the streets doing God knows what. So I just went on with my life, going to work, trying not to worry too much —"

I half listened. Looked at the clock in the kitchen. Paced in front of the picture window. All the while waiting for a gap in her tirade when I could toss in some lame excuse as to why I had to hang up now.

"— been meaning to tell you, but there was just never a good time. You know how it is."

"How what is? And tell me what?"

"Where's your head at, Beam? I swear, you never listen to me. I was saying how I kept telling you one day that I'd let you know more about your father, when you were old enough. Well, you're old enough. But the thing is ... the thing is I ..."

She let it hang out in the open so long I thought we'd been disconnected. Honestly, I'd stopped thinking about it a long time ago, figuring I'd never know.

"It's like this," she finally went on. "I can't tell you who he is."

"Why?" I blurted. Even though I'd put it out of my mind, it didn't mean I wasn't curious. Maybe my real dad was out there somewhere, wondering about me. Or maybe he didn't know a thing about me, considering Lana had probably told him she was on the pill.

I steeled myself for the revelation.

"Because I don't know," she said.

"Don't know what?" Where he lived? What his first name was? I needed more to go on. Maybe a few years down the road, I could hire a private investigator, track him down.

"I don't know who he is, all right? Where he is, or what he does now, if he has a family of his own — I don't know any of that."

It felt like she'd just shot a cannonball through my gut. I left the room, unaware of what Buzz or Noreen might have heard so far. But whatever Lana was about to say next, I wanted it to be between the two of us. Fisher darted out the back door in front of me, his attention immediately captured by a monarch butterfly on a nearby azalea, fanning its wings as it soaked up the morning sun. The kitten crouched, waiting for the insect to move within reach.

The stifling heat closed in on me. I kept walking — down the back steps, past the garage, toward the neighbor's pasture. Weed stems lashed at my bare legs. A fly buzzed around my ears. "You said his last name was Bellamy."

"Yeah, about that ... It wasn't. Not as far as I know. He went to Bellarmine University for a semester, then dropped out. That's about all I remember. He didn't talk much. He kind of had one thing in mind. He was drunk. Well, we both were." Big surprise. A few breaths, then, "Somehow it stuck in my mind as Bellamy University. Wasn't until after you were born and I'd already named you that I figured out that was wrong. Anyway, we were only together that once. I never saw him again. I was young and stupid enough to get pregnant ... Sorry, that came out wrong. I didn't plan on getting knocked up ... I mean, you happened, and I didn't know how to deal with a baby. Felt like I'd disappointed my parents. They weren't easy to please. Dad never said much, but Mom ... she was a hard woman to live with. Always pushing me to do better. To be someone important. To have a career. There was just no pleasing her. So I gave up."

I almost said nothing. Almost. But this little confession about not knowing who my father was had turned into another 'I'm the victim' rant and I was so tired of that.

"You gave up on everything," I said.

"What?"

"Your mother, yourself, me ... Oakley." Most of all Oakley.

"Don't go there, Beam. I did my best with him. Just leave it at that."

"No, I'm not going to drop it. He needed help learning to brush his teeth and tie his shoes. Lots of help. You couldn't handle it. You checked out. If you weren't drunk, you had drugs in your system. Whatever it took to make *yourself* feel better — or just not feel at all."

"I kept a roof over your head!"

"By jumping from bed to bed? Do you realize how creepy some of those guys were that you made us live with?"

"Just because they weren't college graduates —"

"That has nothing to do with it. You slept with a bunch of losers because it was the easy thing to do. And because you thought you didn't deserve better."

A pause. A very long one.

When she finally spoke again, the edge was gone from her voice. Like I'd finally hit on a nerve.

"I suppose I didn't," she said. "Noreen was right after all. My real momma didn't want me. No one does. Not even you." Then so softly I almost didn't hear her, she said, "Can't say I blame you."

It was the way she said it that stopped me from going on. It wasn't totally clear to me whether she was fishing for pity like she always did, or if something had really, finally sunk in and she was starting to unravel. Not in a going insane kind of way. In an inner reflection way. Like she couldn't deny any longer who it was she'd really been all these years.

277

For the first time ever, I felt the tiniest bit sorry for her.

"I'm sorry I was such an awful mother to you, Beam. And I'm sorry what happened to Oakley."

It was a start. A turning point. But it didn't erase all that had happened.

"Do you think you could ever forgive me?" she asked. "Not right away, maybe. But eventually?"

I turned that over in my head a dozen ways. But no matter how I looked at it, it was still as though she was asking me to hug a prickly cactus. I'd need a thicker skin for that. Maybe a suit of armor.

"I don't know. Ask me in a few years."

"A few ...? Beam, that's not fair. I'm trying. I really am. I want us to be a family again. I really do."

"I *have* a family now, Lana." I used her first name on purpose. To make a point I was sure she couldn't miss, because I'd never called her that to her face before. It was just how I thought of her. As Lana. Giving birth hadn't made her a mother in the fullest sense of the word. But I was over blaming her for the way things were. Had been. I held my future in my own hands now. So to drive my point home, I added, "I'm *happy* here."

And it was true. It wasn't a perfect situation, but maybe that was the point. We loved each other in spite of our flaws.

"Listen, Beam. I know you think that you're —"

I hung up.

Forgiveness wasn't a single act. It was a process.

Someday, maybe Lana and I would talk more. But for now, I needed time away from her. To find purpose in it all. I needed the security of miles between us. Needed to fill my life with new memories. Better ones.

I started back toward the house. Buzz was standing at the door, looking out at me.

The butterfly flapped its way across the lawn, looping mere feet above a black-and-white kitten honing his hunting skills. When the butterfly disappeared into the leafy green canopy of a catalpa, Fisher raced to me and rubbed his head against my shins. I stopped, not wanting to trip over him. He lifted a paw and tapped me on the kneecap, a signal to me. I scooped him up in my arms, looking back to the screen door, where Hush had joined Buzz.

Serenity lifted me up like a gentle wave swelling on a calm sea. I was glad I'd almost hit Buzz that day. Gladder I hadn't. Indebted to a dog who'd taught me to judge each creature as an individual. Grateful for the many events that had delivered me here.

In walking away from the drama that was Lana's life, I'd chosen my own course. Where I was going from here, though, I had no idea. All I knew was that for now, this was where I was meant to be.

chapter 22

Buzz

Hunter shifted the truck into park and turned the ignition off. "So you never really filed a report when I dropped you off here before, did you?"

They sat in the parking lot of the sheriff's station, neither of them moving to go inside. Only Hush seemed eager to get out of the truck. He lifted the paw of his newly healed leg and rested it on the top edge of Buzz's seat. Other than the long patch of shaved hair barely grown back on the inside of the dog's leg, you'd never know he'd ever broken it.

"No." With one word, Buzz felt shame bear down on him. He'd lied to Hunter that day. Had lied to Beam about why he was homeless. Had lied from the beginning to Noreen by hiding his past. Still had things he hadn't spoken of.

"Well ..." Hunter's gaze wandered from the law enforcement building, to the grocery next door, and then to the road that wound over the low hills of Adair County. "I suppose if I'd been in your shoes, I would've done the same."

A weight, a very small weight, lifted from Buzz's shoulders.

He didn't doubt it was an honest sentiment, but still, he couldn't help but wonder if they didn't resent his dishonesty. Life was ambiguous like that. You could see things two ways at once. Like any decent human being, Buzz valued honesty. But more than that, he valued love and loyalty.

Then, as if he were reading Buzz's thoughts, Hunter said, "Few things in this world are ever black and white, Buzz. I once judged a neighbor harshly, assumed he'd done something horrible to my daughter — all because I'd jumped to conclusions without knowing the full story."

Buzz could sense there was more coming, so he waited, even as Hush began to pant because the AC was turned off and the windows were still up.

"So …" Hunter drew in a big breath and let it out. Then, as he pulled on the latch of his door and nudged it open, his mouth quaked with the hint of a smile. "You still going by Buzz Donovan — or do you prefer Carroll?"

"It was my maternal grandfather's name. He was Irish. Had a brogue so heavy when he first came here at twelve that he got beat up twice. For the rest of his life, he worked hard to lose that accent, but every once in a while it would creep in. Especially when he drank. And the more he drank, the more he talked. I used to love to listen to him then, how his voice would rise in a lilt at the end of a sentence." Buzz smiled, too, lost in the memory. "But no, no one ever called me Carroll. It's always been Buzz."

They both piled out of the truck, Buzz making sure Hush stepped down carefully, rather than leaping and tumbling.

"And Donovan?" Hunter shut his door and came around the hood of the truck to walk beside Buzz. "Another family name?"

"Nope. Buzz Donovan just had a nice ring to it." Buzz planted his walking stick with each step, more for balance than support. Every once in a while his vision went blurry or things seemed to tip sideways or his legs felt wobbly. He hadn't mentioned it to anyone, but he was sure they'd noticed how unsteady he was, although maybe they'd just chalked it up to aftereffects of the shooting.

Inside, Hunter escorted him to the front desk. The cheery receptionist was there again.

"Morning, Doc Hunter!" she chirped.

"Morning, Roz. How's Cookie doing lately?"

"Back to her old ornery self! Those antibiotics did the trick. I was so worried about her. Never knew they could fall ill from a tick bite. We couldn't figure out what was wrong with her, but you picked up on it right away. Thank you."

"You're welcome. And Jazzman? How's that old draft horse getting along?"

"Still kicking — figuratively speaking. Did you come for Mr. Buskirk's belongings?"

"We did. Could you tell us where —?"

She aimed her pencil over her shoulder. "Down that hallway, turn right at the end, second door on your left. Just go on in."

Before they could go down the hallway, they had to pass through a metal detector and get a quick pat down from a gray-haired deputy who wished them a nice day, then waved them on. When they arrived at the door, Hunter reached for the doorknob, but Buzz stopped him with a hand on his wrist.

"Do you mind if I —"

"Go ahead." Hunter touched his friend lightly on the shoulder. "I'll wait out in the lobby."

Buzz looked down at Hush, then at Hunter. "Do you think you could …?"

"I'll keep an eye on him. Sure you'll be okay?"

"Yeah," Buzz breathed.

Seconds passed while Buzz stood facing the door, Hunter's and

Hush's footsteps receding behind him. He half-turned, almost called out to Hunter to come back, go in with him, but this was something he had to do alone.

He gripped the cool metal orb, turned it, pushed. The door itself was heavy, solid, probably bulletproof, its tiny square window at eyelevel crisscrossed with fine wires. He opened it just far enough to slip through. Harsh fluorescent lighting repulsed him momentarily. He squeezed his eyes tight, kept his head down, and trudged up to a bare counter manned by a dower-faced, baldheaded deputy. After a short but pointed interrogation, Buzz was presented with his backpack across the counter. He waited until the deputy disappeared into a back room filled with shelves and cubbyholes before pulling it to him.

It looked deflated and more worn than he remembered it. But yes, it was his. There were gaps where the stitching was pulling lose and the first hint of a hole in one of the bottom corners. Not until he picked it up by the top loop strap did he realize it was empty. His heart sank. He pulled open each zipper one by one, dipped his hand inside, fished around, found nothing.

So much for retrieving his past.

He wasn't sure whether to just leave it or take it with him. It was just a material thing, void of the memories it once contained. He turned to go, empty-handed, and made for the door.

"Wait!" the deputy barked in a voice so commanding Buzz stopped in his tracks. "There's more here."

The crinkle and plunk of plastic hitting laminate sounded. Buzz turned, saw several clear bags being fanned across the counter as the deputy arranged them for visibility.

One at a time, Buzz opened them. The first was a larger one containing his toothbrush, a comb, a nearly empty shampoo bottle, and various other personal hygiene items. He moved on to the next: his wallet, empty of bills but still containing his driver's license with the name 'Carroll Buskirk'. Another bag held a map of the United States so creased it was nearly falling apart. The yellow highlighter that marked his route was still evident, although it had faded over the months. He glanced at the names of the towns and cities he'd passed through, a cascade of memories flashing through his mind. Inside the same bag was an envelope with a few more items: a photo of him standing beside four-year-old Patrick in front of the zebra enclosure at the zoo, another picture of his son in full military formals, a purple heart, and his son's death certificate.

For a long time, Buzz looked at those four things, both mournful for the brief time he had known his son and grateful to have fathered a young man who gave his life in service. Buzz had once had the same dream, trained as a medic, and was weeks away from deployment. He'd wanted to help others, train in the medical field somehow, but growing up poor he'd had no way to pay for schooling, so he'd chosen the army. He'd loved the discipline of it, the orderliness, the purpose. It had suited him. Although divorced, he still had visitations with his son. Life had had its bumps, but things had begun to smooth out.

And then ... he'd gone to pick up Patrick for a weekend. Gabriella had met him at the door, nervous, her face veiled in the shadows, a faint blotch of purple showing above one cheekbone. It had all seemed so strange, so unlike her to turn him away. They had quarreled often before their marriage broke apart, but she'd never denied him his son. Angered and confused, he'd staggered off, intent on finding a lawyer who would set her straight if she refused to let him see Patrick again.

The next day, the police came. A different kind of lawyer, a public defender, had urged him to confess to domestic abuse, saying his sentence would be lighter if he didn't fight the charges. How stupid of him to have agreed.

His whole life, Buzz had tried to make sense of it all. It wasn't until more recently, when he'd learned of his medical condition, that he'd given up trying to.

Life was seldom fair. Kindness was sometimes met with cruelty. Karma often failed to even the scales. The only revenge he could muster, ultimately, was to live with peace in his heart.

And he had. For although he had little control over how others treated him and often none over what life dealt him, he *could* choose how to react to mistreatment and adversity. He'd started out on his journey as a means of honoring his son. It had turned into so much more. He'd seen fantastic sights and spoken to people whose stories were sometimes heartrending and at other times inspirational. If he'd never decided to take Patrick's ashes to Chincoteague, he would never have met Beam. And Hush's future would have been uncertain.

Everything was as it should be. Despite all his fears and doubts, all the sadness and every injustice, everything *would be* all right.

"I can take these now?" Buzz asked the deputy.

"Yes." The man slid a paper and a pen in front of him, pointed to a fuzzy line at the bottom. "Sign here first, acknowledging that you received the items."

Buzz signed and placed his belongings in the backpack.

In the lobby, Hunter met him with a questioning look. "Everything there?"

"Everything that matters," Buzz replied.

—o00o—

A quiet calm enveloped Buzz as he got out of Noreen's car and pulled himself to his feet with his walking stick. Buzz, Beam, and Noreen had been invited to the McHughs' for a Sunday dinner. Hunter's wife, Jenn, greeted them in the driveway with a young clone of herself.

"Hi," Jenn said. "This is our oldest daughter Maura. She's on

285

summer break from college in upstate New York. And over there" — she waved toward a large tree, where a young girl was spinning in a tire swing — "that's Hannah. She can seem shy and unengaged, but she's not ignoring you really. She has mild Asperger's and isn't always sure how to handle new people. Just give her time and she'll be fine."

At first sight, Hannah McHugh looked like any other ten-year-old. She was as perfectly formed as any child could be: pale blond hair that swept her shoulders, longs legs with slightly knobby knees, eyes as bright and blue as a summer sky. It had taken a couple of visits to the McHughs' home for Buzz to gauge that she was different somehow, but when Beam met her for the first time that June day it was apparent that she instantly knew.

Buzz heard a low growl in Hush's throat. Puzzled, he looked down at the dog, then followed the line of his gaze. Under the sprawling shade tree where Hannah was swinging lay her dog, Echo, another Australian Shepherd. Unlike Hush with his spots and patches, Echo was nearly all black. If not for the strip of white on the underside of his muzzle and his white toes, Echo would have been lost in the shadows. Hush woofed again softly. Echo lifted his head to regard Hush defiantly, his regal look a bold declaration that he was standing watch over his girl and this was his territory.

"Enough, Hush," Buzz said. Hush looked up at him out of respect. The standoff broken, Echo laid his head down. The message had been sent, the understanding received.

"It'll be fifteen minutes or so until dinner is ready," Jenn went on. "Somehow the apple pie was ready before the pulled pork. Rather than start with dessert, I figured we should probably wait for the main course. I hope you all don't mind."

"That's no problem at all, Mrs. McHugh," Noreen said. She clutched an oversized handbag to her middle, as if she wasn't quite sure what to do with it or herself.

"You must be Noreen." Jenn offered her hand and Noreen

returned the handshake with business-like formality. "And Buzz, this must be your young friend, Beam. Is that right?"

Taking it as a cue, Buzz introduced them all. The moment he was done, Beam asked, "Is it okay if I talk to Hannah?"

Jenn and Maura exchanged a glance.

"Sure," Jenn said, "but don't expect that she'll answer."

"Oh, and don't get too close at first," Maura added. "Every once in a while she still freaks out and runs off. But she's better than she used to be. When she was little, sometimes she'd scream if you accidentally brushed against her."

"Got it. No problem." Beam ran off, slowing as she neared Hannah. Instead of approaching the girl directly, she knelt tentatively before Echo and offered him her hand to sniff. Once the introduction was sufficient, he allowed Beam to stroke the top of his head. Then she began to rub behind his ears. Soon, her fingernails were scratching at his withers and spine. Stretching his neck, Echo leaned into her touch.

Hannah dragged her toes in the dirt to stop the tire from spinning. Her cheek pressed against the thick rope, she studied Beam and Echo.

"Would you like an iced tea, Buzz?" Jenn asked.

Startled, Buzz glanced at her. "Yes, please."

While he and Noreen settled in the Adirondack chairs on the front porch, Jenn and Maura disappeared inside. Hush leaned against Buzz's chair, watchful yet relaxed. In a paddock to the side of the house, two horses grazed, their tails swishing away the flies. Farther down the road near another smaller farmhouse, sheep roamed over a hilly meadow.

It was as peaceful a day and place as Buzz had ever known. Yet the greatest wonder of all was what was happening under the big shade tree.

Hannah was crouching beside Beam, pulling a finger through the dirt in intersecting swoops and arcs, as if she were drawing a map. Although he couldn't hear her, Buzz could see Beam speaking to Hannah, smiling at her, nodding. Soon, Hannah took Beam by the hand and pulled her across the lawn, up the steps, and inside the house. Echo stopped just beyond the porch and lay down, yawning, one watchful eye on Hush. Beam gave a quizzical shrug as they passed by.

A minute later, just as Jenn and Maura reappeared with the drinks, Buzz heard Beam say from inside, "Ohhh, Hannah, those are so, *so* beautiful! I've never seen anything like them. The colors!"

Beam was talking about Hannah's paintings that lined the walls of the McHughs' home, each one framed and positioned like the finest showing at a gallery.

Maura sat on the porch rail, balancing with her legs stretched out like a cat on a lazy afternoon, while Jenn claimed the porch swing.

"Hunter said it's almost ready," Jenn informed them. "Shouldn't be but a few more minutes. He has a special recipe for the barbecue sauce. If you don't compliment him on that, he'll mope all evening."

She went on talking to Noreen, asking her about the bank she worked at and whether they'd had many loans defaulted on. Buzz's attention drifted away as Beam's voice carried through the open picture window.

"That one ... Is that your dog?"

He wasn't sure, but he thought he could hear Hannah's whispered replies. In the several times he'd visited the McHughs' house, he'd never once heard Hannah speak out loud. That Beam had somehow connected with her through the dog amazed him, to say the least. Especially given the fact that a few months ago dogs were Beam's greatest phobia.

A wet nose tickled his fingertips. He turned his hand over, let Hush sniff his palm. For a moment, he was concerned that maybe Hush was alerting him again, but there was no worry in his friend's gaze, no frantic licking or nudging at his knees.

There was only love. And that was all that mattered.

chapter 23

Beam

Lana Adelaide Larson clacked over the sidewalk and up the front steps wearing a new black leather coat and tailed by an even newer boyfriend. This one had money, lots of it. He wore a suit jacket: navy with thin lapels, tapered fit at the waist, with a gray-toned sweater beneath and under that a silky white shirt, no tie. Overdressed for a summer day, but I'm guessing it was a fashion statement, not a practical matter. His white slacks were pleated and cuffed at the ankle. His suede shoes were a light gray. He probably didn't have socks on, but I couldn't tell. A platinum watch flashed on one wrist and on the opposite hand, a single gold ring set with a sapphire adorned his pinky. He had one of those dark, perfectly trimmed beards that looked like it was painted on, and when he smiled my way, it was to show off unnaturally white teeth.

I didn't know him, but already I didn't like him.

At least the tattoo-sporting, beer-guzzling truckers that Lana more normally shacked up with were real. If this guy had been any more fake, he'd have been a plastic blow-up doll.

Lana stomped to a halt before me as I stood just inside the front door, nothing but a flimsy screen between us. "Get your things. You're coming home."

"Hello, I'm fine," I replied with false cheer. "How are you?"

"Don't get smart with me, Little Miss Bellamy Adelaide."

I cringed. Every time she used my middle name, which was also hers, it reminded me just how self-centered she truly was. I hated my middle name even more than my first.

With a patronizing tilt of her chin, she flicked a hand at the door handle, as if to tell me I should stop defying her and just fling it open. "Get your stuff. Let's go home."

"Where's 'home' now?" I asked, cynical. Obviously the guy with her wasn't from Flint. Had she given up on settling for her usual pond scum and worked her way up to being a call girl? She seemed a little old for that, but whatever.

"Traverse City." Lana grabbed the screen door handle and tried to turn it, but I had it locked.

"Since when?"

"You'll like it there." She jiggled the handle several more times, persistent. "We have a place on the lake. Real nice. Two stories, four-car garage. Covered porch out front and a great big deck out back with a barbecue and everything. A boat, too."

Ralph Lauren eased up to her shoulder, a broad smile plastered onto his peachy spray-tanned face. Closer up, I could see he had his share of age spots and a fine fanning of crow's feet. He was older. Well, older than Lana. So she had herself a sugar daddy. Good for her. Must be her retirement plan.

Lana pulled at the handle again. "Get your things. Hurry up."

"This is your mom's house," I said. "Don't you want to say 'hi' to her?"

"No, I don't." A look of panic crashed over her features. "Is she here?"

"You're safe for the next half hour. She's at work."

"Good," she breathed, her eyes fluttering upward in relief. Then she fixed me with her best I'm-your-mother-so-do-what-I-say glare. Remorseful, slightly apologetic Lana had disappeared. The old Lana was back. "Listen to me, Bellamy, because I'm not going to say this again. You need to get your stuff and get your butt out in that car" — she jabbed a glittery-nailed finger at a black foreign SUV — "so we can get back to Michigan. Now, come on out." Both hands latched on the door handle now, she pitched her full weight into it.

"It's locked, sweetheart," Ralph Lauren murmured calmly behind her.

"I know!" She pounded both palms on the screen then. That's when I saw it: the big diamond ring. B-I-G big. Sunlight bounced off its facets like a strobe light off a disco ball, almost blinding me. "You come out here this instant, Bellamy Adelaide Larson!"

"Are you engaged to him?" I asked, point blank.

Ralph Lauren smiled sheepishly. I might have felt some admiration for him if he'd at least tried to calm her down, but he stood there, cowed, while she carried on, screaming at her only child. If she'd been a reasonable person, she would have asked to come in and sit down to talk with me. I would have given her an hour. At the end of that, I still would have refused to go with her, but it would have been nice to see her grovel. Ralph Lauren laid a hand on her shoulder, but she pushed it away. Okay, now I saw it. He wasn't that much different from the rest. He just had money. "Who is he, anyway?"

"This is Alonzo." She didn't give a last name. I suppose it didn't matter. He'd be gone in a few months, tops. "We're married."

Or not.

Leaving would require filing for divorce. Ah, I got it. If she could last a while with him, she could sue for alimony. Still, that sort of scheming seemed too complicated for her.

"You're what?"

"Married, Bellamy. Married."

"Since when?"

"A month ago."

I didn't ask how long she'd known him before then or why she hadn't told me about this before now. You'd think if your kid ran away — your straight-A, college student at fifteen kid — that you'd make getting her home a priority. But the fact that she dragged her boyfriend ... husband here with her said a lot. "Oh. Oh. I see. So that's why you didn't come down right away to fetch me? You two had a thing going on and you didn't want to interrupt it."

"If this door wasn't between us, I'd slap you right now."

I looked at Alfredo, or whatever his name was. "Are you going to let her talk to me like that? She's threatening to abuse me."

Flinching, Alberto backed away. He was so far whipped he probably didn't even have his man-parts anymore.

"Bellamy!" she screeched. "Do not speak to your father like that."

"He's *not* my father."

"All right, stepfather, then."

"He's not anything to me. I don't have a father. Step or otherwise. I had a sperm donor. One of your many, *many* good lays. I'm surprised you married this one. Lose your job? Need health insurance for an STD?"

Lana's face twisted angrily. "I am going to call the cops and have you forcibly removed from here, do you hear me?"

"Hang on," I said. "I'll get the phone. After you tell them how I ran away, I'll fill them in on your ... habits." I glanced at Alejandro, but he was studying his suede shoes like he was inspecting them for lint or flecks of mud. "Then, I'll give them a list of all the men you've lived with over the past ten or so years and which ones supplied you with what. I'm sure a few of them have police records. Or maybe they're in jail right now."

"Bellamy, no. Don't do that." Her features softened. The tears

293

that she was so good at summoning on command spilled down her cheeks. She pulled a tissue from her purse and blotted around her eyes before her mascara could run. "You wouldn't do that to your mother, would you? Alonzo and I ... we've got a good thing, sweetie. We're happy. I'm ... I'm starting over. Cleaning up my act. I don't do those things anymore."

I'd heard that bit about getting clean a hundred times. Usually she was hungover or coming down from tripping out when she gave it. This time it was a little different, though. *I* was different. I no longer felt like she was my responsibility. "Then prove it. Leave me here. Come back in two years when I'm eighteen and you've been clean that long. Until then, I can't watch you mess up your life again. And I won't let you get in the way of me living mine."

She shook her head. "Bellamy, Bellamy. I want you with me. I need you. Honey, I love you, I do."

Wanted, needed ... yes, she did. Love me? If she did at all, it wasn't enough.

"Beam?" a voice gruff with age called from the yard.

Standing by the old water pump was Buzz, one hand clutching his walking stick for support and the other holding a pair of pruning shears. Dirt smeared his forehead. Setting the shears down, he pulled off his gardening gloves and stuffed them in the front pocket of his overalls. Hush leaned against him, his bad leg barely touching the ground. They must've come from around back.

"Who's that?" Lana whispered. "Mama didn't say anything about getting married again — or is she just living with a man?"

"His name's Buzz," I told her. "He's a friend. And he's just fixing the place up."

She looked at him like he was an apocalypse zombie and if he got a step closer she'd catch the plague from him. "He's the one, isn't he? The one who stopped the robber." Her lip curled into a snarl. "Not what I imagined."

"Is everything okay, Beam?" Buzz came closer, Hush limping ever so slightly beside him, until they stood at the bottom of the porch steps. Blinking hard, he rested the walking stick against the column.

My heart grew ten sizes at the sight of them. I wanted to wrap my arms around them both and absorb their energy. Their bond — between that old, failing man and a dog whose sole purpose was to make sure he made it one more day every morning they woke up — *that* was what love was. Unconditional.

It was the same thing I'd had with Oakley.

"Everything's fine, Buzz. Just fine. Everything." I unlocked the door for him and held it wide. "Come on in. I made scrambled eggs for supper, just like you like 'em. I think there'll even be enough for Hush."

Lana took a step toward the door, ahead of Buzz.

I warned her off with a glare. "Go home, Lana — wherever that is for you this week. *This* is my home. Here, with Noreen — and my friends."

Head down, Buzz brushed past her. He bumped into the doorframe, as if he didn't see it, then disappeared behind me into the living room. Lana balled her fists, her jaw muscles twitching as she bit back whatever caustic words she was holding in. Hush stopped to sniff her feet, her shins, her knees. He looked up at her, his gaze not unkind, but something else. Protective? The slightest growl vibrated in his throat.

Lana's mouth fell open. She scooted back, stopping just short of the porch's edge.

Slipping a hand through the crook of her elbow, Alonzo attempted to usher her away. "Why don't we go, Lana? Let her think about it."

She took several quick breaths, like she was working up something to say but couldn't quite find the words. She took half a step toward me. In a blink, Hush moved to stand between us, his hackles bristling.

This time he growled louder.

Lana sidestepped her way to the steps. Once she was at the bottom and was certain Hush wasn't going to lunge after her, she clung to Alonzo's jacket sleeve and hurried to the car.

Before getting in, she shouted, "I'm coming back tomorrow! Have your things packed. You're going home with us."

"Thanks for the warning," I mumbled.

"Your mother?" Buzz said behind me.

"Yeah."

He nodded in that way that wise people do. "I understand now."

We got each other that way, Buzz and I. We didn't have to have long drawn-out conversations. We listened to what was said and what wasn't. Words, after all, don't mean half as much as how someone treats you.

I watched Lana and her new husband speed off down the curvy lane, not at all sad to see them go. Not angry, either. She wasn't worth the trouble.

In the kitchen, I served Buzz a plate of cheesy scrambled eggs with little bits of green peppers and sausages thrown in. On the floor, Hush ate his and licked the plate halfway across the kitchen before I snatched it up and put it in the sink. Then I let him lick clean both our plates.

Buzz sipped at his coffee.

"Hey, Buzz?"

His eyebrows lifted.

"You still want to go to Chincoteague?"

"I'd like to, but ..." His eyes settled on Hush, who was slurping from his water dish in the corner, right alongside Fisher. "The dog would probably make it farther than I would. We tried. Maybe that's all that matters. Some things aren't meant to be. I guess it's just not going to happen."

"It will." I reached across the table and laid my hand over his. "I know how you can get there."

chapter 24

Buzz

"You sure this is okay?" Buzz gazed out the window of the truck as they cruised down the highway, Beam driving. It had been weeks — no, months now since he and Hush had first staggered into Faderville during that ice storm. Things had been so much clearer then, figuratively and visually. He remembered the sharpness of images: the glassy coating of ice that had encased every tree limb and surface, the way the sunlight shone off of it all the next day, the contrast of wintry earth beneath a watery sun.

Now, no matter how hard he blinked or rubbed at his eyes, everywhere he looked it was like peering through a piece of frosted glass. Edges had lost their definition, details were missing, and colors were muted like an old faded Polaroid. He could still see the outline of mountains in the distance, but objects closer to him were so fuzzy at times as to be unidentifiable. He'd meant to continue on once Hush was healed, but because of his own problems it had become impossible. Not being able to complete the journey he'd set out to do last year had been devastating to him, but in being stranded in

Faderville, he'd become surrounded by familiarity over time.

And now, even though they were headed toward the coast, his apprehensions got the best of him. He was more reliant on Hush and Beam than ever. It was asking so much. Too much.

"I'm not sure I'm comfortable doing this. I think we should go back."

"Relax, Buzz. It's all good." Confidence infused her every word.

To Beam, this was an adventure. To Buzz, it was a risk — danger abounding in strange territory. There was so much that could go wrong. Clearly, she hadn't thought this through. Clearly, neither had he.

"So, you didn't actually talk to Noreen about it?"

Beam hesitated. They'd left right after Noreen had gone to work for the day. As casually as if they were just making a trip into town for supplies. "Well ..."

"Tell me you left her a note, then? You did, didn't you? You didn't just up and leave."

"I'll call her when we get there."

"When we —? Sunbeam, you can't be serious. Turn around right now."

"Not a chance. You've been kidnapped. Look, I know how important this is to you. And you're important to me. So we're going, okay? We'll be back in a few days. It'll all be fine."

"No, it won't. You still don't have a license."

Sitting between them, Hush leaned into Buzz to get closer to the window. Buzz rolled it down a crack and Hush pushed his nose closer to all the scents rushing in, sniffed the air, then snorted in Buzz's ear.

"Ah, you're wrong. I do." Nylon rustled as she rummaged through her backpack sitting on the floor between them. She pulled something out of her wallet, a card, and pressed it into his left hand. "See? Remember when I had you sign those papers a few days ago that I'd done all my driving hours? Well, I went down to the county license bureau two days ago and took my test. I'm a —"

"You drove yourself?"

"Well, yeah. How else was I supposed to get there? Surprised you didn't notice I'd left."

"I did, but I thought Noreen was with you."

"She wasn't home from work yet. Besides, you know she doesn't like riding in the truck."

"Right. True."

"Anyway, I'm a legal driver now."

Buzz flipped the card over, brought it closer to his face. In one corner was a picture. Beam, he guessed. He couldn't tell for sure. He couldn't make out any of the letters printed across it. For all he knew, it was her student ID, anybody's maybe. But he wasn't going to question her about it because he didn't want to let on that his vision was as bad as it was.

He tucked it back in her wallet. "I just hope we don't get pulled over."

"Thanks for the vote of confidence."

The miles blurred by. Hills transformed into mountains, crouching shapes of deep green against a backlit sky, the sun a pale disc that peeked from behind sluggish clouds. Scents of summer wafted in through the window: clay earth, damp wood, and freshly cut grass. If Buzz thought hard enough, he could recall the sight of morning dew glistening on lawns like hand-flung pearls and the season's first flowers, small and delicate whorls of white and pink, hidden among the tender blades at his feet.

He'd heard people say that if you lose your sight, your other senses took over and sharpened. But it wasn't quite that simple. If you couldn't see, it was true that you had to rely on hearing, smell, and touch, but none of those things gave you a sweeping assessment of the world like vision did. In a glance, you could see the sprawling outline of a big city: the stair step silhouette of a skyline, staggered gray blocks

300

against a clear blue sky, sunset reflected in mirrored plates of glass; the low jumble of steel-sided, rust-pocked warehouses and red brick factories hugging the rail yard; the crowded nests of houses with patchwork fencing and secondhand yard furniture; the modern chain stores and fast food strips on either side of a long boulevard thick with traffic.

To Buzz now, those things were little more than fuzzy shapes in colors that all melted together. He smelled the chemical smoke and burning engine oil, heard the honks and the screech of brakes, felt the bumps and vibrations of Beam's old truck as they passed these places, but it was just random bits of information that he couldn't quite piece together. He wanted to ask Beam the details, so he could make sense of it all. Yet he sat silently. Too much time to think, to wish things were different for him. It was hard not to sink into a darkness of spirit, hard not to mire in self-pity. And if it hadn't been for Beam, for Hush, he would have.

With Hush's shoulder pressed into his, Buzz fell asleep. He didn't dream, he didn't rest. He simply stopped thinking for a while to let his headache dull.

When he awoke, it was hours later. For a few minutes he was disoriented, couldn't remember where he was or why he was going anywhere at all. The confusion, as it often did, spawned a sense of panic in his chest. He was alert, his senses — what was left of them — were heightened. His dread, mounting. And yet, he felt locked into his current state, nowhere to flee, no knowledge of what it was that he might run from.

And then ... then a muzzle pressed softly against his sinewy thigh. His fingers wove through silken fur. A dog sighed, sat up, snuffled at his neck. Whiskers tickled his ear.

Hush. Yes, this much he remembered. His dog.

The rest came back to him much more slowly. Until then, he kept his eyes shut. When he finally pried them open, the sun was higher in

301

the sky.

"You awake?" Beam said softly. She turned the radio down. He hadn't even noticed it was on until then.

"Yeah. Where are we?"

"Almost in West Virginia. I wanted to stop a while back, but you looked like you needed the sleep. I'm about to burst. There's a rest stop coming up. We could stop there, let Hush out to potty, have some lunch. I brought some bologna and cheese to make sandwiches. Noreen didn't have a lot of food in the house. She never does. But if you don't mind having nothing but sandwiches and apples for a couple of days, at least we have something to eat. Sound okay?"

The thought of eating anything was about as far from Buzz's needs right now as a trip to the moon. His appetite had waned over the last few weeks, along with his weight. If it wasn't nausea that prevented him from eating, it was his lack of appetite. And his memory. He knew he still needed food to provide him with energy, but honestly, sometimes he just plain forgot to eat.

He mumbled his agreement and promised himself that he'd eat for Beam's sake, for all the trouble she'd gone to.

At the rest stop, Beam walked Buzz to the restroom. When he was done, she walked him to a concrete picnic bench. Cellophane crinkled. Hush rested his snout on Buzz's lap and sniffed. Beam put something in front of him, but he had no idea what it was.

She guided his hand to it. "Your sandwich."

He thanked her and just as he had his mouth full, Beam said, "I know, Buzz."

His mouth was dry and he struggled to swallow the stiff lump of bread and bland bologna before asking, "Know what?"

"That you're having trouble seeing. Don't worry about it, though. Hush and I will help out. Just don't be afraid to ask if you need anything or have a question, okay?"

He wasn't sure whether to be grateful or embarrassed. Either way, he felt like a burden. Like he wanted to withdraw from the world to some tiny padded cubicle where he wouldn't hurt himself or misplace things. Independence, however slight, was a source of pride. Having that taken away was like going backward in age and becoming an infant again.

Then, a pop tab snicked open and carbonation fizzed from the soda can Beam placed in his other hand. "Root beer. I wasn't sure what you liked. I hope that's okay."

He smiled. "It's my favorite, thanks."

A cold wet nose sniffed at his pants leg. Buzz stroked the fur on top of Hush's head, felt the warmth of the underside of the dog's chin as it came to rest on his lap. Hush had performed so many selfless acts on Buzz's behalf. Lived off crackers and dabs of peanut butter. Accepted discarded dumpster remains. Slept next to him on the cold hard ground, always vigilant. Walked beside him through sleet and snow, gale force winds, and heat waves so intense he was afraid Hush would burn the pads of his feet and so he'd made little boots for him out of strips torn from one of three T-shirts he'd owned at the time or his last spare pair of socks. Despite all that, the dog had chosen to follow him. To guard him. To offer comfort in the worst of conditions. Even though the dog couldn't possibly have had the slightest inkling why Buzz was marching the breadth of a continent on a mission.

Beam understood, though. Her heart was every bit as big as Hush's.

Still, he couldn't let her do this. The root beer can cool against his palm, he set it down. "I want you to take me back, Sunbeam. Back to Noreen's."

"Why would I do that?"

"Because it's too much, what you're doing. Patrick's gone. I wasn't there for him growing up. It's time I let go and just —"

"Buzz, stop." She clamped her hand on his. Hard, so he'd know it

303

was a signal to shut up, because she was about to say something important.

chapter 25

Beam

"Do you ever listen to yourself?" I pressed my palm more firmly over the cool, paper-thin skin of his hand. "Not being there when he was growing up — that was something you couldn't control."

Eyes pressed tight, he inhaled, let it out slowly.

"I bet in the time you did have with him, Buzz, that you were the best dad you could be."

He scoffed.

"Let me do this. For you. For Patrick. And you ... do this for me. Please. Go with me there. To Chincoteague. Show me the ponies and the sea. Tell me about Patrick along the way. I've never seen the ocean. I've never ridden a horse or even the ponies at a carnival."

He turned his face away. "But why?"

"Because ..." I gathered my courage. Speaking from the heart wasn't something I had much practice at. But what I felt was so strong, so real and true, I didn't want to let a moment more escape without saying it. "Because you're the closest thing I've ever had to a father."

A silence settled between us. A minute without words, during which we both tried to grab a hold of the thing I'd said and wrestle it into some new kind of normal.

And then, he laughed.

"What was that for?" I punched him in the upper arm. Not hard enough to bruise, just hard enough to make him stop laughing.

He was still smiling, though. "More like a grandfather, wouldn't you say? You're young enough to have been my son's daughter."

"It's not about the age difference," I barked back, a little wounded that he'd taken my confession so lightly. "It's how … It's the way …"

"How what? What way?"

"It's hard to explain. I suppose it's how, when I drove into that ditch, you stayed with me until help came. It's the way you listen to me when I talk about my life back in Michigan. The things you say that have made me see Noreen differently — more kindly. The way you explain all your power tools to me and how to turn off the main breaker in the electrical box, even though I have no idea what you're talking about." I smoothed the wrinkles on the cellophane, noticing how haphazardly I'd wrapped the sandwiches up, but not really caring, when normally it would have spurred me to re-wrap them. "Most of all, it's how you encourage me to be something more. To dream about the future. To figure out who I am."

"And do you know yet — who you are, what you'll be?"

"Not a clue." I tugged a loose scrap of bread crust free and tossed it to Hush. "But I want to be someone who helps others. A doctor, maybe. A psychiatrist. A teacher. I don't really know. I'm just beginning to think about it."

"Sunbeam" — he laid his hand over mine —"I believe in you. You can be *anything*."

I didn't know it until then, but I'd needed to hear that. More than I'd needed a nice house to live in. More than I'd needed a perfect childhood.

I didn't have to stay stuck to my past. It was like someone had suddenly turned me around, so I was looking forward instead of backward.

He squeezed my hand. "If I were to pick a daughter, it would be you."

My heart expanded. A lump formed in my throat. I squeezed his hand back. "Thank you, Buzz."

Not knowing what else to say, I unwrapped my sandwich and started eating. Pretty soon, we were sitting there with nothing but crumpled cellophane and empty pop cans. Air brakes burped as a semi pulled into a parking space. Hush was sound asleep in the shade cast by Buzz's body.

A van pulled up in the parking lot. The sign on the side said *Camp Evergreen*. Kids in matching neon-green shirts piled out, noisy and happy. I wondered what it would have been like to be one of them.

We watched them for a few minutes.

Then, out of the blue, Buzz said, "Do you ever wish you could go back in time, Sunbeam, and do something differently?"

And just like that, visions of a sun-dappled forest and campers in their khaki shorts were replaced by a smoky screen of darkness, orange and amber flashing from busted windows, a tattered curtain whipping outward as it danced with flames, smoke scouring my mouth and throat, the chemical smell of burning plastic, the waves of heat. And somewhere amid the roar and hiss of the fire, the sound of a tiny kitten meowing.

"I should have gone back in after him."

Should have.

The words bounced around in my brain like live grenades with their pins waggling loose.

Before I knew it, my body folded. Any hope for the future or sense of worthiness I'd embraced vanished in a puff of exhaled breath.

Tears came not in hushed sniffs or muffled sobs, but body-wracking, soul-drenching wails, like the young bride who's learned her husband will never return from war. I covered my face with my hands — a dam of straw against the rushing wall of a five-hundred-year flood.

It had been a Saturday night, the 5th of June. Warm, like today. The day had been nothing out of the ordinary, yet I remembered every detail about it as if it were yesterday. Oakley had eaten a bologna sandwich for breakfast and another for lunch. He didn't see the difference between breakfast food and stuff you ate for lunch or dinner and most of the time we didn't have anything healthy around to eat like fruit or oatmeal, so it was eat whatever we had or starve. After lunch, we'd walked to the corner dollar store. Oakley had gazed at all the toys, asking if he could have one, and I'd had to tell him no twenty times. Most of the time, if you just told him 'Maybe later' he'd put the toy back, satisfied that someday he'd find those toys under the Christmas tree or wrapped inside a box on his birthday. But that Saturday, he'd been enthralled with a toy race car. One that looked very much like Jeff Gordon's car, complete with a bright yellow '24' on it. Jeff Gordon was his hero. He'd taken to him after Gordon's win at the Brickyard 400 a year prior.

He kept asking 'Why?' I told him we didn't have enough money.
"Why?"
"Because Mom doesn't make enough."
"Why?"
"Because some jobs pay less than others."
"Can she get a different job?"
"Not one that pays more."
"Can her boss give her more money?"
"No, it doesn't work like that."
"Can we ask her for some of the money she gives that man Russell?"

Russell had been Lana's previous dealer. Until he got thrown in jail. It still baffled me how Lana never got arrested herself. In some ways, I wished she would. But the prospect of ending up in a foster home had always terrified me and in all likelihood Oak and I would have been separated. I couldn't abide by that.

"You mean Marcus?" Marcus was her current provider at the time. He had managed to elude local law enforcement long enough to buy himself an Acura MDX and a small yacht. My guess was he had friends on the force. He was also smart enough not to get personally involved with Lana.

Oakley shrugged. He couldn't discern between the dozens of men who came and went in Lana's life, never judged them as bad or good. Oakley trusted everybody. It was what I loved about him. It also scared me to death.

His lip jutted. "Please? I saw money in her purse last night."

"Sorry, Oak." Who knew where she'd gotten it from or if she still even had it? Besides, Oakley couldn't read. It could've been two dollars or two hundred. We needed it for food more than anything else.

I took his wrist and gently pulled him away. We made it as far as the double doors when the cashier stopped us. "You gonna pay for that car, little man?"

Confused, I looked at Oakley. He lowered his eyes, his right hand fiddling with a lump in the pocket of his too-big shorts. I let go of him and he took a step back, his eyes shifting from the floor to the door.

"Oakley, put it back," I whispered.

He drew it from his pocket. Turned it over in his chubby hands, the brightly colored ads and shiny metal reflecting the overhead fluorescent lights. "Can we pay for it later? If we promise to?"

"Put. It. Back," I repeated. I was as mad at him as I was brokenhearted. He never asked for anything of his own. And even though there was a lot that escaped him, he also knew stealing was wrong. Laying a hand on his shoulder, I turned him around and marched him back to the toy aisle. There, in plain sight of the observant cashier, he put the car back on the shelf he'd taken it from. On our way out, I mumbled, "Sorry, he doesn't always under—"

"Hey, no worries," the lady said, waving a hand at me, her multi-colored plastic bracelets clacking. Her name tag said 'Marquita'. "I know how it is with his kind. I got a slow cousin like him."

I wanted to punch her. She was trying to be nice, yet she was talking about him like he wasn't even there.

Then she pointed a fuchsia fingernail at me. "But if I *ever* see you lifting stuff, I'll stick the cops on you — and don't you dare use your kid brother to do any dirty work, got it?"

"Sure." I fisted my hands, my chest hot with indignation.

Her eyelids were purple. Her skirt a black faux leather. Her hair a shade of red that doesn't occur in nature. If I thought a little harder, I could recall the flavors of chewing gum in the display racks of her lane and the candies hanging in little clear plastic bags there: Lemon Drops, candy hearts, Red Hots, Pixy Sticks … Details often rushed to me in a wave like that. Sometimes it was enough to make my brain explode.

I grabbed Oakley's hand, tugging him toward the exit. Just before the automatic doors, he twisted around, waved at Marquita, and said in his characteristic monotone drawl, "Have a nice day."

I suppose he was reminding her, in his own way, that she'd forgotten that part of her job.

That night, everything changed. Oakley never got his car. And I lost my little brother forever.

Drowning in bittersweet memories, I arose from them with an arm around my shoulder and the bristly feel of a short beard buried against the crown of my hair.

"It's okay, Sunbeam," Buzz murmured. "It wasn't your fault. You didn't know he went back in. You thought he was safe."

My cheeks were wet, my sleeve drenched.

A highway patrol officer approached from across the parking lot, stepping up onto the curb and striding toward us with equal doses of concern and urgency. My heart faltered. Had Noreen called the authorities after all? Were they searching for us? If I was going to have a meltdown, the least I could have done would be not to have it in public and call attention to myself.

"Is everything all right here?"

Buzz patted me on the back. "On our way to her grandmother's funeral in Maryland. Not my wife's. Other side of the family. They didn't see each other often but talked on the phone a lot."

The officer stopped on the other side of the picnic table, looking us over. His eyes were flint-hard, like he'd been told one too many unbelievable stories over the years. Then he reached around to his back pocket — and handed me a tissue.

I stared at it. He extended his arm to dangle it closer.

"Go ahead. It's clean. I promise." A kind smile spread slowly over his mouth, reached up into sincere eyes. His shoes were polished to a reflective sheen. The mic clipped to his shoulder crackled with bits of dispatcher-talk. He glanced at Buzz. "I always keep a spare or two. When you come across accidents as much as I do, people are bound to be emotional."

"Thanks," I said, finally realizing he wasn't going to arrest us after all.

"No problem." Backing away, he tipped the brim of his hat. "Sorry about your grandmother, miss."

"Thank you, sir." Buzz squeezed me to his side. I leaned into him, the bones of his shoulder protruding, sharp but solid. He raised his other hand in a salute. "Have a nice day!"

My heart clinched so hard I gasped. Buzz turned his face to me, but I could tell by the way he was squinting and his pupils wandering that he couldn't quite make out my face.

"What is it?"

I sniffed a few times before remembering the tissue in my hands.

I unfolded it and blew my nose. "Nothing, really. Just something Oakley said once."

"Have a nice day?"

"Yeah, that. It's like you …" I shook my head. "Never mind."

For several minutes neither of us said anything. I was still trying to swim above the guilt, with Buzz's shoulder as my buoy, when he cleared his throat.

"I need to tell you something, Sunbeam."

Good news never started out that way. I already knew he was dying. What else could he have told me that was any bleaker than that?

"This may sound a little … 'out there', but you have to believe me. Because it happened to me. I swear it did. One day, before I knew all this about the tumor in my brain, I was at work, helping a guy named Burt on a wiring job. We were always careful, but there was some miscommunication. Nobody's fault. I went to grab a bundle of wires, thinking they were disconnected. Turned out they were live. It was like someone cracked me with a whip." He snapped his fingers, but the sound came out muffled. He'd grown weaker lately. It was obvious even in that simple gesture. "I didn't come to for over an hour. Woke up in the hospital. Confused as hell."

"You got shocked? That had to hurt."

He breathed in softly, like he was concentrating on the air whistling through his nostrils, rushing down his windpipe, and into his lungs. "My heart stopped. I died."

"But they brought you back? Just like after the robbery?"

"They did." He turned his face to me then. "And for a long time afterward, I wished they hadn't."

I tried to dissect that, but no matter what there was only one way to interpret it. "I don't get it. Are you saying you wanted to die?"

"Oh, no. Not that. I didn't want to come back to *this* life. Not after I'd been there — on the other side."

This was getting more bizarre by the second. I was starting to think Buzz's condition had addled his brain, jumbled it up like a skillet of scrambled eggs. "Where's 'there', Buzz? Are you talking about … Heaven?"

"I don't really know, Sunbeam. I'm not the religious sort. Never have been. So I don't know I'd call it that. All I know is that I wasn't *here*. Not in my body. Not in this … plane, for lack of a better word. Same thing happened this last time at the hospital, too. They were sure they'd lost me. But they didn't give up. And I came back. Again. For a time, though, I was … I can't explain it — somewhere else, I guess."

Honestly, he'd lost me when he mentioned 'the other side', but I went along with him, because, well, because he was Buzz. "Like some other dimension?"

"More or less."

"Right. Sounds like one of those *Star Trek* episodes where there's an alternate universe." Again, I couldn't help it. Sarcasm leaked out of my pores. There was no keeping it in.

"I suppose it does." An amused smile flitted across his lips but quickly fell away. "Your brother, Oakley … I know he died that night. His body ceased to function. But it wasn't the end for him. He still … he still *is*."

My fingernails pierced my palms. I didn't want to hear this nonsense anymore.

"We should get going." Standing, I started to gather up the trash, cellophane crinkling as I balled it up in my palm. "There's more in the truck if you want any."

I grabbed my pop can and stepped over the bench.

Buzz didn't budge.

"Are you coming?"

He lifted his chin, turning his head slightly. "Sunbeam."

"What?!" I bit back, my irritation evident.

"He doesn't blame you."

I dunked my trash in the waste receptacle so hard the lid banged.

"How would *you* know? Have you talked to him lately, huh?"

He patted the bench beside him. "Please, sit."

From beneath the shade of the picnic bench, Hush observed me with mild curiosity. He tipped his head up and squinted into the sun, his tongue lolling to the side. He yawned wide, coppery cheeks bunching, and slowly flopped back over onto his side, his speckled legs stretching lazily, as if to say he wasn't ready to go anywhere just yet.

There was a time when those wild-colored eyes and shiny white teeth would have propelled me into a state of absolute fear. No more. He'd licked my tears, saved my life, and earned my trust a hundred times over. I'd tried not to like him. Buzz, too. Instead, what I felt for both of them now was much stronger than mere like. Strong enough to suck me beneath the surface like an undertow.

Against my better judgment, I sat. Part of me wanted to get in the truck without them and just keep driving, no plan but to put distance between myself and Buzz's wild ideas. Another part of me yearned to listen, to gather every word so I could believe in something bigger and become the better person for it.

Two starlings landed on the far end of the table, alternately hopping forward, then back as they eyed the crumbs of our lunch. Hush popped his head above the table edge and they exploded upward in a burst of beating wings and startled chirps.

"What if you knew that he was still here, Beam? Not in the physical sense as you and I know it, but his energy."

"Okay, now you're talking crazy. Let's just drop this and —"

"Listen, please. The place he's in" — Buzz lifted a hand from the table, moved it slowly upward, as if reaching toward something unseen — "it's much better than ... than *this*, even as beautiful as this world can be. But this world can also be mean and ugly. There's none of that where he is. None. No hate or neglect or selfishness. No guilt or shame. He doesn't get tired or sick, or sad or lonely. He feels only joy and wonder. He is energy, pure and simple and complete, connected to every living thing, past and present." Then, as if aware he'd gone a little too esoteric for me, he started over. "Beam, he had Down syndrome, right? You said he tried to be friends with everyone, trusted too much sometimes. I bet he was the embodiment of innocence, right?"

I didn't say anything. Oakley may have been innocent, but he wasn't as dumb as most people believed.

"Do you think that Oakley, being Oakley, would have blamed you for what happened? Would Oakley hold a grudge, or be suspicious, or harbor jealousy toward anyone? Did he ever do any of those things, Beam?"

"You didn't know him."

"But you did. Tell me — would he have done any of those things?"

"No, but he ..." I didn't know where I was going with that, so I just let it hang there.

"You shouldn't either, then. We can't blame ourselves for what we didn't know. And even if we make a mistake, it's just that — a mistake."

All the fight whooshed out of me. Deflated, I sat there for a good minute, trying to think of some way to argue with him. In the end, I couldn't. "So who's healing who in this relationship? I thought the old dude was always the Yoda."

"Does it matter?"

"Guess not."

He nodded. "You know, I bet Oakley made a lot of mistakes."

By most people's terms, yeah. Like a million. But he just kept on going, no regrets, no kicking himself in the pants. Which was Buzz's point.

"You're saying I should be more like him?" I said.

"I'm saying don't make waste of what he taught you. And know

315

that where he is … everything's just fine." A pause, then, "You still don't believe me, do you?"

"I don't know, Buzz. But if I was going to believe anybody, it'd be you."

He nodded. "That's a start."

A busload of senior citizens on a sightseeing tour had pulled into the far side of the lot and were piling out. Clusters of old ladies in stretch slacks with oversized purses slung over their bony shoulders. A stoop-backed man leaning on the arm of his plump wife. Other couples who looked barely past retirement age. The bus driver himself. All weary and worn. But content.

Then one elderly lady disembarked, her raspberry-pink visor slanted just so, her beaded coral necklace complementing the tangerine of her glittery earrings and bracelet, her white slacks and peachy golf shirt straight out of a golfing magazine. At the bottom of the bus steps, her hand still on the rail, she took in the view, breathed in the mountain air. A smile as wide as the sky, she looked all around — at the children playing beneath the oaks, at the pair of fluffy white dogs prancing through the grass at the end of rhinestone leashes, at the truckers leaning against their cabs as they chugged energy drinks. She looked like a five-year-old who'd just walked through the gates at Disney World, not a seventy-five-year-old beaten down at the end of her life.

For the briefest of moments, as her gaze panned the rest stop, her eyes came to rest on us. Even from fifty yards away, I could sense her brightness, her spirit.

Oakley had effused joy like that. You couldn't be around him and not feel it. Sometimes that was downright exhausting, though. Still, in trying to be the grownup of the household, I'd abandoned that part of me that found wonder in the simple things.

"I've missed him so much. It's just hard to think that he's … gone. I mean, I still don't feel like he is."

"Because he's not. Look around you. Just *look*."

Ironic, coming from a guy who was losing his sight. I shut my eyes. Turned his words over in my mind. Thought of Oakley. Of how much I loved that silly kid. How his hug could make even the worst day better. How he loved to sing, loudly, even though he couldn't carry a tune or remember the words. How he could remember the names of race-car drivers and their numbers, but couldn't add or subtract. How he could sit on the stoop and blow bubbles for hours, no greater care than whether his next bubble would be his biggest yet.

"His last breath," Buzz said, "it's air now, someone else's breath, maybe. His words, his smiles, what he did — they affected you and those around him. Remember the good. Always."

I opened my eyes. Saw a sky, blue and vast and brilliant. Mountains, broad and numerous, blanketed with forests so thick that you could get lost in them half a mile from the highway and never find your way out. I saw cars zooming at dangerous speeds down ribbons of interstate that stretched the length of a continent. Trucks, heavy with freight. Steel and concrete barriers. Grassy strips of manmade prairie, where groundhogs and field mice thrived. Hawks and buzzards floating on thermal winds. Sparrows and robins and birds I'd never seen before and didn't know the names of, hopping along the ground to quarrel over crumbs and flitting from branch to branch.

I listened, too. Heard the echo of Oakley's laughter in children playing. Heard the sound of his footfalls in people walking by. Farther away, a car radio boomed with a Beach Boys' song. I imagined Oakley, making up the words, strumming an air guitar.

The smell of asphalt, heated rubber, and engine oil made me think of how Oakley would watch every minute of a stock-car race on TV and cheer no matter who won.

In the cherubic smile of a baby being carried on the hip of a passing young mother, I saw Oakley's joy and innocence. His love of life.

"Sunbeam?"

"What?"

"You called Noreen, to let her know about this trip, right?"

"I texted her. Told her about Lana showing up. She said she never saw her. My guess is Lana went back to Michigan already. She was never one to follow through on her threats. But yeah, I told Noreen where we're going and why."

"What did she say?"

"She said to be careful on the interstate and not to fall asleep at the wheel."

"Huh. That all?"

"She said to take good care of you."

The truth was that in between the platitudes Noreen had sounded pretty mad, but I wasn't going to tell Buzz that. As long as she didn't send the cops after us, I could take a little heat.

"One more thing." He folded his hands together. "My driver's license ... it says I want to be an organ donor. When I ... when I go, will you see that that's honored, please? I don't even know if it's possible, me being as old as I am, but if it is ..."

"Sure, Buzz. If that's what you want." Rising, I placed a coaxing hand on Buzz's shoulder. "Come on. Let's hit the road."

"Sunbeam ... about Oakley —"

"I get it, Buzz. I do." I helped him up and gave him a moment to steady himself before we turned and started toward Carlos.

Trotting at Buzz's left, Hush gave a soft *woof*, as if to remind us of his presence. Then with a buck, he leaped ahead and raced to the truck, his leash trailing behind.

"I thought you had a hold of him," I said to Buzz.

A smile curled Buzz's mouth. "Funny, I thought *you* did."

chapter 26

Buzz

They sat in the bed of the truck, the three of them — the old man, the young girl, and the dog — facing east. There, the sun's corona fanned its golden fingers outward, a thin band of yellow and pink showing where clouds of purple marched toward the horizon. Beneath it stretched the mirrored surface of the ocean, reflecting the sky above in a shifting iridescent mosaic of turquoise and violet and amber.

They'd been waiting a long time for the sun to rise, waking in the middle of the night, sleeping in shifts once they arrived, and then … Hush had woken them up with a series of soft *woofs* when a flock of seagulls had landed farther down along the shore.

Although the finer details were lost to him, Buzz was sure he'd never seen so many colors all together before, not even on those rare occasions when he'd gone down to Venice Beach at sunset. That beach, too, even in the hours before the sun came up, had never been this quiet, this undisturbed. Being here this morning with Beam and Hush, it was like watching the dawn of time. If he forgot the fact that they were in a truck, it was as if there were no highways, no cities, no crowds, no wars, no abuse or neglect or apathy. There was only this moment, this place; the earth, the sky, the wind, the water.

With a sigh, Hush stretched his legs and squinted into the brightening sun. Buzz ran a calloused hand over the dog's foreleg. The hair was still growing back where Hunter had had to shave it to put in the pin, and Hush still had a slight but distinct limp. Otherwise, he looked like any healthily aging, well-worn dog: a bit grizzled around the muzzle, his coat a little duller than it once had been, and his muscles slightly leaner for all the miles he'd covered in the past year.

"What are you thinking?" Beam asked, her voice mingling with the lap of waves against the shore.

The sea wind scrubbed at Buzz's face. He tugged at his beard, wondered what it would be like to be clean shaven and feel the wind and sun upon it fully. "That I'd do it all over again, just to be here with the two of you and Patrick."

"All of it? Even the hard parts – getting hurt and robbed and ending up in Faderville?"

"All of it." He gave a sidelong glance in her direction. "Especially Faderville."

She shrugged, unconvinced.

"What? You wouldn't?" He arched an eyebrow at her, the implication clear.

"Well, I did meet you guys. But my life in Flint, living with Lana …"

"I'm sorry you had to go through all of that."

She scoffed. "Sure."

"I am."

"But …?" she prompted.

Buzz smiled. He had to. "You're a better person because of it. A pretty amazing one." She didn't know it yet, but in time she would.

"If you say so."

"Believe me." With a grunt Buzz set himself down on the sandy beach. He held onto the tailgate, steadying himself as he waited for the wave of dizziness to pass. Only it didn't. Not even when he was lying down these days. The world around him spun so fast that nausea filled him constantly. Fighting it exhausted him.

Ears perked, Hush sat up. Before the dog could leap off the back and break his leg again, Buzz gestured for Beam to help him lower the dog. As Beam reached out to lift Hush's back end, Buzz said, "But if you don't believe me, believe the dog. He thinks you walk on water."

As they lowered Hush to the ground, Beam let out an airy laugh. "I can prove that theory wrong."

She took off for the ocean, pausing partway to tug off her shoes and socks. Hush loped after her with his stilted gait. Together, they raced through foamy waves along the shore, where sea met sand in an endless pulse, birds bursting upward in an undulating cloud of white wings. Hush barked at Beam's heels as she kicked up sprays of water. Stopping, she laughed, her arms spread wide as she turned in a circle.

Although she was little more than a fuzzy blur, watching her made Buzz even queasier. He had to look away. Too soon, he realized it was the bad kind of queasy, the kind where it felt like his guts were spilling out around him. He grasped at the tailgate as he leaned against it, but everything felt suddenly sideways, like the earth had tipped and he was sliding down a steep hill.

His knees gave out. He hit the sand with a soft thud. Saw Hush's legs weaving around him. Felt the dog's tongue flicking over his face ...

—o00o—

A blanket lay draped over him. Buzz blinked at the light, opened and closed his eyes. Things just weren't staying focused anymore. A blurry shape knelt before him.

"Hey, Buzz."

He knew the voice. But whose?

"It's me — Beam."

Beam? A girl's voice. He thought about it. Did he know someone named Beam? She sounded young.

The girl helped him sit up, his back to the tire of an old, rusty truck. Gently, slowly, she brushed the sand from his cheek and clothing. She handed him a bottle of water. He sipped at it, but most of the water dribbled down his chin.

Long minutes passed before his vision became sharp enough to make out her face. Even as he stared at her, she didn't look away; she just held his gaze patiently, waiting for him to remember. And he did, eventually.

"How long was I out?"

Beam smiled at a couple passing by who couldn't seem to help but gawk. The sea breeze tossed her long brown hair across her eyes, but she didn't push it away. "I don't know. A couple of hours, maybe?"

"Did anyone … ask?"

"Ask why you were having a seizure and if they could help? Close to a dozen, I'd say."

"What did you tell them?"

"The truth: that you had a brain tumor and this was normal. Well, normal for you. I told them there was nothing they could do. That it was best just to let you wake up on your own."

"Was it ugly?"

"You flailed around like a fish on a boat deck."

"That bad, huh?"

"Yeah, but you were in a good place." She swept an arm outward, indicating the sand around them. "Good thing we weren't at an ice rink."

"I suppose so." He was glad she'd been there so no one could take him to the hospital and separate him from Hush. Still, he wasn't comfortable with it. Beam was taking on a lot for someone her age by looking after him. Yet if she hadn't volunteered to drive him here he never would have made it.

"I also told them you were here to spread your son's ashes today. They understood."

The grass on the dunes rippled in a gust of wind. Couples — some old, some young — walked along the shore hand in hand. Buzz imagined them smiling, swinging their hands as they chatted about their futures and remembered their pasts. He didn't do much of either these days. It was all about the present and what was right in front of him.

What he could see of the world now was like looking through a telescope, the lens of which was covered in frosted glass. His sight at the edge of his vision was diminishing. Every day, his window to the world shrank a little bit more.

The laughter of children playing broke above the buffeting wind and rush of waves. He could barely make out their tiny forms, hunched over heavy buckets, plunging flimsy plastic shovels into the sand to add one more scoopful, then flipping the buckets over to build their castles — creations that would dissolve with the first strong tide, like a storm surge taking down a beach house.

The cry of gulls was distant in Buzz's ears, even though the flock was all around them, and he realized that that sense, too, was fading fast.

Smells, if they were strong, brought on unbearable headaches. The scent and taste of food, even foods that he had once loved, made him nauseous. He might have found sustenance in blander foods, but his craving for such things had all but ceased.

Because he had no appetite, he didn't eat enough. Because he didn't eat enough, he was always tired. Because he was tired, his headaches worsened. And because of his headaches, he found it hard to think.

He wanted to hide from the world, retreat, pull so far into himself that no light, no sound, no smell could reach him.

Even as hard as it was to be here, to be present, he wanted to grasp at every last sensation. Hoard them away in his memory, as many as he could: the salty taste of sea air on his tongue, the wind pulling at his hair, Beam's bubbly voice as she chattered on about colleges and careers, Hush's cold nose pressed against his palm as he begged for a treat, and the sand shifting under his feet as they walked along the shore.

He wanted only simple things. The things that reassured him that he was yet alive.

Beam spread a blanket on the sand and helped him to it. Then she flopped down on her back, hands behind her head, and looked up at the clouds. "Tell me about him."

"Who?"

"Your son." She turned on her side to look at him, the dog stretched out between them. "What was his name?"

"Patrick. Patrick Carroll Buskirk."

"Carroll?"

A grin flitted over Buzz's mouth. "That's my real name: Carroll Buskirk. I didn't want him to have it, but his mother insisted."

"Oh, I see why you went by Buzz. How old was he when ...?"

"When he died? Twenty-four."

"That's young. Really young. How did it happen? A car accident?"

"War. Afghanistan. At first they blamed an ambush by local insurgents. It later came out that he was a victim of friendly fire."

Gulls jeered overhead, filling the sorrowful silence between them.

"How long ago was that?" Beam finally asked.

Buzz thought about it. "Eight years? Ten? I don't know, really. He'd made a career of the army. Got higher in rank than I ever did. Since I was his only living relative, they gave me his ashes. When Hush and I left L.A., each day when I woke up, I took a pinch of Patrick's ashes and cast them into the wind, so that he'd be everywhere — from the Pacific to the Atlantic, in the desert sands of New Mexico, the wheat fields of Kansas, the muddy Mississippi, the mountains of Tennessee ... Everywhere."

"That's beautiful, Buzz. You must've been very close."

"I hadn't seen or talked to him since he was six."

"Why?" Beam sat up and crossed her legs Indian-style. "Did he live far away?"

"No, not far. His mother and I split up when he was only two. It was obvious we weren't meant for each other, even in the beginning. We tried — although we probably shouldn't have. I wasn't the most ..." — What was the word he wanted? It finally came to him — "*attentive* of partners. I had a lot of growing up to do, even at thirty. She lied a lot. Made up excuses. Blamed others for things not going right. She liked to fight, made reasons to. I preferred to run away. It wasn't a good situation for our son."

"She got custody when you split?"

He nodded. Even now, it still hurt his heart to think of those times.

Beam waited for him to answer, but finding the words was becoming increasingly hard for him. It took so much of his energy. Even when he knew the words, putting them in order, waiting for the right one to come to him, *that* was what frustrated him more than anything. Sometimes it was impossible.

"She had a new boyfriend. A jealous bastard. Whenever I'd come to pick Patrick up, he was there, watching, making sure she didn't speak to me more than she needed to. I worried for her — and for Patrick. Then, one day, I came to pick up my son. It was Patrick's birthday. He was supposed to stay with me for the week. I knocked, but his mother, she ... she wouldn't open the door. I got mad. I shouted at her." Even now, the anger surged within him. He clenched his fists, pushed it away, reminded himself that was long ago. "I

325

pushed at the door to go in and saw … her eye, swollen, purple. She shut the door and locked it. Her boyfriend was in there. I know it."

Tears burned his eyes. Buzz shut them tight. He didn't always remember the details, but the emotions were as strong as ever. "The next day, they came to arrest me."

If Beam was shocked, she didn't let on. Instead, her voice remained soft and low. "For what?"

"Assault. She said *I* hit her." Opening his eyes, Buzz's face twitched with a snarl. "I would never have hit her. Never. It was him. *Him.*"

"But if you didn't do it —"

"I said I did, because the … the …" He rubbed his forehead. Wanted to rap his knuckles against his skull and jar the words loose.

"The defense attorney?"

"Yes. He said if I confessed, I'd get out in a few years. And if I didn't, I'd be in for a long time. So I went to prison, got out in eighteen months on good behavior, but she still wouldn't let me see my son. And when I tried to approach her one day to talk, she said I threatened her. My parole officer told me if I violated the restraining order, I'd go back to prison." Those days had been so dark and lonely. The only thing that got him through was the hope that he could rebuild his life and make Patrick proud of him. Yet she'd found a way to thwart that, too. "I never saw Patrick again. But I always remembered the promise I made to him."

"What was that?"

He gathered his memories like drifting tufts of cotton – fuzzy, scattered.

"To take him to see the sun rise over the ocean for his birthday. To see the ponies run along the shore. You see, when his mom and I split up, I'd call him at bedtime and read to him. I'd bought a secondhand book from the corner thrift store: *Misty of Chincoteague.* I read it to him over and over again, and almost every night he'd say,

'Will you take me there someday?' And I promised him I would."

Buzz broke down then. Years of buried pain pulling him under. Down to a place he'd long feared to venture into.

And in doing so, he released the grief that had cloaked his heart for decades. Purged himself of an unspoken sadness. Of regret and loss. Of unfulfilled dreams. Of lost moments.

In their place, an unexpected brightness entered. His love for his son who was long gone. For Hush, who'd saved his life countless times. For Beam, who'd made this day possible. Even for Noreen, who'd opened her home to him.

Beam wrapped her arms around Buzz and held him until his sobs ebbed.

When Beam finally let go, Hush rooted at Buzz's tear-soaked hand. Buzz turned his palm over and the dog licked it clean, as if to tell him there was no need for tears, so long as he was at his side.

—o0Oo—

The next morning, Buzz could barely see the sunrise, yet he felt it fully. It heated his skin, hurried the blood in his veins, quickened his heart.

This was the day he'd worked toward. The day he fulfilled his oath.

The better part of a year ago, he and Hush had set out from Los Angeles. Put miles upon miles of asphalt behind them. Marched beneath the desert sun. Climbed mountains. Braved wind and rain and hail and snow. Dodged traffic and snakes and coyotes. Slept beneath overpasses of concrete and steel and under star-filled skies. Hungered and thirsted. Bled and suffered bruises. Been robbed and nearly run over.

All for this: a promise.

Yesterday, they'd gone to the marshes on Assateague Island

where the ponies wandered in bands. Sadly, they'd missed the Pony Penning on Chincoteague by days, so the herds had already been returned to the larger island. It made them a bit harder to locate, but rather than being packed into corrals for the annual auction, they were happily grazing at a distance.

Beam had described it all in detail: how they grazed upon the cord grass, how the salty water made them drink more and distended their bellies, how their tails and manes were tousled by the sea breeze, how they kept a watchful distance, guarding their young. She described their colors and markings: dun with white socks, deep black with a narrow blaze, chestnut, sorrel, and gray, piebald and pinto. In his mind's eye, he saw it all: the different shades and patterns, their coats, glistening under a summer sun, their shaggy manes and swishing tails, their hooves splashing up sprays of water as they trotted away. He wished he could have seen it clearly with his own eyes. Wished that Patrick could have, too.

When the herd moved out of sight, they'd returned to the seashore. Beam guided him into the water one cautious step at a time until he stood waist-high in the ocean, an occasional wave splashing up past his navel. He clutched the jar to his chest, afraid the tide would pull him under. It hadn't seemed appropriate to carry his son's remains around in a plastic bag anymore, so Beam had fished up a jar out of a trashcan and rinsed it clean.

He twisted the lid open. It smelled faintly of pickles. Or maybe sauerkraut. He used to be able to tell the difference.

"Go ahead," Beam said.

"Is anyone watching?"

A pause. "Just the dog. And some guy about half a mile down the beach. But don't worry. He looks pretty drunk to me."

He put the lid in his pocket and tipped the jar. "Is anything coming out?"

"No, don't think so. More."

Placing his other hand at the bottom of the jar's mouth, he tipped it more. The slightest of weight shifted inside. He shook it. Ash spilled into his palm. For a moment, he held it there, fingers closed loosely, the remains of his fully grown son reduced to fine papery flakes. The son he hadn't seen grown up. The son he'd loved with all his heart, even though miles and years and death had separated them. And then ...

He let him go.

Because he knew they'd meet again.

The ashes floated from his palm to join with wind and sea. To become a part of them. To drift on an ocean breeze that encircled the earth. To mingle with waves that lapped at sandy shores continents away.

Unceremoniously, Buzz turned the jar upside down and shook it hard, ashes plopping softly in a heap upon the water's surface before slowly dissipating and sinking.

"You made it, Patrick. All the way to the Atlantic Ocean. I told you we'd come."

—o00o—

Buzz leaned his head back, every stone and pothole of the road reverberating through his bones. Almost home now, he and Beam had barely spoken the past two days. What more could they have said?

"Buzz?" Beam shifted down as Carlos strained to climb a hill. The pungent scent of freshly cut hay poured in through the open windows. "About the operation, I understand if you don't want —"

"I'll have it," he said bluntly.

"You will?" When he didn't answer, she went on. "I thought you didn't want to risk it."

"I'll have it — if they say it's not too late to try."

Beam reached across the seat and took his hand, holding it long

329

after the truck had crested the rise and started back down hill. Finally, Buzz nudged her hand away.

"Shift," he said, "before you ruin the gears."

chapter 27

Beam

Static surrounded me, jittery electrons bouncing around in barely contained orbits. I jumped back from the window, fairly warned, my skin tingling.

Lightning cracked, its fiery tendrils splitting a tree branch between the house and garage. Across a moody sky, bursts of white flashed and flickered. In the strobe of light outside, a knife of wood plunged downward, spearing damp earth.

A moment flashed into my memory: the day after Buzz and I arrived in Faderville and we were out in the driveway, clearing it, when the heavy coating of ice cracked a thick tree limb and brought it down. Buzz had been wearing my grandfather Roland's clothes, which hung on him so loosely he looked like a scarecrow.

If I kept my eyes closed, I could see Buzz as clearly as if he were standing right in front of me. I could even sense him.

Earlier in the week, Hunter had arrived before dawn to drive him up north to a hospital several states away. Buzz hadn't woke me up to say his goodbyes, but the night before he had hugged me hard and given me his walking stick, telling me he'd be using a wheelchair for a while anyway. It rained that night and had every day since.

Until the lightning came, today's storm had been nothing but a daylong gray deluge. A reflection of my outlook.

This was the day Buzz was to have his operation. By now, it might even have been done. They hadn't said how long it would take. I only knew that the outcome wouldn't be known until after he awoke — if he did at all. The risks had been enormous. But without the attempt, Buzz would have died soon, anyway.

He'd been trying to prepare me for that all along. It still didn't make it one iota easier. There are some things you just can't accept, no matter what. Someone you love dying, for one.

Still, there was hope. Always hope. However infinitesimal.

I'm not sure how long I stood there, mesmerized by the blear of images as rain poured down from the clouds and dripped from the trees. It could have been minutes. It could have been hours. Time had no measure. All I could do was wait. For something to happen. To move forward. Or backward. Something to remind me that I was still alive, because I wasn't all that sure I was. I was numb from the inside out. Drained. Hollow. Inert.

Until the phone rang.

It startled me like a four-alarm fire bell. Rattled me to the core. Shattered and upended me.

Noreen stood, her feet hitting the floor like boulders dropped into a deep well. She trudged to the phone, lifted it from the receiver.

"Hello?" Her breaths amplified against the mouthpiece. "Yes, speaking. Who's this again?" A pause. I turned my head to look at her. I didn't like what I saw. Her brow folded. In concentration or concern, I couldn't really tell. "Uh-huh ... Uh-huh. I understand, yes. Uh-huh." Another frightening pause, then, "Oh, I see."

Groping behind me for the couch, I stumbled to it, folding into its depths as the back of my knees hit a cushion. A shapeless heap of sorrow, I stared at the lines in my knuckles as if seeing them for the first time. Buzz's hands had so many scars and calluses — there must have been a story for each one: a house he'd built, a night in the wilderness, his days in the army. My hands were soft and smooth, untried in the world.

For a few minutes more, I was aware of Noreen's mumbled replies, her words blending into a meaningless buzz. It wasn't until I heard her breath catch before the first sob broke from her chest that I looked up again.

She clutched her arms across her chest, rocking softly. Then she looked up, toward Heaven, and I knew in that moment —

"Bellamy ..." She walked toward me. "It's for you."

I shook my head. What would I have to say to the doctor? Thanks for trying? No, I couldn't. Not without breaking into a million pieces.

"Take it, please." She held the phone out, practically shoved it into my hands. "You'll want to hear this."

I took it, pressed it to my ear, listened. It was warm where she'd gripped it with her own hand. I summoned a single word. "Yes?"

"Just confirming. Is this Bellamy Larson?"

"Yeah."

"This is Doctor Rafalski at Johns Hopkins in Baltimore. I wanted you to know that we began surgery at seven a.m. this morning using a specialized type of laser therapy to ablate the affected tissue and slow or perhaps even stop the growth of the tumor, but we won't know the efficacy of the procedure for some time. We'll monitor him closely over the coming weeks. There are other medications and treatments we'll administer, but I want you to know we've passed the first hurdle."

His words wafted past me like a swarm of flittering moths. I was aware of each individual one, but couldn't quite sort them out. Was he saying that Buzz was okay?

A silence opened up on the other end.

"Miss Larson, did you hear me?"

"About the operation? Yeah, I think … yeah."

"Good. Mr. Buskirk would like to speak to you."

"What?" I was sure I'd heard wrong. It had taken a moment to register that Buskirk was Buzz's real last name. To me he'd always be Buzz Donovan.

"Here, hang on." Then I heard the doctor's voice, more distant, as if he'd handed the phone to someone else.

"Sunbeam?" The voice, groggy, crackled with strain. It was Buzz.

Something like an infant's mewl leaked out of me. I swallowed my disbelief. The words, then, tumbled out. "It's you. It's really, *really* you?"

"It is."

My throat constricted. Tears squeezed from my eyes. I couldn't speak, despite what I wanted to say. Snuffles turned to sobs.

"Hey, now. None of that. I thought you'd be happy."

"I am. I am." I sucked back a glob of snot and swallowed hard, summoning words that deserved to be said. While I had the chance. "I love you, Buzz."

"Love you too, Sunbeam. How are you, anyway?"

"I don't know." Happy wasn't a strong enough word. Yet I was too shocked to be jubilant. Mostly, I just felt an overwhelming sense of peace, like being buoyed on calm waters after a hurricane. "Relieved, I suppose."

"Me too." He tried to laugh, but it came out as a cough. "Ow, can't do that."

After he'd regained his breath, he asked, "How's my dog?"

I looked over to where Hush was lying next to the cold, empty hearth. He let out a hefty sigh of longing. The dog hadn't been himself ever since Buzz had left. He'd been moping around, barely eating, and watching the door for hours on end. "He wants you to come home."

Maybe 'home' wasn't the right word, since Buzz really wasn't from around here, but the fact of the matter was that Buzz belonged wherever his dog was.

"Me too, Sunbeam. Me too. Tell him I will."

"When? Did they give you a day?"

"Soon, okay?" Then after a long pause, he said in words more air than spoken sound, "Tell him."

But even as he said it, I heard the wispiness in his voice, the fragility. I also sensed he was telling me what I *wanted* to hear.

"Sunbeam ...?"

"Yeah?"

"Take care of him for me, okay?"

I started to tell him I'd do that until he got home, but Dr. Rafalski came back on. He explained the probable course of Buzz's recovery, that it would be slow and difficult, that he would tire easily and have to re-learn some basic things, like maybe how to walk, and that he might never, ever again be able to do many of the things he used to do.

He also said there were still risks and that Buzz wasn't in the clear yet. I figured he was saying that to cover his butt. Medical science had come light years in the past few decades, but there were still things it couldn't accomplish yet. Doctors weren't perfect, either. And they couldn't predict the future.

As he was speaking to me, it occurred to me he probably had no idea that I'd only recently turned sixteen, because he was talking to me like an adult, using a lot of medical terms. I welcomed that he would entrust me with the information. And yet —

"Doctor ...?" I meant to say his name, but I wasn't sure I'd pronounce it right. "Why are you telling me all this? I mean, I want to know, I appreciate it, but ... why?"

"Why you? Right. He listed you as his adopted daughter. His only relative. Is that right? We can't give out this information to anyone but family. I suppose I should have asked first. I know the last name's different, but I just assumed —"

"No, that's right," I interrupted, before he could hang up on me. "He's my father."

And it sounded right when I said it.

"Good, then I can ask you to confirm. He wanted any viable organs donated, should he become deceased — is that correct?"

"I guess so." It seemed like an odd question, but I suppose there was probably some protocol to make sure family was on board with a person's requests in matters like that. Then I remembered: that day at the rest stop on our trip to spread Patrick's ashes. He'd mentioned wanting to be an organ donor then. "Actually, yes, I'm positive. That's what he wanted."

If he died — I still couldn't bring myself to say 'when' — then perhaps he could give life to someone else.

A minute later, the doctor had said all he could. I gave the phone back to Noreen and relayed everything I remembered. She didn't ask any questions, didn't offer empty platitudes of sympathy. Instead, she just folded me in her arms, soft and comforting, until I yielded to her embrace.

I wept softly on her shoulder. When my tears stopped flowing, which was some minutes later, she released me and said, "I hope he comes home soon ..."

The words 'but if' hung unspoken in the air between us, as delicate as icicles in a spring thaw.

Her arms no longer holding me up, my knees were threatening to collapse beneath me, so I sank into the safety of a chair again. Hush padded over to me and rested his chin on my knee. His limp was barely evident now, but on chilly mornings when he first woke up it still showed as a hitch in his gait.

Sitting at my feet, he studied me with those wildly intense eyes, swirling in blue and brown, his coppery eyebrows twitching quizzically. I scratched the fur on top of his head, wondering what it was he was thinking, wondering if he understood that had been Buzz on the phone. Maybe I should have let him listen to Buzz's voice?

I leaned forward to kiss him on the muzzle. Just as I pulled back, his tongue swiped away the salty trail of my tears.

—o00o—

The days that followed were the longest I'd ever known. There wasn't enough I could do to fill them up. I pored through the college sites on the web, but without seeing those places in person, I couldn't get a feeling about any of them. They were just pictures, carefully selected to show students at their happiest and most productive: smiling on their way to classes, intensely observing a chemical reaction in a test tube, studying in a spacious, multi-level library, and sometimes frolicking in a game of Ultimate Frisbee on a grassy quadrant. Almost all of the students they showed were the usual ages of eighteen to twenty-two. I couldn't help but expect that if I went to one of those places, my age would set me apart — and not in a good way.

Still, the more I stared at the pictures, the more I realized they were someone else's dream of a bright and budding future, not mine. I didn't know where I belonged. Except here.

If the days were long, the nights were eternal. I'd lie in my bed, gazing out at the stars through a patched-up screen, listening to the crickets chirp and hounds bay in the distance and cows call out to their calves.

This place ... this was my dream. My home.

I tried to ground myself in those bucolic sounds, to be grateful that I wasn't in Flint anymore — where I could get shot at — and that Noreen had intervened to rescue me from having to join Lana and her sugar daddy in Traverse City, but my mind always drifted back to Buzz and all the conversations we'd had in the few short months since I almost ran over him. He'd helped me look at the world differently and accept what was. That didn't change that I wanted to believe he'd come back to us, even though I realized he might not. It did help me to let go of all the resentment I'd once harbored toward Lana. She was who she was. For reasons all her own. I could only be responsible or me.

Dr. Rafalski called every few days to report on Buzz's condition. I wish I could say 'progress', but that would imply that in some way he was improving. He wasn't. Complications had set in early: a stubborn infection that left his body weaker, a buildup of fluid in his brain, trouble speaking and remembering, more seizures ... There were more setbacks, it seemed, than advances.

I hadn't spoken to Buzz since the day of his operation. That alone told me things were not going well. All the waiting forced me to realize there wasn't anything I could do and that my worrying about him changed nothing.

The time also gave me the opportunity to witness that the Earth around us continued to spin on its axis. The sun rose and set. Storms rolled in and sunny days followed. The TV, which was almost constantly on whenever Noreen was home, provided evidence that the lives of others hadn't slowed one bit: people went to work, commercials urged parents to shop for back-to-school clothes for their kids, and news was still happening all around the world.

I began to adjust to life without Buzz, however empty it seemed at first. Hush and I went on walks through the surrounding fields. Sometimes we just piled into Carlos, windows down, and drove the back roads to see where they led. I discovered so much and took hundreds of pictures: leaning tobacco barns, mobile homes clinging to hillsides, a goat farm with kids clambering over rusty barrels and sagging planks, and old tractors abandoned in weedy fields. Back in Flint, I would never have wandered around like that. Here, the undiscovered called out to me. I existed in the moment, Hush at my side as he listened to my every spoken thought as if it were Martin Luther King Jr.'s 'I Have a Dream' speech.

During those days, I stopped wishing for 'what might have been'. I didn't regret any of my yesterdays or fret about all my tomorrows.

I simply *was*.

—o0Oo—

Hush and I returned one day from one of our drives. It was as if I'd been in search of something, even though I had no idea what that was, and come back empty-handed once more. I'd thought I would get home before Noreen — I was supposed to have filled out and sent in a college application, but I hadn't even started. When I pulled in, though, I saw her car sitting out front. It never sat out front. She always put it away in the garage.

I knew then. And I didn't want to go inside and hear it. So I parked the truck a hundred feet from the house and stared at the front door, trying like heck to gird my insides so my heart wouldn't drop down and blast a hole right through me and on out the floorboards.

Eventually I got out. Only because Hush was pawing at the door and I couldn't stand it anymore. Noreen met me on the front porch.

I looked into her eyes. "Is he —?"

She nodded.

Buzz, she explained, had died a few hours ago. At his request, his organs had been donated to those who needed them. There would be no funeral, no memorial. Who would come, besides Noreen and me and maybe the McHughs? Buzz Donovan, once known as Carroll Buskirk, was gone. A blip on the census. A passing statistic. A homeless man, scorned by those more fortunate. A nameless face passed by many as he walked the breadth of a continent, forgotten shortly after his image faded from the rearview mirror. Handyman. Father figure to me. Hero for a day …

Although I'd expected it, it didn't seem real. His body had ceased to function, yet it still felt as though he was there, somewhere.

I inhaled deeply, resisted exhaling, but too soon my body craved another fresh lungful.

When I let out that breath, it was as if all the air had been sucked from my body by a powerful vacuum.

No one ever lives forever. Nothing lasts. Even mountains wear down to hills, and hills to plains, and plains to valleys. And sometimes the earth thrusts upward to create new mountains. The new from the old. Mass changed, shifted, recombining in various forms to recreate itself continuously.

But Buzz wasn't just a physical being. He was *energy*. And energy was never destroyed. It just *was*.

He'd tried to explain it to me more than once. At the time, I couldn't quite get my mind around it. I still struggled with the concept. But ... I was beginning to understand.

Finding Buzz, getting to know him, becoming his friend, and losing him — it had to *mean* something.

Maybe, just maybe, he wasn't really gone after all. The energy that *was* him, it had merely been dispersed. Taken another form. Droplets of water vapor rising up into the clouds to later rain down on parched earth. Molecules of gas filling the air. Particles of dust scattered amid the dirt.

His last breath, it's air now, someone else's breath, maybe. His words, his smiles, what he did — they affected you and those around him. Remember the good. Always.

Ah, Buzz. How could I forget?

—o0o—

Buzz would've told us not to, but Noreen and I had a memorial for him anyway. With Hush between us, we stood atop the highest hill within sight of Noreen's home. Up there, you could see for miles and miles. Stretches of woodland where human feet had never once trod. A patchwork of pastures and fields nestled between the hills. Dotting the view was a scattering of homes — some grand, some humble — along winding roads. And far in the distance, twin ribbons of asphalt: the Cumberland Parkway.

Squinting against the noonday glare, I shaded my brow with a hand. "He'd be pretty hacked off about this, you know."

"Buzz Donovan hacked off? I doubt it." Noreen tugged the brim of her sunhat down. In her other hand, she clutched Buzz's walking stick. "More likely, he'd just shrug and ask us what the point was."

We remained there for a long time, not saying anything. Eventually Hush lay down and closed his eyes. His exhaled sigh expanded to fill the silence.

Inside me, the sadness that had been so persistent was gradually ebbing away. In its place was a longing — for what had so briefly been and what would never be.

For days after learning he was gone, I kept thinking Buzz would show up at the door, or that I'd see him somewhere. Once, while in Faderville, I was almost sure I had. Until that person turned around. An older man in well-worn jeans and a faded work shirt. He hadn't even looked like him. It had just been something about the way he carried himself, his bearing, an aura.

Every night when I went to sleep, I hoped I'd dream of him. I never did. I had very little to remember him by. Just a few pictures I'd snapped on the sly —

And his dog.

As if he knew my thoughts, Hush looked up at me, sunlight sparkling in his marbled eyes.

We meandered along the hill, then stopped at the edge of the woods, the tree trunks standing sentry like soldiers guarding another realm.

Noreen tipped her hat back. "So, which tree?"

I looked from one to another to another. No one tree was more special than any other. "Does it matter?"

"It should." Her head swiveled left, then right. "I see dogwood, catalpa, honey locust, and shagbark hickory … Black walnut, I think, over on that slope."

About fifty feet to our left, slightly downhill, stood a spindly sapling. I pointed to it. "What's that one?"

When she reached it, she inspected several leaves. Some were in the shape of spearheads, while various ones resembled mittened hands, and yet others looked like the footprints of three-toed animals. "Sassafras. Each leaf is different. You can brew a tea from its bark. My mama used to make it. I haven't had a glass of sassafras tea for ages. What a treat that was."

A wry smile twisted her mouth, revealing bittersweet memories. "Course, she also used to lash the back of my legs with a willow switch. Can't say I miss that. Or her, most times. But that was how they raised kids back then. Maybe that's why I was the way I was with Lana. We didn't believe in coddling children. We were tough on her because we expected a lot. My mama and daddy wanted me to have a better life than them and we wanted the same for our daughter. In my day, we weren't allowed to make mistakes or break the rules. We were supposed to be normal, average, hard-working folks, not different for the sake of being different. Certainly not insolent or freewheeling."

She hadn't said any of that as an excuse, but it was like a door of understanding had just been opened for her. I knew she'd still be hard on me. That she'd never be the kind to shower me with praise or ruffle my hair for no reason. But I knew that she cared and, in her own way, she'd never fail to demonstrate it.

"That one, then. The sassafras." Not that it had anything to do with Buzz, but the fact that you could make a tea from its bark, well, that was kind of the cycle Buzz was always babbling about, so it fit him.

With careful consideration, she propped the walking stick so that it rested between the two boughs, each about as big around as my wrist. We both stared at Buzz's stick a while. Like we were making sure it wasn't going to fall over. I went and nudged it a bit, just to be certain. A stiff wind couldn't have knocked it loose.

Then, Noreen did something very strange. Very … not Noreen-like. Taking my hand, she squeezed it lightly and kissed my cheek. I glanced sideways at her. But only for a moment. Just long enough to see a trickle of moisture leaking from the corner of her eye.

I squeezed her hand back. "I know it was kind of a surprise when I showed up here. Well, not kind of. More like a complete surprise. And I know it stirred up a lot of painful memories for you" — still holding hands, we turned and began the long trek down the hill — "but I really think things are going to turn out all right."

After the slightest pause, I added. "And I'm glad I came."

"Me too, Bellamy," she said, her voice cracking as she said my name. "Me too."

Our hands drifted apart and a comfortable silence settled between us. The first of its kind I could ever remember. But I was sure it wouldn't be the last. There'd been a shift between us, a meeting in the middle. We still might not have understood each other completely, but we were both trying, and that was more than I could ever have said of Lana.

Strange to say, but if it weren't for Lana, Noreen and I would never have ended up like this. Lana had driven us apart and brought us together again. Somehow, I'd like to think we were both stronger for it.

"Did you ever decide what you want to study?" Noreen asked.

She probably wanted me to say a doctor, a lawyer, or even a banker like her. But I told her the truth. "Photography. I want to take pictures of ordinary things and ordinary people who really aren't so ordinary after all. I don't know if that'll be a career or just a hobby, but I like the idea of telling stories through pictures."

Her mouth tightened and I could tell she was trying hard not to convince me otherwise.

"Some days, though, I also want to be a neurologist," I added, because I still wasn't all that sure. "Or a pediatrician. Or a social worker. Someone who helps other people. Who makes a difference." Saying it out loud, a realization gelled inside me. It was like I'd been wandering around without a map all these years, and someone had finally pointed out the way. "I know now."

"Know what?"

"What I want to be. A teacher for kids with special needs. Kids like Oakley or Hannah."

After a few moments, she said, "It takes a special person to fill a role like that. You're perfect for it."

I smiled. Whether she meant it or was just being nice, I didn't know, but just hearing it made all the difference in the world.

We climbed a short slope and I sprung up it, propelled by hope and possibility. Her breath coming in labored grunts, Noreen struggled behind, hampered by her aging knees and extra weight. I stopped next to a twisted juniper to wait for her. Small blue berries speckled the ground beneath it.

"Gram?" I said as we turned and continued on together. I was just getting used to calling her that. Before a couple of weeks ago, I hadn't addressed her directly at all. Just blurted out whatever it was I had to say. But the more I called her Gram, the more accustomed to it I became. And the more I liked being with her.

"What is it, Bellamy?"

She still never called me Beam, but I didn't hate that she didn't anymore. Bellamy had a grown-up ring to it. A measure of respect.

"You still have the Mason jar?"

She nodded. "It's back at the house. In my top dresser drawer."

"When are we leaving?"

"Day after tomorrow. You sure it's what he'd want?"

"He didn't say so, but yes, I'm sure. It's where we spread his son's ashes."

"That seems more than right, then." We went through an old gate separating two pastures and came in sight of Noreen's back yard. "By the way, your mother called this morning. Says she's been clean and sober for eighty-four days now. She's hoping she can come and see you again sometime. Maybe on her first anniversary."

"Why so long?"

"Said she wanted to prove to you she could make it that far."

Maybe people do change. If they have reason enough to.

We must have gone a quarter mile before the sound of wood being dragged over sticks and earth made us both turn around. Higher up on the hill, on the path we'd come from, stood Hush.

"We forgot the dog," Noreen said. "Why don't you call him, before he runs away?"

"He won't run away." Heaven knew he'd had plenty of opportunity in his life. The only time he'd gone out of sight had been to seek out Buzz in the hospital. "But if it'll make you feel better —" I slapped my leg and whistled.

Hush lifted his muzzle proudly.

"Why is he fetching you a stick?" Noreen asked, puzzled.

"He's a dog. He just wants to play." I slapped my leg again. "Hush, come on!"

His body twisting sideways, he began to trot toward us. But the stick he was carrying ... it was huge.

It was Buzz's walking stick.

"Oh. My. Lord." Noreen shook her head. "Suppose he's trying to tell us something?"

I thought about it. "He's telling us that Buzz is still with us.

345

Always will be."
    Just like Oakley.

epilogue
Beam ~ four years later

The ducks paddled their way across the quad pond, dipping orange bills beneath the water and preening their feathers as they floated in safety far from the banks of vulnerability and Hush's ever watchful eye. Sometimes, we'd come down here to the middle of campus and sit for hours, me studying for Adolescent Psychology or taking random photos of passersby, and Hush transfixed by the web-footed creatures bobbing on still waters. Even when they came ashore, he never chased or frightened them. But he was endlessly fascinated to the point of obsession. In the evenings, when I gathered his leash and a textbook or two, he knew where we were headed and raced to the door, slobber dripping from his long tongue to pool on the tiles until I was ready to go.

Without that dog, I don't know how I would have gotten through these last two years, since I'd moved on from taking online courses to living in my own apartment just off campus, several hours from home. Funny how easily I'd taken to calling Noreen's little cottage just outside of Faderville 'home'. I missed the place. I missed all the once broken things that Buzz had fixed and made look new again. Missed the rambling board fences and rickety gates. Missed the cattle grazing contentedly in the neighbor's pasture and the cricket song drifting through patched-up screens. I missed the rolling hills and how they changed with the seasons: from the gray of winter, to the vibrant green of spring, to the water-parched yellows and muted olives of summer, to the jewel tones of fall. I missed that mischievous cat, Fisher, who'd steal the tuna from your sandwich if you left it unattended on the kitchen table. I even missed Noreen.

Leaving had been surprisingly hard. Hush had made it easier, though. He didn't regret yesterday's cotton-mouthed speech in communications, or dread tomorrow's statistics exam. He reveled in the moment, quick to take joy in the ordinary: a walk at dusk, weekend mornings when we lazed side by side on the futon, and a bone stuffed with peanut butter to keep him busy when I left for class.

Best of all was when I came back to my apartment every day, sometimes more than once a day, and he was there to greet me, wagging and wiggling, slathering me head to toe with sloppy dog kisses, leaping and spinning as if I'd been gone for months, not hours.

My heart was never empty. Hush always filled it to overflowing. My journey would always be his, no matter the path life took me down. With Hush at my side, there was no burden too great to bear, no worry that could not be lessened, no grief that could not be comforted.

I hadn't forgotten about losing Oakley, but I'd forgiven Lana. She'd cleaned up her act and stayed with Alonzo for four whole years now but, like the dried-up pit of a plum that is never watered and thus will never bear fruit, her personality hadn't changed much. Her addiction to regular soakings with alcohol and occasional forays into recreational drugs had simply been replaced by shopping binges and expensive vacations. She looked healthier, but that was about all the good I ever came away with when we met once or twice a year.

Family, I'd concluded, was not defined by blood, but by acts of love.

Somehow, Buzz's loss had bonded Noreen and me in ways that normalcy never could have. We'd loved, however briefly, and lost. Quarreled and compromised. Bickered and hugged. The day she dropped me off at the university, she'd told me she was proud of me.

I knew Buzz would have been proud too. In a month, I'd be graduating. But I wasn't done with school, as much as I wanted to be. Come fall, I'd begin my graduate studies in education and psychology at this same school. I had plans. Big plans. For all I'd endured and lost, there was so much more ahead. Everything I'd been through had given me a purpose, fueled by an intimate understanding of the struggles that kids like Oakley and Hannah were faced with daily.

Still, I had four exams next week. And all this information wasn't going to enter my brain through osmosis, no matter how often I fell asleep with my cheek on my textbook. Hush lying beside the bench where I sat beneath a weeping willow tree, I cracked open the spine on my Literacy Assessment book, found the study guide to Chapter 18, and started reading.

Five minutes later, I was reading the same paragraph for the fourth time. I could not, for the life of me, stay focused. I was antsy, alert to every passerby, studying faces near and far. I'd purposely left my good camera back at the apartment, so I wouldn't let myself get distracted from my studies.

Popping into a sit, Hush whimpered softly. I laid a hand on his withers.

"Quiet, buddy. Nothing going on here."

His whining escalated. His body began to quiver, vibrate almost, like a jet plane powering up for takeoff.

I tapped him hard on top of his skull to get his attention. "Those nerds going down the steps by Waverly Hall on their skateboards again?"

I looked where he was looking. Didn't see anything but a pasty,

349

middle-aged guy sitting on a low concrete wall next to Waverly swiping a finger over his tablet. I went back to reading the study guide and decided to take out a pencil to start writing notes the old-fashioned way. Maybe it would trigger some latent learning pathway, so I could get through this course with a respectable grade.

I had the dull lead point pressed to a piece of yellow notebook paper when Hush sprang to his feet and took off around the duck pond faster than I could figure out what the heck was going on. Like a hound taking off after a jackrabbit, he flew over the open ground in a blur, ignoring the ducks entirely, his leash whipping along behind him. He'd always been so reliable about sticking with me that I'd neglected to tie his leash to the bench leg.

I stood, cupped my hands to my mouth like a bullhorn. "Huuush, come!"

He kept going, flying over the trampled grass, his legs stretched to full stride.

"No, Hush! Get back here. *Here!*"

Starting forward, I spewed every command I could think of. And a few curses for added emphasis. The couple of dozen people scattered around the quad heard every colorful word of exasperation. They pulled their own dogs back, stepped out of the way, got out their smart phones and started videoing the unfolding scene, just in case something hilarious or criminal happened.

The man who appeared to be the object of Hush's laser focus looked up, startled, and dropped his tablet in the grass beside him. Hush, propelled onward by some invisible galactic force, still wouldn't respond to me. He didn't stop until he'd flattened the poor man who'd been innocently surfing on his tablet onto his back.

Shame slammed my conscience. If the man was hurt, Hush and I would be banished from campus for life. I'd be fined and jailed. Hush could be — I didn't even want to think of it.

I ran as fast as I could, shouting Hush's name over and over.

Lactic acid burned in my thighs. My heart banged so loudly in my chest, I expected my ribs to explode outward from the force. The last time I'd suffered this much horror, I'd paid in scars.

How could Hush, in a matter of seconds, destroy my trust like this?

As I neared them, all I could see were the soles of the man's shoes as he writhed on the ground, crying out with …

Wait. Was he *laughing?*

I slowed to a jog, then stopped ten feet away, my panic ebbing with each heartbeat.

One disadvantage to a dog with only a short bobtail is that you can't see it wagging until you're practically on top of it. Unless, of course, the dog's entire hind end is doing a hula dance of joy. Which it was.

Going forward, I hooked my fingers through Hush's collar to pull him off. It took more effort to unglue him than I'd anticipated, but eventually I was able to drag him back a ways. I slipped the handle of his leash over the top of a metal sign post that urged dog owners to pick up after their pooches. He barked repeatedly, an excited, screechy bark. I told him to shut up, but it wasn't having any effect. Turning around and trying like blazes to ignore the incessant yapping, I hurried back to the victim of Hush's enthusiasm.

I stuck out my hand. "Are you all right?"

Sputtering, he clasped it and I pulled him into a sitting position. After he located his glasses in the grass next to him, I untied the hoodie from my waist and handed it to him.

He stared at it. "What's this for?"

I pointed to his forehead. "You have dog slobber all over you."

"Oh, right." Swabbing his face clean, he laughed. "I suppose I do."

Crouching down before him, I surveyed the damages. Nothing I could see, except for foamy globs of saliva and grass stains all over his suit. I shot Hush a scolding glare. Straining against the leash, the dog wagged his bum harder, not looking the least bit guilty. Then I turned my attention back to the man. Fortyish, he had close-cut blond hair and startlingly blue eyes framed by thick black glasses. Even with him sitting down I could tell he was short.

"Sorry he tackled you like that. I don't know what got into him. He usually ignores strangers entirely."

"Don't worry about it. I like dogs. That was quite the welcome. Made me feel right at home. Left my own friendly mutt back in Wichita. Miss her like the dickens. Adopted her about three years ago. First dog I ever owned, but she won't be my last. I don't know why I never had one before."

"Hush is my first too. Really, are you okay?"

"Fine, fine, just fine." He flapped a hand at me like it was no big deal, then blotted at his shirt front with my hoodie. "If this is the worst thing that happens to me this year, I'd say I'm pretty lucky. For my first day on campus, though, it does make for a memorable experience."

"No offense, but you look a little old to be a student here. Actually, not too old. Too …" — I indicated his suit — "professional."

"None taken. And you're astute. I'm not a student. I just had an interview. Starting next semester, I'm an associate professor here. I'll be teaching Applied Statistics. I'm very much looking forward to it."

If I could have drilled a hole to China and plunged in right then, I would have. That was one of the classes I had lined up for my first term of grad school.

My dog had just flattened my professor on the quad lawn. Lovely. I'd have to report to class in a ball cap and dark sunglasses, sit in the back of the class, and never, ever speak out loud. Maybe I could transfer to another section. Or change majors.

"Again, sorry." I backed up, reached for Hush's leash, looked for the closest door to duck into. "Glad you're okay."

"Never better. A little concerned about the jolt to my new ticker" — he laid a hand over his heart, held it there — "but I think I'll be fine."

"Oh. Pacemaker?" Now I felt really bad. Maybe for an encore Hush was going to bring down an old lady with a walker. I wound Hush's leash around my hand and reeled him in close. He was whining like the guy had a bag full of crack and he was a junkie in need of a fix. What was wrong with this dog?

"Oh no, no pacemaker." The professor fisted his hand, looked at it like he held a precious diamond in his grasp. "Brand new heart." He lowered his hand. "Well, not brand new, but new to me."

"You had a heart transplant?" If the guy was walking down the street, you'd never know he had someone else's heart beating inside his chest. The fact awed me.

"Four years ago." He smiled like he'd just announced the birth of his first child. "Gave me a whole new lease on life. Once I recovered from the surgery, I started having this overwhelming urge to walk and just keep on walking. Last year I hiked the Appalachian Trail. I've been to a dozen national parks. Climbed mountains on four continents. Funny, because before the transplant I barely ever left my desk."

I stood there speechless, a surreal feeling trickling through my veins. It was as though electrons were vibrating in every molecule of my body. And then it dawned on me.

Sinking to my knees, I clutched Hush to my side to restrain him. Stared at the professor so long his smile slipped away and he started to give me one of those looks that you give a crazy person right before you run like hell because you suddenly realize you're in the presence of a psycho.

But then, "Are *you* okay?" he said.

I averted my eyes. "Yeah, fine. It's just ... you reminded me of someone. Someone I was very close to. He died four years ago."

"I'm sorry to hear that. Do I look like him, maybe?"

"Not really."

"How so, then?"

I shook my head. "He once walked across America. Hush was his dog."

His eyebrows lifted. "Ahhh, the hiking. I see. I suppose that was quite an undertaking."

"Yeah. We met when I almost hit him with my truck in Kentucky."

"Goodness. I hope he wasn't hurt."

"No, but I was. Kind of. Ran into a fence post. Slight concussion." Hush was still quivering in my hold. The man reached out to stroke the top of his head. I let out his leash slowly and he immediately curled around and pressed his body against this man he'd never met before, then looked up at him adoringly. It was the oddest thing I'd ever seen from him. Hush wasn't *un*friendly. More reserved, really. At least until he got to know a person. "There's something else, though. He died of a brain tumor, but he donated his organs. His heart was one of them. My friend was sixty-three, but the doctor said he had the heart of a thirty-year-old."

The man nodded in interest.

What I was about to say was as weird a thing as I'd ever said before, but I couldn't *not* say it, because my intuition was screaming it at me. "This is kind of out there, but the way Hush is acting — it's like he *knows* you. You don't know who your heart's donor was, do you?"

"No, I'm sorry. I don't. Sometimes they'll connect you with the immediate family of the donor, but I asked and in my case, apparently, my donor wanted to remain anonymous. So no, I don't have a name. That is a lot of coincidence about your friend, but what are the odds, huh?" He pushed his glasses higher up on his sunburned nose, then handed my hoodie back to me. "By the way, I'm Dr. Jerome Spiegel.

Jerry to most folks. This" — he tipped his head at Hush and the dog jumped as far in the air as his leash would allow — "is obviously Hush. You are?"

"Bellamy. Bellamy Larson."

He offered his hand. I shook it, wholly aware that he would never forget me now. Or I him.

"Nice to meet you, Bellamy."

"Everyone calls me Beam," I said out of habit, even though I was fine with being called Bellamy these days.

"Beam, then." Clapping me lightly on the shoulder, he glanced Heavenward. "Like a sunbeam, right?"

Then ... I remembered. *Everything*.

And I smiled.

The pain *had* faded with time, although it had never really gone away.

But that pain, it was a constant reminder of how lucky I was to have known someone that I could love *so* much.

about the author

N. Gemini Sasson is a serial remodeler, intrepid gardener, dog lover, and Boston Marathon qualifier. She lives in rural Ohio with her husband and an ever-changing number of animals.

Long after writing about Robert the Bruce and Queen Isabella, Sasson learned she is a descendant of both historical figures.

If you enjoyed this book, please spread the word by sharing it on Facebook or leaving a review at your favorite online retailer or book lovers' site.

For more details about N. Gemini Sasson and her books, go to:
www.ngeminisasson.com

Or become a 'fan' at:
www.facebook.com/NGeminiSasson

Sign up to learn about new releases via e-mail at:
http://eepurl.com/vSA6z

Made in the USA
Middletown, DE
28 April 2025

74857604R00220